BLIND FAITH

BLIND FAITH

Patricia Haley

BET Publications, LLC
http://www.bet.com

NEW SPIRIT BOOKS are published by

BET Publications, LLC
c/o BET BOOKS
One BET Plaza
1900 W Place NE
Washington, DC 20018-1211

All Kensington Titles, Imprints, and Distributed Lines are available at special quantity discounts for bulk purchases for sales promotions, premiums, fund-raising, and educational or institutional use. Special book excerpts or customized printings can also be created to fit specific needs. For details, write or phone the office of the Kensington special sales manager: Kensington Publishing Corp., 850 Third Avenue, New York, NY 10022, attn: Special Sales Department, Phone: 1-800-221-2647.

ISBN: 1-58314-300-9

First Printing: June 2003
10 9 8 7 6 5 4 3 2 1

Printed in the United States of America

This book is dedicated to Jeffrey Glass, my incredible beloved husband. You are my very best friend, my encourager, my confidant, my supporter, my travel buddy, and my true love. You have brought so much fun and joy to my life. Thank you for being such a dream.

I'm glad we're able to share this journey together. I appreciate you reading my manuscripts over and over, and always providing a wealth of enthusiasm and suggestions. You are amazing. As I've grown in my writing, you've grown in your editing. At first, you just found typos. Now, I laugh (and cry) every time you give me my manuscript back and see it marked up with red everywhere. Your feedback has evolved into telling me that I need more description here, character consistency there, and scene development in other places. I also love all of the encouraging "you go girl" comments you make to let me know areas that you really like. Every book I write is ours, because you have motivated me to stretch myself into areas of challenge. I love you for it. I am touched that a businessman like you would take the time to learn and understand the techniques of editing, just to help me make my writing better. No one could ask for more in a partner.

I haven't forgotten the time when you got off work, drove me two hours to a signing, even when I told you it wasn't necessary. It took you four hours to get home after taking three trains, a bus, and a cab. There's so much I could thank you for, like standing in hundreds of stores while I do signings, watching but not disrupting. You're as excited as I am when a reader supports me, yet alert at all times. Tears come to my eyes when I think about your love for me. You always verbalize your feelings, yet your actions of love speak so much louder.

This literary journey God has put me on is exciting and rewarding. But the real joy of it all is being able to share it with you. You are an absolute blessing in my life—a gift beyond imagination. Thinking about you, I just shake my head. Never could I have expected God to bless me so miraculously with a husband as compatible as you. You are a constant reminder to me of how merciful and gracious God is. Jeffrey, you are undoubtedly my soul mate, and I love you from the depths of my heart and soul. For every day that I'm alive, my heart is committed to you, now and always.

ACKNOWLEDGMENTS

This book is special to me, but it was written during a time of many challenges; yet God showed himself faithful and ran the words through my head and got them onto paper. I am grateful to God for leading me along this captivating literary journey. I pray this book will reach the eyes of every person he intended to see and/or read *Blind Faith*.

I am blessed with a multitude of loved ones, and I want to use this opportunity to pay special tribute to a few of those key people in my life. The past few years have been filled with loved ones leaving, like my father, Fred "Luck" Haley, who I miss dearly, and I am grateful for his love. Others who have gone on include my Aunt Ivelean Tennin, Aunt Arletha Stapleton, Uncle James Blake, and Uncle O.D. Dockery.

One loss, which threw me for a loop, was the passing of my beloved Aunt Lottie Tennin Flowers, someone I dearly love and treasure. Her list of accomplishments and service to her community, family, and church, was longer than she was tall. Her short stature, five feet tall in heels, didn't reflect the big heart and huge amount of love she extended to so many of us. No matter how busy she was, my aunt always made time for me. Aunt Lottie wasn't in the habit of reading novels, but she made me happier than she ever realized when she stayed up most of the night to finish my first book, *Nobody's Perfect,* and wanted a sequel. Of all the professional reviewers who gave feedback on the book, none carried any more weight than her simple assessment, which came from the heart. She is exceptional and an example of the legacy one's life should represent. She is special to me, beyond measure, and I miss her.

Joan Vaughn Walker, one of my other moms, "added" me to her family, some twenty years ago, after I graduated from college and landed in Pontiac, MI. Her recent passing was unexpected. I am grateful to her for encouraging me, without judgment, during major points in my life. Her eloquent words, graceful style, and abundant support give me something to both shout and cry about. She is one of three women who inspired my recurring character Big Mama (Emma Walker) in my novels. I shall miss Mom Walker's wisdom and presence, but will never feel the loss of her love. To my "little sister" Francis Walker, I am in awe of you for enduring the pain of transition, and making all of us, especially your mom, so proud. I love you, Ms. Saxophonist.

It is difficult to say good-bye, in such a short time, to so many people who have touched my life and helped me to evolve into the person that I am. Without the grace of God, it would be impossible. So, I say thank you, Jesus, for letting me take bite-sized pieces of grief, which are manageable, and which haven't overshadowed the wonderful memories I have with each person. I am grateful to God for allowing these loved ones to pass through my life, and for enabling them to leave a piece of their love, courage, and strength behind for me. I accept this transition period as the price for loving unconditionally.

I am surrounded by a host of supportive and loving family and friends, and I can't name them all. Thanks to my mother—Fannie Haley, Bob Thomas, Lorena Skelton, Fred and Geneva Haley, Freddy Deon and Umeka Haley, Robert and Diedre Campbell, Walter and Jeraldine Glass, Anthony and Bonnie Hargrove, Brendon and Brice Simpson, Margaret-Ann and Rayford Reed, Donald and Mary Bartel, and Nadine Washington. I appreciate the support from all of the Haley, Tennin, Moorman, and Glass family members. I particularly want to acknowledge Benn Tennin and Nic Tenner, two cousins of whom I am incredibly proud for making lemonade out of lemons. I'm looking forward to the same from you, Aymond. As always, I honor the memory of my brother, Erick, whose endearing love inspires me.

I do want to acknowledge my advance readers, who get better and better each time around. I hope you know just how grateful I am to each of you for your comments. You have truly helped to make each of my stories better. Thank you to Emma & John Foots, Laurel Robinson, Varinia Robinson, Dorothy Robinson, Dr. Leslie Walker, Attorneys Tammy and Renee Lenzy, Kirkanne Mosely, Christina Fryman, Rena and Roscoe Burks, and my incredible hubby.

I am blessed to have my faith-based sisters and brothers, who I've enjoyed touring with and writing our *Blessed Assurance* anthology with. Victoria Christopher Murray, Jacquelin Thomas, Marni Williams, Maurice

Gray, Terrance Johnson, and James Guitard, you are each a blessing to me. Thanks, Audrey D. Williams, for coordinating the tours and publicity for the faith-based group, as well as for me personally. You are truly wonderful in this arena.

I am grateful to my sorors of Delta Sigma Theta Sorority. Special thanks to my own chapter—Valley Forge (PA)—for kicking off the chapter's book club in 2003 with *No Regrets*, as well as Milwaukee (WI), Houston (TX), Rockford (IL), San Francisco (CA), Schaumburg Hoffman-Estates (IL), Palo Alto (CA), Pontiac (MI), and Stanford Univ.—Omicron Chi. Thanks to Alpha Kappa Alpha, Zeta Phi Beta, and Sigma Gamma Rho.

I am grateful to the BET family—Linda Gill, Kicheko Driggins, and Guy Chapman for your energy and enthusiasm in constantly seeking out new promotional venues for the New Spirit Line. Jessica McLean-Ricketts, thank you for your getting my books on the store shelves. Glenda Howard-King, you are a phenomenal editor. You truly helped to make *Blind Faith* happen. Thanks for giving the idea a chance.

Thanks to a long list of individuals who helped me in different ways. I am grateful to my agent Claudia Cross, Patricia Hill, Gary Murphy, Rose Coit, Mariah Carlisle, New Covenant Church (Trooper, PA), Dominion Christian Center (Rockford, IL), Nancy Arnold, Pam Perry, Shawna Grundy, George and Monica Lloyd, Cabrina Robins, Will and Kimberla Roby, Thelma Gould, Lana Edwards, Karen Portis, the Bernoudy women (Cynthia, Monique, and Mea), Trevy McDonald, Monique Ford, Dr. Lola Richardson, Marina Woods, Claudia Bell, Sharlene Scott, Cheryl Charity, Beverley Saxon, Teresa Pullett, Gazelle Robinson, Vincent Alexandria, Nicole Bailey-Williams, Wilma Wilkerson (shopping mama), Katie Armstrong (Ingram), Stephanie Perry Moore, Pat Byrdsong with Shades of Romance, Nancey Flowers with QBR, Bernadette Connor, Tamlin Henry (WDAS), Mary Ann Edmonds, Derrick and Jennifer Wooden (Jade Designs) for the outstanding web site creation, Sarah Granlund (Montgomery News), Gary Puleo (Times Herald), Rawsistahs, and Kim Collier.

Special thanks to B. Dalton, Waldonbooks, Book World, Rockford Library, Houston Library, South Dade Library, Broward Library,

Univ. of Southern Florida, Macedonia Baptist Church (E. Norriton, PA), Delta Authors on Tour (DAOT), Paine College, Howard University, Philadelphia's Art Sanctuary, a long list of independent African-American booksellers—House of Peace, Afrocentric, Cultural Connection, True Vine, Truth, Apple Book Center, Our Story, Kujichagulia, Basic Black, A&B Distributors, Culture Plus, Mind & Soul, Expressions, Karibu, Sepia Sand & Sable, Medu, African Spectrum, Shrine of the Black Madonna, CushCity, Jokae's, Black Images, Treasures of the Heart, Heritage Books and More, School House, Montshu, Print Emporium, Books for Thought, Sibanye, LaUnique, NuWorld of Books, Eso Won, Psalms 23rd, X-pressions, Dygnyti, Fellowship Chapel, Haneef's, Ligorius, Reading Room, Community Book Center, Afro-American BookStop, Gospel Lights, Pyramid Books, and Masters Hand. I am grateful to the book clubs— Extra Special Women (IL), Ebony Girl Talk (TX), Good Girls Book Club (on-line), Cover Story Book (TX), Sistahs with a Vision (NJ), Atlantic Bookpost, Circle of Strength (PA), Stars Book Club (PA), Beloved Women of God Ministry (NJ), NoName (NJ), and Felicity Women's Discussion Group (PA).

As always, I acknowledge you, the readers. My literary journey would not be complete without your support. I appreciate each and every person mentioned, and those inadvertently omitted. Thank you for touching my life and may each of you be blessed in return.

There is neither Jew nor Greek, slave nor free, male nor female, for you are all one in Christ Jesus.

—Galatians 3:28-29

CHAPTER 1

The phone was ringing but the apartment door wasn't cooperating. Courtney shifted the oversize duffel bag on her shoulder, trying to keep it in place as she wiggled the key in a lock that was as old as the turn-of-the century dwelling. One day she would demand that the landlord replace the antiquated lock with a modern one, but tonight it didn't matter. The fun she'd experienced over the weekend overshadowed any small inconveniences. So long as she could get inside and hop into bed, all would be well with the world. A few more jiggles and the door was finally open. When she entered her starter apartment, the caged heat lashed out at her. The humidity wasn't showing any mercy on August. Before she could get situated, the phone rang again. She dropped the bag in the middle of the floor and snatched the phone up from the table in the dining area. She wasn't shocked to hear Paul on the other end.

"Where have you been?" he blasted through the receiver.

Courtney pulled the phone back and rubbed the temple of her ear. "You knew that I wasn't getting back until today."

"Yeah, but you were supposed to come back this morning. You had me sitting around here waiting for you all day."

Her original flight was scheduled to get in around noon, but two of her college friends, Ashley and Larry, had talked Courtney into going standby on a later flight so she could stay until the very end of the weekend with everyone else. She could have left early Sunday morning, but there was more fun to be had in the afternoon. Being among peers that she related to on multiple levels made the decision an easy one. If only she had more friends like that at home, ones who looked like her, thought like her, and had the same idea of fun. "I'm sorry if you were waiting around for me, but I called and told you that I wasn't getting back until late."

"So, being with your friends is more important than coming home and being with me? I guess you don't care if we spend time together anymore."

"You could have gone if you wanted to, Paul." She stood with her feet planted, eyes rolling toward the ceiling, and lips pursed. "I asked you to come with me."

"I haven't lost anything in Chicago. This is where we live and you need to remember that, sweetheart. School days are over. Philly is home and this is where you and I live, not halfway across the country with your so-called friends that you keep trying to shove down my throat."

"I can't help it if my friends are important to me. Why do you make such an issue about them?"

"How am I supposed to feel if you put them ahead of me all the time? You messed up this weekend and I deserve an apology."

"This is crazy. I am not going to apologize for having a good time this weekend. If you didn't want to go, that's on you." Courtney waited for Paul to respond, but nothing came so she jumped back in. "Paul, it's after midnight. I need to go to bed so I can get up for work in the morning."

"What's more important, me or your job? Don't get me wrong, I'm glad you have that job, but it's not all that. I should come first. Courtney, you really need to get your priorities straight."

"One of us needs a real job in this relationship," she blurted out.

"Ever since you came home this summer, we've had nothing but problems," he told her.

"Huh, you think it started this summer? Well, I can go back a lot further than that." She tilted the phone away from her mouth and let her eyes span the room with her teeth clenched so tightly that a nut would have cracked under the pressure. "I'm really tired. I'll have to talk with you later." She set the phone down and rested one arm on the back of the chair and the other on her hip, shaking her head in the process.

Absence over the weekend hadn't made her heart grow fonder. The relationship with Paul was still limping. Maybe she could find the spark they needed. Then again, it would take more like a bonfire. Whatever the problem was in the relationship, it would take more than a five-minute analysis to solve. At the moment sleep was her priority. She kicked off her shoes, shed her clothes along the short walk to the bedroom, threw on her gown, and jumped into bed. Sleep swooped in as soon as her head hit the pillow.

CHAPTER 2

Courtney wasn't as tired as she had anticipated when morning came. With a burst of energy, she wasted no time getting dressed. Paul was probably expecting a call, but why take a chance on ruining a perfectly good morning? She was already running a little late. It would be better to let the day get started and touch base with him later. She grabbed a piece of fruit from the counter and headed to work.

The office was already hopping when she arrived around nine, taking full advantage of the flex-time policy. She walked along the row of window offices that were reserved for management. One day she expected to be sitting in her own plush office. She jockeyed through the maze of cubicles and administrative stations, greeting the secretaries and the security officers as part of her normal routine. For now she had to be content with her walk-in-closet-sized cubicle.

She set her apple on the desk and retrieved her messages.

"Hey, Courtney . . ."

The voice of the first message was familiar but she couldn't place it right off.

"I got your number from the alumni association. Looks like I will be in Philadelphia this week to check out Penn's law school. If you're in town, I'd like to take you up on the offer that you made at graduation. If you're free Friday, I'd love to have you show me the sights."

"Oh my goodness," she said, sifting out the New England accent in a few of the words spoken. "Sebastian!" she mumbled with her heart picking up tempo. "Law school, here?"

"I don't know any other Northwestern alums in Philadelphia. If you know of anybody else, maybe we can all hang out together. It'll be a blast. Give me a call." He rattled off his phone number. "Talk to you later, buddy."

She had made a courteous gesture at graduation, telling him that she would show him around Philadelphia if and when he came to town. She was stunned that he had gone through the trouble of getting her number and had actually called. She couldn't forget how his smooth skin wore a tan like drizzled molasses on a gingerbread cookie.

If she agreed to go with Sebastian, what would they do? She had pushed the envelope so many times with him over the four years at Northwestern. They often ran into one another at the fitness center, spent hours talking afterward, and had lunch together on a few occasions. Nothing serious ever transpired. It couldn't. She was black and he was white. Eating lunch together had been challenging enough. How many times had she been on pins and needles trying to avoid running into her friends with Sebastian and having to explain an innocent lunch? The impending grief from her close friends had been one of many deterrents keeping her from really getting to know him. Paul was another factor. Most of the time they were on shaky ground, but he had still been her boyfriend of record for the entire stay at Northwestern.

"You're back. It's about time," Brice teased when he found Courtney sitting in her office.

She turned toward the entry of her cubicle and couldn't speak past the bite of apple in her mouth. The average-height, medium-built coworker came in and took a seat.

"How was your little weekend? And don't even try to pretend that you had a real party."

She swallowed hard and wiped her mouth with a napkin.

"I had a good time, and what if it was a 'real' party?"

"Oh, *please!* A school like Northwestern doesn't know anything about partying. What you had was a little reunion."

"Oh, so what are you saying, that your alma mater is the only place that can have a party?"

"No, I'm not saying that Howard is the only place. There are a bunch of black colleges that know how to do it too, like FAMU and Jackson State. Now, they know how to get down."

Courtney knew she was headed for a no-win Black Power session with Brice.

"Anyway, my reunion or whatever you want to call it, Mr. Militant, was fun."

Brice held up the closed-fist Black Power sign and tucked his head with his eyes closed for a second.

"One of these days, you're going to get busted doing that in here," she told him.

"I'm not afraid of these people. I'm black and I'm proud."

"Keep it up. I'm going to see how proud you are standing in the unemployment line."

At times she found his perspective confusing given the complexion of his skin. He wasn't just "high yellow," as her aunt used to describe a lighter-skinned black person. His skin reminded Courtney of December, when color drained from the plants and didn't return until the sun came out in the spring. Add his tight, short curly locks of hair to the package and European blood sang from his veins.

He flopped his hand up and down. "Enough with all of that. Did you hang with the peeps or did you blend in?"

"Peeps?"

"Peeps, you know, the folks, the brothers and sisters. Come on now, you're from Philly. I know you can talk the talk, I don't care how many degrees you got. You know what's up."

"I'm sorry, but I can't keep up with your slang. I don't know how you can be an assistant manager and get away with so much slang. It's unbelievable how much street talk you do around here."

"I might be down with the black folks in here, but I know how to be straitlaced with the rest of the group."

"Oh, so you change up?" she asked.

"Noooo, don't say that." He waved his hand frantically. "I'm true to myself and my people," he said, slamming his closed fist into his chest, "but it's better for the cause if I keep this good job. Another unemployed brother on the street isn't my idea of a rebel."

"So you're fighting the revolution from your BMW."

"No doubt. Better a BMW than a Pinto, and I did see one of those on my way into work this morning."

"You remind me so much of somebody that I know from Northwestern. Neither one of you has any sense."

"You like us and what does that say about you?" He gave her a wink.

"Anyway, what did I miss on Friday?"

"Nothing, not a single thing. Oh yeah, that's right, except for Joe Bob checking out your cubicle every couple of hours. He was crying because you didn't come in Friday," Brice said, sniffling and pretending to wipe tears from his eyes.

"Who?"

"You know who I'm talking about, the guy with the four-inch-thick glasses."

"Who, Wally, the new co-op student?"

"Wally! You have got to be joking. Now you know he's not black. No self-respecting brother is going to use a name like that. That would get changed with a quickness. He'd get called something like Big Wal or B.W. or anything but Wally. Please."

"If that's what his mama named him, that's what he gets called."

"Nah, nah. Brothers have enough troubles. Can you imagine being in the hood with a name like that!" Brice stated.

"He's a nice guy. You should leave him alone," she said, unable to hold a straight face.

"Nice! Forget that, he just better find someone around here that's more up his alley. You're off-limits."

"Who says so?"

"I say so. You don't have any brothers, so I'm looking out for you the same way they would to keep you out of trouble."

The phone rang, displaying an outside number. Courtney answered it.

"Hey, Paul," she said loud enough to be heard in her cubicle but not to spill over into the aisles.

Brice got the hint and waved good-bye before departing.

"I'm still waiting on my apology," Paul stated over the phone.

"For what? I'm glad that I went to Chicago. You should have come with me." She twirled her pen and pressed the receiver tight to her ear, letting no words escape.

"I keep telling you that I don't need to hang around uppity people who think they're better than I am."

"My friends are not like that. They are simple, down-to-earth people who like having fun."

"What, do you think I'm stupid? I know they talk about me behind my back just because I didn't go to college."

"Why would they spend time talking about you?"

"That's what I'm trying to figure out, but they can say whatever they want to about me. It doesn't even matter. I'm happy with who I am."

She was quiet briefly before attempting to move to another subject. "One of my college friends is coming to visit Penn's law school. They want us to show them around the city Friday. I know Thursdays and Fridays are our nights, so maybe we can take them Saturday." She gave Paul time to respond while squinting her eyes nearly shut.

"I'll pass."

"That's fine. I'll go by myself."

"I knew that you would," he fired back.

She should have told him the friend she was talking about was a guy. Maybe it would have made a difference. After all, Sebastian was at most a friend. There was no reason to keep him a secret from Paul, but she felt the need to be evasive and didn't know why.

"Have fun with your little college friends."

"I am so sick of your attitude about Northwestern and the people I went to school with. None of them have done a single thing to you." She spoke with a heavy voice, drilling the words into the mouthpiece. "Look, I have work to do. I'll talk to you later."

She dropped the phone into the cradle, rested her forehead in her hand, and sighed. So much stress for so little contentment in return. No sense praying for wisdom. God had already answered that request. Eventually she'd get around to doing what needed to be done. The presence of someone nearby shocked her back into the confines of the office.

"Oh," she said, turning, "Cara, I didn't hear you come in."

A vanilla-candle-colored woman with bright red lipstick accenting her round lips stood in the cubicle, fumbling with the hair clip that held her tightly drawn kinky blond hair in place.

"I'm sorry. You were so deep in thought that I didn't want to say anything. I should have announced myself."

"It's okay, come on in."

"You sure? Because I can come back later. I didn't want anything really. Just wanted to chat for a minute before my meeting." Cara took a seat and crossed her legs. "I looked for you this morning but you were nowhere to be found."

"I got in a little late this morning. You know that I met a bunch of my friends back at Northwestern over the weekend."

Cara tapped Courtney on the knee and raised her voice level. "That's right. Oh, that should have been so cool. What did you do?"

"I spent most of the time running around with a couple of my close friends. You name it and we squeezed it into the weekend."

Courtney didn't think Cara could relate to her kind of entertainment. There was no need to tell her about the mini-reunion party at Ashley's, where the gang of eight people watched movies and played cards late into the night while embellishing every racial issue that they could collectively discuss. It didn't help change the state of affairs, but they all seemed to feel stronger, more empowered sharing their thoughts in a humorous way with those who could relate.

"Did Paul go with you?" Cara asked.

As far as the people at work knew, Courtney's relationship with Paul was perfect. No need to divulge personal information to coworkers who sat on opposite sides of the social train tracks and didn't try to develop a friendship that oozed outside the Monday through Friday corporate bubble.

"No, he couldn't go. He had to work."

"Oh well, welcome back." Cara stood up and took a brief stretch. "I better go. I have to print off the agenda for the two o'clock meeting. You going?"

"I'm going to pass. I have enough other work to do since I was gone Friday."

"Okeydoke." Cara stopped before she got all the way out and said, "I keep forgetting to give you the invitation to my art party. I finally agreed to host one for my sister-in-law. It would be great if you could come. The party is Saturday, but I'll drop the invitation off with the directions sometime this week."

Saturday. Courtney was relieved to already have an out, thanks to Sebastian. Close call. She enjoyed talking to Cara and going to lunch and breakfast with her, but socializing after work would require too much sifting in her everyday life. The restaurants they went to were good, but every now and then Courtney wanted a good old-fashioned platter of smothered chicken over rice with two sides and a dessert.

That was out of Cara's league. Whenever people from the office wanted to go out for lunch, it was to the mainstream restaurants. When specialty spots serving Thai, Indian, Greek, or Japanese were selected at times, Courtney went willingly with the group. No one offered to go with her when she suggested soul or Caribbean food. For once, she wanted to take them to a restaurant where she could get a bottle of Louisiana hot sauce and not have to settle for a bottle of Tabasco sauce. When it came to venturing out into the ethnic waters, she was on her own.

Work had its moments, but nothing like personal life. Constantly arguing with Paul was draining, but she refused to let him penalize her for going to college and making friends outside of west Philadelphia. She would call Sebastian and confirm their meeting for Saturday. Why not? It would be something to do in an otherwise empty weekend.

CHAPTER 3

The week had gotten off to a bumpy start with Paul, but like other weeks, the dust had settled in time for their recurring Thursday night outing. Courtney entered the room. The pastel-colored sleeveless summer dress draped her like dainty sheer curtains swaying to the breath of the wind. She stood in the living room of her apartment gazing at Paul, who was sporting a pencil-thin tie and matching royal-blue leather shoes and belt.

Courtney favored bright colors, but had never considered how they would look on a pair of men's everyday shoes. She guessed that his outfit might be considered *GQ* in some European circles, but in Philadelphia it was in poor taste.

"Where are we going?"

"Let's grab some Popeye's and then head over to the pool hall."

"Pool hall! Aren't you tired of hanging out there? I know I am," she said.

"That's where we always go on Thursday night. We've been going since our junior year in high school."

Paul walked over to Courtney and wrapped his arms around her.

She wiggled her shoulders and pulled back. "That's exactly what I mean. That was six years ago. We were only sixteen then. We're in our twenties now. Come on, there are other things we can do on a Thursday night for fun. We don't always have to hang out at the pool hall. I'm tired of that."

"Well, I'm sorry the pool hall isn't good enough for you anymore. I guess we don't party like the big-time folks at Northwestern. Before you went to school, you didn't have a problem hanging around with the folks from the neighborhood."

"And I still don't have a problem hanging out with folks from the neighborhood. I don't even have a problem with the pool hall. The only real problem I have is with you."

"Oh, what, so I'm not good enough for you either?" He leaned his back against the door with his arms folded tight. His neck stretched and retreated like a turkey. "My, my, it looks like a diploma isn't the only thing you picked up in college."

Courtney planted her feet in the wooden-framed atrium that separated the kitchen from her closet-sized eating area, with both fists locked into her side.

"What exactly does that mean?"

"Courtney, what do you think it means? Nothing around here seems to be good enough for you anymore. Now that you have your degree and your big-time job downtown, you think I'm not good enough for you, especially with your friends coming to town or whatever."

Her friends had nothing to do with her being tired of the same drama with Paul. Her "friend" was coming to town, but Paul had no idea who. She realized he was just talking and it was better that way. No need stirring the pot when nothing was cooking between her and Sebastian.

"Hmmph. You don't know what you're talking about," she responded.

"Oh, I don't, huh? Well, check this out. Everything was cool with us before you got your job. Now, all of a sudden, all you do is nag at me about getting another job. You never had a problem with it before, and I've been working at the Hoagie Shop since my sophomore year in high school," he said.

"You don't get it, do you?"

"Obviously, I don't. So why don't you tell me, Ms. Courtney, since you're the smart one with all the answers?"

"You've had the same job since your sophomore year in high school and you don't see that as a problem? It might have been all right for spending money back then. You're a grown man now. How long do you plan to work there? That can't be your dream in life."

"There's nothing wrong with my job. I like it and I'm good at it. I can hook a cheese steak up like nobody in town. That's how I got promoted to grill chief. I'm the one running the grill. No matter what you think, that's pretty good."

"That's great, Paul. Just great. Is that what you plan to do for the next thirty years?"

"Maybe."

"What about getting married? You keep asking me."

"And you keep saying that you're not ready," he was quick to say.

"That's right, because you're not in any kind of position to get married. You can barely take care of yourself with the job you have."

"I just got promoted and you know that. It's going to make a big difference."

"How! Your so-called raise was next to nothing. It will barely buy your monthly bus pass. Forget about moving out of your mama's basement."

"So what? I have more money saved than you, sweetheart. Most people my age don't have nineteen thousand dollars in the bank."

Courtney hated to acknowledge it, but he was right. How he got the money was what concerned her. He was constantly in some type of car or bike accident and he didn't even have his own car. Each accident led to a lawsuit and three to five thousand dollars. It had turned into supplemental income. She couldn't figure out how Paul, his parents, two brothers, two sisters, uncle, and grandparents could all be so accident-prone with at least two going through a lawsuit or related medical treatment at any given time. She had to wonder if they were creating accidents and maybe intentionally pulling in front of unsuspecting drivers. Either way, it might be money Paul could count on, but not she. Money had been a sore subject for at least the past year, with each related conversation ending badly. She knew it would be better to move on to something more tangible and less volatile.

"What about benefits? You don't even have medical benefits."

"Don't need them. I don't plan to get sick."

Courtney stood silent for a moment. "What happened to your plans to go to college?"

"That's all you talk about, college. Everybody doesn't have to go to college to be successful. I have other plans." He eased his hands into his pants pockets and paced in a small circular path keeping near the door.

"Like what, real estate!"

"Yeah, I admit that the real estate classes didn't work out, but there are other trades."

"So, what are you saying? You planning to go to trade school?"

"Maybe. What does it matter? You don't seem to want anybody unless he has an Ivy League degree like you."

"For your information, Northwestern isn't an Ivy League school."

"I know that, but somebody needs to let you know. Matter of fact, Northwestern is no better than City-Wide Community College, and CW is just as popular too. They have students from all over the world going to that school. It's definitely big time, no doubt."

"CW doesn't have on-campus housing."

"So what?"

"So, where do all of these world-class students live?" she asked.

"Haven't you heard of apartments? There are plenty of rooms around the college," he said. "You have all of that so-called education and no common sense."

"So what? You're uneducated with no common sense. There, we've finally found something that we have in common." Courtney shook her head, wondering exactly at what moment over the past six years Paul had become so ignorant. "Whatever, Paul."

Courtney dropped her arms and took the short walk to the dining area and took a seat. She locked her hands together and rested them on the table, rolling her thumbs around each other. "Where is this conversation going? Where are we going?"

"Well, it definitely doesn't look like we're going to the pool hall. Look, I'm out of here." He turned to leave the apartment. With one hand on the knob he turned back toward Courtney. "You take it easy, Courtney. If you come down off of your high horse, you know where to find me."

"If you climb out of the hoagie pit, you can give me a call," Courtney squeaked into the hallway as Paul pulled the door shut behind him.

The warm tears streamed down her air-conditioned cheeks. They were coming against her will. Another would-be fun-filled evening had ended in an argument. Weekend after weekend, argument after argument, being with Paul didn't feel good anymore. She felt love for Paul or something like it. She missed him when he wasn't around, somewhat, but not like she had at the beginning of her freshman year in college. She loved how much they had had in common back then, church, the neighborhood, friends, and grand ideas for the future. She dwelled on how much they enjoyed hanging out, although it had been a while since their weekends had left her with breathtaking memories. The more she thought about it, the fewer happy moments she could conjure up. She didn't feel like they belonged together. Prayer after prayer had left her with the same feeling for the past three years. It didn't quite sit right in her spirit. Still, so many aspects of her life had changed since leaving Philadelphia and heading off to Evanston. Maintaining some sense of familiarity by dragging on with Paul hadn't been totally bad, just mildly miserable. He was lukewarm water on a chilly night. But the time had come to start afresh.

It had been a long time coming, calling it quits. The thought of splitting up with the only boyfriend she'd ever known was more agonizing to her than actually being apart. Breaking it to her family was going to be another unpleasant scene. The hopes and dreams her family had for her went beyond education and career. They permeated deep into her personal life, including her choice of mates. They knew Paul from childhood, knew his family, and liked his roots to the neighborhood. Letting go of the man her family had deemed to be her mate would take some preparation. She had two weeks before the family party, Labor Day weekend, honoring her graduation and a few other family birthdays. For one reason or another it had gotten rescheduled over and over this summer. It was bound to happen this time, while the warm weather was still holding up for an outdoor cookout. She stretched out across the bed, screaming inside without a sound breaking free. For now she would suppress the sadness the way she'd done for the past three years with Paul, sharing her discontent with God alone.

CHAPTER 4

Courtney didn't have to punch a time clock, but all employees were expected to arrive somewhere between seven and nine. This Friday morning she made it into the office around eight-thirty and was hoping for enough zest to get through the day.

She listened to her voice messages and picked through her e-mail.

"I thought I heard you over here. I'm running down to the cafeteria to get a bagel. You want anything?"

"Sure, Cara, I'll go down with you. Just let me grab some money."

The ladies walked and did small talk. Courtney greeted a host of secretaries along the way. While she was waiting for the elevator, a black man stood behind her. She turned around and said hello. The elevator stopped at the fifth floor, a black woman got on, made eye contact with Courtney, and they spoke to one another.

Courtney wasn't sure what she wanted to eat. She and her coworker went from station to station perusing breakfast dishes. After talking with practically every grill person, cafeteria worker, and cashier in the place, Courtney was ready to leave with her discounted bowl of fresh berries to go with her oatmeal.

"How do you know so many people?" Cara asked. "You started the same time I did. I don't know nearly as many people."

It would take too much explaining to convey that she didn't personally know all of the people she spoke to and who spoke to her. It was a neighborhood thing. Courtney remembered excitedly walking down the street with her grandfather, a tall strong black man whose hand swallowed hers as he held it. He would wear his hat and topcoat down Fifty-second Street nodding his head at passersby, shaking the hand of a few and talking with others. Everybody around the neighborhood did it back then. It was like one big family.

Cara stopped at her cubicle, two rows before Courtney's.

"Thanks for going down to the cafeteria with me. I'll see you at the status meeting at eleven," Cara said.

Courtney went to her cube and ate her breakfast. She was tossing the container in the garbage when her boss, Sheila, entered.

"Hey, lady," Sheila said.

Courtney patted the guest chair in her cubicle gesturing for her to sit down. "I haven't had a chance to talk with you all week."

"I know. It's been crazy. I don't know if I can take another meeting this week. How have you been? How was your trip to Illinois last weekend?" Before she could finish, Brice entered the cubicle. The ladies acknowledged his presence without breaking the flow in the conversation.

"Sheila, it was a good trip. I am so glad that I went."

"You still talking about that little party? One of these days I'm going to take you to a real party. Matter of fact, the next time I go to my homecoming at Howard, I'm going to let you go with me so you can see how it's really done," Brice said, bopping his head to the beat of an unheard song.

"I keep telling you that you remind me of this friend of mine from college. He's crazy just like you," Courtney told Brice.

"What's his name? I might know him."

"Never know," Sheila said. "We all know it's only about one or two degrees of separation between professional blacks. Everybody knows somebody who knows somebody. It's a small world for most people, and a downright shoe box for blacks like us."

A middle-aged black man stopped his mail cart outside the cubicle and briefly chatted with the three that were huddled in Courtney's office before heading on his way.

"How's Paul?" Sheila asked.

Sheila and Brice were Courtney's closest coworkers being that they were the only three salaried blacks in the entire North American marketing research team. They had similar backgrounds, all coming from inner-city working-class backgrounds with pit stops in top-caliber schools. Her frequent conversations with Sheila and Brice, and involvement in various social activities outside of work, gave them firsthand knowledge about Paul.

"Not good. We don't get along anymore. We argue all the time about our jobs and money."

"You need to cut that trick loose. He's not going to be able to hang with a sister like you. It's just a matter of time before he really trips about your job and all of that long money you're making. He's not good enough for you," Brice said.

"Just because he doesn't make much doesn't mean he isn't good enough for me."

"The money is not the problem. It's his attitude. If he's tripping about you doing well in this entry-level position, how's he going to feel when you get a management position? He can only move up so much at the Hoagie Shop. It's not like he's going to take over the owner's spot. Face it, his gig has limited potential, which means the brother has limited potential. That's why I said that he's not good enough for you. You need a man like me."

"You need to quit. Brice, you have at least three girlfriends that we know about, let alone the ones we don't know about," Courtney reminded him.

"Yeah, yeah, but none of those are serious. I'm just checking things out."

"Well, you won't be checking things out with me, Mr. Gigolo."

A five-foot-eight pale-complexioned coworker came around the corner and was startled to see the crowd in Courtney's office.

"Oh, I'm sorry. I didn't know you had someone in your office."

"You need to see me, Jason?" Courtney asked.

"No, I can come back later. It's nothing important."

"Are you sure?"

"Sure, no problem. Hi, Sheila and Brice," the guy said as he exited the scene.

Sheila covered her mouth slightly to ensure that he didn't hear her. "He is on you, girl."

Courtney sighed.

"No, he's not. He stops by in the morning and says hello, that's it."

"Girl, please, you might be young but you are not dumb. Men are men, across the board. I don't care if they're black or white or yellow or purple. Men are all the same when it comes to chasing a woman. Now, I know you can tell when a man is interested in you. That man is on you. He's not coming by here just to say hello. Every time you see him he says, 'Hi, Courtney.' His eyes are all wide with a big ole smile."

Courtney knew Sheila was right. Sebastian had shown interest for years at Northwestern, but it wasn't feasible for her to act on it. What would be the point? They couldn't date in Illinois or Pennsylvania, regardless of how much charm flowed from his tall, athletic body that had an array of females from various ethnic groups looking him over every chance they got. Playing his trumpet in the school band had helped to lengthen his list of interested women.

"Wait a minute, now, Paul's got issues, but I know you're not rolling like that," Brice said in a firm tone. "There are plenty of women in this department. I know that he's not coming around here looking to get with you two. Slavery is over. The master can't roll through here and drag our women away while us brothers sit and watch. He'll get dropped acting a fool up in here. Biff better roll on."

"Biff! No, you didn't go and rename the man."

"That's right. No different than us getting called Bubba. It doesn't matter what I call him as long as he rolls on, because I know you're not interested."

"I don't even think of Jason like that. He seems to be a decent guy. That's all."

"That better be all!"

"Why, what if I did like him?" It was friends and family who thought like Brice who would help to keep her focused away from a Sebastian type. "You have some nerve telling me who I can and can't like with twenty women nipping at your heels."

"Like I said, Paul might be a trip, but you have other options. Going that way is a bit extreme," Brice said with his face twisted as if he'd been sucking on a lemon. "How is he going to come up in here and try to get with one of the finest sisters in this joint? He must be crazy. He better roll on to one of those temps who are always trying to snatch a man up in here. You two sisters are off-limits."

"So, Brice, are you saying that you wouldn't date a white woman?" Sheila asked.

"I'm not going to say that I won't date one, but I'm not going to marry one. Nah, nah, I might play around outside the yard, but when it's time to go home, it's to a sister."

"So, the only woman you're willing to marry is a sister?"

"Yep."

"What about Italian? They can be pretty dark," Sheila said.

"Nah, even though they don't get treated much better than the blacks around here. But nah, I'd have to say no. I'm not coming here to get beat up because I'm messing around with some Uncle Tony's niece and he doesn't want her hooking up with somebody that looks like me."

"You have a point there," Sheila added. "When we talk about interracial couples, we usually think of a black and a white, but it could be Jewish and Italian, Irish and Italian, or something Chinese and Jewish. You know any of those combinations would catch flak from their own kind just like a black and white couple would from some of us."

Courtney was reminded why someone like Sebastian wouldn't come up in a conversation like this, friend or not. "What about Hispanic or Asian or Native American or even somebody from the Middle East?"

"Now, Hispanic and Native American, I might have to think about that one because they're like pseudo-sisters." Brice stretched his hands out and floated them down, swerving in and out like the curves on a tight two-lane road overlooking the ocean. "Hispanic women might as well be sisters. I'm cool with them. I really can't say much about Native Americans because you don't really run into them too often around here. I'm not sure about Asian women either. I don't have a problem with them, but I have to marry somebody that can hook up a sweet potato pie and some collard greens at the drop of a hat, and I don't know if they can do that. See, that's why a brother has to be careful about marrying outside of the race. You might have to give up too much."

"And I guess you're not ready to give up sweet potato pie for true love?" Courtney asked.

"You know it. What about you, Ms. Thang?" Brice asked Sheila. "Would you marry a white guy?"

"Nope, that's a special calling and it's not for me. Too much drama. Relationships are enough work as it is. I'm not trying to complicate anything. I'm going to wait for my black knight in shining armor to drive up and whisk me out of my office," Sheila said.

"What if he doesn't show up around here for a while?" Courtney asked.

"No matter how long it takes, I'm going to wait for a brother. That's all there is to it."

"Speaking of knights in shining armor," Courtney cut in, "I still want you to come to church and my aunt's for dinner on Sunday."

"I was planning to come, but it looks like I have to run down to Baltimore to check on my mom. She was admitted to the hospital yesterday for chest pains."

"Is she all right?"

"She's fine." Sheila stretched her body out vertically in the chair and toyed with the security badge dangling from the long thick string around her neck. "They thought it might have been a heart attack, but it turned out to be gas. I really hate that I can't go with you Sunday. You know your family can hook up some good food. And I know that fine cousin of yours will be there."

"Who, Edwin?"

"Who else?"

"Hey, wait a minute. I'm the only fine brother around here," Brice said with his chin in the air.

"Will you please be quiet for just a minute?" Sheila said, laughing his way.

"I'm sure he'll be there. He doesn't miss too many of his mother's Sunday dinners." Courtney knew it was a different story with his brother. There was no telling about Jay, who wasn't always in a legal position to come.

"Man, I'm really disappointed now."

"Why don't you give him a call? I'm sure he'd like to hear from you."

"No way, girl. I am not going to call him. I'm not throwing myself at any man, not even your super-fine cousin. He knows my number. I'll let him call me."

"So why don't you just call him? What's the big deal?"

"See, that's the problem with sisters. Don't sit back. Show a brother you're interested. Men love when a women makes a move toward him," Brice shared with them.

"When a man is interested, you know it. You don't have to chase him. He comes looking for you."

"Do you like Edwin?" Courtney asked.

"I like him and all. I really enjoyed myself when he took me to dinner that time."

"I know he likes you."

"Well, that's all well and good, but he made it clear that he didn't have the time to dedicate to a serious relationship. If a man is up front enough to lay that out on the table from the beginning, then I have to respect that. For me to pursue him now would only be throwing myself at a man who has made it clear that he's not interested. A sister has to move on. What other single uncles or cousins do you have, since you don't have any brothers?"

"There's my uncle Raymond and my cousin Terry."

"What side of your family is Edwin on?"

"My father's. His mother and my father are brother and sister."

"What side are this Uncle Raymond and cousin Terry on?"

"My father's side."

"Oh no, then I can't go out with either of them."

"Why not?" Brice asked.

"Because they're related to Edwin. I can't go out with any of them since I've already gone out with him. You know the rule."

Courtney agreed, recalling the unspoken dating protocol she had been raised on.

"What rule?" he asked.

"The rule says that if you go out with somebody, then you wipe out any chances of going out with their friends, their roommates, and definitely their relatives. We don't play that," Sheila explained.

"That might be true for a close relative, but you have to do a lot more than just go out on a date for that rule to apply," Brice contested.

"If you go out with somebody just one time and you don't even hold hands, it still counts as a date. That means you have to take their entire set of family and friends off your list of possibilities. That's the way it is," Sheila reiterated.

"Hmmph. When I was in college, you would have been amazed at how people were hooking up with everybody. Nobody was off-limits," Courtney added.

"Not even the sisters and brothers?" Brice wondered.

"Let me put it this way, not the sisters that I knew."

"That's what I thought. The brothers got busy with whomever they wanted to, right? Men are going to be men. I go out with whomever I want to go out with. Rules don't apply to me," Brice said.

Relationships were tough. It didn't look like she was headed for a future with Paul, but there was no need to tell everything just yet. She thought they had broken up several times in the past and those turned out to be false alarms. She decided not to share the actual status with Sheila and Brice until some days of certainty had passed. If and when she told them about Paul remained to be seen. Telling them about Sebastian was definitely out. No need to rock the racial boat with her friends.

CHAPTER 5

The morning flew by and Friday afternoon had rushed in again to bump Courtney into a much-needed weekend of recovery.

"Knock, knock," the man said without going through the actual motion of rapping on the carpetlike walls of the cubicle.

Courtney spun around and looked up to see Jason standing in the doorway.

"Jason, come in."

"Wasn't sure if you were still here."

"I'm packing up now. What's up?"

"A group of us are going to Friday's for happy hour. Thought I'd check to see if you were interested in coming."

Courtney normally passed on going to happy hour with the group, but now that she and Paul were over, she had no other plans for Friday night. It wouldn't hurt to stop by Friday's. Making an appearance every now and then might strengthen her image as being a team player.

"Why not? Sure, I'll go."

"Really?" he said, sounding surprised that she'd accepted. "I mean great."

Courtney knew Jason had expected her to say no like she had for the past three months. "I have to finish up here. I'll meet you over there in about forty minutes."

"Good deal. It's the one on City Line Avenue." Jason turned to leave and then turned back to Courtney. "I know you're not married, but is that your boyfriend?"

Courtney picked up the five-by-seven gold-framed picture that sat prominently inside her desk hutch. She held it for a moment, opened the lower drawer of her desk, and tossed it inside. "Not anymore."

"Really? That guy must be crazy!"

Courtney took the comment as a compliment without expounding on it. Jason didn't have a chiseled body like Sebastian or a smile that lit up the place, but he did have interest. She hadn't given herself a chance to get to know Jason. Happy hour would be his time to impress.

"So, we'll see you in forty," he said.

Courtney reflected to her conversation earlier in the day with Sheila. She could tell Jason was interested in her. She wasn't sure how receptive she was to a white coworker. Brice would be the least of her problems if she went there.

She was still feeling the aches of having to prove herself in every meeting. Many of the men in the group had started after high school as interns and worked their way up to analyst and in a few cases, management. They were locally bred and attended Greater Philadelphia University as their school of choice. Fresh out of college, she knew most people saw her as a rookie marketer who was still wet behind the ears. Having a degree from Northwestern should have been a ringing endorsement that she was intelligent enough to handle the job. Once they learned where she had gone to school, she found herself being challenged with project after project. She was making an effort to be a team player but not everyone was accepting her. Jason seemed to be.

Mrs. Ellis, the elderly cleaning woman, shuffled in to empty the trash like she did every day. Courtney always knew to expect her around five during the week and about four on Fridays.

"Heading out for the weekend, huh?" Mrs. Ellis asked.

"Yes, I am, Mrs. Ellis. I'm out of here. You should be getting out of here too. Don't stay too late. It's Friday."

"I won't be long. Soon as I finish cleaning that mess those nasty bigwigs left in the conference room, I'll be leaving too."

Courtney knew she was referring to the quarterly review meetings that had gone on all week with the vice presidents and directors. The working sessions were scheduled to start at six each morning and go well into the night, which meant they ate every meal and snack in the conference room, day after day. They cut out early this Friday, and all the gobs of food that they hadn't touched were eaten by anybody that could get in there fast enough and grab some of it. The scavengers were the real culprits, but Courtney decided against sharing that piece of information.

"You'd think since they got all of those big titles they'd know how to clean up after themselves. It's a shame how they left that place. You know, you can't buy home training. They all so used to having a maid clean up after their nasty behinds at home. I guess they think I'm their mama. Been here thirty-two years and it don't never change. This is 'bout the nastiest bunch I've seen."

Courtney gave a grunt of acknowledgment and kept quiet, knowing the old grandmother was just talking to be talking.

"Have a good weekend, Mrs. Ellis."

"You do the same," the cleaning lady said as she left with the sound of the cart's wheels fading as she continued down the aisle.

Courtney shut down the laptop, secured it in her hutch, turned the key in the lock, and was officially off work. She wasted no time getting to her car. She pulled her Honda out of the parking garage and casually headed for Montgomery Drive. The sun was beaming, people canoeing down the river, couples holding hands and strolling along the waterfront. She felt relieved to finally be free from the ball and chain Paul had around her leg, but sad not to have someone to hang out with on such a beautiful day. She believed God had someone lined up for her now that she was being obedient and had let go of Paul. By some miracle, maybe he would show up before this gorgeous afternoon was over so they could capture the warmth together.

She parked in Friday's lot and went inside. Courtney was about to ask the hostess to direct her to the group right before catching a glimpse of them at the backside of the bar. She took shallow breaths along the cloudy path. The cigarette smoke latched on to her clothes and suffocated her hair.

Jason saw her approaching and waved her over to the crowd.

"Courtney, glad you could make it."

Greetings and acknowledgments poured in from her marketing coworkers.

She took a quick survey of the group and was disappointed to see only two other women, at a smaller table to the side of the bar, who were being pawed by four men. Her definition of being social with a virtual group of strangers was straightforward. No personal matters discussed. Hi, bye, and how's the weather squeezed in the middle, summed up the tone of her conversations. Having someone touching and groping her was completely out of the question. Courtney had no intention of joining that intimate group. Instead she mingled with the guys sitting at the bar.

"Courtneyyyyy, woffff. How the heck are you? You want a beer?" Bill asked.

Courtney didn't want to stand in his space. She figured the man had been there no more than an hour, and the tomato-red color in his face gave indication that he was already drunk. The smell of di-gested beer ravaged her nose. She took a step back to avoid letting him put his arm around her with a mug of beer clutched in his fist. She was running scenarios around in her head of how to react if he spilled any of it on her. She didn't want to act a fool in front of her colleagues, but wasn't going to walk away wearing a ruined dress with-out someone catching it.

Jason pulled her away. "Come on, dude, she just got here. Give her a break."

The staggering coworker slurred his puzzled words while lifting his mug to Courtney as a toast. He stumbled to the bar stool and guzzled the remaining brew.

"Can I get you a drink?"

"Cranberry juice and ginger ale mixed," she said.

"That's it?" Jason asked.

"That's it."

He put the request in with the bartender.

"So, Courtney, I've never seen you at a happy hour."

Adam was in earshot and overheard Jason talking to Courtney.

"It's about time you came. We have a blast." Adam held his head back and poured the shot of gin into his mouth followed by gulps of beer.

It was difficult for Courtney to see these people as the sober, mild-mannered colleagues she worked with every day. In the office they were polished. Tonight they looked like a bunch of drunken, out-of-control schoolkids. This group was slightly older, but no different than the slew of students she had spent four years avoiding in college. She hated when the dorm would buy kegs for the few extreme partyers, using money that had been allocated for all students. She didn't drink and didn't want her money to go to the borderline campus alcoholics who couldn't get a weekend going without jump-starting it with a mug in their hand. They'd drink beer and other alcohol until they either passed out at the party or puked along the way to their room. The worst times of the school year were the fall and spring quarters when the fraternities and sororities held their rushes. Anything went. Many of the girls in her freshman dorm had been sexually violated time and time again because they got drunk at a party, passed out, and couldn't remember how many guys took a turn on them. Different city, different people, same experience.

"I understand you went to Northwestern."

Courtney couldn't figure out why some of her coworkers made such a big deal out of where she went to school. She was proud of her alma mater, but wasn't wearing it on her sleeve. She didn't approach other people by asking where they went to school. It didn't matter. She assumed anyone on the team was qualified.

"Are you from Illinois?" asked DeWayne, another one of her many young male coworkers.

"No, I'm from Philadelphia."

"What part?"

"West Philadelphia, the Overbrook section."

"Wow, so how did you end up at such a good school coming from that part of town?"

"They recruited me and made me an offer I couldn't refuse."

"Boy, wish I could have gotten an offer from Northwestern. I couldn't get any special program, so I stayed in Philadelphia and got my associate's from CW."

Courtney knew where he was headed and didn't feel like defending herself. She could have told him about her scoring in the top 3 percent on the ACT or getting a score of 1500 on the SAT, but opted not to bother. She would go another route.

"I have a cousin that's an accountant. He was accepted at CW."

"When did he graduate? I might know him."

"You know what, he ended up not going there. He decided to go to Georgetown. They have a better basketball team."

The guy retreated back into his mug of magic and took a swallow.

Courtney took a long look at her watch, wondering how thirty minutes had already gotten sucked up. She had made an appearance and it was time to go. She recognized the warning signs. A few more shots of whiskey and a little more time would loosen the tongues of her colleagues, empowering them to feel comfortable crossing the line and saying whatever rolled into their heads. It had happened time after time during her summer internships. She'd go to happy hour and it was just a matter of time before one of her alcohol-influenced coworkers would forget that she was a black woman and embark on conversations that were inappropriate. A few had even been crazed enough to approach her in a sexual way. What was said after she left was out of her control. But she was responsible for the moment and could comfortably exit with a clear conscience.

"I'd better get going."

"Why are you leaving so soon? Hang around for a little while longer. The party is just getting going," Jason told her.

"Where do you people hang out on a Friday? Maybe there's a place we can go dancing, you and me," Adam slurred with his glazed red-tinted eyes fixed on Courtney.

A blank stare was the only response she offered.

"I have to go. I'll see all of you next week. Have a good weekend."

Courtney waved bye and rushed from the smoke-filled pit to the fresh air outdoors. She felt the blistering stares.

After she left, the handful of men still lurking at the bar talked about how attractive she was and how they wouldn't mind spending some private time with her.

"I'd spend time with her," Adam said.

"No way, dude," DeWayne said.

"She's gorgeous," Jason said, nursing his beer. Any other feelings of interest that he had for Courtney were kept to himself.

She didn't see happy hour at Fridays as being much different than going to the pool hall, except those that drank there held their liquor better. Puking in Big Pete's Billiard Hall was a no-no. It couldn't hurt to do some kind of bonding with her coworkers, but going to drunken happy hours wasn't the way. Courtney pulled a handful of hair around to her nose and gagged on the odor. Now she had something to do tonight, go home and wash her hair. With guys like Paul and Jason, she was sure to have a healthy, well-washed head of hair.

CHAPTER 6

Saturday rolled in with a touch of melancholy. Courtney wasn't eager to admit it, but there was a faint ache for Paul, or was she getting that feeling confused with the longing for companionship? Like a dog returning to a buried bone, she considered giving him a call. She had picked up the phone time after time yesterday. Thank goodness she'd been able to fight the demons of complacency. It would be easy to resuscitate the dead-end relationship with Paul. They had both done it so many times over the past three years. The relationship had begun showing signs of illness in her sophomore year in college, suffered a massive attack in her junior year, and had been on life support ever since with shutdowns along the way, each time resulting in a resuscitated reunion. How many times could her heart keep starting? She understood the framed poster in her office that showed a cat squeezing through a tree hole and a scripture across the bottom that said something about him not knowing how to go out or come in. That was it. She was stuck in transition.

Bad matters worse, she had to meet Sebastian today. The happy hour last night was enough of the team player act for a while. Her washed hair was just relaxing back into place. Another afternoon of the same drunken ignorance didn't yield a pleasant feeling. It was too late to get out of it. She had made the promise and planned to stick with it, but hopefully it wouldn't consume the entire afternoon. It was two o'clock. She fired up the Honda and drove to Dave & Busters on the waterfront. If they could finish up by four o'clock, there would be enough time left for her to see a movie before the day was over.

Courtney saw Sebastian standing at the top of the stairs. His six-foot stature had reaped the benefits of his consistent fitness training, and he was wearing those dark khakis and cream-colored polo shirt. He still wore his dark hair short and combed back away from his face.

"Thanks for hanging out with me," Sebastian said as she came up the stairs.

Courtney responded with a smile. "I hope you don't mind coming here instead of taking the city tour. It's too hot outside for me."

"Are you kidding? This is awesome. I've spent two days at the law school and the business school. Any break sounds good to me."

They walked into the main area. The place was sectioned off with stationary rides in one spot, basketball hoops and other games in another, lines of billiard tables, a bar, and rows of booths clumped together in a restaurant section. Seen through the twenty-foot-high windows was the river and the massive Ben Franklin Bridge hoisted hundreds of feet in the air, serving as the backdrop to the indoor amusement park.

"What do you want to do first?"

"You're the guest. You choose," she offered.

"Let's shoot some hoops."

They kicked the afternoon off with basketball and moved to skeet ball, playing game after game.

Courtney felt like she had twenty years ago when the state fair came to town. She wanted to play all of the games, but first things first. "I'm getting hungry," she said.

Sixty seconds and they were transplanted from the play land to the refueling station. They sat in a booth and combed the menu.

"Let's get the chicken pizza and some of the nachos," Sebastian suggested.

It felt like old times back at Northwestern to Courtney. They placed the order and their food came in less than fifteen minutes.

"Are you seriously considering Penn?" It would seem weird if he actually ended up in Philadelphia, so close by.

"I am. This trip was just a formality. I'm in."

"Wow! Congratulations," she said, wanting to offer a compliment without showing too much or too little excitement. She'd known Sebastian for four years. She couldn't explain why all of a sudden she was feeling giddy around him.

"Yeah, thanks," he said, bobbing his head up and down trying to get the dangling cheese to break free from the slice of pizza he was holding in midair.

"Haven't the fall classes already begun?"

"Oh, I didn't tell you. I'm starting in January," he said, wiping his hands on a napkin.

Courtney scrunched her face. "I thought everybody started law school in the fall. Won't you be off cycle?"

"I'll start law school next fall, but I'll start the business school program in January."

"You're going to do both the J.D. and M.B.A. combined program?"

"Crazy, huh!"

"No, I guess not," she stammered. "Not if that's what you want to do."

"I do. It's time to get serious. It's taken a great deal of last-minute maneuvering but it's what I want to do. Deep down I'm a business-man."

"Why are you going to law school?"

"Two words—my family. My dad inherited the family law firm from his father and he took it over from his father. I will be the fourth gen-eration, and my dad is adamant about me taking over the practice. Pursuing any other profession is absolutely unacceptable to him."

"I know all about doing something you don't want to do just so your family will be happy."

"Stuff happens. What can you do?"

Courtney grunted, thinking about her constant need to please her family when it came to whom she dated and what kind of decisions she made with her career.

"How about another round of skeet ball? I know I can take you this time."

"You're on."

Three rounds of skeet ball later, a couple of simulated motorcycle races, a turn with the virtual reality set, and several rounds of squirt-ing water into the mouth of an electric clown rounded out the after-noon. Courtney and Sebastian cashed in their six-foot-long trail of game tickets. They salivated like kids in a candy store over the five rows of stuffed animals, colorful kiddy toys, and the few prizes appropriate for adults.

"What should we get, Court?" Before she could respond, he covered his mouth and yelled, "Oops. I forgot, Courtney. Please, please, mademoiselle, don't thrash me, please." He could still feel the pangs of the swift and direct correction that she had put on him in their freshman year when he made the mistake of shortening her name and calling her Court. "Please, mademoiselle, please," he went on.

Courtney couldn't believe how silly he was willing to be in a public setting. She was more amused than embarrassed, which came as a surprise. "Okay, okay." Staring up at her were his perfectly rounded deep brown eyes framed by his neatly groomed thick eyebrows that melted any inkling of unrest that she might have lurking inside. She pulled him up from the bent-knee position he had assumed. "Get up."

"Yeah!"

Courtney was having so much fun that the moment of would-be humiliation floated by.

"Which prize? We have enough tickets to get one of the jumbo prizes," he said.

"I don't know, let's get the stuffed elephant."

After pledging the sorority and becoming a Delta in college, she picked up an elephant every chance she got. The four-foot fluffy elephant would be a welcome addition.

"You heard the lady, give me the elephant, please."

They walked out the door, and the dash of dusk startled Courtney. It was after seven o'clock. She had completely lost track of the time. She hadn't laughed this much since the reunion with the crazy bunch. It was refreshing to have a few hours where she could be as silly as she wanted to be without feeling childish.

The day was gone but it had been well spent. A pleasant surprise. She had expected him to be the kind of partyer the other men at work were. The ones she'd seen in action as recently as yesterday. He was different, at least for an afternoon.

"Once I get settled, I'll give you a call."

"I'd like that." She dug around in her purse and came out with a pen and piece of paper. "Take my home number in case you can't catch me at work. By the way, I don't know if you remember me telling you about my cousin Edwin?"

"He's the one that went to Yale."

"That's the one. Maybe he can give you another perspective on law school."

"Cool. Let's blow this pop stand. Where's your car?"

"I parked in the lot next door."

"I'll walk you there first," he said, still holding the four-foot elephant. "Then I'll grab a cab."

"No, you won't. I'll give you a ride. It's the least I can do since you've been so good about carrying that humungous elephant around for me."

"Awesome. It will give us a chance to talk a little longer."

The elephant hogged the backseat, and conversation consumed the front. Fifteen minutes, door to door. Courtney dropped Sebastian off at the hotel and went home. She was too tired to stay out and see a movie. Tonight she would have to settle for a good book and turning in early. The rest would do her good. Besides, she needed to get ready for church tomorrow and dinner at her aunt's house. That would be another bright spot in the weekend if both of her cousins, Jay and Edwin, showed up.

CHAPTER 7

Courtney flashed her badge across the scanner, and the turnstile opened to let her enter the building. Two of her favorite security guards were on duty. She knew most of the guards and they went out of their way to accommodate her, like carrying packages to her car, walking her to the garage at the drop of a hat, and letting her enter the building without filling out the proper paperwork the times she'd forgotten her badge. She didn't know exactly why the guards showed her so much favor, but figured that being friendly and treating them with respect, unlike the way she'd seen some of her colleagues act toward them, had something to do with it.

She plopped her portfolio down on the desk and set the brown paper bag next to it. Her morning routine was the same, retrieve voice mail messages, read e-mail, and go to the cafeteria with one of her coworkers. Since she hadn't answered or returned Paul's phone calls last night, she was bound to hear from him today. Right or wrong, she had successfully managed to duck out of church yesterday, barely escaping his attempt to catch her in the vestibule. Nearly breaking up and getting back together was a game they'd played for so long. Eventually she'd have to deal with him, but not right now.

Jason paid Courtney a visit not long after she got back from the cafeteria. Seeing her on the phone, he mouthed the words that he'd come back later. By mid-morning Shelia and Brice had stopped by to highlight the events of the weekend.

"What's up, Ms. Courtney?" he said, sauntering into the cubicle with his arms raised to half-mast and index fingers bopping up and down.

"Brice, it's early on a Monday morning and you're already prepared to act a fool," Courtney said.

"That's why I don't let him hang out in my office," Sheila said.

"No, it's because you're a director and that means you can't have three blacks in your office with the door closed. People might think it's a conspiracy," he said.

"Especially with you in the office."

"See, little worker bees like me don't have to put on airs. I can hang out and act a fool up in here and they don't pay me any attention. You see, you're management, part of the establishment. You is the 'man.' "

"See how crazy he is? Pretty soon you won't be able to let him come into your office either. Why do you have to be so loud? Anyway," Sheila said, while putting her hand with fingers spread apart in Brice's face and turning her conversation away from him and toward Courtney, "what did you do this weekend?"

"I went to happy hour with some of the people from our group on Friday and to D and B with a friend of mine from Northwestern on Saturday," Courtney told them.

Brice's eyes opened wide and his mouth hung open.

"I can't believe you went to happy hour," he said, shaking his head. "They got sloppy drunk, didn't they?"

Courtney concurred.

"Yeah, after a few drinks they forgot all about you and started letting the words fly?" he said.

"I didn't stay long enough for all of that. A quick half hour and I was out of there. That's all I could take."

"Was it all guys?"

"A few women from creatives were there. They were all over them too and at least one of them is married. I can't believe they let those guys treat them the way they do. I'm not having it."

"That's why you need to keep Joe Bob from sniffing around your desk."

"What about this friend from Northwestern? Is she a fine sister? If she is, you have to hook me up."

Courtney fidgeted in her seat. In light of the happy hour fiasco she had just reported, blow by drunken blow, it would be difficult to explain that going out with Sebastian had been a totally different experience. Brice would wonder how that could be. Sebastian was a white man, and Brice believed that all of the millions or billions of them walking the face of the earth thought and acted exactly the same in every situation. He told her that whatever treatment the brothers got, that's what he was giving back. Whoever fit his profile was in trouble.

Cara came around the corner. "Excuse me, Courtney, I have the pricing team on the phone. They need more time. They want to know if we can push the status meeting back to this afternoon, around one?"

Courtney swiveled around to her on-line calendar and took a look. "I'm free from one to three. That should be fine."

Brice took a long look at Cara while he waited for Courtney to conclude their business.

"Great. I'll send a notice out to the rest of the team. Thanks." She didn't offer a formal apology for barging into the conversation, but directed a smile to Sheila and Brice. "See you this afternoon, Courtney."

As soon as she cleared the area, Brice said, "That's a sister."

"What made you say that?" Courtney asked.

"She definitely has some black in her. She doesn't have the nose, but look at those lips," he said.

"I was wondering about that too," Sheila said.

"When in doubt, remember roots," Brice added.

"Alex Haley's movie, *Roots*?" Sheila asked.

"No, hair roots."

Sheila and Courtney looked at each other and bent over in muffled laughter, clutching their abdomens.

"You are something else," Sheila said.

"It's true, the hair doesn't lie. She might have blond hair, but that stuff was Negro nappy."

"She could stand a perm," Sheila interjected.

"She's carrying a lot on that back end to be so skinny. That's a sister, no doubt," Brice added.

"How do you know she's not Hispanic?"

"Because they have hips and sisters have behinds and there is a difference," Sheila answered.

"It's hard to tell sometimes. You can't always go by the complexion since we come in every shade from white chocolate to dark chocolate," Courtney said.

"I don't like white chocolate. Give me a nice piece of milk or dark chocolate," Brice said.

"You're sick. Can you think of anything else but women? Good grief, you are pitiful."

"Yeah, but you love me because I'm the number-one player in the house. I know the ladies, even when they're trying to go undercover like Ms. Cara. I might have to go introduce myself to her again and spend a little time getting to know her since you two sisters haven't fallen for my magnetism yet."

"Please," Sheila said, chuckling. "Since you only date sisters, you better make sure about Cara first."

"Yeah, right, it's not like I'm going over there and ask her if she's black and passing for white."

"You better find out, she might be."

"You think there are fair-skinned blacks still trying to pass for white?" Courtney asked.

"Never know. Far as I'm concerned, if you look black, you're black. But if you need proof, you say go for the hair roots. I say show me a picture of her grandparents. That says it all. You can find out a whole bunch of family secrets when you start pulling out those old photos," Sheila said.

"That's true, because my grandmother was part Indian, Cherokee," Courtney said.

"You and every other black person up in here has a grandmother that's part Cherokee. What a trip. Everybody and their brother is supposedly part Cherokee in Philadelphia, but I never run into any real Native Americans. What's that about?" Brice asked.

"Don't know," Sheila said, stirring her coffee with her legs crossed. She stared at the hutch for a few moments trying to figure out what was different. "What happened to your picture of Paul?"

Courtney pulled her desk drawer open, exposing the facedown frame.

"Hey, that's my signal, male-bashing time." Brice tapped his fingertips repeatedly against the adjoining thumb. "I'm out of here. Catch up with you at lunchtime."

"Oh, Brice, I almost forgot." She handed him the brown paper bag. "My aunt sent you some fried chicken, greens, and sweet potato pie."

He opened the bag, submerged his nose, and drew a deep breath.

"Umph, umph, umph. See? This is what I'm talking about. This is how you get a man. Is your aunt single?"

"She would be considered too old-fashioned for you. She believes in one man to every woman."

"Just think about it. You can have food like that every day. All you have to do is give up those other ten noncooking women you're seeing. How's that sound?" Sheila asked.

"Well, let's not make any hasty decisions. Looks like I'll have to start this thing off slow with Auntie. Keep bringing the grub and I'll see how it goes."

"That's what I thought. Get on out of here and do some work," Sheila said.

"Yessah, Boss," Brice said on his way out.

"So what's up with you and Paul? Did you break up?"

Courtney pushed the desk drawer shut and spun around to face Sheila, nodding.

"Get out of here. When did this happen?"

"Actually, it was last weekend."

Jason came around the corner and stuck his head into the cubicle.

"Hey, Courtney. I'll come back later."

Sheila gripped her cup and eased back in the chair, smirking. When he left, she leaned toward Courtney and said in a whispering tone, "You know he's on you, girl."

"That's the second time he's come by today."

"Oh," Sheila said with a mischievous-looking expression, "let me leave."

"No, you don't. Hang around a little longer, in case he comes back. I really don't want to get into a conversation with him. He's the one who invited me to happy hour and it wasn't my thing. I don't want to get too friendly with him."

"You sure? Because I don't want to stand in the way of true romance."

"Don't even go there. Speaking of true romance, what about going out with Edwin?"

"Girl, we've already been down that road. He hasn't called me and I am not calling him. Period."

"I talked to him about you at my aunt's house yesterday. He likes you."

"If he likes me so much, why hasn't he called?"

"Because of his job."

"Job, we all have a job. What does that have to do with it?"

"He's been really busy with work and personal stuff, but he really likes you. He told me he was planning to call you this week."

"You shouldn't have said anything to him about me. I don't want to go out on any charity date. I'm single, but I am not tripping about being alone. I'm just fine."

"Please, last week you were talking about how fine he was and how you wouldn't mind going out with him again."

"Okay, but I'm not desperate."

"Not saying that you are. All I'm saying is he likes you and you like him. Go for it."

"Well, let's put it this way. I won't throw myself at him, but if he calls I'll go out with him. How's that, Ms. Matchmaker?"

Courtney gave a thumbs-up.

"You need to stop worrying about me and work on your own romance. Paul is buried in the drawer and Jason is in hot pursuit—too much drama for me."

"I'm not interested in being with Paul or Jason. I just broke up with Paul. I need to breathe, although I would be willing to go out on a double date if it'll help you and Edwin get together."

"Huh!" Sheila glanced at her watch. "Let me get to my office. I have an interview candidate coming in at eleven and I haven't read the résumé."

"Let me know when you hear from Edwin," Courtney said.

Sheila waved and turned the corner, disappearing into the office madness. She got back to her office in time to catch the ringing phone.

"Hello, Sheila. This is Edwin Williams. Do you remember me?"

Sheila eased down in her chair and let hints of her smile peek between words. "Of course I do. It's good to hear from you."

The conversation was short, but she felt encouraged. By the time it was over, she had agreed to join Edwin for dinner soon. The week was looking up. For now, the order of business was getting that résumé read in ten minutes. Working under pressure was a regular state of being, and Sheila felt an extra jolt of motivation, thanks in large part to Mr. Williams.

CHAPTER 8

Sebastian shuffled the boxes around in his new apartment. His plan was rolling right along. The first step had been completed, make contact with Courtney and go out with her. As long as he got to spend time with her, it didn't matter how it was labeled—dating, hanging out, a friendly visit. Last Saturday had gone well. She was the one, the reason he'd elected to forgo his acceptance at Yale's law school and come to the University of Penn. The way he saw it, there were several exceptional law schools, but only one Courtney.

There was the issue of her boyfriend, the one she had had in college. Strange, she hadn't mentioned him that Saturday. Maybe he wasn't in the picture anymore. Sebastian would have to find out the next time they met, without being too obvious.

Unpacking could wait. The phone was working and the most important item on his agenda was to call Courtney and see if she was interested in going out again.

"Courtney Young, it's your buddy Bas. How the heck are you?"

"Hey, Sebastian. When are you coming back to Philadelphia?"

"As of yesterday, I'm officially a Philadelphia resident and I'm unpacking as we speak."

"That was quick. You were just here a week and a half ago trying to get your plan together."

"I'm loving this place. Sometimes your heart tells you what to do and you just do it. My heart says Philadelphia is the place to be, so here I am."

Courtney wanted to melt listening to the melodic ring in his voice, which rivaled sounds he used to create at school with his trumpet.

"How'd you like to get together on Saturday for another skeet ball tournament? I deserve a rematch," he told her.

Courtney thought about the afternoon they'd spent at Dave & Busters a month ago. It had been more enjoyable than she'd imagined. Going out for another round of pure silliness might be just the ticket. At least there would be something to do this weekend.

Courtney didn't take time mull it over. She wanted to go. "I'd love to go."

"Awesome, how about we meet after you get off work this Friday?"

"I'll take off a little early. That way we can meet around four."

"See you then, Ms. Young."

Nice and slow was his approach. If she was for him, and he knew in his spirit that she was, this was one of many weekends to come with Ms. Courtney Young.

CHAPTER 9

The rest of the week zoomed by without incident, dumping into Friday. She had survived the second Thursday without Paul, and Courtney wasn't feeling the sting of loneliness. She rushed to meet Sebastian at their hangout spot by four o'clock. After she parked the car and buzzed to the front of D&B, she saw him standing outside in a pair of jeans and a T-shirt. She was becoming convinced that he could wear any outfit and make it look appealing.

"You're here. Hope you haven't been waiting long," she said.

"Just got here myself."

It would have been an awkward greeting had she taken time to think about the appropriate move. He was a friend but not a friend-friend. Something more than a plain hello and a lot less than a hug would work. Before she could think it all out, he embraced her, clutch and release, quick and easy.

"It's good seeing you, buddy."

"Welcome to the fine city of Philadelphia. I'm glad you decided to go to law school here. You didn't waste any time making up your mind."

"No time like the present to start chomping away at this four-year program. I don't officially begin until January, but they let me get into an economics class and an elective. I started late, but it shouldn't be a problem since econ was my undergrad major. All things considered, it actually feels good to be back in school. It gives me a few more years of simple living, so long as my trust fund holds out."

"Can't complain about that."

"Do you want to go inside?" he asked.

"I'd rather stay out here for a little while. Would you mind if we take a walk along the waterfront?"

"Are you kidding! That's perfect."

The two sauntered north, letting the riverfront walkway be their guide.

"Sometimes I think about taking a sabbatical and going back to get my master's."

"Go for it."

"I don't know. Half the time I want to be back in school. The rest of the time I'm glad to be out working. I guess I'm not really sure what I want to do right now."

"No pressure here. My philosophy is to enjoy life and be true to your heart. You have your entire life to be a responsible adult working a thousand hours a week and wearing a stiff suit. One day I will have to conform, but not yet."

"The next four years won't be easy. Let's face it, Wharton and the law school aren't easy gigs."

"Still beats work."

It was early, so the dinner clubs and nightspots weren't in full gear, cutting down on what would be a congested thoroughfare. A few passersby rushed along the walkway, bypassing the slow-moving Courtney and Sebastian.

"My dad thinks business school is a waste of time."

"Wharton is one of the top business schools in the country. It's going to be hard."

"All he sees is me wasting an entire year getting a degree that I won't need to run the family's law firm. The sooner I can start generating billable hours, the better."

"Doesn't it matter to him what you want?"

"No. If pursuing law was good enough for him and Grandfather, then it has to be good enough for me."

"What about your other brothers and sisters? Do they have to practice law?"

"If I had some they probably would, but I'm the only pup in the litter. All of the family aspirations fall squarely on my shoulders. My mom died when I was a baby. My father remarried right afterward and my stepmom is my mom. They didn't have any more children, so she tends to be overprotective when it comes to me. I can write the book on dealing with family pressure. There's a constant balancing act between making them proud and keeping myself happy."

"I'm an only child too," Courtney told him.

"Get out of here. How cool is that?"

"Sometimes it's too much pressure being an only child. It would be nice to have someone to share the stress with," she shared.

The sidewalk could comfortably hold four people standing shoulder to shoulder, so Courtney didn't pay much attention to the man approaching. Of course she would speak, as was customary, as soon as he stopped drilling his eyes into Sebastian and looked her way. He pushed passed them, leaving room enough for two others on his empty side. No street greeting came this evening.

"You've been all over the world. What place do you like the most?"

"That's hard to say. I have so many favorites. The more I see the world, the more I realize how much we Americans take for granted. In Europe the vehicles are small. It takes like four upgrades to get a car not much bigger than a Yugo. People live on much less than we do. They eat tiny little meals. Our appetizers would be full-course meals for them."

Courtney could only imagine the Young family in Europe. They'd starve. If Uncle Raymond couldn't have two choices of meat, six or seven side dishes, and at least two desserts to choose from, he would consider it a light weekday meal, not to be confused with the all-important Sunday dinner. She didn't even consider him getting into a Yugo. If it wasn't a Cadillac, he wasn't driving it. "I've never gone to Europe."

"No? Well, we need to correct that."

Maybe for people of European descent, but that didn't register high on her list. "I've always wanted to go to Africa. That's my dream vacation."

"Africa is unbelievable. After I cruised Europe for a few weeks this summer, I took some money from my trust fund and spent a month on a mission trip in Africa. It's the best money I've ever spent. That trip changed my life, and the beauty of Africa, it's so hard to describe. The people, the culture, it consumes you."

Courtney didn't expect a man with undeniable European heritage to be so captivated by Africa. It was supposed to be her homeland. She wanted to feel the overwhelming sensation of setting foot on her motherland and be able to tell the story to the masses. Instead she had to see it through Sebastian's eyes.

"Did you feel awkward being a white guy in Africa?"

"Not at all. The continent is mixed with so many countries filled with people of different colors and beliefs. Some are Muslims, Christians, medicine men, bush people, hunters, kings, leaders. Some are dark, some light, mixed, you name it. The only other place that I've seen such a mix of people was in South America."

"What do you mean?"

"Brazilians are all part of one big pot of mixed people. Imagine this, most of the people with blond hair were your skin tone or darker, holding hands with someone my complexion that had very dark kinky hair. Race wasn't a factor because everyone is Brazilian."

"Are you telling me that Brazil doesn't have any discrimination?"

"I don't know about that, but if they do, it's not by race. They're divided by religion and socioeconomics."

"Oh, you mean the haves and have-nots, or as they would call it in my neighborhood, the ones with money and the broke folks without it."

"Exactly," he responded.

"So they do have some kind of discrimination."

"Every place in the world does. If it's not race, it's religion. If it's not religion it's gender, or in India it's your social class. Who knows? There are probably places in the world where it's by your toe size."

"I never thought about it like that but I guess you're right."

"Every society finds a way to make one group feel superior over another. It goes way back to Bible days, like with Pharaoh and the Egyptian slaves. Someone always wants to be on top."

"You're religious?"

"Not so much religious. I'm a little afraid of that term after seeing so much injustice and hatred around the world done in the name of religion. I believe in God and I follow the teachings of the Lord."

Courtney's eyebrow arched.

"You look surprised?"

"I'm sorry," she responded. "I didn't mean to. It's just that you don't strike me as someone who would know the Lord."

"Why, because I'm a genuinely debonair fellow?"

"Something like that," she said, laughing. "I don't know."

"What, it couldn't be because I'm white? You know, some of us serve the Lord too."

"I know that," she said, looking away, "and it's not just because you're white. You're from a well-off Boston family, and usually people like that don't think they need God."

The forty-minute stretch deposited the couple at Penn Treaty Park. The rows of weeping willows swayed to the tease of the baby wind. It wasn't time for the season to claim the colors, so the green grass was still able to leap up and meet the low-lying branches, escorting a calming feeling into the park. Courtney had seen this place from the street many times but had never set foot in the park. It was more breathtaking up close than it had been from her car.

"What makes you think I'm well off?"

"Come on, anybody who can fly around the world all summer on their trust fund, and then have enough left over to pay for a combined Ivy League law and business school degree, after spending four years at Northwestern, come on."

"What if I had financial aid?"

"Did you?"

"No."

"That's what I thought."

"But you weren't sure."

"Any time you have enough of your own money to spend twenty-five to thirty-five thousand dollars each year for four years of undergrad, plus another four years of graduate school, you have money."

"My dad might be well off. I'm just a poor student trying to get an education."

"With a trust fund!"

"Okay, I acknowledge that, but it's a far cry from being rich. I could go to law school on my own, but why if the money is there for that purpose? Wouldn't you love to be able to pay for your children's education?"

"Sure, who wouldn't?"

"That's what my trust fund does and I am grateful to my dad, but I'm my own man. I will have to make my own money after graduate school, and I'm not afraid of that."

"Being a poor student is one thing, but being poor for real is another."

"When you sleep on the ground under the smoldering heat during the day, and shivering cold at night in tents that have no doors, no air-conditioning, no heat, and on top of it you're surrounded by thousands of sick people who don't have decent running water, you realize the worst conditions in America are like country club living to some other countries."

The couple leaned on the railing that separated land from sea. The Ben Franklin Bridge was to their backs and the Philadelphia skyline sat before them, punctuated with buildings of all shapes, heights, and colors, vying for their space in the scene.

"Every time I used to run into you at school, it was by the water," she echoed softly.

"We're both water lovers."

"Oh, not me."

"How can you not love the water? The beach is my favorite place to be in the summer, running barefoot through the hot sand and jumping into the cold water," he told her.

"I love the beach too. What I'm not crazy about is the dirty water. When we go to the shore in Atlantic City, I don't put a single toe in the water."

"Well, Ms. Young, you'll have to come to St. Thomas with me. The water is so clear you can practically use it as a mirror."

"I'm glad we came here. It's peaceful. It reminds me of how big God is, looking at the vastness of the water."

"We'll have to go to church together sometime," she added.

"Sure."

Courtney didn't have a clue as to where, but it definitely wouldn't be Fifth Baptist. They might have surrendered parts of their lives to God, but they were holding certain racial views with a death grip. Taking Sebastian to Fifth Baptist would be like Daniel wrestling in the lions' den. He could survive, but it would take boatloads of faith, the kind that couldn't be acquired from mere talk. They'd attend another church, one of the other thousands in the Philadelphia area where no one could recognize her and run back telling Reverend Tyler and the congregation about what they thought they saw. Better safe than sorry.

"I attended a church when I was here last time. It was a lot like my old one in Chicago. I wasn't expecting to find a church with so much diversity praising the same God. It's hard to find a church that has it all, a mixed crowd, strong teaching, and good music. The music is a must for me," he said. "Most churches have one or two, but not all three. You were right about something you said earlier, but it was such a good debate that I couldn't backtrack."

"What?" she said with a sheepish look.

"Where I grew up, there weren't any of those three factors in my church. Our one-hour service included a host of people who looked exactly like me. We might have had one Italian person. That was as dark as it got in St. Paul's Episcopal Church. The minister did a fifteen-minute speech. Every now and then he'd turn pages in the Bible. I think it was to shake the dust off."

His church sounded like Fifth Baptist to Courtney, except darker.

"The only music we got was Mrs. Miller banging on the cathedral organ. That's the sum total of my religious pursuits in my youth."

"So, what happened? What made you change to a different kind of church?"

"I played with a few of the other musicians in the area. We did a few pickup gigs. One guy invited me to his church and the rest is history. I accepted the Lord as my savior and began to learn about what rights and privileges came with that."

Courtney longed to get into a church where she could learn more about rights and privileges too.

"What kind of church do you go to?"

"I go to my family's church. Great music and good people but it doesn't have everything that I want," she told him.

"Anything in particular missing?"

"Mostly the teaching. I would like more of what I got back in Evanston. My church back there taught me about the promises that God has made to us, as believers. I really started to learn about faith and I want to keep it going. I'm not getting that right now. I have a wonderful pastor and he really cares for the people and the community, but he concentrates on the Ten Commandments and empowering the people through social action. I know we need that, but I need more. I've been thinking about looking around, but for now I'm staying with my family."

"The most difficult piece for me is finding decent music. It's difficult to find a church that gives a strong message and can carry a tune."

"That's not shocking coming from a trumpet player."

"Ah, my trumpet. Take a look around. You see the trees, the river, and the bridge?" Sebastian raised her hands in his.

The warmth in his hand sent an electric charge surging through her body, ending with a spark deep inside that she wasn't prepared to kindle.

"Now close your eyes. Can you imagine being serenaded on a warm sunny day when the trees are blossoming, the birds are chirping, and the soothing sound of the water hits against the rocks?"

She was sailing in the moment until reality clipped her wings. Courtney rubbed her hands softly along her arms and took a step back from Sebastian.

He sensed her uneasiness and gave her breathing room. "I'm hungry, are you?"

Courtney nodded.

"Let's go eat, and don't tell me you want barbecue chicken pizza with red onions and pineapple again."

Courtney wanted to keep the endorphins flowing. It was easy to have an enjoyable time with Sebastian. He was funny, smart, and fine. He would fit right in with Edwin and Terry at the family cookout on Saturday. Too bad he couldn't come. If she brought him, Aunt Sis would have more than the grill lit up. Nah, she was enjoying her meetings with Sebastian. Why expose their friendship to the family and have them misinterpret the relationship, potentially blowing it out of proportion? No sense messing up a good thing.

They picked up the pace and scooted down Delaware Avenue in search of food and more conversation.

CHAPTER 10

The last room at the end of the two-story boardinghouse offered more privacy than the other nineteen, which was what attracted Jamal to it four months ago when he revolved back into society. The full-sized sofa bed gobbled up much of the unoccupied space, leaving enough room for a clothes rack masquerading as a broken chair, a portable TV sitting on the floor near the door with the extended rabbit ears grazing the chipped-paint-covered walls, and a thirteen-by-seven-inch rickety wooden table that held a charred hot plate.

September had rolled in with the fury of a lion, refusing to be outdone by the Africa-hot heat that had scorched the town in August. The sweaty thickness in the air swooped down into the hallway, creeping under every door, without invitation. Inside room number 10, Jamal got some relief from the window fan, which was a welcome intruder in his space.

The bang on the door startled him. He rolled over and buried his head under the pillow. The rap on the door intensified. The landlord was tough about having too many visitors. No one got into the building unless they belonged there. Jamal didn't know who was at the door, but he didn't want any company. Whichever one of his fellow residents it was had picked the wrong day to pay a visit. In nothing but his boxers, he jumped up from the bed on the side that didn't squeeze

his bike against the wall. He made the five steps to the door and
snatched it open.

"Philadelphia Police Department."

The officers remained in the hallway.

"Detectives," Jamal said, smirking.

"Mr. Williams, we'd like to talk with you," the shorter, wider officer
said with his polyester-blend suit screaming for mercy as the buttons
were stretched to their limit across his midsection.

"About what?" Jamal extended his right arm up the door for support, scratched his head, and yawned, showing no fear or interest in
what the detectives had to say.

"We'd like to ask you a few questions."

"Well, I'm not interested." He pushed the door with enough force
to slam it shut and turned his back to walk away. He'd had enough
run-ins with Crawford and Holmes to know that the matter wasn't
over, but he enjoyed the brief moment of control before feeling the
bloodcurdling crack across the back of his legs that slumped him to
his knees, barely missing the corner of the bed.

"Let's try this again, Mr. Williams. We'd like to ask you a few questions."

His legs felt like logs throbbing to the beat of his pain. "I'm not answering anything without a lawyer."

"You hear that, Sam? He wants a lawyer."

Jokes were in the air, and laughter fought with the stifling heat for
center stage.

"I'll be asking the questions," said Detective Crawford.

He was being overpowered, but Jamal didn't want to roll over and
take his beating like a little boy. He felt like a man, even in the presence of terror.

He squirmed trying to get free, only to worsen his situation by en-
ticing Detective Holmes to get in on the free-for-all. It was hard to tell
which culprit sent the crippled table crashing to the floor with the
hot plate following suit. Jamal's face was square into the floor and he
found himself gasping for air at times. Crawford had already pinned
Jamal's arms behind his back and slid the nightstick under them,
forcing the stick up toward the shoulders. Holmes gave Jamal a firm
size-twelve steel-toed stomp in the middle of his back.

After the first few moments of pain, it all felt the same to Jamal. As
the pain elevated, so did his contempt.

"I haven't done anything."

"Oh, we can always find something that you've done. That's not a problem."

"Why are you hassling me?"

"Hassling you! We're just asking for a little cooperation," Crawford said.

"I have rights?" He squirmed a little more to ease the pressure on his left arm since it was going numb faster than the other.

No mercy came from Crawford. He responded by tightening the grip he had on the nightstick. He bent down to be within whispering distance of Jamal's ear. "You have the right to shut up. We're not arresting you, not yet. All we want to do is ask you a few questions. We can do it here or we can take you downtown, which one you prefer?"

"I'm not saying anything."

"That's your choice." He snapped the cuffs on Jamal and the two officers snatched him to his feet.

"Why are you cuffing me?"

Jamal was restrained but didn't feel subdued. Maybe he could get lucky enough to break free. He rocked his shoulders with enough vigor to shake his arms out of their sockets, like a wolf willing to gnaw his paws off in order to set himself free from a hunter's trap. After his efforts, both his arms and cuffs were still in place.

"It's your lucky day, Mr. Williams. We're giving you a chauffeured ride downtown to the County Hotel."

"What did I do?" Jamal said with attitude.

"What did you do?" Detective Crawford laughed.

"You resisted arrest, Mr. Williams. You're going downtown."

"This is bull. You don't have anything else to do but jack around with me. Why are you here? What was the charge in the first place?"

"We don't need a reason to stop by, Mr. Williams." Crawford patted Jamal on his back. "You're a criminal with a record. That gives us the right to pay you a visit any time we choose. Got that? Now let me give you those rights you've been begging for."

Jamal recalled how the rookie cop, who had arrested him four years ago, had pulled a little card out of his pocket to ensure that the Miranda rights were quoted accurately. That was such a long time ago and he had found out such care was rare. The other cops he had dealings with recited what they could remember. Whether it was correct or not didn't seem important. Once they randomly decided he was getting arrested, his rights were squashed.

"Mr. Williams, you have the right to remain silent."

Jamal knew one thing was certain about Philadelphia's finest; even when they were cracking him upside the head with a nightstick, they were courteous enough to call him Mister Jamal didn't find much appreciation in the officer's pseudo-home training during his beating.

"Can I at least put my pants on?"

Detective Crawford gave it a second thought, realizing the cuffs would have to come off in order for Jamal to get properly dressed.

"Sam, toss him those pants on the chair there." He turned to Jamal and looked him dead in the eyes. "Detective Holmes is going to take the cuffs off. If you try anything, and I do mean anything . . ." He took a few steps back, unsnapped the holster, took his gun out, and switched off the safety. "You decide how you want to go downtown, on your feet or in a body bag. It's all the same to me. That's your right, you little punk. Now get dressed and hurry up. You're not the only joker we have to deal with today."

CHAPTER 11

Edwin maneuvered the two-seater convertible along the narrow one-way street lined with boarded-up houses and abandoned cars. He felt troubled every time he came to his old home. He blocked out the war-zone remains, which were left from the stench of drugs, unfounded police raids, and untamed poverty. This was the neighborhood of his youth, the one where children played kick ball after school until the streetlights came on, signaling that it was time to get on home. Every neighbor knew his name and cared whether he got home safely from school. This was where he could sit on the front stoop playing pinochle for hours at a time. Growing up on the block lined with well-maintained homes seemed like an eternity ago.

He kept his eyes peeled for a parking space. Coming up empty, he settled for his unofficial reserved spot. He rolled the car up to the soft curb straddling the corner, leaving enough room to open the door without scraping the fire hydrant. He didn't worry about the safety of his car. The same guys that had labeled him as a brainy kid and teased him from elementary school on up about his thick glasses were the same ones who now hailed him as a hero. He knew they looked up to him and took pride in his accomplishments as though they were their own.

Edwin hopped up the newly cemented steps two at a time. He already had his key out, the same one he had gotten on his twelfth birthday seventeen years ago. He walked through the dark living room toward the light whimpering from the kitchen. Slicing through the dining room, he was careful not to bump up against his mother's prize china cabinet. Every knickknack and family memento she'd collected over the past thirty years was securely tucked inside.

"Mama, I'm here."

She slowly raised her head from the table as Edwin entered the kitchen. The weight of her tears dominated her thin frame and resisted her effort to sit up straight.

"Jamal's in jail."

"Jail!" Edwin plopped down in a chair. "For what? He just got out."

"I don't know. Lord Jesus, what am I going to do?" She clasped her hands together, cupped her nose, and shook her head relentlessly.

Edwin grabbed her hands and pulled them to him.

"Mama, it's going to be all right. Don't let yourself get worked up like this. It's not good for you."

"I have to get my baby out of jail." She scrambled to get up, moving but not getting anywhere.

"Mama, please." Edwin got up and put his arms around her. He could feel her heart racing. "You have to calm yourself down and tell me what happened."

"I don't know what happened. He called and said they'd locked him up. He was waiting for a bail hearing. I called the number to the station but they won't tell me anything. I know he needs somebody down there with him."

"Why didn't he call me?"

"You know why." She took the damp paper towel and dabbed the corners of her tear-soaked eyes. "He's ashamed of always having to ask you to come get him out of jail. Lord, the poor child just can't seem to get himself straightened out. I have to go get him."

She pushed back from the table, attempted to stand, and slid back down into the chair.

"Mama, just wait. It's three o'clock in the morning. You don't know where he's being processed."

"I know he's downtown."

"Where, the Filbert Street jail, the Roundhouse, or headquarters?"

"I don't know. Oh God."

Edwin felt the piercing cry of his mother's voice slice into the innermost sections of his soul. Whatever she needed him to do he was going to have to do, no matter what.

"Edwin, you have to find out where he is and get him out. I can't leave my baby down there. You know how bad those cops beat him last time. I just couldn't take seeing him like that again. They almost killed my child."

Once she was steady on her feet, Edwin gently eased his mother back into the chair.

"Let me call around and see if I can get some information," he said.

"Can you take me to the courthouse?"

"Do you mean the courthouse or the jail?"

She hunched her shoulders, not knowing the answer.

"Let's wait at least until I can find out where he is."

His mother banged her fist against the table, and her eyes enlarged to the size of quarters.

"Wait for what, for them to kill him this time! I'm not waiting on anybody or anything." This time she was able to make it to her feet and stood with head held high. "I'm going right now. If you can't take me I'll get a cab or take the bus."

"Mama, I don't mind taking you. You know that. I've gone every other time and you know it. I'm an attorney. They'll let me in faster than they'll let you in," he said in a soft-spoken, calming tone. "All I'm saying is that we should find out some information before we go running down there."

He was talking, but wasn't sure if Mama was listening. He had seen her act like a she-lion whose vicious protective instincts kicked in whenever danger surrounded her offspring. He knew she was capable of going down to the police department and causing a major incident if she didn't get answers soon. She wasn't going to be right until she saw with her own eyes that Jamal was okay.

She reclaimed her seat and grabbed Edwin's hand.

"The bail is always around a thousand dollars. I hate to ask, Edwin, but I'm going to need the bail money from you."

"Whatever it is, I'll get it, Mama. Don't worry about that."

Edwin still felt guilty for not coming up with the money the last time. He had finally put his foot down and told his mother he wasn't going to bail Jamal out every time he got into trouble, no matter how much pressure she put on him. The first and only time he hadn't given his mother the money that she was asking for, it had almost gotten his brother killed. Telling his mother no this time wasn't a consideration.

His mother took a deep breath and relaxed her body in the chair.

Edwin grabbed the wall phone and prepared to make the necessary calls.

"Oh, Mama, I almost forgot. I meant to bring the check with me. I'll have to bring it back tomorrow."

"What check?"

"The one to fix the roof."

"Oh, that, it's no hurry. You have plenty of time to get it. They won't start working on the new roof until Monday." She rubbed his hands. "I'm glad you're here, Edwin. I don't know what I'd do without you."

Edwin didn't know what she'd do without him either. He couldn't remember the last time she'd tried to handle a serious matter on her own. Whenever there was a problem or financial need, he was the first person she called, saying she didn't want to burden Jamal since he had enough struggles of his own. Half the time Edwin didn't know what to do about being saddled with the responsibility of taking care of his mother and Jamal. He needed to be a good son, but some boundaries were going to have to be set. It had already cost him his engagement. He needed to do something, but tonight wasn't the time to figure it out. His mother needed him.

CHAPTER 12

The hustle and bustle, phones ringing, and wall-to-wall people packed into her parents' home were to be expected for such a monumental event. Courtney knew her family would spare no effort in celebrating. They told her it wasn't every day that someone in the family graduated from such a prestigious school like Northwestern with honors, although every few years it seemed like someone in her generation was doing just that. Her graduation was a family affair, warranting due recognition in Young style.

Courtney remembered when her parents had moved from the old neighborhood to the larger suburban middle-class house in Wynnewood. The rest of the family had deemed their place to be the site for all major family events since the twelve-by-twenty-foot deck was ideal for grilling and the half-acre lot perfect for seating a hundred or so people at any given time. The grill was fired up. The dining room table was decorated with a host of dishes situated like a patched quilt, colorful, all different, and completely covering the table. There wasn't an empty space to be found. In a few hours the backyard would be covered with loud talkers, boasters, well-wishers, exaggerators, and some straight-out liars, all sharing the common purpose of showing support for a family member who had gone and made the family proud.

Time had not stood still. Three years had elapsed since the last graduation party was held for cousin Terry, who had gotten his engineering degree from Drexel, and five years since Edwin finished law school at Yale. The family was due a party. No other reason was needed.

She stood at the dining room window peering into the backyard, watching the people arrive, and reflecting on her college days back in Illinois. The four years hadn't been all glitz and glamour for Courtney. It was hard to leave the comforts of a loving home when there were so many people around the old neighborhood that looked and lived like her. Leaving a place where she was in the majority, to be reduced to a minority, had required discipline, faith, and prayer to survive. The four-year journey had been worthwhile. She'd met a host of special people, including Sebastian. Now she had taken on the corporate world. There were new challenges, but seeing Sebastian helped her escape back to the less responsible college life. It was nice having him around. Perhaps they would find something else exciting to do together over the next week or two.

Her face lit up when Edwin entered the backyard. He waved and beckoned for her to come outside. In the meantime, he was summoned by an older gentleman who sat in a lawn chair with his legs crossed, cap cocked to the side revealing a short gray patch of roughly plowed hair. He held a mason jar filled with sun tea and a touch of something else. Balancing a lit cigarette between his lips and the remaining fifteen teeth that were randomly scattered throughout his mouth, he took a puff from time to time without raising a finger. As the smoke rose toward the blue sky, he cringed his eye to avoid the dose coming his way.

"Hey, Edwin. How you doing with the law firm? Are they treating you right?"

Edwin cooled his arm with the sweating bottle of Coke.

"I can't complain, Unc."

"Well, you got a good job. You hang in there. We're proud of you. Where is that brother of yours? I haven't seen him in a while. He coming?"

Edwin held his head down, knowing it was just a matter of time before he was going to have to go through the spiel about Jamal's familiar set of circumstances.

"He got locked up last night."

"Locked up! What did he get into now? I hope he ain't still messing around with that dope."

"I don't really know, Unc. I'll let him tell you."

"That poor boy. He just can't seem to stay free. Every time I turn around he's in some kind of trouble. It seems like trouble just follows him."

"Sure does."

"I can't figure out why he always has to get locked up on the weekend. Can't he do his dirt up in the week and keep the weekends open for himself? He won't ever get married if he's going to stay locked up every weekend."

Courtney tapped Edwin on the back. "Hey, cuz."

Edwin gave her a tight squeeze, lifting Courtney off her feet. "Congratulations."

She blushed.

"You already told me congratulations three months ago when I first got home. I've already cashed the check you gave me for graduation."

"Hey, look, I'm just going along with the flow. You know how your family has to throw a party every time anybody does anything."

Courtney playfully punched Edwin in the upper arm. "My family! These are your folks too."

Edwin looked at Uncle Raymond and then back at Courtney, taking a swig of his Coke.

"Ummm, that's your uncle," he said, trying to hold back his smile, which wasn't cooperating.

"You know you're wrong." She chuckled.

"Just kidding. You know I love Uncle Raymond. He's crazy as all get out, but he's family," Edwin said.

"Speaking of family, where's Jay?" she asked.

"He got locked up last night."

"Oh no, you should have called me." Courtney took a deep breath, closed her eyes, and blew out slowly. "For what?"

The smoldering fear in the pit of her stomach ignited a flame and burned her insides. No matter how wide the river was between her pursuits and those of Jamal's, the two had a special bond and nothing could hinder it. "I wanted to see him today."

"Well, he got out this morning and you know that you're his girl. So, he just might make it over here."

"Did they . . ." she said as her eyes filled with tears. "You know?"

"Beat him? Not this time, thank God. Mama would have ended up in jail too. It hurt her so badly the way the cops jacked him up last time, and over some dumb stuff."

"Wasn't it about an argument at the basketball court or something like that?"

"Every time I think about it, I get mad all over again," Edwin said.

"You know Jay doesn't bite his tongue for anybody."

"Yeah, right, but that stuff is going to get him killed. Sometimes you have to take the low road. You know how the cops are around here. They will jack up a brother in a minute and ask questions later."

"We had the same problem in Illinois," Courtney told him.

"Yeah, I heard about the cops in Illinois and they are no joke."

"They were unbelievable. A couple of police were caught beating up black teenagers and then dropping them off on the other side of town, in an area everybody knows is racist. Then they were beaten again by a group of guys in that area."

"That's messed up. I'm not surprised though. Didn't Dr. King say something like the racism and hatred he experienced in the South didn't have anything on Chicago and the North?"

"Well, this one specific area in Chicago was so filled with hatred for blacks that we had a rule. If you're driving through this one particular section and happen to get a flat tire, just keep driving. Ride the rim until you can get to safety."

"Oh," he said, chuckling, "no, you didn't."

"Yes, we did too. It's easier to replace another rim than to wind up with a crack upside your head."

"It's wrong, but what can you do? I'm in an awkward situation because Mama thinks that I can fix all of Jamal's legal problems and straighten out the whole legal system. She doesn't want to hear that I'm doing all I can do to get him out when he's sitting in jail waiting on his arraignment. I don't know what else I can do to keep my mother happy. I can't keep forgoing billable hours to represent Jamal. The firm is only going to tolerate so much."

"What choice do you have?"

All Edwin could do was shake his head. He hunched his shoulders, held his head down to brace himself for the weight of his mother and brother across his back.

"You know, we all think you're the Johnnie Cochran of the family. Big-time lawyer at Gershwin, Peters, and Myers."

"Right, a corporate law firm and half the time I'm running around trying to help the family with custody cases, divorces, accidents at work, and all kinds of other craziness. You know I don't mind helping out, but it's gotten ridiculous. Somebody in the family is calling every week asking me for money or legal advice. Do you know Uncle Cletus called me last week and asked what he should do?"

"Do about what?" Courtney asked.

"He found a bone in his fish fillet. On top of that, his fries had been soaked in hot oil and they burned his tongue. He was talking about how nobody gave him a warning."

"What did you tell him?"

"I told him to go back and ask for a free sandwich and a cooler order of fries."

"No, you didn't."

"Yes, I did. He wanted to know if there was a case in it. I told him that unless his tongue was completely burned off, he didn't have a case. He said he was just checking because he had heard about some people who had gotten burned from their coffee and were able to file civil cases behind it. I told him he should have gotten the coffee then. He said, nah, that already has a warning label on it."

Edwin shook his head, and Courtney laughed so hard she gasped for air.

"Don't worry, now that you're back you're going to get your share too," he told her.

"I don't think so. I'm not a lawyer like you or an accountant like Deon or an engineer like Terry. I'm just a plain old marketer. Nobody in the family needs my help."

Edwin chuckled at Courtney's innocence.

"It doesn't matter what degree you have. As far as the family is concerned, you are college-educated and an automatic jack-of-all-trades. That means you're smart and every time they need money or something done, you're getting called. Take my advice, cuz, get ready for the phone to start ringing."

"I forgot to tell you about this guy I know from Northwestern. He's coming to Penn for law school. Before we graduated he was thinking about Yale, but he decided to come here. I've been showing him around town, but maybe you can talk to him about your experience in law school."

"Now, that's the kind of man you need. Is he a prospect?"

"Oh no, he's white."

"Really!"

They both looked down and moved a few blades of grass around with their feet.

"So, where have you been taking him?"

"We've gone to D and B and walked along Delaware Avenue. Why, where were you thinking?"

"No place in particular, so long as it's not around here, especially after last night. Mama isn't feeling too good about white people right now."

"I know better than to bring him around here, but you're right. She needs time."

"A whole lot of time, maybe more than we have in a lifetime."

Courtney heard someone yelling, "Ce-Ce," and knew it could only be one person. She swung around, with joy rushing from her face and arms extended. "Jayyyyyyy."

There stood her cousin in a pair of low-hanging baggy jeans, starched white-ribbed T-shirt, with a Sixers cap tilted to the side, and a four-inch gold cross blanketing his chest. He swaggered toward her, moving with the beat of the music. Five feet nine and a hundred and forty pounds, Jamal couldn't hoist Courtney over his shoulder, but he did snatch her up and twirl her around.

"What's up, cuz?" he said.

"I was wondering if you were coming."

"Now you know I wouldn't miss out on a party, college girl. I'm proud of you, Ce-Ce. I always knew you'd be big time."

They embraced. Jamal and Edwin followed with their palms slapping together, fingertips sliding out to a clutch, locking and shaking.

"Where's Mama?" Edwin asked his brother.

"She took some food into the house. Man, ah, thanks for hooking a brother up with the bail money. I owe you and I'm going to hit you up a little something something as soon as I get my hands on a little paper."

"Don't worry about it. It's all good. You don't owe me anything. You're straight with me. Just handle your business and get yourself together."

"That's what I'm trying to do, man," Jamal blurted out, slamming his fist into his open hand. "If these cops will leave a brother alone. It's hard for a brother out here, man, when they're trying to play you and break your will. But I ain't having it. It's all right, though. I'm going to handle my business later. But for right now, let's get this party on. Woo, woo," Jamal said, dancing in place with his hands in the air and shoulders rocking.

Courtney felt the warmth of her two older cousins, who were the brothers she didn't have. The afternoon was shaping into a bowl of warm apple pie, one of her favorites. Perhaps she could top it off with a scoop of ice cream. She would call Sebastian as soon as the party was over to see if he was up for another evening out on the town.

The family picture was now complete, painted with personalities from executives to thugs. Everyone had arrived.

CHAPTER 13

Courtney didn't normally go to an evening service, but what choice did she have when Sebastian asked if he could come to Fifth Baptist? She guessed it was the right decision saying that she preferred to go to his church, since it was more casual. Sebastian was someone she looked forward to spending time with, as long as it wasn't on her home turf where familiarity had a price. The farther away from west Philadelphia, the freer she felt. Fifth Baptist was up close and personal and carried a steep price tag. God was forgiving and merciful. Some of the church members weren't.

She grabbed a bulletin from a stack in the vestibule and crossed the threshold into the sanctuary. She thumbed through the pages, careful to watch where she was going. She stopped a few rows from the front, directly across from the sold-out sections of the Jones and Sims families. No need to hang the reserve sign behind the church mothers sitting on the first two rows. That's where the Young family sat. Regular members of Fifth Baptist Church knew that and bypassed the rows looking elsewhere for a seat. Her father and Aunt Sis had been young teenagers when their parents helped start the church forty years ago. The old wooden pews had held four generations. When Aunt Sis married Edwin Senior over thirty years ago, the addition of the Williamses spilled the family over into the second pew. Older fam-

ily members had gone on to glory and new ones had been born, net-
ting a consistent family presence every Sunday, come rain or shine.

Courtney got to church early enough to get an aisle seat but late
enough to skip Sunday school. Aunt Sis and Edwin were already
there. Courtney saw them in the back hallway leading to the pastor's
study. She knew whatever they were talking about had to be important. Not just anyone could enter into the area, behind the sanctuary,
without permission from Reverend Tyler. He said he needed one
place that left him free to think, pray, and wait on God. The back corner of the church seemed to serve his purpose.

Service got under way and the choir led Fifth Baptist into the spirit,
preparing the way for Reverend Tyler to bring the message. He stood
in the pulpit wearing his black robe. He didn't open with a scripture as
usual. Today he began with an announcement about Jamal's situation.

"Church, we need to rally around Sister Cleora and the entire Williams family. I'm not sure if you've heard, but the police arrested
young Brother Jamal again Friday night. From what I'm told, they busted
into his place and arrested him for no reason. He's out, praise God,
but we just can't keep letting this happen."

"Oohs" and "ahs" sprinkled with whispers were heard throughout
the sanctuary.

"I don't have to tell anybody that these are good people. You all
know Deacon Young and Trustee Edwin. This family has been a part
of Fifth Baptist since the beginning. Their folks helped start this
church some forty years ago. I was no more than ten years old back
then. Ain't that right?"

Nods and affirmations came in various ways from the Young and
Williams families who were now sitting tall and proud.

"They have been blessed with a lawyer, an accountant, two or three
electricians, an engineer, and I believe a nurse too, isn't that right,
Sister Cleora?"

"Yes, sir, Reverend," she responded with arms folded across her
chest and her hat-covered head titled slightly to the side.

"You know our very own Courtney just graduated from Northwestern
University this year, all the way out in Chicago. Stand up, Courtney."

She was not expecting to be the center of attention and looked
around at her family before moving. Encouraged and prodded by
them to stand up, she did, clutching the pew in front of her.

"Amen, amen. Fifth Baptist, give our young sister a hand-clap. We might be looking at the next CEO of one of those big companies downtown. Amen. If you don't know her, you better get to know her. She might be the very one giving you a job in a few years. Thank you, Sister Courtney. God bless you."

She eased back into her seat and took a deep breath, thankful to God that she didn't have to speak.

"How many people made it over to Sister and Brother Young's house yesterday and got some of those ribs and barbecued chicken? Oo-wee, Deacon Williams, make you want to slap somebody upside the head and get to Holy Ghost dancing right here. Amen. I tell you, that was some good eating. Oo, Lord."

Courtney wished her parents had been able to make it to church. Her father would have soaked up the accolades about his world-famous barbecue. After the party yesterday, they were exhausted and opted to rest up for their upcoming road trip.

"You know Brother and Sister Young were blessed to be able to take retirement from the gas and electric company a few months ago. We're sure happy for them, but I hear tell they're thinking of moving down South. Well, I don't know about that. God might have something to say about that. The way Brother Young put a hurting on that barbecue yesterday, I don't think his calling has been satisfied around these parts just yet." Reverend Tyler chuckled himself. "Amen, church."

Courtney respected Reverend Tyler. He spoke in plain language for the common people to understand. His members were folks who were, or used to be, residents of the neighborhood. He commanded the full attention of the congregation whenever he stepped into the pulpit. He was someone to be trusted. When a family was out of work and needed food on the table, Reverend Tyler made sure the church supplied meals to fill in the gaps. If someone ran out of oil in the middle of the winter, they were either given money from the collection plate to buy some or were allowed to sleep in the church until times got better for the family, or the weather broke, whichever came first. Whatever the people needed, Reverend Tyler tried to help get it. He didn't have a problem preaching Sunday morning and heading down to the mission on Broad Street to spend time with the homeless. Fifth Baptist relied on Reverend Tyler. They knew he cared about the people and the neighborhood. So, when he made a request or offered an opinion, right or wrong, a line of faithful supporters followed without hesitation.

He leaned on the podium and pulled the microphone closer so that his voice was strong and precise without his having to yell. He patted his forehead with his large white handkerchief.

"This is a serious matter. I don't have to tell anyone in here what the police are capable of doing to our young men in this town, and some of the black cops are just as bad as the white ones. Church, you know that I'm right about it."

More "oohs" and "ahs" saturated the church.

"We all know the kind of treatment they put on us and expect us to just lie down and take it. We haven't forgotten what they did the last time."

Courtney remembered when she was younger and Jamal talked her into being on the junior usher board, since he was on it. He used to love coming to Fifth Baptist before all of his troubles began. After spending time in and out of juvenile, he would come to church and be determined to stay out of trouble and on track. When he turned twenty-one, five years ago, his troubles landed him right into city jail, on and off. After getting out of jail, he didn't seem to have any interest in coming to church to hang out with a group of people that wanted to tell him what a mess he was making of his life.

"It's shameful how they beat young Brother Jamal within an inch of his life. Now, beloved, we have rights and we have to start exercising them. When those politicians fill our churches come election time, we have to start making them more accountable," Reverend Tyler said.

Anybody that wanted to get elected in the area came through Fifth Baptist. With the help of the church, Tyler had endorsed black, and in many cases white, officials who he believed could improve the community. He did everything from campaigning for them, on occasions having the church going door to door, to making financial pledges. Each candidate he endorsed went on to victory. The word had spread to the masses. Whenever a problem came up, Reverend Tyler was called before the local NAACP. He believed the church was intended for more than Sunday worship. He was known for calling a rally at the first sign of injustice. Courtney had stood on the steps of the courthouse downtown, with the church and other people from the community, more than many attorneys from the suburbs. Maybe that had something to do with Edwin wanting to be an attorney. He had seen them all the time, thanks to Reverend Tyler and Fifth Baptist.

He unwrapped the microphone from around the podium, pulled the robe at both shoulders, and took to his stage. He glided down the aisle, making eye contact with the church members along the way.

"We've got to stand up for ourselves and for our men. We can't let these cops have their way in our community. They talk about how dangerous and violent our neighborhoods are. The only violence many of us have seen has come from the police. Dear God. This time it was Sister Williams's son."

He went as far as the corded microphone would allow and spun around to head back up the center aisle. He stopped along the way to wipe his brow. He leaned on the ninth pew from the front and told the lady sitting on the end, "Next time, Sister Jones, it might be your boy."

He walked up three more rows and shifted to the other side of the aisle.

"I don't know, Brother Henry," he said as he tapped the corner of the pew and then ran to the front of the church with the robe breezing behind him in dramatic fashion. He put his foot on the first of the three steps leading to the pulpit and turned to face the crowd.

"It could be me next time. We don't know. I don't have to tell you how many times the police have been caught arresting the wrong man in our city this year. It's gotten so bad that none of us are safe, except for the protection of God."

He leaned back with the microphone in the air like a singer hitting the final note of a love ballad, and patted himself on the chest with his hanky. "Oh, Lord."

He went up the last two steps, placing him on the landing in the pulpit. He bent slightly and spun around two full circles with the black robe swirling like a debutante's dress at a ball, before resuming his original place back at the podium. He reinserted the microphone into its stand. He lifted the shoulders of his robe and let them plop back down to get them repositioned after his performance.

He leaned into the microphone and said, "All I know is that we can't let this go on. Somebody has to take a stand. Yes, Lord. You don't hear me, Fifth Baptist." He slapped the corner of the podium and turned like he was looking for a response from Deacon Young. "I said we have to take a stand to save our young folks. You know what we have to do."

A few weak "amens" came forth, and Reverend Tyler went back in for more.

"You don't hear me. Ooo, Lord, I said you know what we have to do. We have to rise up and walk downtown to let them know we are not taking this sitting down. The sixties are long gone. This is a new day. Amen and amen."

The people were awake, throwing out "amens" and "yes, Lords" as if he'd preached a sermon straight out of the gospel. It wasn't clear exactly what a rally could do about stopping the police violence, but if Reverend Tyler said that it needed to be done, then so it was. Only God in heaven could come down and say different.

After service, Courtney waited in the vestibule for Edwin to finish counting the collection plate money. She wasn't expecting to see Paul, and there he was. When he did come to church, it was to the earlier service. What was he doing at the second service? She put on her shades and pretended to read the bulletin, avoiding eye contact with him. If she could only let him get out of the church without seeing her. Wishful thinking. She felt him approaching.

"Courtney, how you doing?"

Like a fly caught in a web, Courtney stopped fidgeting and slid her sunglasses down to the edge of her nose.

"Paul!"

"I saw you standing back here and didn't want to leave without saying hello."

"That was nice of you." Courtney felt relieved to finally be broken up with Paul. "You don't usually come to the second service."

"I'm doing a lot of things different these days."

Courtney didn't want to ask for clarification, fearing it might lead into a deeper conversation than she wanted to jump into.

"Your parents here?" he asked.

"They stayed at home today. They wanted to get some rest before heading out for a trip to North Carolina this week."

"Vacation?"

"Kind of. They bought the new Buick and have to put it on the road. You know my father doesn't feel like his new car is right until he's taken it down South with the sales sticker still pasted to the window. His car isn't christened until he pulls up in my Aunt Cat's yard and everybody comes over to take a look and get a ride."

"That definitely sounds like your dad."

"Hey, more power to them. I'm out of college. I'm glad they both took the early retirement. They deserve to be happy."

"I guess you went out with your college friends a few weeks ago, huh?"

"Sure did."

"Figured that. I bet you had a good time and 'thangs' with them. That's just the kind of uppity people you're looking for."

The "them" he was referring to was a "him," but she wasn't about to tell Paul. The last thing she needed was for him to find out that Sebastian was white and go around blabbering to those in the church that already saw her as a little too proper for the neighborhood.

"So, you still high-riding?" he asked.

The soft seductive tone in his voice gave her ease. The sting of the knock-down, drag-out argument they'd had was softening.

"Are you still pitting?" she asked.

"Ah, we got jokes. Yes, I'm still working at the Hoagie Shop and lovin' it."

Paul felt the calmer waters too. They hadn't talked in nearly two weeks, which was a first, but it was becoming more and more difficult to jump back into the relationship. Given a long couple of weeks and how good she was looking, he wasn't sure that calling it quits was the right move.

"What are you doing for dinner?" he asked.

Before Courtney could respond, Edwin entered the vestibule.

"Paul, what's up, man?"

The men clasped fists, shook, and released.

"It's all good in the hood, partner. How's the big city treating you?"

"Can't complain, man." Edwin didn't know how to take the interaction between Paul and Courtney. Was he intruding on a possible reconciliation in the works or rescuing her from a not easily forgotten predicament? "Paul, man, it's good seeing you. Cuz, I'll catch you later."

Courtney didn't want to go with Paul. Her spirit wouldn't allow it. It was over this time for sure. She had prayed religiously for guidance and she believed Paul wasn't the man God had for her. Playtime was over. She felt as if her heart were pounding loud enough for others to hear. She needed to mark her relationship with Paul a thing of the past, dead and buried, no matter how much her flesh wanted to settle for something less than what God had. She needed to figure out an escape route to get away from him, and it came to her. "That's fine. Where is it going to be, at your mama's?" she asked Edwin.

Edwin felt puzzled and unsure of what Courtney was doing. He'd have to play along in ignorance. "My mom's. That's it."

"I'll see you in a few," she told him.

Edwin acquiesced and went outside to wait for his mother.

"I was going to take you out to dinner, a nice place too, not the Hoagie Shop. But I see you already have plans."

"How nice of you, Paul, but yeah, I'm meeting the family over to my aunt's."

"I know all of your family. If you want some company I don't mind going with you."

Too little, too late. When Edwin left, Courtney felt like her mission had been accomplished. The gate was open and she was headed for the open pasture. She had wiggled out of a dinner date with Paul. Inviting himself to tag along was putting that pasture in the far distance. She didn't know what else to do to free herself from his offer. It was refreshing to be on speaking terms with him again, she had to admit. After all, she had spent the past six years of her life committed to him. Getting along was different than getting together. She didn't want to do it, but decided it needed to be clear to Paul that they were officially done, for good.

"On second thought, I take that back. Since we're not together anymore, I shouldn't be hanging out with you and your family. Right?" he said.

She remained silent. So far, he was saying everything she wanted him to without her having to utter a word.

"Oh, no comment." His hands slid into his pants pockets. He did a soft lean over his left shoulder. "I guess I'm right then." He rocked his head and cocked a grin. "All right then, Ms. Courtney. Tell your parents I asked about them and I'll see you around the way."

"You take care of yourself, Paul."

She didn't feel the same longing for Paul in his presence as she had in years past. She and Paul had gone round and round long enough to know she could survive without being with him. The companionship hadn't been easy to write off, at least until the New England breeze had swept past Africa and guided Sebastian Whittington to Philadelphia. Courtney had a new friend to hang out with, and the weekly arguments she'd endured for months with Paul weren't missed.

She walked out of the church with her shades back in position and head held high. It was a glorious afternoon.

CHAPTER 14

She drove to her aunt's house, parked, and strolled up the steps. The front door was open and she could see through the screen.

"Knock, knock," she yelled through the screen while simultaneously pulling the door open.

Aunt Sis came out of the kitchen wearing an apron and holding a towel that she was using to wipe her hands.

"Hey, baby."

Courtney dropped her purse on the couch and keys on the cocktail table. She gave her aunt a peck on the cheek.

"Hello, Auntie."

Aunt Sis took the backside of her arm and rubbed it up from the top of her eyebrows to the temple of her head, annihilating any sweat along the way, careful not to drip any oil-tainted flour from her fingertips.

"I saw you sitting on the end this morning. You got out of there so fast, I didn't get a chance to say hi. You taking care of yourself?" Aunt Sis asked.

"I am."

"Jake and Bee coming?"

"I doubt it. You know they're heading down to Aunt Cat's tomorrow, and Daddy likes to leave early in the morning when he's going to North Carolina. They'll probably take it easy and rest all day."

"That's right. He did say they'd be gone for two weeks."

"What is that? Something smells good," Courtney said.

"I'm frying up a little chicken and cooking up a few greens to go with the spaghetti and potato salad I brought home from the party yesterday."

"Ooh, no, you didn't say greens and fried chicken."

Auntie was pleased to see the joy her food brought to her family. It was one of the few gifts she had to give.

"It'll be ready in a few minutes. Get them plates and glasses out of the cabinet for me. We're going to sit down to the table as a family today."

"Where is Edwin? I saw his car parked in his spot across the street," Courtney said.

"He's upstairs checking on the plumbing in the bathroom. I need some work done up there and he's going to pay for a plumber to come out and do it next week. He'll be right down. Come on into this kitchen while I fry up this chicken."

Courtney followed her aunt into the kitchen and took a seat at the table. "Did you bring any ribs?"

"Uh-uh, ooo, no, that pork runs my blood pressure right up. If I'd thought about it, I would have brought some for you all. You're young, you can still eat it," Aunt Sis said.

"Your chicken is fine with me."

Her aunt rested one hand on the corner of the counter and in the other she took the fork and rolled the pieces of chicken over in the hot grease, leaving the golden-brown side exposed.

"Paul didn't come with you?"

The only person Courtney had told about breaking up with Paul was Edwin. Even her parents didn't know. When she told them Paul couldn't make it to the party, they assumed he had to work. She didn't offer any clarification and they didn't ask. Aunt Sis was just like another parent to her and would need the update at some point, not necessarily today.

"He mentioned it, but decided against it."

"He should have come. He knows all of us, has all of his life. That boy knows he can come here and get a meal. He doesn't need a personal invitation. Next time I see him, I'm going to tell him so."

Courtney sat quietly. She was grown and shouldn't be afraid to tell anyone she'd broken up with the family favorite, but revealing the truth didn't feel right at the moment. It would have to come later, after her stomach had been massaged with some of that potato salad and chicken.

"What's for dessert?"

"Look under the plastic cover over there, underneath the cabinet where I keep the plates. See if there's some 'tata pie left."

"Oooo. Yes, potato pie. I came to eat on the right day. Auntie, you know how to hook up some Sunday grub." She broke off the front corner of a slice and wolfed it down, holding her hand like a catcher's mitt near her chest, in case some morsel tried to escape the clutches of her sweet tooth and scamper to the floor. She gave her aunt another kiss on the cheek.

"Girl, did you wash your hands?"

"Oops, sorry, Auntie. Let me wash them now before I get a whupping."

Aunt Sis adored her niece. With two sons and no girls, Courtney was like a daughter. Aunt Sis couldn't ever remember spanking Courtney in her childhood, but always spoke like she was going to, on the rare occasions when she used to act up.

Courtney had favor with her aunt and knew it. Being an only child wasn't painful growing up with aunts and uncles who treated her like their children, and cousins who were like siblings. Staying tight and looking out for one another was a must in the Young family, and Courtney liked it just fine.

Edwin came down the stairs and went into the kitchen. His mother was putting a fresh set of flour-dipped chicken into the cast-iron skillet.

"You made it," he said to Courtney.

"Sure did. You know I wasn't going to sit up in my little old apartment and have leftovers by myself when I can come over here and eat Aunt Sis's cooking."

"Need any help?" Edwin asked his mother.

"Nope, I'm about done."

"I'm going to watch a little football until the food gets ready."

"It's not cold outside yet and that football is on already."

Edwin gave Courtney a nod toward the living room.

"I'm going to check on the game too, Auntie Sis. Let me know if you need me to help."

"I'm almost done and that cousin of yours better be here by the time we get ready to eat. He told me to fix these greens and he better get here."

"Oh yeah, I have to remember to take another piece of pie and a tiny bowl of greens to my friend at work again. He's the one I fixed the food for a few weeks ago. He's always talking about soul food, but he didn't know anything about good food until he had some from our family." She knew Aunt Sis was soaking in the compliment.

Courtney went to the living room and plopped down on the couch next to Edwin, who was flipping channels with the remote, in search of the game.

"You already know what I'm getting ready to ask you."

"What?"

"You and Paul back together?"

"No!"

"You sure?"

"Positive. That ship has sailed."

"The two of you looked awfully cozy at church. I didn't want to interrupt."

"Stop." Courtney gave Edwin a playful pluck on his shoulder. "Paul's a trip. I think we broke up for good this time. No going back."

"It was just a matter of time. I'm surprised he lasted as long as he did. You outgrew him four years ago. I just knew you were going to cut him loose after your freshman year."

"You might feel that way, but the rest of the family really likes Paul. They think he's the one for me. Both of our families have been at Fifth Baptist for years."

"Nobody really thinks Paul is right for you, except maybe Paul. You two don't have anything in common, except that you grew up in the same neighborhood and go to the same church. That's it. You have so much going for you, little cousin. Paul doesn't have anything, doesn't want anything, and has the nerve to try and trip with you because you don't want to eat discounted cheese steaks every night for the rest of your life."

"I tried to talk to him about going to college to give himself more options. He wasn't interested. On top of that, he told me Northwestern was for snobs. Funny, he didn't seem to have a problem with Northwestern when I took my work-study money and helped buy his plane tickets to come visit me while I was in school," she said with her arms crossed.

"You can't even get mad at him for not wanting more out of life. If it works for him, it's fine. You might think someone like him should be dissatisfied or unhappy, but then again he might not be. He can only dream as far as his exposure allows him. That's just the way it is."

"He thinks I'm putting down his job. I'm not. I'm just saying some people don't get a chance to go to college or trade school or whatever. When you get an opportunity and you don't take it and then you sit back and complain about what other people are doing, that's when I have a problem. There's nothing wrong with him working at the Hoagie Shop, but he's just doing it because he's lazy."

"I still can't believe he let those basketball scholarships go just because he was too lazy to take the SAT exam and fill out the application. How many people get offered free rides to Temple, Duke, and Georgetown? I wish they had given me the money that he didn't use. I just finished paying off my Temple loan and have a long ways to go with the ones from Yale. He wasn't for you, Courtney. Eventually he was going to resent you for being successful, put you down, or flat-out hold you back."

"I know, he already told me Northwestern was no better than CW."

"CW who?"

"City-Wide Community College."

Edwin's muffled grunt gained momentum and escalated into roaring laughter the more he thought about Paul's comment. "That tells you what kind of a person you're dealing with."

"I don't want to be seen as a snob, but I don't want to hang out at the pool hall every Thursday night either. I did that for years."

"Don't let the stuff he says bother you. Bottom line is, you've matured, and he hasn't."

"I still don't want to be seen as a snob in the neighborhood."

"You're not. Courtney, they love you. Ms. Arnold, the Chapmans, and I can't even think of all the people who talk about how proud they are of you. They talk about you as if you were Oprah. When you did that summer internship last summer, Mr. Peters told everybody you were like second in line from the CEO."

"No, he didn't. I was one step above the administrative assistant."

"Didn't matter to him. You might as well have been his daughter. The people in the neighborhood are happy for you. When you make it out, it's kind of like they make it out."

"The older people are happy about us doing well, but what about people our age?"

"You'll always have a few like Paul. With them, you're wrong if you do and wrong if you don't. If you had stayed around here, gotten pregnant, and were a single mother living in government housing, his kind would be talking about how smart you used to be and how you'd wasted your life. Going to college like you did and getting a little exposure and learning how to think outside the neighborhood, all of a sudden you're too good. You can't win with his kind. All you can do is what makes you happy and forget the rest." He gave her a hug and wondered what part of the advice he could digest for himself. "Did you go out with the guy from Northwestern?" Edwin whispered.

She affirmed that with a nod.

"How'd that go?"

"I actually had a great time. I wasn't expecting to either."

"Don't let Mama know anything about it. You know how she feels about white people."

Courtney's eyes widened and lips tightened. "I wasn't going to say anything anyway. He's just a guy from school, no big deal." If she said it enough, maybe she could believe it.

"Oh, it's a big deal around here. Don't even think that his being a student from Northwestern makes him all right. I've seen how Mama and some of the family treat my white colleagues. You don't want to subject him to it. As far as they're concerned, he fits the profile for every cross-burning, plantation-thinking bigot just because he's white. Mama still hasn't let go of her anger for those people in south Philly, and every white person that comes her way has to pay for it."

What had happened to Uncle Eddie was a faint memory. Courtney was a little girl when it happened, but every now and then some of the other family members would retell the story to keep it fresh. From what she had heard, Uncle Eddie had gotten certified as an electrician in a union where he was the only black. He made good money and decided to move out of the neighborhood and buy a house down in south Philadelphia where the only sprinkles of black were found in pepper shakers. The first night in the new house, somebody spray-painted profanity all over the front of the house. A week later, they threw a brick through the front window, wrapped in a burning rag. Uncle Eddie refused to be run out of his house.

One afternoon somewhere between three and seven men broke

into the house. Every time somebody told the story now it had a different number, but the consistent part of the story was that they attacked Uncle Eddie and broke both of his knees and arms. He had surgery right after the assault and came through with flying colors. He could handle what was happening, but didn't want his wife and two sons in danger. He decided to move out of the house as soon as he got out of the hospital. Then, without any warning, he got a blood clot after the surgery. It went to his lungs and killed him. The family was upset, but Aunt Sis took it the hardest. Daddy helped her move back to the old neighborhood. They said she almost had a nervous breakdown because of it.

The police never did find out who was responsible for beating Uncle Eddie, even though he gave them descriptions. He wasn't sure of exactly how many, but there were a lot of them. Everybody knew it was more than the one nineteen-year-old Aunt Sis saw running from the house and was able to identify. In the end, it didn't matter. Even he was found not guilty due to a lack of evidence. From that day, Aunt Sis vowed that white people couldn't be trusted and she wanted nothing to do with them. One time Aunt Sis said she'd get justice any way she could, no matter how long it took.

"If you're white, Mama doesn't like you. No other characteristic is necessary. When you fit the profile, nothing else matters. Little cuz, don't get involved unless you've weighed the cost. Trust me, it won't be cheap to get involved with somebody like him in this family."

"Well, for the record, I'm not seeing him in a romantic way. I am footloose and fancy-free, waiting on the man God has for me."

"I'm glad to hear it because I know someone you might be interested in meeting. I wouldn't normally introduce any of my crazy friends to you, but Roger is different. He's a decent brother, church-going, and a good businessman. He's got his act together. I know he's a little on the old side for you, being almost thirty and all, but hey, you've always been mature for your age. You can handle it."

"Umm, I don't know."

"Look, anybody beats that clown Paul. Let me set you up on a date."

Edwin's humor found a smile in Courtney.

"Okay. I'll go out with him when you go out with Sheila again. It's been eight months since you took her out the first time."

"I know, but I'm working on it. I called her right after we talked about it over here a few weeks ago. We were supposed to go out Friday but I had to cancel because of the thing with Jamal."

"I hope you rescheduled."

He propped the remote vertically on his thigh and rubbed his chin with his other hand. "Don't worry, I will. It's just that work is killing me right now. I've been working on lawsuits for the past year. Everybody and their brother seem to be suing our corporate clients. But I will make time for Ms. Sheila. I'm going to see if she's free for dinner on Thursday."

"Good, because you can't be standing up my friends, and she's my director on top of that. What's wrong with you?" she teased.

"But you don't have to wait on me to meet Roger."

"Yes, I do. If you go out with Sheila, I'll go out with Roger. That's the deal."

Edwin wrapped his arm around Courtney's neck in a loose choke hold and rubbed the top of her head with his fist.

"Get your plates," Aunt Sis shouted from the kitchen. She came to the doorway. "Edwin, I almost forgot. I want to go to the outlets down in Delaware one night this week. Since you're getting the bathroom done, I might as well get some new towels and fixtures to go with it. What night can you take me?"

"Let me look at my schedule, Mama. I'll let you know tomorrow."

Courtney knew who was rushing up the front steps. "It's about time you got here, Jay."

"Ce-Ce what's up, girl? Eddie, Eddie, Eddie, what's up, what's up, what's up, bro?"

The brothers extended their hands, letting their fingertips lock and then snap back.

"You got it, bro," Edwin responded.

"Where's Mama?"

"In the kitchen, and you narrowly escaped a whupping. She's been ranting about you not being here."

"Squash all of that. She knew I was coming. Since my license is suspended and my bike needs the tire fixed, I'm limited. I have to catch the bus or wait on somebody to give me a ride, and you know I'm not into begging for a ride. I gotta get here on my own, the best way I can. Oh yeah, and, man, I've been thinking about the bail money that you keep putting out for me. I don't want you to do it anymore. I told Mama to stop asking you. If I get locked up again, I gotta just do the time and wait until I can get out on my own, but she doesn't want to hear that."

Courtney excused herself and went to help Aunt Sis.

"It's cool, li'l brother. Let's eat. Mama, your baby boy finally got here. Can the rest of us starving folks eat now?"

Edwin rose to his feet. He raised his fist like a boxer getting ready for a match and extended a fake punch to his brother. Jamal jerked his head back in slow motion as if he'd caught the fictitious jab on the cheek. Edwin put his arm around Jamal's shoulder and they hesitated no longer in making their way to a table filled with Aunt Sis's delicacies.

Courtney proceeded to set the table. Her heart was warmed in the presence of family, but there was also a tug to get home and call Sebastian.

Night had sauntered in and Courtney was finally home. It had been a long and satisfying day. She changed into loungewear and fixed herself a snack before snuggling into her seasoned chair, in a living room that doubled as a den. When she was at Aunt's Sis's, Courtney had looked forward to seeing Sebastian at the Sunday evening church service that they had gotten out of an hour ago.

Going to his church, this evening, had been an experience. It was the first church since leaving Chicago that she'd gone to with a mixture of races, all singing and praising the same way. Courtney had to admit she was a little skeptical about the quality of the music since there was no organ. At Fifth Baptist, Brother Brendon would have those keys humming. When the music got really good and the church broke loose and leaped to their feet, it was all he could do to keep the organ from lifting up on one side and trying to go airborne. Much to her amazement, the lightweight band comprising a drummer, keyboard player, and bass guitarist had Sebastian's church rocking.

The minister didn't have the same flare behind the glass podium as Reverend Tyler did when he took to the aisles, but Courtney was moved by the message. The words kept ringing in her head, over and over, "A double-minded man is unstable in all of his ways—choose this day whom you will serve, for the day will come when right will seem wrong and wrong will seem right." She wasn't quite sure why she couldn't let it go.

CHAPTER 15

Edwin didn't practice being bicultural. It came natural. He could stand on the steps of Mama's house and shoot the breeze with the neighborhood fellas for hours, reminiscing about the good ole days and talking about the war wounds of Philadelphia, but when he walked across the threshold at Gershwin, Peters, and Myers his bilingual street savvy was checked at the door.

Before jumping into the fishbowl every morning, he made the appropriate adjustments in his conversation and stiffened up his walk. Countless discussions about the stock market had yielded a couple of profitable additions to his portfolio as a result. People in the office came from money, had money, and made money. They weren't better than his friends from the neighborhood, just saw life through a glossier set of eyes.

Being a team player was his focus. He tried his hand at golf, but it didn't beat shooting hoops on the court with the fellas. His guard was kept on automatic, never letting himself get too comfortable. He didn't mix business with culture. Politics, affirmative action, views on dating, and the legal system were a no-no. The heated discussion he had years ago, with a fellow attorney about the racially biased death penalty system, had gotten out of control. If that hadn't been enough, he'd allowed himself to be lured into defending his position on why Haitian refugees should be able to stay in the country, like every other immigrant, instead of being put back to sea on the two-by-four board they sailed in on. Since then, he had learned to smile with his peers and practice law, leaving the real Edwin at home. Certain issues would have to be addressed in a circle of his other peers, the ones outside the office.

The heart of the city skyline positioned itself outside Edwin's fifteenth-floor windows. Floor-to-ceiling bookcases were packed with journals, case law books, research manuals, and a few law school remnants. The secretary announced an incoming call to Edwin, who was juggling the stack of folders sitting in front of him, trying to grab the one for his two o'clock meeting. He put the call on speaker.

"Ms. Spencer, what a surprise."

"I hope a pleasant one."

Edwin didn't encourage Mandy when she made overtures. He was conscious not to cross the line and lead her into believing there was romantic interest on his part, yet he cherished her friendship. Their camaraderie had begun eight years ago when they met in law school at Yale. He remembered her wild-eyed enthusiasm in class discussions, but reserved, almost docile style in moot court. They joined study groups together and helped one another get through. He knew she'd make an excellent attorney.

"It's always good to hear a friendly voice. To what do I owe the pleasure of this call?"

"I guess you forgot about our conversation a few weeks ago, the one where I told you I was going to Washington for the legal conference. You said to stop in Philadelphia on my way down so we could have dinner. Did you forget, Mr. Williams?"

Edwin dropped the red-tabbed folder on top of the stack and planted his feet on the floor. He leaned back in the seat, stretched his arm, and gave it a slight bend. He hung his head and let his hand glide from the front of his head to the back, several times, before resting it under his chin.

"I am sorry, Mandy. I did forget. You wouldn't believe how busy I've been. It's crazy around here."

"That's what happens when you graduate with honors and go to work for a big firm like GPM. You get plenty of opportunity to show what a top-notch attorney you are, and you, Mr. Williams, are phenomenal."

"Phenomenal? I wouldn't go that far. Overworked, definitely."

"At least you can't say underpaid."

"You're right about that, I can't. Still, it's days like today I consider taking one of those nice nine-to-five corporate jobs like you have. Is Johnson and Johnson looking for attorneys?"

"Probably, but a man of your caliber needs more challenge to keep him fully satisfied. I don't think you'd get that here unless you were given the chief counsel position, which doesn't seem to be readily available."

"Thanks for the vote of confidence."

"I believe in you and I know you'll make partner soon."

Edwin didn't have the same assurance as Mandy. He had worked hard for the firm over the past five years, sacrificing personal time and happiness outside the four walls of Gershwin, Peters, and Myers. He left no stone unturned in presenting himself as partner material. He passed the bar exam the first time around and then sat for the Jersey, New York, and D.C. exams to boot. He could have waited a few years, had the exams waived, and gotten licensed in the other states, but chose to proactively get licensed in them, in case that was needed.

Highly respected for his legal prowess and client rapport, Edwin didn't feel like he was a part of the elite club. He was well paid, but the title of partner seemed to elude him, no matter how many tough cases he won. He couldn't pick up the phone and call in favors from the district attorney or from the police chief whenever Jamal got into some bogus trouble. His connections weren't solid. He was popular in the neighborhood, but in the legal arena he was John Doe, Esq.

What he had accomplished would be fine for some, but he wanted more. Before crying racial wolf, he wanted to do everything on his end to eliminate the race factor and prove himself, even if it meant working five times harder than his peers. Experience, extensive educational and professional credentials, an exceptional win-loss case record, well-satisfied clients, and an impeccable reputation were in place. An average attorney in a major Philadelphia law firm took eight years to make partner. His record spoke loud and clear. He wasn't average. A brother couldn't graduate from Yale with honors and be just average. With a handful of black students in attendance, getting in required a miraculous move of God alone, never mind graduating on top. He would give Gershwin, Peters, and Myers another year before hitting the road if they didn't step up with a promotion to partner.

"About tomorrow, what time were you thinking about meeting for dinner?"

"My train gets in around six-thirty, so how's seven o'clock?"

Edwin looked at his calendar. "Ahh, that will be too tight. Seven o'clock won't work."

"I can be flexible. I can come earlier or later, whatever works best for you."

"Maybe we should just pass on dinner this trip, but I'll do a better job of coordinating next time."

"I know you're busy, but you have to eat sometime."

"I know, but I've got a pile of work here. I've been staying until six and seven every night, but tomorrow I was planning to leave by five so I can take my mother to Delaware."

"I don't want to disrupt your plans, but I'd love to see you. Tell you what, why don't I come around five and get a room downtown and wait for you? That way you'll have time to do everything you have planned. We can eat afterward. How's that sound?" Mandy asked.

"I might not get free until nine or ten and that's too late to take you to dinner."

"No, it's not. I can cater to your schedule. I'll be ready whatever time you get free, it can be seven in the evening or one in the morning, doesn't matter. If you don't want dinner, we can grab a cup of your favorite Chai tea from Starbucks. Since you work around the clock anyway, the tea will be a really good late-night boost."

"It's tempting but I think we should pass. I wouldn't want you waiting like that."

"Are you canceling because you're concerned that I'll be inconvenienced having to wait for you?"

"Yes, I don't want you to take the train here, only to end up meeting me late in the evening. I don't want to waste your time like that. I wouldn't feel right having you wait around for me."

"Don't worry about it, just say yes."

He gave her proposal consideration.

"Please, Ed, don't be concerned. I would love to see you. I'm coming tomorrow night, and I'll wait for you at the Marriott. I'm giving you my cell phone number. I know you already have it, but I don't want you to take the time to look. It's just as easy for me to give it to you again, just in case."

"You always make it so easy for me. You're a good friend, Mandy. Thanks for forcing me to take a break. I'll see you tomorrow."

After Mandy got off the phone, Edwin held the receiver for a moment. She wasn't his type, but she made it easy on him. He placed the receiver on the cradle and went back to business. There was enough work to carry him into tomorrow, without blinking.

Edwin couldn't believe it was already Wednesday. He thought leaving work at five would get him to Delaware long before six. Mama would have a couple of hours to shop and he'd have her back home by eight-thirty. That would put him at the train station by nine to pick up Mandy. He hadn't counted on his mother wanting to make a few other stops.

"Mama, I have plans later."

"That's fine. You can drop me off at home and I'll see you tomorrow night around six."

"Tomorrow night?"

"For the counseling class that the court is making Jamal go to. What time did you want to pick me up?"

"I didn't know anything about it. I have other plans."

"What could be more important than family?"

Edwin pressed the clutch so hard the car jerked.

"Your brother needs your support. You know the 'white folks' killed his father."

"He was my father too, Mama."

"Yes, but you made out okay without your father. Jamal hasn't had it as easy. You know the problems he's had. It would mean a lot to him and to me if you made time to go."

"What about my job and my plans?"

"You can always get another job and run errands. You can't get another mother or brother."

Stillness hovered inside the car.

"What time do I need to pick you up?"

"Why don't you get me by five? That will give us plenty of time to eat down at the little Jamaican restaurant that I like off of South Street, and still get to the class in time. See you tomorrow, son. I just love you."

After Edwin dropped his mother off, he retrieved Sheila's phone number from his electronic organizer, but paused before making the call. It would be awkward, and he felt embarrassed about canceling again on such short notice. This was the second time in less than a week. He played the scenario repeatedly in his head so it would be smooth when he shared it with Sheila. She was on the line and they exchanged common greeting courtesies. No need to beat around the bush.

"Sheila, I'm sorry, but something came up with my family again and I'll be tied up until late tomorrow evening. I'm really sorry. I know you must think I'm a total jerk."

Quiet choked the line.

"Do you want to meet afterward?" she offered.

He was reluctant to schedule a time now and have to cancel again. The unpleasant experience was one he didn't relish with his past two girlfriends and he wasn't quick to make the same mistake. "I'm not quite sure how long I'll be unavailable. I'd rather change it to another day altogether."

"I understand. Maybe some other time," she said, twirling the phone cord.

"I'd like that. Again, Sheila, I truly apologize for canceling at the last minute. I was really looking forward to seeing you again. I hope you give me another chance in the very near future."

Edwin could tell by the gaps in the conversation that Sheila didn't like being stood up. He felt awful. While driving, he contemplated what he needed to do to get his professional and personal life in balance. Not every woman in his life was going to bend over backward to accommodate his obligations. He was seeing Mandy as the exception, not the rule.

CHAPTER 16

Three more days in a row, but who was counting? They had dinner at the Cheesecake Factory in King of Prussia, had gone to the aquarium across the river in Camden Saturday evening, and finished the week off at Sebastian's church last night. Visiting his church again didn't require much convincing. The previous message had pricked her curiosity, and Courtney had a taste for more.

Faith Christian Center was supposed to be her haven, but the burning eyes of judgment sitting in the pews singed her soul, the same way the ones walking along the street did. Then again, why wouldn't they, Courtney admitted. Church was a place to learn right from wrong. The rest was a matter of free will. The church wasn't obligated to use the teachings, except maybe on Sundays, in front of the minister, while he was standing at arm's length from God. There was no guarantee any other time. There was something positive in everything. Church was helping to settle some of her haziness about race. Religion was ideal for preaching on the healing powers of God, help in finances, and problems in a marriage, but race wasn't in the lessons at Fifth Baptist or Faith Christian Center. No one seemed to want to hear from God on the subject. People, whether they were black or white, churched or not, were on the same page when it came to racial matters, divided.

Planning to see Sebastian this evening was another easy decision. It was what they'd done consistently since he moved to Philly two weeks ago. The only piece requiring any extra thought was what theater they should go to. Courtney ruled out Sixty-ninth Street because she was sure to be recognized, and even worse, she didn't feel like paying money to listen to people narrate the movie from their seats. The riverfront theater had more selections, but the happy hour crowd was known to crash the theater in drunken stupors. Both theaters were to be avoided. That left the artsy theater in Society Hill, nestled in the heart of the upscale section of downtown, or the more traditional one in Old City. Courtney was comfortable with either. They presented the lowest risk of running into someone and having to explain why she was at the movie on a Monday night with someone like Sebastian. Catching a movie and having a good laugh without being interrogated was the goal.

"When we leave here, how about going with me to Delilah's soul food restaurant at the train station or the Caribbean Delight on South Street?" Courtney asked.

"Sure, let's do it."

"Do you have a preference?"

"I haven't been to either before. It's totally your call," he said.

"All right then, let's go to the Caribbean Delight. It's closer. Maybe we can do Delilah's next time."

South Street was going to be a haven. The block was speckled with novelty shops that featured everything from African artifacts and trendy clothes to tattoo parlors and condom shops. With all of the distractions, nobody would have too much eyeball energy left to stare at the two of them.

Walking along the cobblestoned road should have given Courtney a flash of nostalgia, but it didn't. This was old Philadelphia, five blocks from the Liberty Bell, the place where America took a stand on freedom, or so she'd heard. None of her friends frequented the tourist attraction. No need based on the philosophy taught to them growing up. Black Americans could acquire freedom two ways, with an education or a high-priced attorney, and sometimes it took both.

"Do you realize we've been out together four days straight?"

"I want to see you every day," he said, resting his arm across her shoulders.

"I still owe you a tour of the city," she reminded him.

"Yes, you do and I'm keeping it on radar."

"What about tomorrow?" Courtney asked.

"I have a study group tomorrow night, but how about Wednesday?"

She drew a slow breath and let it seep out as her shoulders tightened. "I can't go out with you Wednesday night. We're having a surprise party for my cousin Edwin."

"The one you want me to meet?"

"That's him, the attorney in the family."

"Well, what about Wednesday? Sounds like the perfect time to meet him."

Courtney gulped and searched for a response that would be a nice way of telling him that he couldn't come. It wasn't that she didn't want him there. Just the opposite, but bringing him to a family function at Aunt Sis's would be the same as tossing a piece of red meat to a pack of starving wolves.

"It would give me a chance to meet your cousin and spend another evening with you," he added.

"I don't know if they're planning for a limited numbers of guests."

"I'm not that big." He scrunched down and tucked his head in, making himself look slightly shorter. "Come on, I won't take up much room."

"I'm not sure if I can bring a guest."

"Courtney, is there some reason you don't want me to go?" he said with firmness in his voice.

How had she gotten into this situation? They were having an enjoyable time, and now this. What was she going to do? On the bright side, it would give her a chance to see him another night, and it was Edwin's party. She could always say he was a student from Northwestern who wanted to talk to Edwin about law school, if anyone asked. "You're right. I'd like for you to come to the party. It's a great idea."

The line for tickets was short. Suggesting the matinee was the right move. Courtney was hoping that most folks were still at work. Fewer people meant fewer stares, even from the ones who wouldn't make eye contact but burned the back of her neck after passing by. It was a good thing Sebastian was only a friend; otherwise this fishbowl factor would be a problem.

Sebastian stepped to the window in front of Courtney.

"Two tickets for the matinee please."

The gentleman inside the booth, who looked to Courtney as if he were born a few days after Moses, gaped at Sebastian, then down at the tickets, and repeated the combination three times before pushing the tickets out of the slot with his wrinkly hand. Courtney watched him watch Sebastian and cut his eyes in their direction as they entered the door. The chill she shook off wasn't from the warm air. She leaned back, caught him staring, and couldn't resist. She waved at the gentleman, wanting him to feel a pinch of the awkwardness he was sending her way. At least people were consistent. She went inside the door Sebastian was holding open.

"Want popcorn?"

"Of course. I want the works."

"And that would be?"

"Small bag of popcorn since we're eating later, a bottle of water, and my favorite almond roca," she said from a slightly squatting position, peering into the glass case overflowing with treats. "That's why I love coming down here. They have the good stuff. You can't get these kinds of snacks anywhere else."

Sebastian moved closer to the counter and placed his order with the waiting attendant.

"We'll have a large popcorn, two bottled waters, and a box of almond roca, please. That should do it." He turned to her with one arm leaning on the counter. "Did I miss anything?"

Courtney attempted to pull her wallet out but Sebastian touched the top of her hand, pushing it back into her purse.

"You haven't missed a single thing, yet."

The attendant placed both bottles of water, and the candy into a cardboard carrying tray, making room for the bag of popcorn last. He made several attempts to fit it into the tray neatly, to no avail.

"Don't worry about it," Sebastian said. "I'll carry it."

He juggled the tray and the bag. Courtney reached out to get the popcorn. She nibbled on a few of the kernels, and Sebastian followed suit, a few steps, and a few more kernels. She ate the popcorn without hesitation, bumping fingers with his a few times in the bag.

She thought back to nearly a month ago at D&B, when she was meeting Sebastian out of courtesy. She grabbed a few more kernels before taking a seat in the empty theater. A few hang-ups about being in public with him were on vacation. Not quite all of them. Edwin's party was the day after tomorrow, and she didn't have a warm fuzzy feeling about taking Sebastian. There might not be anyone else like him there, another student, that is. At some point he could have met her family and friends, but why Wednesday?

CHAPTER 17

Courtney sat at her desk and jotted down a few notes for her up-coming meeting. Didn't take long for her mind to drift to the time she'd been spending with Sebastian. They hadn't been dates, but whatever her outings with Sebastian were called, Courtney was en-joying every minute and anticipated more of them until he got settled into the area and expanded his circle of friends.

"Hey, lady, you have a minute?" Sheila asked. "I want you to take a look at the projection reports my assistant put together. They're based on your numbers from last week."

"Sure, you want me to come to your office?"

"Please, but give me five minutes. I need to make a quick stop first."

Courtney got her calculator and went to Sheila's office. It took nearly an hour but she was able to explain the information and give Sheila what she needed.

Edwin's party kept popping in and out of Courtney's thoughts. She wanted to invite Sheila, but how could she do that with Sebastian coming? What would Sheila think? Then again, if she rehearsed her line enough times, she could convince everybody that Sebastian came to the party to meet Edwin, in hopes of getting insight into law school. The only consideration to be flushed out was how to keep Sebastian from hearing her tell the story. She had time to work out the details, but the plan was solid enough to extend an invitation to Sheila.

"What are you doing tomorrow evening?"

"Let's see, Wednesday," Sheila said, glancing at the calendar. "Nothing, I don't think. Why?"

"I want you to come to Edwin's surprise birthday party."

"Girl, you don't know how to quit," Sheila said, shaking her head and pulling the identification tag hanging around her neck.

"Come on, what can it hurt? You already said you aren't doing anything. Come on, please."

"Why do you keep pushing for me to get with your cousin? How many times have you told me you're waiting on God to bring you a man?"

Courtney raised her hands with an uncertain look. "A few."

"Well, why do you keep trying to matchmake us heathens?"

"You're right. I'll back off."

"Good, because I told you I'm not going to chase Mr. Edwin Williams. He canceled on me twice and danced around setting another date the last time. Since he's so busy, let him stay busy. He doesn't need me disrupting his world and I don't need him disrupting mine."

Today wasn't out of the ordinary for Edwin. Three hot cases being prepped simultaneously with briefs due in a week, plus new cases being assigned every day. Thank goodness for the new intern and paralegal he'd gotten to take some of the administrative load off him. They would be great assets to the firm when they got up to speed, but right now he didn't have the time to break them in. Whatever they could do on their own was all the help he would be getting until his three major cases cleared litigation.

The intercom buzzed and his secretary announced a call from Mandy Spencer on line one. He took the call.

"Mandy, don't tell me, you're coming to Philadelphia for a conference."

"Not quite, I'm coming to Philadelphia, but not for business. My visit is strictly personal."

Edwin leaned back in his chair and propped his hand on the armrest.

"Really? So don't keep me in suspense, what's bringing you to Philadelphia?"

"That does it, I know you're working too hard. I hope you didn't forget about your own birthday."

"Birthday!" He flung his arm in the air and let it fall to his head and slide down the back.

"Yes, birthday. You know, the little thing that comes every year?"

"Oh, Mandy, I have been so swamped with all of these takeovers and mergers, I haven't thought about much of anything else."

"I guess I can take that to mean you don't have any plans."

"I guess I don't."

"Well, carve out some time tomorrow. I'm taking you to dinner, and I won't take no for an answer. Do you understand, counselor?"

"Fully. Dinner sounds fine. What did you have in mind?"

"How about the Fountain Restaurant at the Four Seasons? I've already checked and they will have your favorite on the menu, roasted duck."

"I can't pass that up. I'm sold. What time will you arrive?"

"My train gets in at five-thirty. I'll take a cab over to the Four Seasons. It should get me there by six. So, I'll confirm a six-thirty reservation."

"That's fine. I'll pick you up at five-thirty."

"Oh no, absolutely not. I know how busy you are. Don't worry about picking me up. I'll take the cab."

"Mandy, I'm picking you up and I'll tell you what you told me, I'm not taking no for an answer."

"As you wish, counselor, see you tomorrow."

CHAPTER 18

Courtney felt in control. She was spending time with someone who was flying high and didn't mind watching her soar. She was in a good place emotionally and her project was reaping the benefit. She checked the white boards to make sure they were supplied with markers. Flip charts were positioned around the room, handouts ready, and refreshments set up. The only task left was to lower the overhead screen and the meeting was ready to go.

Having major responsibility on such a visible project, Courtney felt the thrill running from her head to her knees. She didn't have the confidence at first, but Sheila convinced her she was the best person to do the marketing analysis. This was Sheila's baby, but Courtney was grateful she'd gotten the opportunity to push the stroller.

Sheila entered the conference room wearing a tailored black suit with a stiff wide-collared white shirt and four-inch-thick cuffs. She dropped her portfolio on the table. "Okay, girlfriend," she said, and kept walking toward the front of the conference room where Courtney was standing, "are we ready to go?"

Courtney clasped her hands together and brought them to her lips momentarily and said, "We're ready to go."

Sheila initiated a mid-range high five.

"I expected no less, Ms. Young."

Courtney surveyed the room again. "I want everything to go just right."

"Don't worry about it."

"You can say that. It's no big deal for you. This is new to me. Having all of these members of the executive staff in my meeting, woooo." She took a deep breath.

"Don't get intimidated. Treat them just like you would in a regular staff meeting," Sheila said, giving Courtney a brisk rub across the shoulder.

Courtney had been so consumed with preparing for the presentation that there hadn't been time to dwell on the magnitude of the meeting, until this morning. Any new product slated to generate double-digit millions in revenue naturally got the attention of the executive staff, but watching the twenty seats surrounding the conference room table fill with vice presidents, directors, and managers melted the remaining shred of calm she had lingering. The other ten chairs, lining the window, couldn't hold the entire supporting cast, and so the remaining participants spilled onto windowsills and crammed into standing-room-only space.

"You will do fine. If you get in trouble, don't worry. I'll jump in," Sheila said before taking her seat.

Having Sheila as a friend and mentor was more than she'd expected. The first time she had interviewed with Sheila, in her sophomore year, they'd connected. Most of the new hires in the group hadn't done any internships with the company and a few had done one. Courtney was glad to have done three.

Speak loud and slow to overcome fear, was what Courtney kept telling herself. The presentation was packed with marketing jargon and statistics that seemed to pique the curiosity of the vice presidents. Five minutes into the discussion, the anxiety eased as her confidence with the information grew. She could tell the audience was on board by the questions and ongoing discussions. An hour later, the data had been provided and all questions addressed, with Sheila having to jump in only a few times. Enthusiasm about the project poured in from the executive staff as they left, including the senior vice president of marketing. Courtney felt relieved and pleased with her performance.

"Excellent job, Courtney, excellent," Sheila said, and gave Courtney a hug. "I knew you could do it. How do you feel?"

"I guess okay. Mr. Hodges gave me a compliment."

"That's not all that old cow wants to give you," Sheila said, rolling her eyes and crossing her arms.

"What?"

"Nothing. Stop by my office later. I want to review the list of action items."

Sheila grabbed her portfolio and left the conference room.

Courtney tidied the room, collected her presentation materials, erased the white board, and ripped off the large flip chart notes before returning to her cubicle. When she got back to her office, the phone rang. Shortly into the conversation, her lips trembled and her back stiffened.

"Yes, I'm prepared to give Mr. Hodges more clarification on the numbers. Four o'clock is fine and I'll bring the supporting statistics and marketing segmentation." Courtney twirled around in her chair and jumped up to go share the good news with Sheila.

She could see through the glass windows that her mentor was alone, but she knocked on her office door anyway. Sheila beckoned for her to come in.

"You were impressive."

"Thank you," Courtney said, sitting in one of the four father-bear, wingback guest chairs in the office.

"You took your time and answered the questions. You didn't let yourself get rattled. I was so proud of you in there. You have come a long way from that shy little college girl who came in here three years ago for a summer job. I'm glad you took a chance on this project. You don't realize it yet, but this was really good exposure for you," Sheila said.

Courtney sat up in the chair and wiggled her feet, causing her legs to rock slowly.

"I know. Mr. Hodges wants to meet with me this afternoon."

Sheila dropped the pen she was holding and reared back in her chair.

"Don't let your guard down with him."

"What do you mean?" Courtney asked.

Sheila spread her hand out across the lower part of her face.

"Nothing, you just be careful with him. Keep everything on a high-level professional basis. You understand what I'm saying?"

"Not really. He's the only black senior vice president in the company. Don't I want to have his favor?"

Sheila walked to the door and gently pushed it shut.

"Listen, Courtney. You're in a much better position than I was in when I came here eight years ago. There were less than a handful of blacks, women, and young people in the entire group, let alone management. I had to prove myself, but that was okay. I was a Harvard graduate and had it all figured out. This job was going to be my first of many executive-level positions. Mr. Hodges was director of marketing research then. He was like a mentor to me. He recruited me and helped me get assigned to visible projects. After a while, he got a little too comfortable with me. One thing led to another and every time I turned around he was scheduling an after-hour meeting."

"Did he, you know . . ." Courtney began asking and stopped.

"Make a pass at me?"

Courtney confirmed her question without uttering a sound.

"He tried a lot of things with me when I was about your age."

"Did you . . ." Courtney asked, shifting her weight in the chair and stammering.

"I did some things when I was young that I'm not proud of, and letting myself get blinded by his charm was one of them."

Courtney didn't know what to say. The news came as a shock. Sheila was dynamic at work, highly regarded, and always in control.

"Wasn't he a lot older than you?"

"He was older but he didn't act old."

"I can't see what would make him think someone like you would be attracted to him. He's an older . . ." Courtney paused.

"Go ahead and finish. You were going to say, unattractive man?"

Courtney felt too embarrassed to acknowledge her thoughts. "Actually, I was going to say short guy."

"Believe it or not, he is suave. He took me to the Four Seasons for working lunches and five-star restaurants for dinner meetings. One time I got to sit in on a meeting with him in New York. We took the limo up and before we left, one of the vendors gave him two tickets to a Broadway play. The meeting finished early and we caught the play before we came back to Philadelphia. You probably wouldn't think it, but he was a lot of fun."

Courtney couldn't picture the two of them together socially. Images raced through her mind. She didn't know what to say or think. Regardless, Sheila was her mentor and friend and she refused to stand in judgment. Dating Paul had created enough of her own challenges where relationships were concerned. Thank God she hadn't compromised her future by staying in the lifeless relationship with him. There were only three irreplaceable items in Courtney's world, all of which she cherished, her faith, her family, and her ability to give herself fully to the man God had established for her. Men like Mr. Hodges were big bumps in the road she was hoping to avoid, now that Paul was out of the way and she was back on track.

"Were you interested in him?"

"No, not like boyfriend-girlfriend."

"So why did you hang around him?"

"At first he showed interest in my work and he really was an effective mentor. He made sure that I was on the right projects and in front of the right people. He helped me get promoted to manager quickly, although my degree from Harvard didn't hurt. Life was good. Everything was on the up-and-up, until he started making advances."

"Was he married then?"

"At the time he was single, but it didn't matter. I wasn't interested."

"What did he say? How did he approach you?" Courtney slapped her hands on her thighs. "I'm sorry to be asking so many questions, but I just can't picture it."

"I keep saying you can tell when a man is interested. For about a month straight he kept hinting around at getting together beyond meetings. I tried to avoid him, but that doesn't work when he's a director and you're a peon."

Courtney sat on the edge of her seat as Sheila continued with her recollection.

"He's good for scheduling meetings late in the day. Watch that. This particular evening, we had our regular status meeting, which could have happened any time during the day, but we met at Le Bec Fin around six o'clock. He told me how attractive and how gutsy I was and how promising my future looked with the company. Before we could finish the meeting, he asked if we could go to my place. He said it would have to be our secret because he didn't like his personal matters to be addressed in the business environment. I told him it wasn't possible. He asked me if I had a boyfriend hanging around. He started teasing my hair and telling me how women should be treated. I still remember how my heart raced and my body tensed up. He was my boss. The man hired me, gave me my assignments, and did my evaluations."

"I wouldn't have known what to do," Courtney interjected.

"It was tough at the time. I could tell it was something he'd done before, because it came too easy for him. The more I told him that I couldn't be involved with him, the more he tried to change my mind. I resisted but couldn't erase the thought of losing my job. I kept wondering what my family would think if I lost my job. I'm like the family trophy. This was the best job I'd ever had. Then I thought, what if I turn him in to human resources? Who would believe me? The first question they'd ask is why did I go out with him in the first place. There's no way I could win in a situation like that. When it was all said and done, my future with the company would have been finished. While I was racking my mind about all of the possible scenarios, he asked me if I was mature enough to handle this kind of opportunity. Then he tried to put his hand on me. I pulled back, and he had the nerve to tell me he thought I was a mature young woman who didn't mind a challenge. That was it. I knew exactly what I needed to do. All of a sudden," Sheila said, snapping her finger, "it all became crystal clear, just like that. I jumped up from that table and left."

"What did you say to him?"

"I didn't need to say a thing. I might have lost my senses for a hot minute, but I got them back in check. No meant no, period. He was lucky I didn't give him a knee. I wasn't about to get involved with him physically. He was out of his mind."

"I bet he didn't like it when you walked out on him."

"You have no idea. He was livid. Threatened to demote me, short of firing me. It was horrible. Plus I couldn't talk about it with anyone. I was too ashamed to let anyone know I was that stupid. I still can't believe I got caught up in a situation like that."

"Isn't that sexual harassment?"

"Sure it is."

"He's a black executive. Why would he harass the only black woman in the group?"

"Certain situations don't have anything to do with race, and sexual harassment is one of them. Men, or I guess women too, who are in power take advantage of those who aren't. Trust me, blacks and whites do it."

"Aren't there rules against it?"

"Of course there are, on paper. Try to use them in here and see what happens. It's a good ole boy network. John knows Paul who plays golf with Bob who shares the same broker with Bill, and trust me, they stick together. Some little black girl yelling sexual harassment would have gotten about as far as a snowball in a burning house. I also had to think about the fact that he was the only black in management. How would that have looked for both of us? You know we always have to carry the weight of our race in every step that we take."

"What did you do? Why did you stay here?"

"I stayed because I wasn't about to let him mess up my opportunity here. This is an excellent place to work. He is only one jerk and no way am I going to let him disrupt my program. Every day I come in here, put on my game face, and play hard. Nobody can touch me with projects delivered on time and under budget. I made director whether he liked it or not. I own that title and he can't touch me. I also had a solid rapport with the recruiting team and professors back at Harvard, which didn't hurt. I told him I knew a few people who wouldn't think he was so great anymore if they knew some of the stuff he was doing with new recruits. I knew other people too. I let him know this was only the beginning of his worries."

"And he left you alone?"

"Not exactly. He didn't believe me at first. Didn't matter, the icing on the cake was when Johnnie Cochran came to town. He was very personable and I was sure to get an autographed copy of his book and a nice close-up picture with him before leaving his book-signing. I blew it up to a sixteen-by-twenty-inch picture and put that baby right on my wall, right next to my diploma. Word got back to Hodges. Next thing I know, he wasn't bothering me anymore. After the dust cleared, I went to H.R. and checked my file. I wanted to make sure he hadn't put any crap in there. Since then, we have no conversation other than work related."

"Wow, I don't know what to say."

"That's why I'm saying be careful. I'll look out for you as much as I can, but you're going to have to be smart about how you deal with him. If he schedules a meeting with you and it seems weird, pop in with an administrative assistant or intern. Tell him they'll be taking notes for you. If he tells you to come alone, let me know and I'll go with you."

Courtney felt relieved.

"He knows not to mess with me. I'm not in my early twenties anymore. I'm not playing with him this time around."

The moment was frozen while the two women let the revelation smolder.

Sheila broke the silence and said, "Courtney, this conversation is just between me and you. I trust you."

"I won't say a word."

"You especially can't tell Brice. He couldn't handle this kind of information."

"I promise, I'm not going to tell anyone. What should I do about the meeting I have scheduled with Mr. Hodges this evening?"

"Call his secretary back and tell him I will be joining you. I guarantee the meeting will either be on the up-and-up or it will get canceled."

"Are you sure I can do that?"

"Most definitely! Remember, I'm a director. He can't touch you. Go make the call and don't worry about it. I have your back."

Courtney said okay and reminded Sheila about the party before leaving the office. All she got was a grunt in return. The bits of information drenched her thoughts. She felt an increased level of respect for her mentor and a sense of peace about interacting with Mr. Hodges. God was good about looking out for her at work, even when she didn't know what she needed.

On the romantic end, the road wasn't clear. Courtney was getting a steady spark burning inside and wanted to tell someone. Sheila was the one person in the office she had considered telling about Sebastian, but after the recent revelation, it wasn't going to be today, and there wasn't anyone else. A touch of sadness nibbled at her heart. She had spent many miserable weekends with Paul and there was no shortage of people that she could have shared the news with, but when it came to enjoying a positive stretch with Sebastian, it required a tightly closed mouth. She tried to piece the preacher's words together. It was something like, "Right would be wrong and wrong seems like right." She had to figure out which was which.

CHAPTER 19

The big day rolled in with fanfare. It started off with Mama's call wishing him a happy birthday. Edwin wanted it to be a low-key day, but his office wasn't having it. Balloons and streamers decorated the dining area. A festive lunch had been catered and a cake spelling out good wishes devoured his morning and half of his afternoon. He wasn't complaining. Being appreciated was a satisfying feeling.

He managed to block out the festivities and squeeze in some work. After all, today he was thirty but tomorrow's deadlines didn't care.

Earlier in the afternoon, his mother had called and left a message with his secretary. The note said that Ms. Olympia was giving her a ride downtown and she'd need him to pick her up on the Market Street side of Liberty Place at five. It would be tight, but he would have ample time to drop her off at home and get back to the train station by six. He shut down his laptop computer and got his suit coat from the cherry-wood closet. He hunched his shoulders and the coat cascaded down to frame his six-foot-one, two-hundred-pound physique.

Edwin felt an instance of anticipation. Getting out of work early enough to have a relaxing dinner, with a friend, wouldn't be such a bad way to spend his thirtieth birthday. It took him five minutes to get to Liberty Place once he got his car out of the parking garage. Five o'clock exactly, where was she? Five-ten, no sign of her. He didn't know what to do. He couldn't sit in the bus lane with the flashers on forever. The buses weren't going to keep driving around without incident. He stroked his face with an open hand.

His head dropped down in a rapid motion and he sighed. "Mandy!" He couldn't stand her up again. He fumbled for her cell phone number. He looked in the face of every passerby, hoping to catch a glimpse of Mama. Bobbing around, his head felt like the puppy that sits in the back window of a car. He dialed Mandy and the call went directly into her voice mail. He sighed again and held the cell phone against the steering wheel. Five twenty-five. He ducked down in the car to get a good look around the area one last time before making a decision. He hated when Mama did this, again and again, as if his time were completely hers. He was the oldest son. Looking out for Mama was expected, but it was taking a toll. Too bad Pops was gone. Lost in thought, Edwin didn't see her approaching.

The car door opened and she got in. "Hi, baby."

"Mama," he said in a crisp tone, "I got here at five."

"Oh, I'm sorry, baby. I got to talking in there and lost track of the time. Happy birthday." She leaned over and kissed his cheek. "Come to the house with me. I have something for you."

"I can't, Mama. I already have plans. I'm meeting a friend later."

"A friend, who?"

"Mama, it's a friend. I already canceled on her before. I wouldn't feel right doing it again."

"But it's your birthday. We always celebrate it together."

"Mama, you and I never talked about spending my birthday together. I didn't know you had anything planned. I'm sorry, but I already have plans."

The brief silence screamed inside the small convertible.

"Tell you what, I'll come by after dinner."

"Dinner! I already fixed dinner for us. Why don't you and your friend come by the house instead of going out? That way we can celebrate together."

Edwin hesitated. He didn't want to disappoint his mother, but he was cautious about subjecting Mandy to his mother's sharp tongue. She'd tried to endure the verbal and temperamental anguish his mother had unleashed on her during law school, when she made those few visits to Philadelphia. A quick glance over his shoulder and the coast was clear. He pulled into traffic, making his way to the train station.

"I guess we can do that."

"Well, thank you for being so excited about spending time with your mama."

"Mama, you know I don't mind spending time with you. I just want to have a nice relaxed evening. I don't want any tension."

"Don't worry, baby, you won't get it from me."

Edwin blew the horn and talked under his breath.

"You'd probably do better going down Walnut Street. It would cut down on some of this traffic."

"I'm going to the train station to pick up my friend. I have to stay on Market."

"Oh!"

Edwin careened the sports car, which comfortably held two adults in the front and one child in the back, up to the Thirthieth Street train station. He pulled into one of the metered slots. Before he could open the door, Mandy walked out of the station and scanned the area for his car.

He waved to the woman with the shoulder-length red hair, but she didn't see him.

"Isn't that the white girl you went to school with?"

"Yes, that's Mandy, Mama." Edwin opened the car to get out. "You know who she is."

"Don't tell me she's the friend you're bringing to dinner?"

Edwin put one leg on the ground and left the other in the car. He twisted his body to a point where he could be seen over the top of the car. "Mandy," he yelled, "over here."

She turned in his direction and sprinted toward the car with the glow in her face intensifying as the distance shortened.

Mumblings and grumblings came from inside the car.

"I don't believe you invited that girl down here. Doesn't she have enough friends somewhere else? I don't believe this."

Edwin maintained a smile while ducking his head in and out of the car in order to volley with his mother.

"Mama, please, please don't show out. She hasn't done anything to you."

"Hmmph," she said, folding her arms across her chest and rocking back and forth in the seat.

Mandy made it to the car and Edwin got completely out and walked over to the passenger side to greet her. He extended his arms to hug her. She responded by tightening her arms around his back and holding on for a few extra seconds after his arms had loosened.

"How was the trip?" he asked.

"It was fine. I didn't do any work. I took a nap, can you believe it? Mandy Spencer taking an afternoon nap on the train, how weird is that?" Her words trailed off when she caught a glimpse of Mrs. Williams sitting in the front seat. "Your mom!"

"Yes, she cooked dinner for my birthday. I told her we'd join her for dinner at her house." He flicked his hand in the air. "It came up after you'd already gotten on the train and I didn't get a chance to run it by you. I'm so sorry."

"It's okay. I can call Four Seasons and cancel our reservation."

Aunt Sis couldn't let the window down since the car was turned off, so she pressed her ear close to the window.

"Are you sure you don't mind the change in plans? I'm really sorry."

"I'm sure. It's your birthday. You'll miss out on some of the best roasted duck in the country, but if that's okay with you, it's fine by me."

"You know how small my car is. There's no real backseat. When I offered to pick you up, I didn't plan for her to be with me. I'm so very sorry about all of this. Let me put you in a cab. That way you won't be cramped in some little space all the way to Mama's."

"Absolutely not. I prefer to ride with you. Don't worry about me, my legs can take it."

Edwin let his head drop. "Mandy, thanks for being so understanding."

"It's the least I can do. Besides, it's your birthday. You should be the happy one."

Mandy couldn't hear Aunt Sis say, "The least she can do. Hmmph. The least she can do is to get back on the train and go back where she came from, and leave my son alone. There aren't any black men left now because of her kind." Her face snarled as she clutched her purse.

Edwin knocked on the passenger-side window and his mother looked up.

"Hello, Ms. Williams," Mandy said.

Aunt Sis looked up at Mandy with a distorted look that was a cross between a closemouthed grin and the outward expression of a stomach cramp.

Edwin and Mandy walked around to the driver's side, and he opened the door to get in. He unlatched the seat so it could lean forward, freeing up the eight inches that separated the front seat from the kiddy seat in the back. Mandy turned her back to the car and slid one leg in, wiggling her hips inside like a bird easing into the tiny round entry hole of a birdhouse.

There was nothing Edwin could do to help facilitate the stuffing process. He leaned on the door and felt total humiliation. Here he was, a Yale law grad, and he couldn't offer a full-sized seat to a friend who had taken time out to ride the train to Philadelphia and treat him to one of his favorite restaurants on his birthday.

Aunt Sis continued to look straight ahead, making no effort to help.

Edwin drove faster than usual to cut the twenty-minute ride down to the bare minimum. Mandy made several attempts to start a conversation, to no avail. The tension in the car felt oatmeal-thick to him. No sense jumping in and stirring the pot. Aunt Sis's jaw was as tight as Mandy's body was in the backseat. Edwin worked hard to get to his mother's street as quickly as possible and get parked. He flew down the street without commenting on the familiar cars of family and friends. He pulled up to the soft curb and in an instant put the parking brake on, shut the car off, and popped the seat up for Mandy to get out.

Aunt Sis turned her head slightly toward his door.

Edwin caught the look on his mother's face as he leaned in to help Mandy. It said that she was more than willing to help Mandy get out of the car. One swift kick to the backside would help her get out of the tight situation she'd gotten herself into. Edwin squinted his eye in his mother's direction.

She saw him and retreated to her corner, looking straight ahead.

One final pull and Mandy was free.

"You okay?"

"Fine, really."

Once Mandy was secure, Edwin went around to the passenger side. He knew Mama would not get out unless he opened the door for her. He was grateful she'd taught him how to treat a lady. He was disappointed she didn't give him a chance to practice the techniques on anyone else.

The three crossed the street and got to the door. Aunt Sis fumbled in her pocket for her keys, finally hitting pay dirt. She jiggled the key in the lock and pushed the door open.

"Surprise!" came from inside the house.

Edwin and Mandy stood in the doorway.

"This is why I wanted you to come over."

The room was filled with fifteen people. What a surprise! Edwin wasn't expecting to see Jamal, Courtney, cousin Terry, other relatives and neighbors. He definitely wasn't expecting to see Sheila standing in the center of the room with a birthday streamer. Edwin grabbed the door and motioned for Mandy to go in as he followed.

Courtney didn't know what to do. She'd invited Sheila to the party because she hadn't been able to get her hooked up with Edwin. After Mr. Hodges had canceled the meeting, Sheila decided to come at her insistence, which eventually turned into flat-out begging. Courtney had no idea Edwin would be bringing a date. She didn't know what to do.

Jamal extended his hand to his brother. They did their normal three-part shake, polishing it off by sandwiching their closed fists into one another's chest and hugging with the remaining free arm.

"What's up, man? Happy b-day, player."

"I didn't expect to see you today."

"Now you know you can't miss out on no party that Mama's throwing. You know how she trips," Jamal reminded him.

"Thanks, man."

"Yeah, it's all good. You know a brother's not going to miss out on his big brother's par-tay."

"Jamal, do you remember Mandy?"

"Yeah, I remember you, Mandy, the Yale lady. Yeah, I remember you. What's up?"

"It's great to see you again, Jamal. It's been an awful long time."

"Yeah, it's been a little while. Looka here," Jamal said, directing that to Edwin, "you take it easy and rock it on out. I'm going to holla at Terry." Turning back to Mandy, he said, "You too."

"Why, thank you, Jamal. I will do my absolute best."

Jamal replayed her high-pitched words over in his head, careful not to laugh out loud. A clean-cut Yale girl at a west Philly party was going to be worth hanging around to see.

Courtney waited until the line of well-wishers shortened before she headed over to Edwin.

"Happy birthday, cuz."

"Hey, Courtney," Edwin said, eyeing Sheila. "You remember Mandy from law school."

"Mandy, yes, it's been a while since I've seen you."

"I understand congratulations are in order."

"For what?"

"Your graduation from Northwestern and for landing an incredible job."

Courtney and Mandy continued their conversation.

Edwin used the break as an opportunity to approach Sheila.

She saw him coming and maintained position. "Happy birthday, Edwin." She swished the ice in her glass of juice.

"Sheila, what a surprise. I didn't expect to see you."

"I just bet you didn't," she said, shifting her focus to Mandy.

"Maybe we can get a chance to talk later."

"I'm not staying long. Courtney invited me and I came to wish you well. I've done that and now I can go home."

"Sheila, look," he said, placing his hand on her arm, "it's not what you think." Her eyes burned his hand off her arm, and he pulled it back as gently as he had initially placed it there.

"Think! I think this is a good time to leave."

"Please, let me explain."

"Edwin, you didn't ask me to come here, which means you don't owe me any explanations. This is your mother's house, your party, and your life. None of it gives me a right to say anything. You've made it clear, each time that you've canceled, that you don't have time for me. Now I see why," Sheila told him, throwing a snarl Mandy's way. "Happy birthday."

She left him standing in the middle of the floor and went to get her purse from the bedroom upstairs. Courtney saw Sheila coming down the stairs with her purse and broke away from Mandy.

"You leaving already?"

"Two's company, three's a crowd."

"Come on, Sheila, please stay."

"I don't think so. I'll see you at work tomorrow."

Sheila opened the door to leave.

Courtney felt bad about asking Sheila to the party, not knowing Edwin had already made plans to bring a woman. What a disaster. What would Sheila say about Sebastian after seeing Mandy with Edwin? Why had she opened her mouth and invited Sheila to the party? In a mo-

ment of insanity, she had possibly ruined the camaraderie of someone she respected as a mentor and a friend.

Aunt Sis saw Sheila leaving, and she approached Courtney, carrying a pan full of chicken wings. "Where she going?"

"She hadn't planned to stay long. She's probably tired because she
worked all day."

There was a knock on the door. Aunt Sis didn't have to move.
There were plenty of people in the room to answer it.

"Umm-hmm, she left because that 'white woman' is all up in
Edwin's face. Look at her. He can hardly breathe. I can't believe she's
up in my house. You know I don't allow 'white folks' in here."

Someone yelled, "Courtney, somebody's at the door for you."

By the look on Aunt Sis's face, Courtney knew who it was without
turning around.

"Courtney Young, who is that man standing in my door?"

The plan was falling apart. For a moment she couldn't think. What
was the line? That's right. "He's a friend of mine from Northwestern,"
she whizzed off.

"Slow down. I can hardly understand what you're saying."

Sebastian was introducing himself to people as he moved toward
Courtney.

"He wants to meet Edwin and talk about law school."

"Girl, what do you take me for? Don't you stand there and lie to my
face!" The pan of chicken was trembling in Aunt Sis's hand.

"I'm telling the truth."

"You better be, because I'm not letting any more 'white folks' come
into my house and snatch the life out of any more of my family, especially you and Edwin. You two are the cream of the crop. Can't have
nothing around them thieves."

Sebastian made it to the spot where Aunt Sis and Courtney were
talking. "Hey, Courtney."

Courtney acknowledged him. She wanted to disappear. This was
more heat than she could stand. Should she introduce him or act as if
Aunt Sis weren't there?

The eyes of the lady standing next to Courtney felt like daggers to
Sebastian. He didn't know what was going on but didn't think it was
good.

"Aunt Sis, this is . . ." Courtney was able to get out before her aunt
turned and walked away.

"Every time we get something good, they want it," she blurted out while still in earshot of Sebastian and Courtney.

"Wow, what was that about? Is it something I said?"

"No," Courtney responded, taking a deep gasp. "It was nothing you said."

The worse possible scenario she could have imagined didn't compare to what had happened. It dawned on Courtney that she'd put a "perfect" plan together without once asking God about how to handle the situation. She had been maneuvering through this maze of friendship and relationship with Sebastian purely on her own energy. If it was cloudy before, Aunt Sis's reaction helped bring clarity. She needed to seek God for direction if she was to continue being anything to Sebastian. There was nothing she could do to fix it tonight. She might as well enjoy the party. In an ideal world Sebastian would have been a welcomed guest, but this wasn't ideal. This was home.

CHAPTER 20

The vise grip was tightening, with Aunt Sis on one end and Sebastian on the other. Courtney didn't know how to wiggle free without coming out torn. Being with Sebastian was like dipping her toe in the racial waters and watching the ripples grow larger with each public appearance. What could she do? She wanted to continue seeing him, longed to see him, but the timing wasn't right. A few more millenniums was the amount of time, she'd estimated, that it would take for her circle of friends and family to warm up to Sebastian. Then he could be the one. No sense worrying about the future. She was figuring out how to get through this second.

She sat with her back to the cubicle entrance, doodling on the Post-it note. This was the first time in five months she had broken her Monday morning regimen. She didn't go to the cafeteria with Cara or anyone else.

"Hey, girlfriend."

Courtney swung around and was glad to see her mentor and friend back in the office. This was her first opportunity to apologize about the mix-up with Mandy and Edwin at the party last week, because Sheila had been out on a business trip last Thursday and Friday.

"What's with the long face?"

"Family stuff," Courtney replied.

"Ooooh, I know all about that. Don't they drive you crazy? At least mine drive me crazy but I love them anyway." Sheila commandeered the guest chair. "Let me take a break. I like hiding around here in your office. You get less traffic than I do in my fishbowl."

"I want one of those fishbowls."

"Don't worry, you'll get one. I'm going to make sure you and Brice get one. If it's left up to me, I'll have the whole row full. Now that's my kind of affirmative action. Put a sister in charge and let her do the hiring. This business about not being able to find enough qualified minorities would be solved overnight. If I can find twenty candidates from top-tier schools in three phone calls, I don't know why human resources can't. I don't know where they're looking for blacks and women, but pretty soon it won't make a difference because I'll have it looking like a mix of Harlem and the national women's association up in here." Sheila laughed herself and noticed Courtney was quiet. "Girl, that was funny, why aren't you laughing like you usually do with your crazy self?"

"Ah, just tired of living with drama."

"I hate to break this to you, but that's life. Drama after drama, and we can't avoid it."

"Speaking of drama, what in the world did you get me into last week at that party? Girl, I was totally caught off guard."

"I know and I am so so sorry." Courtney held her head back and looked at the ceiling and took a sigh. "I had no idea it was going to turn out like that. I really am sorry."

"It's not your fault. I should have listened to my first mind and stayed my behind at home. Oh well, what can you do? So, did he marry Plain Jane yet?"

"Marriage! She's just an old friend from law school. He's not going to marry her. My aunt will make sure of that. When Edwin took Mandy back to the train Thursday night, my aunt went with them. They all sat in his two-seater sports car with that pouch or whatever you call it in the back."

"I thought he finished law school five or six years ago."

"He did."

"Looks like school is still in for her," Sheila said, twirling her fingers and turning her cringing face slightly to the side without losing eye contact with Courtney. "Enough of that, let's talk about something more positive. What's going on with you, now that Paul has been buried in your drawer or probably in your trash by now? Any prospects?"

"Not really."

She wanted to bring up Sebastian but wasn't quite sure how to do it. If Sheila had stuck around a little bit longer at the party she could have met him, as planned. "Edwin keeps trying to get me to go out with a friend of his. Apparently it's some guy who has his act together."

"Nice, does he have any brothers or friends or uncles?"

"Edwin."

"Oh, girl, *please!* Not Edwin again. I'm sorry, but he is a tired brother. I know he has it going on at work and in the family, but he's not available."

"What are you talking about? I told you he's single. I don't know why he can't seem to hook up with you."

"He might as well be in a relationship."

"Why do you say that?"

"For someone with no wife and kids, he sure seems to have a dependent."

"I know. He has to help his brother a lot."

"Hmmph, his brother is not the one I'm talking about."

Before Courtney could get clarification on Sheila's comment, Jason popped in.

Courtney was expecting Sheila to tease her by making facial expressions, with her head turned so Jason couldn't see them, but she didn't.

Seeing Sheila, Jason said, "I'll have the reports on your desk before close of business."

"I know you will," she said, smiling while watching him retreat. After he left she said, "You don't have to worry about him coming back any time soon. He's too afraid he's going to run into me. I hope you don't get mad at me for scaring off your men."

Courtney chuckled, helping to loosen the tightness she was feeling.

"It's about time you started laughing again. I was about to let you take a mental health day and send you home."

"Why?"

"Because you are not yourself today. Having this Mr. Got-his-act-together waiting in the wings is supposed to be a good thing, but you'd never know from the look on your face earlier."

Courtney liked her mentor. Sheila had trusted her enough to share intimate information about her and Mr. Hodges. There weren't lines of people waiting nearby that she could talk to about what was eating at her. She didn't know if this was the time or the place but decided to take the chance.

"Let's go to your office. People are too nosy around here."

Sheila didn't hesitate. She needed to be visible in the fishbowl at certain times of the day anyway. It was a small price to pay for being a director.

They got to the office and Courtney closed the door behind them.

"This must be juicy," Sheila said, pulling the deep-sitting leather chair up to the desk. "What's going on?"

"What if I tell you that I'm friends with this wonderful guy?"

"The one Edwin wants you to meet?"

"A different guy."

"Ummm."

"He's seen so much of the world and has such a compassionate heart for people. He's articulate, fun to be with, and he makes me laugh. When I'm with him, I feel confident and motivated to achieve goals. On top of everything else, he loves the Lord."

"Oooo, look at you. If I didn't know better, I'd think you were blushing. This man sounds too good to be true. Does he work downtown? I want to meet him."

"He's in law school at Penn."

"So, he's a smart one, although Edwin has a law degree too and I don't know that he's the smartest, but let's not go back there. Let's stick to you," she said, fumbling a paper clip on the desk. "He sounds like a dream. You might not know this yet, but it's hard for us to meet men like that once we leave college. We're so spoiled at school and don't know it. All of our friends are just like us, young, educated, motivated, and goal-oriented. We think everybody's like that. Then we get a job and get slapped in the face. Oh, girl, I'm sorry. I didn't mean to be preaching in here."

"No, go ahead. You're right. I just got out and that's kind of how I'm feeling already."

"People at work think we're too ethnic if we eat soul food, talk to the janitors, and read *Essence.* The people at home think we're too uppity if we buy a house two blocks out of the ghetto, have a white friend, and vote anything other than Democrat."

"That's the truth," Courtney said, shaking her head between every word. She hadn't articulated it quite like that before, but it was basically the same conversation she had had with Larry and Ashley back in Evanston.

"When I was growing up, I thought bourgeois blacks were a trip. I thought they were people with a little money and prestige who wanted to be white. I see differently now. Many of them are just trying to find a place where they can share advice on politics and retirement plans, over a plate of smothered chicken and collard greens."

Courtney chuckled along with Sheila. Those were her sentiments exactly. She wasn't alone.

"When they want to send their kids to the good schools, half the time they end up being the only black, out of hundreds of students, and that can't be healthy for them down the road." Sheila plopped her elbow onto the desk and rested her chin inside her cupped hand. "I'm sorry for getting on my soapbox, but this stuff always hits a nerve. Let's get back to this man you're telling me about. He sounds wonderful. So, what's wrong with him?"

"Why does something have to be wrong with him?"

"Because there's always something not quite right. That's what keeps us humble. Does he have a baby from some crazy one-night stand in college?"

"No, not that I know of."

"Is it bad credit? Because I know a brother in law school has got to have some debt."

"I'm not sure, but I doubt that he has credit problems. He uses his American Express card faithfully."

"That's a good sign, because you know AMEX wants the full balance paid off every month. If he wasn't paying, he wouldn't be able to keep using that card."

"I know, that's right." Courtney laughed openly.

"Okay, then, what is it? It has to be something."

Courtney hesitated before talking.

"He's white."

"White! As in white, white?"

Courtney nodded.

"You don't mean fair-skinned-looking white like your girl Cara."

Courtney shook her head no.

"Real white?"

Courtney rested her elbow on the arm of the chair and ran her index finger up and down the side of her face.

Sheila pushed back in the chair with her eyes wide and a grin plastered across her lower face, refusing to blink. "You go, girl. I am scared of you. I don't know what to say. I bet he's fine, isn't he? I know he is."

Courtney fought to contain her smile, but couldn't keep her cheeks from getting puffy.

"I knew it. White or black, you can't help noticing when a man is fine."

"I know what a fine brother looks like. I hadn't thought much about a white guy, at least not until I met Sebastian four years ago."

"Fine is fine. It's a universal language. And he's not from France or Italy or any place like that? You know they love some sisters," Sheila said.

"I wouldn't know. I've never been to France or Italy."

"Let me tell you, girlfriend, some of us get treated better over there than we do in the States. Why do you think so many famous blacks with money move over there when they get a chance? Every time I take a business trip to England, I take the train to Paris or a commuter flight to Rome or Florence."

"Really?"

"Umm-hmm. The first time I got off the train in Paris, it looked like Harlem. I should say it looked like Harlem did before the rest of New York figured out that it was part of Manhattan and started buying up the place."

Courtney held in her laugh but enough leaked out to lighten the mood.

"But Paris was full of blacks from the islands, from Africa, America, you name it. And guess what, they greeted us on the street just like our people do here."

"It must be something we got from our African heritage, because too many of us do it," Courtney said.

"Can't escape those genes," Sheila added.

"I guess not."

Sheila tapped the desk with her pen. "So, girlfriend, you have to tell me where you met your friend, and don't tell me here at work."

"We met in our freshman year at Northwestern. I was a cheerleader and he was in the band."

"Ah, a musician. So, he has a little rhythm. Umm-hmm, they've been known to like sisters. I can't believe you've been undercover all this time."

"It's not like that. He called me when he came to town for law school. We went out and we've been hanging out together ever since."

"Your family must have a thing for old college friends. You go ahead with your bad self."

"I thought you'd be offended."

"Why?"

"Because you're not big on interracial relationships."

"That's not true. I'm not big on dating outside the race for myself and definitely have a problem with brothers doing it. I don't have a problem if another sister wants to, more power to her."

Courtney wasn't sure why Sheila had a double standard. She was either for or against interracial relationships. "That's kind of unfair."

"Now you know life has nothing to do with fairness. I'm not saying it's right. I'm just saying that's how I feel and I'm not the only one. You know sisters get bent out of shape when they see a ballplayer or an actor or some TV personality in an interracial relationship. He can be as popular as all get out, until they show his wife. If she has long blond hair, he's finished on the black female circuit, and you know it's true."

"Why is that?"

"I can't speak for all sisters but I'll say as far as I'm concerned, when a white guy gets a sister, he goes top of the line. If you don't believe me, check it out the next time you're on the street. They go after the fine sisters, with beauty, brains, and you name it. I can't say the same for some brothers. I just want the brothers to maintain the same criteria for other women that they have for a sister. If the sister has to be attractive with five degrees, a chain of businesses, and speaks four languages, not counting English, that's fine. But, I don't want the brother to be eager to settle for someone outside our race who barely has a high school diploma, just because she represents what society has said he couldn't have for hundreds of years. Women aren't trophies. I don't care what race they are. That's what pets are for."

"Maybe they want to feel validated."

"Validated my left foot! If a man, any man, wants to feel validated, then there's something more wrong with him than getting a woman can fix. A therapist might be more along the lines of what he should be looking for."

Sheila always made Courtney laugh. Being in her company today was needed.

"So, you don't have a problem with me seeing someone like Sebastian?"

"Sebastian! With a name like that, you don't need to say any more. He has to be white, because I don't know one single black man named Sebastian."

"Sebastian Alexander Whittington the Third."

"Oh my goodness, definitely white without a doubt. And that's one of those aristocratic names too. Don't tell me, he's from money."

"Not according to him. His father has money but not him."

"Have you met his parents?"

"No, we're not serious like that. We're just spending time together having some laughs, that's all."

"Okay, Ms. Just-spending-time-together."

Courtney's eyes and smile spread. "Really, that's it."

"Please! Which one of us are you trying to convince? Because I'm not buying it. Your face lit up when you were talking about him. I've never seen your face look like that when you were talking about Paul, not even three years ago when you did your first internship here."

"I don't know. I like him a lot, but it feels weird. Wherever we go, we get stared at, and we're not a real couple. That gets tired. People even stare at us in church."

"I thought you religious ones were all about love, God is love, we're love, they're love, everything is love. I guess love isn't blind after all. I can't believe you caught grief up in the Lord's house."

"As much as if not more than I notice on the street."

"Whhhatt! See? That's why I don't waste my time chasing down a Sunday morning church party. That's all they are. Any time you can't go to church and get peace, something is wrong. I keep saying you might as well hang with us heathens. At least you know what you're getting Monday through Sunday."

Courtney didn't have the energy or feel the need to defend the churches. Making distinctions between one church and another was pointless. To Sheila it all looked the same. It was no wonder. Courtney was trying to figure it all out too. Faith Christian Center and Fifth Baptist had different racial makeups, different teaching styles, and different music, but each was praising the same Lord. Some people who would go to Fifth Baptist weren't going to Faith Christian Center and vice versa. Both churches had aspects she liked and disliked. She was starting to see Fifth Baptist with a new appreciation. It might not be the church for her, at this point in her life, but there wasn't anything wrong with it. Fifth Baptist was as critical to God's tapestry of churches as any other confessing and living for the Lord.

"Let me get out of here. They already say you're showing me too much favoritism."

"I say so what. As long as you have the credentials and the performance ratings to back me up, I'm pushing you as far as you can go. I'll promote you over myself if I get the chance."

Courtney got up to leave. "See you at the status meeting."

"Oh, and take my advice. Since you and 'Sebaaaastian' are just friends you might want to keep this to yourself. Some of our coworkers may or may not be as understanding, if you know what I mean. Everyone doesn't need to know your business . . ." Sheila did a double arch with her eyebrows to seal the heart-to-heart discussion. "Especially your boy Brice."

Courtney walked back to her cubicle, thinking about her situation. She was relieved to get a positive reaction from Sheila but confused about her own thoughts. Not so long ago she was the one doing the staring, before realizing how deep eyes could burn. She had been a "them," one of those who kept the racial fires burning. She hadn't thrown in heaps of coal like some, but she'd kicked in some wood chips. There was enough judgment to go around and she had to swallow a dose too.

She felt ashamed to be serving God in some areas of her life but harboring racial biases and prejudices in other areas. She wasn't burning crosses in anyone's yard or calling other races devils, but she was letting her biases, hurtful experiences, fears, and the oppressive pains of her people override the word of God that told her to love her neighbor, which included people that didn't look or think like her. She wanted to repent and ask God to forgive her subtle biases and prejudices. She needed him to help her rid herself of the term "white folks," which was never followed by anything positive. She wanted to love beyond someone's idiotic "you people" comment or asking about the texture of her hair. She had done enough of the same with her private conversations at school with Ashley and Larry, at work with Brice and Sheila, at home with Edwin, and on occasion with a random black cabdriver. It didn't matter. There had always been someone to talk to about "those people." Her well-hidden diplomatic racism and prejudices needed cleansing, as she knew only the Lord could do. It would take time, not as long as Aunt Sis would need, but at least a few weeks. It had taken thousands of years to cause all of this racial dysfunction. She wouldn't change overnight, but acknowledging her contribution in keeping the fire burning out of control was a start. This wasn't the time to talk to God openly. She'd have to wait for a more suitable time.

In a progressive world, where everyone had the principles of God written on their hearts, and not just words in their mouth, Sebastian would be the ideal man for her to get to know romantically. Since that wasn't the world she knew, Sebastian was treading somewhere between friend and silent partner. She liked him and craved to be near him, but nobody could know. She wondered how much longer be would let her get away with it.

CHAPTER 21

Screams and hoopla ricocheted off the Madison Square Garden ceiling during the first quarter of the basketball game. The fans weren't taking the slam dunk sitting down. The Knicks had been up for most of the game, but it looked like the Sixers were on a comeback. Courtney watched the Sixers huddle around the coach, as he sketched plays on a clipboard, five rows below them. This was the way to see a game. One day, when she had the money and the connections, she would buy seats like this for Jamal so he could see his beloved Sixers win in person.

"Go, dude," Sebastian bellowed and dropped into his seat after standing for five minutes straight. "Did you see that! Great game, great game," he said with his fist shaking in the air.

Courtney marveled at his enthusiasm and free spirit. She had taken Sheila's acceptance as encouragement and decided to move a millimeter from "just friends" status toward "relationship." It was safe being in New York, where she didn't know a single soul. It fostered an atmosphere where they could celebrate openly, which came as a relief compared to Edwin's party a few weeks ago.

"These seats are incredible."

"What did you say?" Sebastian yelled.

Courtney scooted closer to Sebastian, putting her hand over her mouth and his ear. "I can actually see their faces."

Courtney couldn't tell who was cheering for whom. She was nestled next to him with no space wasted.

He draped his arm around her shoulder and leaned into her ear. "I know. I can't believe it. My dad really came through this time."

Cheers and screams again. The crowd was on their feet again.

She decided to enjoy the game and save the talking for later.

After six regulation minutes that turned into thirty real-time minutes, the buzzer rang, signaling the end of the game. The Sixers came out on top. She wasn't a big Sixers fan, but knowing Jamal was enabled her to savor the victory.

Courtney and Sebastian rose to their feet. She picked up her coat, which she'd been sitting on. Sebastian reached for it and helped her put it on. They slid to the aisle. Into his first step, he reached back and grabbed her hand. Thousands and thousands, pushing, prodding, running, hustling slowly, dragging hurriedly. The crowd was a mass of ants scurrying for cover when a foot kicks their hill in. He weaved in and out of the herd, making their way to the train station. Penn Station didn't offer any relief from the congestion, but the noise level was lower than it had been in the Garden, at least when the voice wasn't shouting arrivals and departures over the intercom.

"I'm glad you brought me to this game."

"Brought you! You're the only reason I was able to get the tickets."

He was glad his father had been eager to call on one of his Yale buddies for use of his season tickets. Thinking back on when his father had found out his son had befriended a marketing executive from Northwestern, Sebastian could still hear the elation in his father's voice. Most likely his father had interpreted it as a sign that his son was finally taking life seriously and moving toward a solid relationship. His father had sung it repeatedly, like a needle stuck on an old album, "Every successful man needs the right woman." His idea of right and that of his father's were shades apart. One day, in person, he would tell his father more about Courtney. For now he just wanted to soak up her beauty and hang on her every word.

"Can he get more for next month?"

"I'm not sure what the schedule is in November, but these babies were tough to get. This game was sold out and season ticket holders don't usually give away their seats for games like this. Even if we wanted to buy them at five hundred dollars a seat, you can't get them."

"I'm not paying five hundred dollars for any seat anywhere," she was quick to tell him.

"Me either."

"That's right, you're the poor student."

"You got it," he agreed.

"Let's stop at Delilah's when we get back," she said, glancing at her watch. "We should get back just before they close."

"Hopefully the train will get in on time so we can make it."

Courtney and Sebastian must have been in the heaviest-traveled spot in the station, because travelers pushed by without the simplest of courtesies. The departure information for the train going to Philadelphia was shouted over the loudspeaker.

"I couldn't hear what she said."

"Me either," Sebastian said. "We better go look at the board."

In the middle of the station stood hundreds of people staring into the air, all looking in the same direction. Courtney heard a series of clicks, a momentary pause, and then mad dashing. Before Chicago, she had spent all of her time in Philadelphia except for the summer trips to North Carolina. This was her first time in New York and it was a lot to suck in. She clenched Sebastian's hand a bit tighter to calm her rising anxiety.

"Track five, that's us," Sebastian said.

It took a minute for her to realize the clicking was the departure and arrival board posting the new track numbers. They weren't in as big of a rush as the rest of the crowd. The train wasn't scheduled to depart for another ten minutes anyway.

Down the double flights of stairs and to the platform, Courtney and Sebastian stood face-to-face. With her hands in her coat pockets, she leaned into his chest and he put his arms around her. She was un-inhibited. The piercing looks they normally got weren't gone, but were watered down by the gobs of black and white couples in close proximity. This wasn't Philadelphia. This was New York City where millions of people marched to their own drum, and she was doing a little stepping of her own.

She could hear the rhythm of Sebastian's heart. She relished the time they'd spent together, a far cry from the happy hour or pool hall scenes. He made her laugh to the point where her stomach ached and felt as if it would burst open if she laughed one more time. He was an incredible catch for some woman. Hopefully God had a black man just like him for her. The moment was perfect, she thought, and she pushed her head in tighter.

A handful of men, who'd drunk excessively and left the driving to Amtrak, were loud and obnoxious for the entire hour-and-a-half ride back home. Courtney was grateful when the train pulled into the Thirtieth Street station and she was able to rid herself of the adult children. She and Sebastian hopped up the steps, hand in hand. She'd passed through the Philadelphia glass menagerie but had forgotten to switch back to reserve mode.

"Delilah's closes in fifteen minutes. We made it just in time. I can't wait to get a slice of sweet potato pie," she said.

In a piercing second, the shocking eyes of correction coming from a passerby electrocuted Courtney back into her reality. She uncoupled her hand from Sebastian's but it was too late. Mr. and Mrs. Jones were coming out of the gift shop and walking toward her. There was no way to avoid them.

"Mr. and Mrs. Jones, how you doing?"

"We're just fine, Courtney. What are you doing down here at the train station?" Mrs. Jones asked her, but was giving Sebastian a firm looking-over. Mr. Jones looked away.

"We went to the basketball game in New York." Courtney didn't want to be rude and not introduce Sebastian, although she wasn't quite sure how she was feeling about the unexpected run-in.

She introduced Sebastian as her friend from Northwestern and the men shook hands.

"Oh, how nice. Well, when you make the kind of money you make, I guess you can do anything you want. You youngsters got it made. The rest of us old heads have to get by doing the best we can. We're so proud of what you've done for yourself, Courtney. We need more young blacks like you to help get things turned around for us."

Sebastian shifted his weight to the other leg and took a swallow, but it didn't stop the rush of color to his face. Mr. Jones gave his wife a nudge.

"What?" she said. "It's true. We need more educated black women for our black men."

Mr. Jones stood silent.

"I don't mean anything against him, I'm just saying."

Mr. Jones grabbed his wife's hand and gave a strong pull. "It's nice meeting you, Sebastian. We'll see you later, Courtney."

Mrs. Jones spoke up as they left. "I'll see you at church tomorrow, Courtney."

"Who were they?"

"People from my church, friends of my aunt."

Courtney wasn't sure how Sebastian was feeling about the undercurrents Mrs. Jones was sending. It wasn't the time or the place to delve into it. Keeping it simple for now was the plan, and that meant getting to Delilah's before they closed in the next five minutes.

"What are we doing for church tomorrow, my place or yours?" he asked, keeping pace with the strides Courtney was taking.

"Yours."

"You sure? I don't want you to get burned out on Faith Christian Center. I don't mind going to Fifth Baptist. Actually, I look forward to meeting this dynamic pastor of yours. I'm intrigued with his focus on social action. I'd love to have some of that in my church. Maybe I can talk with Reverend Tyler and get some insight on how to make that happen."

Oh no, she thought. One day he could go to church with her, but she wasn't ready to make such a major move. Acting on impulse had backfired with Edwin's party. Moving with caution, behind enemy lines, was best.

"Yeah, but let's go to your church tomorrow. We can go to mine some other time."

Sebastian was still learning to read Courtney. He sensed her uneasiness but didn't want to raise the awareness until she initiated the issue. He planned to spend many days to come with her, and it would get addressed.

CHAPTER 22

Jamal sat with his back against the headboard. He ate the bag of chips, chasing it down with a lukewarm can of ginger ale. Sixers up by ten, eight minutes left in the fourth quarter. He felt it. Victory was in the air. The three-game losing streak on the road was about to be history. They were going to win.

The thumping music tore through the paper-thin walls and brutalized his ears. Jamal jumped up from his sofa bed, slid his feet into a seasoned pair of Nikes, and snatched the door open. He didn't bother to tuck his extra-long ribbed T-shirt into his jeans, which hung seven inches below his waist. His firm deliberate steps deposited him at door number 3 in a hot second.

Two solid bangs on the door generated no response. The bangs intensified.

"Leroy," Jamal said, standing with arms braced against both sides of the doorway. "Open this door, man, or turn that noise down." He banged again. "Don't make me miss the rest of my game. I ain't playing, Leroy, you better not mess up my game." He kicked the door one time and got no response.

A few other residents stuck their heads into the hallway to check out the commotion. Seeing it was Jamal, they retreated into their abodes.

He went back into his room and shut the door. A few minutes later, he heard banging on his door.

"I know that fool ain't banging on my door unless he's gone crazy, rolling up on me like that, and while my Sixers are playing." He chuckled about the gall Leroy had.

Jamal bounced up and opened the door. He gritted his teeth, hung his head to the side, and rolled his eyes.

No need to close the door; it would only encourage them to break it down. He could feel his blood percolating. Detective Holmes and Crawford were two people he didn't care whether they saw the light of day.

"Well, well, well, if it isn't Mr. Williams," Detective Crawford said. He pushed the door wide open so they could enter. "Hello, Mr. Williams. It's been a long time since we've paid you a visit. Hope you didn't think we'd forgotten about you."

Jamal kept quiet.

"Did you miss me? I'd like to spend time chatting with you and catching up on old times, but I'm here on business. You remember Mr. William Lovett, your delinquent friend, a.k.a. Pee Wee Muhammad. Seems he's gotten himself into some trouble and we want to talk to him about it. Word is on the street you used to run together. Once I heard that, I said, this is my lucky day. My old pal Jamal Williams will tell me everything I need to know. So, I said, Sam, let's stop by and see my old friend Jamal. Aren't you glad we stopped by?" Detective Crawford put his foot on the bed, nearly touching Jamal's leg, and propped his elbow on top. "Aw, Sam, I don't think we came at a good time. Jamal doesn't seem as excited about seeing us as we are about seeing him."

"Man, what do you want? I'm trying to watch my Sixers game."

Sam shoved the TV off the chair, sending it toppling to the floor. It had survived several previously unprovoked attacks and managed to keep on playing, a little more battered on the outside but rock-solid on the inside, where it counted. No matter how much abuse the officers gave, they couldn't finish off the TV.

A short scuffle ended with Jamal's head down in the bed and both officers pressing a knee into his back.

"Why do we have to go through the same routine every time?"

"Because you keep coming out here playing games. I don't care what you do, I'm not going to let you punk me. Do whatever you gotta do, but I don't know nothing about what Pee Wee's into, and even if I did I wouldn't tell you." Jamal struggled to get into a comfortable spot, despite the pressure on his back.

"We'll see. Let's take our ride. You know the routine."

"Fine, I guess you don't have anything else to do but bust me for something I didn't do."

"Sam, did you hear our friend? The same line he gave me ten years ago."

He mustered enough strength in his legs to stand on his feet without assistance. He didn't know if Detective Crawford would ever let it go. Ten years seemed like yesterday when Crawford had busted him and his boys for possession of marijuana, with the intent to sell. He wasn't selling drugs, but that didn't stop him from hanging around Monk, who was running a street operation. Crawford could have taken them to juvenile, but instead he chose to cash in. He made weekly visits to pick up his five hundred dollars. It was the price Monk paid to keep his pharmaceutical business rolling. After eight months, Monk cut it off. Crawford must have gotten used to the money by then, because he tried to demand the money from Monk and the rest of the group. When no one gave in, he locked up everybody that was on the scene when the initial bust had gone down.

Jamal could still remember the cops banging on the door at his mama's house and dragging him out. He was innocent of the charges, but he might as well have been guilty. The officers applied pressure during his interrogation, forcing him to go without food or water or a chance to go to the bathroom. They tried to make him testify against the other suspects by threatening to crack a few ribs and hurt his mother as a bonus. It didn't work. He wasn't a rat. Most sixteen-year-olds would have cracked, but he held strong.

In court, the judge saw his honor-roll grades and let Jamal off with a few hours of community service. Jamal reported Crawford's actions but nothing was done. Crawford had made sure that he paid the price every day since.

"Yeah, I know you were a drug dealer back then and people like you don't change."

"I got off, didn't I? That's because I was innocent."

"I don't care if you did get off. You're a dealer and the court might have let you go, but I've held my own trial, and guess what, you're guilty. So, it's up to me to enforce my sentence. I hereby sentence you." Crawford taunted him with the look of humor dripping from his face that was instantaneously replaced by a staunch piercing stare. "Joke's over, boy."

"*Boy!* I got your boy."

"Maybe." Crawford put the nightstick under Jamal's neck and pushed it up.

Jamal tried to resist the pressure but was unsuccessful. His head was forced back, making it difficult to breathe.

"Right now, boy, I'm your daddy." He snatched the enforcer away from Jamal's neck. "You know the drill. Get your shirt."

"For what?" Jamal said, rubbing his throat and coughing.

"You're going downtown."

"For what?"

"Aggravated assault."

"Assault! Who did I assault?"

"Me, of course. Sam, I think I've been assaulted. Don't I look assaulted?"

"You look like you've been assaulted to me."

"That's what I thought. Let's go, Mr. Williams."

"This is a bunch of crap. How long do you plan to do this? You must have something better to do than to harass me."

"Nothing that gives me more pleasure. Let's go." He clicked the cuffs in place.

"I don't know why you're doing this. I'll be right back out, just like the other times."

"I know, smart boy, your brother is the big-time lawyer. So tell me, Mr. Williams, since you're so smart, how did your brother get stuck with a loser like you? What happened, was your mother one of those welfare crack-heads?"

Jamal wrestled. "Don't you talk about my mama."

"Or what? What are you going to do?" Crawford pulled out his revolver and put it to Jamal's head. "Go ahead, smart boy, give me a reason to put you out of your misery."

"While you're down there, we might as well throw you into a lineup."

"How you gone do that? I haven't committed any crime."

"You fit the description."

"What description?"

"A black man."

"Just any old black man?"

"Close, but not exactly. Today I'm looking for the one who robbed a liquor store Wednesday night around seven. Where were you?"

"I was at my brother's birthday party with plenty of witnesses."

"Really?"

"Yes," Jamal said, rocking his head back and forth, "really. So you gotta back up off of me."

"Not so fast. I'm sure there was another crime just like it around midnight. You can have that one."

Jamal closed his eyes and hung his head with a smirk. It was too comical to be serious. "You're kidding me, right?"

"Sure I am and you'll see just how funny it is soon enough." He snatched Jamal by the shoulder and shoved him out the door. "Let's go."

Twenty-three minutes, give or take a few seconds, was all it took to get to the city jail. Jamal knew it without having to see a clock. Once he was processed, that's when he would normally make his phone call. He didn't want to call Mama, because she would get upset and call Edwin for help. He had already helped too much. This time he'd sit it out in this infested hole where the smell of digested food, which had baked in hundred-degree weather, would be a more pleasing aroma. Enduring the stench, instead of calling Edwin, was the right thing to do.

CHAPTER 23

Sebastian pulled his car out of Faith Christian Center's parking lot with Courtney sitting on the passenger side.

"I can't believe I've been to your church four or five times already."

"But this is the first time you've come for the morning service. We're making progress," he teased.

She would have gone to Fifth Baptist, but her run-in with Mrs. Jones at the train station yesterday was fresh and required a cooling period. If she had gone today, it might have fanned Mrs. Jones's fiery discontent for Courtney's choice of companionship and cause it to spread through the church like wildfire.

"I've been going to the evening service because I thought it was the one you preferred," she told him.

"No, actually, I prefer the morning, but that's when you go to Fifth Baptist. I've been willing to go in the evening because it's the only time we can go to church together, and I feel that's important for a couple." He picked up her hand and kissed the back of it. He was pleased when she didn't pull away.

"My aunt would have a fit if she knew I had skipped out on Fifth Baptist to go to someone else's church. Let her tell it, God only stops by one church in Philadelphia on Sunday, and that's Fifth Baptist. Every other church gets a messenger."

The two laughed together as they drove along Main Street.

"One day I'd like to go and check out Fifth Baptist myself, if you'd let me."

Courtney kept quiet but gave a soft brush across his hand, which was resting on the gearshift. The bonding continued as they ate lunch and added another hour to the mountain-high list of conversations they'd shared.

Courtney basked in the moment. She kept dashing water on the emotions, on the spark that had been ignited in Penn Treaty Park.

Sebastian opened the car door for her. She tossed her purse into the backseat and sat down, drawing her leg in so he could shut the door.

"How about taking a ride down to South Street?"

"Don't you ever study?"

"Doesn't look like it, huh?"

"You can't have any time left to study. I don't want you flunking out of school because I'm taking up all of your time."

"Not a chance, my classes are a breeze. I could easily have taken another class this time around but the dean wouldn't approve it since I started late. Having a lighter load is working out better anyway."

"Why?"

"I have more time to get to know you without being strapped to my desk. Being in Philadelphia with you is worth investing in another four years of grueling academia."

A humming sound rushed from Courtney's purse. She wrestled with the seat belt, finally breaking free, and reached into the backseat for her purse. The noise had settled down. She pulled out her cell phone and the display showed a missed call.

"Oh, how funny is this. It's Aunt Sis's number. She left a message. We must have talked her up." Courtney dialed into the message center. "Hmmph, that's weird. She said it's important that I come to her house as soon as I get this message."

"Is everything okay?"

"I don't know. She didn't sound right."

"Should you give her a call and find out what's going on?"

"I'd rather just go over there." The pounding pressure in her chest harmonized with the one in her head. She sucked in small pockets of air, trying to get a grip on her fear.

"No problem. We're on our way."

"I hope nothing happened to Aunt Cat or my parents. I talked with them this morning and everything was fine."

"When do I get to meet them?"

"Whenever they stay in town long enough to unpack. They went to North Carolina right after Labor Day. It was supposed to be for two weeks but my Aunt Cat is sick, so they're staying longer. They came home last week for a few days and turned right back around and went back. They've always talked about moving down there after retiring."

Courtney couldn't sit still for the twenty-minute drive. They crept down the block, eyes peeled for a spot. There were none directly in front of the house, which meant they'd have to park around the corner. It would be okay since she wasn't alone. She parked two to four house-lengths from Aunt Sis, but that was like three miles on a day when the pharmaceutical street salesmen were open for business. Edwin had offered to buy Aunt Sis a town house somewhere else. She refused to leave the old neighborhood and her way of life.

Walking to Aunt Sis's house from the car, Courtney saw the two-seater in its reserved spot. "Good, Edwin is here." Courtney slowed her walk to a crawl. "My aunt can be pretty opinionated, but she's a good woman. Don't take her too seriously. Her bark is much worse than her bite."

"Gotcha." Sebastian took two steps alongside Courtney. "Are you sure you want me here? I can wait in the car if you want me to."

"No, that's not necessary. Come on."

Courtney bounced up the stairs like she had a million and two times. Sebastian didn't move as quickly behind her. When she walked into the house, Aunt Sis and Edwin were talking.

"Hello, everybody," she said, holding the door open for Sebastian. "Aunt Sis, I got your message and came right over. What's wrong?" Courtney didn't know what to think. Aunt Sis's reaction was causing her worry meter to rise by the second.

"Oh, I'm being so rude. Sebastian, this is my—"

"What in the world!" Aunt Sis took a few steps toward the living room. "You have the nerve to bring him here again. What did I tell you about bringing 'white folks' in my house? If you think he's coming in here, you got another think coming. It would be over his dead body this time."

Courtney stood completely naked in her heart. She kept telling herself to wait, slow down. It was confusing. The pounding wasn't in sync like it had been in the car. She couldn't tell if the pounding was coming from inside her chest or her head. Whichever it was, it couldn't be good. She needed to slow it down, collect her thoughts. How could Aunt Sis go there! The weight of the embarrassment was overwhelming. She feared it would drill her straight into the basement, like a tornado, leaving nothing with feelings in her path.

"Mrs. Williams," Sebastian started to say and thought better of it, too late for rescue.

"Don't say my name, don't you say a word to me," she screamed with her head frantically shaking back and forth. "It's your kind that killed my husband and has my baby locked up like some animal. I'm so sick of y'all. Every time I turn around, there you are. 'White folks' begging for votes at my church, 'white folks' in my business, but I can bet you there won't be any more 'white folks' in my house," she shouted with the blood vessels in her temples bulging and her hands shaking. "Get out."

Sebastian had prepared himself for another welcoming session like the one he had had with Mrs. Jones. This he wasn't expecting. His mind was working and the signals were going to his legs but they weren't moving fast enough.

"Get out," Aunt Sis yelled, throwing her hands up.

"Mama, Mama," Edwin screamed.

Courtney stood in the archway, dividing Sebastian in the living room from Aunt Sis in the dining room. "Aunt Sis, please."

"It's all right, Courtney. I'm sorry for upsetting you, ma'am," Sebastian directed to Aunt Sis and then faced Courtney. "Take your time. I'll be waiting in the car."

When Sebastian closed the door, Courtney didn't know whether to go out and check on him or to stay and try to comfort her aunt. She'd worry about what she needed for herself later.

"I wish they'd all take the boat back to where they came from." Aunt Sis leaned both arms on back of the chair. "And you ought to be ashamed of yourself, bringing that devil into my house. I didn't expect this from you, Courtney. You weren't raised like this. You know better. You have disappointed me, Courtney."

Courtney stood without offering a word of defense.

"Mrs. Jones told me she saw you at the train yesterday, all hugged up on some white man. I know she's a godly woman, but I all but called the woman a liar because I knew she couldn't be talking about my niece, not the child I helped raise. Well, I guess I'm the liar. I didn't expect this from you, Courtney."

The tears swelled in Courtney's eyes.

"It hurts me to know that you looked me in the face a month ago at Edwin's party and lied to me." Aunt Sis walked into the kitchen, leaving Courtney standing alone.

Courtney collected the ton of disappointment and converted it into chunks of rejection. She felt as if they were being shoved down her throat and would make her gag at any minute. It hurt coming from an aunt who was more like her other mom.

"I haven't done anything," she blurted out.

Edwin walked toward the front door and Courtney followed.

"I know, but why don't you and Sebastian go ahead and leave? I'll stay here with Mama until she calms down." Edwin put his arms on Courtney's shoulders and tried to console her.

"Sebastian didn't do anything to Aunt Sis either."

"I know, but you have to understand where she's coming from." He kept his voice low so his mother couldn't hear him in the kitchen. "She sees the men that beat up Pops in the face of every white man. No one is exempt."

"Sebastian didn't beat up Uncle Eddie."

"Doesn't matter. He looks like the man who did. As far as she's concerned, that automatically makes him an enemy."

"But Sebastian isn't her enemy. He's a good person."

"And I don't doubt that, but she can't see it. Hatred can cloud your ability to see rationally."

"I don't want her to be upset with me." Courtney made a step toward the kitchen.

"She doesn't mean it," Edwin said, holding her back.

"It sounds like she does."

"I'm not making any excuses for her. I've been through this before with Mandy when we first met in college. She came down a few times and Mama was so mean to her that I didn't invite her or any of my other friends to come home with me after that, not even the black ones. Take my advice, leave work and your friends like Sebastian in your other life; that way you can both be spared the humiliation. I'm sorry about this, little cuz."

"It's not your fault. Poor Sebastian." She covered her face with her hands. "Let me go check on him. I don't know what to say to him."

"I'll go with you."

They made the short trip from the house to the car parked around the corner. Skipping from the street, up the steps, and into her aunt's nurturing territory took a hot minute on any other day. The same distance on this trip seemed like an endless road.

Sebastian was leaning on the car when they came around the corner. A man walking by got off the sidewalk and stepped toward the car, letting his eyes rove up and down Sebastian, brushing against him, and keeping his eyes fixed on him after passing by.

"What's up, partner, you lost or what?" the man asked.

Edwin saw the man and picked up his pace. "Hey, Boost, he's with me."

Boost and Edwin did the slap, clutch, flip, and knock shake.

"All right now, what's up, Money? I didn't know that 'old boy' was with you. I'm just trying to keep the streets safe around here, man, you know how it is."

Gershwin, Peters, and Myers wasn't the language on the street. Edwin was like a foreigner who could speak English to some, and in the same conversation switch with ease to his native tongue when talking to fellow countrymen.

"It's all good, man."

"You know this."

They knocked fists one last time.

"I'm out, Ed. Stay black, man."

"I'm going to do what I can."

"Peace," the man said, heading into the clutches of the neighborhood.

"Sebastian, it's good to see you again. Look, I apologize for what my mother said to you." Edwin reached out to shake Sebastian's hand. "I'm sorry."

"I understand, Edwin. Perhaps I'll get a chance to talk with you again, under a different set of circumstances."

"I look forward to it."

Courtney gave Edwin a hug. "I think we should go. I'll talk to you later."

Sebastian opened the door for her. Once she was in, he went around to the driver's side and got in.

Edwin pulled his pants up to generate enough play in the knees for him to squat comfortably next to Courtney's window. "I'll be at home if you feel like talking."

"Oh, I almost forgot, how's Jamal?"

"I'm not sure. I went to bail him out and he wouldn't let me."

"That's strange for him to have you come down there and then not let you bail him out. That doesn't make any sense."

"He didn't call me, Mama did."

"But he knows calling her is the same as calling you."

"He didn't call her either. We went by his place after church to drop off some food. His landlord told her he'd been arrested last night."

"It just never ends."

"Not according to Mama, but don't you worry. If Jamal was in serious danger, he would have let me get him out. I'm still going to follow it up on the legal side, to see what's what. It's going to be all right."

"I believe that. I need to get more serious about praying for all of this chaos. God is the only one who can fix this much craziness," she said.

"You got that right," Edwin responded. "See you later, cuz." He leaned in and gave her another hug for the road.

CHAPTER 24

Courtney didn't bother to fix any dinner. She couldn't eat. Replaying the look on Aunt Sis's face, and layering it with the words she had spewed, was enough to digest. She turned the ringer off the phone in the dining room-office area. A few moments of quiet would give her time to weigh it all out. Courtney couldn't get Aunt Sis's words out of her head, "You've disappointed me." It hurt, coming from someone she'd spent much of her life trying to please, for her loyalty to be questioned over a harmless friendship wasn't going down easy. Aunt Sis just couldn't stay mad, she kept telling herself.

She turned the TV on but couldn't muster enough concentration to make it worthwhile.

God, I don't know what to do. I want to keep seeing Sebastian and I want to keep my family happy too. What do I do?

She was praying for God to order her footsteps in all parts of her life. He got her through Northwestern and was guiding her through the corporate maze, filled with land mines of socially accepted prejudices, buried in a few cubicle conversations, here and there. Relationships were an animal of a different color.

She wanted to figure out the winning formula. Paul was someone she didn't want to be with, but her family liked him. Sebastian was a good friend but Aunt Sis didn't like him. If only she could come to a place where there was someone they all liked. She wanted to be with someone who had all of the pieces. Sebastian had traveled the world and could talk about issues with intelligence. She was in awe of his ability to make her laugh in one sentence and motivate her to pursue her dreams in the next. She didn't know anyone else who could play the trumpet and then quote economic theory like he could, and make both sound good. She tried, but couldn't get Sebastian out of her head.

When she was going back to campus a few months ago, she couldn't wait to see her friends. Times were rough with Paul and she clung to the idea of going back to the protective walls of college life, checking out of reality for a well-deserved weekend. That was then, and Sebastian was now. She doodled his face in her mind, letting the pleasant memories etch in the rough spots. They'd spent every free minute together for nearly two months. The time amounted to a tall glass of lemonade on a hot summer day. Good conversation without a single argument, great food, and clean entertainment, enough sweet to take the edge off the bitter. It was day and night compared to Paul. Sebastian didn't look like her, but he sure thought a lot like her, not in every area, just when it came to their views on education, their careers, the Lord, their families, and even their ideas of how to have fun. Wasn't that what she'd hoped and prayed for in a man? But he was the wrong color. In hindsight, she hadn't specified race in the prayer. Surely God already knew that part. Sebastian couldn't be the one for her. A relationship with him would require a special kind of person for a special calling. God had given her challenges in the past, but nothing like this. She was already pressing against the racial pendulum at work, trying to keep balance between being a team player and not compromising her sense of self.

Courtney couldn't believe she was back in this position, not knowing what to do. She was praying and pondering, pondering and worrying. She believed God would answer her prayer and make it plain and clear about what she needed to do. There wasn't a response bullhorned into her living room or a ring on the phone or a knock at the door. She knew her peace and direction would have to come the oldfashioned way. If she kept praying and had faith, He would give her some answer. Reverend Tyler had mentioned faith a couple of times earlier in the year during the anniversary celebration, but nothing recently. His strength was in making people who had been made to feel like victims gain the power they needed to stand up for themselves.

She could use a combination of what she had learned about faith in Sebastian's church and how to equip herself to win a cause from Reverend Tyler.

"A double-minded man is unstable in all of his ways." That's what Sebastian's minister had said. Being stuck like the cat in the painting, not knowing how to go out or come in, was a feeling she had right before cutting Paul loose. Maybe that was the solution, cut Sebastian out of the picture. It had worked with Paul and maybe it could work again. She prayed that God would help fix a situation that had gone bad.

In the meantime, the decision seemed clear-cut. She would take the low road and not rock the boat with her family. They were the ones who stood by her during every challenge that had come her way. They were always there for her. She couldn't jeopardize that.

Her mind said that not seeing Sebastian anymore was the right move but her heart wasn't in agreement. With Paul, it had been easy. All they had left to share was their race, Fifth Baptist, and Aunt Sis. Severing ties with Sebastian was a different story. The thought of not seeing him created a mist in her heart, a feeling that wasn't pleasant but she could live with. Family came first.

She picked up the phone to call Edwin, the one person who could understand some of her pain. If he was home, she would find out what she could do to mend fences with her aunt, even if it meant not seeing Sebastian. Hopefully that would keep Aunt Sis happy. She would work on her own happiness later.

Chapter 25

Sebastian was worried about Courtney. She was visibly upset when he dropped her off earlier. He wanted to stay with her but she said no. It was an awkward situation all around. He had expected some uneasiness, but Mrs. Williams's reaction was over the top. It was a setback, but all wasn't lost. If he could win over the family, Sebastian knew Courtney would relax into the relationship. He understood her reservations. It wasn't anything she'd spoken out loud, but he felt it when she pulled away in familiar settings and never let him visit Fifth Baptist with her. He had asked every weekend for a month and then quit. She gave the same reason each time. Fifth Baptist didn't have a faith-building message. Maybe that was true, but the admiration and respect she had for Reverend Tyler implied there was something being taught at the church that was worthwhile.

He'd called several times with no answer. He wasn't sure how to help her past the moment, but he knew who did. He dropped to his knees and leaned on the exercise bench with his hands clasped and head bowed.

"I don't know what it will take, but, God, I know you do. Help Courtney and her family to see me through your eyes. Help my family to see her in the radiance in which you created her, beyond her color, her religion, and even her title."

His body was in a humble position but his words were bold. Her peace would have to come from God because he was the only one who could bring it.

"Let them see her heart, the heart that you have drawn to me. Let your love cover her heart. When I asked you for my soul mate, I had no idea you would make her so beautiful, so radiant, so perfectly suited for me. Let the walls of racism fall down far enough so Courtney and I can climb over into the land that you have established and purposed for us before the beginning of time. I thank you, God, from my inner being, because you are awesome. Amen."

He rose to his feet and stared into the glistening lights of the city from his seventh-floor apartment. It would be an uphill battle with the families. He had already forgiven Aunt Sis and hoped when the day came, Courtney would be able to forgive his father.

He didn't know how the puzzle pieces would fall into place, just that they would. The soothing warmth in his soul calmed the fluttering anxiety. That was all the confirmation he needed. Knowing that ultimately he could win her heart would be well worth the journey. His trust was in God and in no way could he be let down.

It might not be a bad idea to make an appointment with Reverend Tyler. He was highly regarded in the church, the community, and with Courtney's family. Reverend Tyler might be able to help him figure out how best to develop a rapport with Aunt Sis and the rest of the family.

He turned on the light switch and pulled the vertical blinds shut. Six o'clock, the football game was still on. On the way to the living room, he tapped the trumpet resting on the tripod with its black case sitting below. After the game he would practice some more. When the spring came, he would be ready to serenade her in Penn Treaty Park just like he'd envisioned from the beginning. He turned on the TV to see what kind of pounding the Redskins were putting on the Eagles. In an hour or so, he'd call again. If he didn't get an answer by then, he'd drive back over to her place to check on Courtney himself. Eventually it would be his full-time role, he was 100 percent sure. For now he would accept the part-time gig.

Chapter 26

The call came in on Tuesday. Aunt Cat had passed and the Phila-delphia clan went into instant travel-preparation mode. Anybody that had time or could get time off work was expected to make the trip. Courtney hadn't been to North Carolina to visit her Great-Aunt Cat in several years. The funeral was Sunday afternoon, but they wouldn't get back to Philadelphia until Monday morning. Just in case, Courtney asked for the day off. Sheila and Brice were the only ones who seemed to understand why she had to go to the funeral of what seemed like, on paper, a distant relative. The Youngs believed family was family, five and six generations removed were as important as those living under the same roof.

It would have helped her case if she'd known Aunt Cat's real name, Artinci. When they'd asked Courtney at work the first time, she didn't know it. Didn't need to—wasn't like she had ever called Aunt Cat by her first name. There were a few instances in her childhood when Courtney slipped up and referred to an adult by a first name. She was immediately chastised. The standard phrase of correction in the family was "you better put a handle on that, young lady." No matter how old she got, she would never be old enough to address one of her seniors on a first-name basis. She heard her coworkers talk to their parents on the phone in ways she couldn't truly comprehend. She couldn't imagine disrespecting her parents in such a way. They wouldn't stand for it.

She called Sebastian to let him know she'd be gone for a few days. There was nothing he could do, although he offered. This would be the second weekend they'd spend apart in over two months. Last weekend was hard, but she needed to start pulling away. The longer she saw him, the more painful ending the friendship would be, which was why she had avoided seeing him this week.

Eight o'clock Saturday morning, the cars lined up on Aunt Sis's block. Courtney, Aunt Sis, Uncle Raymond, and Jamal rode with Edwin in the minivan that he'd rented. The nine hours of traveling were consumed with laughter, storytelling, a few rest stops, and occasional naps from the nondrivers. Edwin did all of the driving. Jamal couldn't drive because his license was suspended. But he sat up front to keep Edwin company.

Courtney jumped for joy when the eight-car caravan had to stop for gas. She was able to go to the bathroom, leaving time to get real food and stretch her legs. It drove her crazy when everybody had to get something different to eat. Some wanted chicken, some burgers, others pizza, and Uncle Raymond wanted true soul food, but ended having to settle for a spicy two-piece with dirty rice, mean greens, and a fast-food version of peach cobbler.

Dusk ushered in the evening, saying farewell to the daylight. The lead van moved slowly down the two-lane paved road.

"Slow down, Edwin," Aunt Sis said, leaning forward to see out of the front window.

"There it is. Ah, that's it now," Uncle Raymond echoed.

A mailbox marked the graveled path that was sandwiched between a cluster of trees and a rickety old wooden shack that leaned to one side. It could have passed as uninhabitable except there was a car pulled up to the door and smoke coming from the chimney. The rocks kicked up as the cars meandered down the makeshift road. Twenty car-lengths from the main road, nestled behind the front house, was a slightly larger home that rested on stacks of cinder blocks.

Courtney looked at the house. When she was a child, they had told her time and time again how setting the house up high helped to keep the snakes out, but it still didn't make sense to her.

Everybody pulled into the yard. The lights in the house were on and the front door open. The car doors slammed. In no time, the yard was speckled with stretches and yawns as passengers rolled out of their vehicles. The family inside the doll-sized house came out to greet the northern tribe of Youngs. "Heys," "how yous?" and hugs bounced around the yard. Aunt Cat's oldest daughter led the pack.

"You all made good time. All right now, Courtney, you come on over here and give me a hug. We so proud of you."

"Thank you." Courtney studied the group. "Where are Mommy and Daddy?"

"In the house," Aunt Cat's daughter answered. "Sharene, go tell Cuttin' Jake and Bee that Courtney's here."

The little girl standing on the porch, with a head full of braids and barrettes that were color-coordinated with her outfit, did as she was told.

A tall, three-hundred-pound man with gray hair came outside with a shorter, round woman.

"Mommy, Daddy," Courtney screamed, running into their arms.

"Hey, baby," her father said, kissing one cheek, Courtney's mother kissing the other.

"I miss you two."

"We miss you, baby girl," he told Courtney. "We'll have a house down here as soon as everything gets settled after the funeral and we get time to find one. You can come down on the weekends."

"Sounds good to me," Courtney said, standing between her parents and locking an arm with each.

"We heard what happened at Cleora's house with your friend," her mother brought up.

She couldn't escape it. Courtney didn't know why she had thought the Sebastian drama would stay in the Philadelphia city limits and let her retreat to a small country town, nestled in North Carolina.

Her father put his index finger under Courtney's chin and lifted her head. "I know we only got half the story from her, but the part we did get, we didn't like."

Courtney looked away in shame.

"I asked Cleora if she'd lost her mind."

"Jake, not so loud," his wife whispered. "You know she's over by the van."

"I'm not biting my tongue. My sister was wrong and she knows it. And she's the very one sitting in Fifth Baptist every Sunday and don't know how to treat folks. I'm not saying she have to like the man, but you don't have to mistreat nobody either. That's why we can't get kids in the church now. It's because of how us old folks act. I told her not to ever treat a child of mine like she did. I'm never too far away to look out for my baby."

Courtney's eyes watered. "What did she tell you about Sebastian?"

"She said he was white and we told her you're grown," her mother said, patting her hand. "Courtney, you are smart and you're beautiful."

Her father jumped in and said, "You have a good head on your shoulders. We wouldn't have left if we thought you couldn't take care of yourself."

"We raised you to think for yourself. We trust you and we support you, Courtney. You pick who you want. You see what I picked." She tickled her husband's beach-ball-sized stomach.

He let Courtney go and gave his wife a hug that completely consumed her. "All I have to say is that I prefer for you to get a black man. There are a lot of people that feel like Cleora, and it wouldn't be easy for you with somebody white. But, I want you to know that I don't care what color he is, so long as he treats you right. If he acts up, I don't care what color he started off with, he'll be black and blue when I'm finished."

"Jake."

"What? I'm just saying."

Courtney felt the lump of heaviness that she was carrying about Sebastian breaking into pieces. They weren't falling away but seemed to be more manageable, now that she had the support of her parents. Was it enough to overshadow the views of the Aunt Sisses and Mrs. Joneses of the world?

"We have to take the clothes to the funeral home and then meet with the reverend at church. We'll be back later. We love you, baby." Her mother kissed Courtney again and followed her husband to their car.

Courtney went into the house to be with the women, who were most likely in the kitchen. Others stayed outside to swap the same old stories about the ride, the South, and the progress the family had made. A few knew it was the only place they would be able to get a nip of liquor in peace. She'd heard it enough times to miss out on one session. From the front door she could see straight out the back. Granddad used to call it a shotgun house and it made sense. If a bul-

let was shot in the front door, it could fly straight through the house
and out the back door without touching anything in between.

The old-house smell rushed to greet her nose. No matter how she
tried to avoid it, the mothball aroma saturated her clothes like smoke
at a happy hour. The three-photo clock still hung above the couch—
Robert Kennedy on the left, John on the right, and Martin Luther
King in the middle. It had fake green leaves lined across the bottom
and a dim light positioned at the top, which could be turned on from
the long cord that fell behind the couch. Nothing had been moved as
far back as Courtney could remember.

The living room was large enough to hold eight people comfortably. The fifteen to twenty that had squeezed in were making do, careful not to upset any of the knickknacks situated in every nook and
cranny. Courtney continued down the hallway to the kitchen, past the
two bedrooms, which were running over with pallets on top of pallets;
blankets, sheets, and pillows quilted the floor. The four-chair metal
table was pushed against the wall on one side eliminating one seat.
Cakes and pies covered in foil and some with plastic wrap, which wasn't
working, were stacked in no real order. The counter held the alu-
minum pans most likely filled with the standard prefuneral menu of
spaghetti, potato salad, home-cooked chicken, store-bought chicken,
and more chicken—none of which would ever be as good as Aunt
Cat's. Her cooking was done now. Warmth covered Courtney's heart.
She had seen Aunt Cat stand at that stove and fry her meat so many
times during her summer visits to North Carolina. The tin cans whose
labels had worn off long ago were still on the stove. One for chicken
grease, the other for fish, because Aunt Cat didn't like mixing the
two. It wasn't proper etiquette. She said it took a couple of uses before
the oil was seasoned just right. Whatever the secret, it worked. None
of her chicken saw the bottom of a garbage can, unlike some of the
unseasoned store-bought chicken on the counter.

"We're tired. We better get sleeping arrangements set before we
get to running our mouths. There's so many of us, we'll probably
need some hotel rooms this trip," Aunt Sis said.

"Hush that talk. Madear wouldn't have stood for it and we won't either. Ain't no family of mine staying in no hotel," Aunt Cat's daughter
told Aunt Sis. "We got plenty of space. Some can stay here in Madear's
place and some can come home with me. Cuttin' Levy got an extra
room down the way a little piece. Some of the menfolk can stay down

there. Nee-Nee just moved into her brand-new house and her double-wide is nice and big."

"Ernestine got a new trailer since I came down here in the spring?" Aunt Sis asked.

"Sho' did and Li'l Mama got her old one. They both parked up there off the main road, over there by the church."

"I don't know about staying with Little Mama. She keeps a nasty house. She's not like you and Ernestine," Aunt Sis was quick to say.

"Nee-Nee house so clean, you can eat off the floor."

"I'm not eating a thing from Little Mama's house. Some of the kids can stay up there. I didn't bring any roaches with me and I'm not taking any back home. I'd have to take the hotel over Little Mama. It just doesn't make any sense how she keeps her house and always has new furniture with her nasty self. She was raised better than that," Aunt Sis stated.

"Well, she still keeps her place 'bout the same as she did when you was here last time. Don't too much change with her. You can stay at my place. Ain't nobody else spoke about staying there, except Big Mama. Somebody went to pick her up from the train station. They'll be back in a little bit."

"Cousin Emma coming! I didn't think she'd make it. You know don't too much get her out of Detroit," Aunt Sis said with amazement.

"You should have known she was coming. She hasn't missed a funeral in the family as far back as I can remember, and Madear said they were close coming up. They were first cousins, but you know she was always like a sister to Madear. I knew she was coming," Aunt Cat's daughter reminded Aunt Sis.

Courtney looked at the stacks of pictures on the table while they talked.

"It'll be good to see her. Looks like I'll be staying at your place then, if you're sure it's not too much trouble."

"No trouble at all."

"You sure I'm not crowding you out?"

"Between all of us, we got room for all of you, if you don't mind bunching up."

"We don't mind at all, except for that wife of your cousin Deon. She's too good to stay with any of us when they come to Philadelphia. I know she'll end up staying at the hotel."

"Well, she got to learn about the Youngs. Family is family and she isn't good for any of us. Which one is she, the high yellow one with that ole stringy-looking hair?"

"That's her, uppity as she wants to be, like she somebody," Aunt Sis snarled.

"Umph, well, she got a good man. She better act with some sense and learn how to treat folks."

"She sure wasn't my choice for him, but you know how these young folks don't listen." Aunt Sis glanced at Courtney before continuing the conversation with her cousin. "She chased him down and finally caught him. I hope she doesn't ruin him," she said.

"Could be worse. He could have married a white woman. You know they do that now, all the time."

Courtney fidgeted in her seat, hoping that Aunt Sis didn't put her into the conversation. She was content sitting and listening.

"Oh, you don't have to tell me. Every time you turn around they're sniffing around Edwin. Oh, I pray he doesn't give in to one of them. She just gone end up divorcing him down the road and trying to take everything that he's worked for. They the only ones that do that, you know," Aunt Sis said.

Courtney wondered if they were talking in the moment or if they really believed white women were the only beings on the face of the earth capable of capitalizing on an unfortunate situation. Maybe Aunt Sis had forgotten about Uncle Raymond's black wife, the one who cleaned out both bank accounts and all of the furniture in the house when she left town with her boyfriend. All she left him was some bills and his old Cadillac. The only reason she didn't get the car was that she made a mistake and broke the key in the lock. She didn't have time to get it fixed before he got home. Courtney would have to keep that memory to herself. She sure couldn't jump into this conversation. She kept listening and looking at the pictures. She was grown, but having a sit-down chat with the older women didn't feel right. Times had changed since college, but not that much.

"I don't know why they so bent on getting our men either. Got to have a black man. What's wrong with their men? They don't want him until he's done something of himself," Aunt Sis preached.

"Nah, they sho' don't want them before that."

"They have plenty of their own men. A white woman can get married any time she wants to and it doesn't matter how she looks. She can be wide as this table or skinny as that broomstick."

"They always get them big diamond rings too," Aunt Cat's daughter said.

"And then they go and get one of those big houses."

"You sho' right. I cleaned for a couple of them and they don't have no money left for furniture half the time."

"House poor, that's what it is. But no matter how much they spend on a house, the women always get to stay at home and I don't know what for because they don't know how to raise their kids. They let them bad kids run all over them."

"Don't they?"

Courtney knew a few house-poor blacks, but they didn't want to hear that.

"I wouldn't keep any of their kids to save my life. I've seen times at the store when the kids are whupping their mothers. Talking about letting them set their own boundaries."

"We know how to set the boundaries for our kids, don't we?"

"We sure do, between a switch and a belt, there's no confusion."

"That's why our kids don't grow up acting a fool with all of those problems that theirs have."

Aunt Sis was really having a forgetful day. If she thought about it for a second, at least one person, who had encountered a few problems, should come to mind. Then again, Aunt Sis was talking about the perfect blacks, not the ones they knew.

"I just hope Edwin gets a decent black woman."

"We just have to keep praying for our men."

"They'll be all right. How you and everybody holding up around here?"

"Best as can be expected. We knew she was getting low, but we didn't know she was going to go just like that."

"When Jake called us, he couldn't tell us much."

"Well, you know she had shuga'. She let it get so bad off. She wouldn't quit eating all of the things the doctor told her to let alone. She ate whatever she wanted. I guess she just got tired of taking them shots every day. They had to take one of her legs a few months back. She was doing fine. Cuttin' Jake and Bee been staying with her the whole time. Last weekend she was complaining about being tired. When we checked on her Tuesday morning, she was gone. We don't know what all happened. The doctor wanted to do an autopsy but we said no. Ain't no sense." Aunt Cat's daughter sniffed a couple of times and took one of the napkins off the table and dabbed the corner of her eyes.

"Umph, umph, umph. Boy, I'm sure going to miss her homemade cakes."

"Madear sure knew how to cook, didn't she?"

The eyes of the women got teary.

"How did she get the name Aunt Cat?" Courtney asked.

"They say she was sneaky when she was a li'l girl, like a cat. That's how she got that name."

"I'm surprised the name stuck, because you know a lot of black folks don't like cats," Aunt Sis pointed out.

Courtney wanted to tell them she did, but decided against interjecting, seeing that she must be one of the few blacks in America who liked cats.

"Sure don't, do we?"

Aunt Sis cut a sliver from the sweet potato pie sitting in the middle of the table.

"You all set for the funeral? You have flowers and all of that?" Aunt Sis asked.

"That's another story. We gone have to get the family together tomorrow and see if we can come up with enough money for the burial. Mr. Harvest is going ahead with it, but I told him we'd get the money to him by next week."

"Didn't Aunt Cat have insurance?"

"She did, but it was one of those old Metropolitan policies."

"That's right. I remember the insurance man coming to the door every month when we were children to collect the money. What happened, she let it lapse?"

"No, she kept that policy for over sixty years, paid it every week. When we called a few days ago, they said it was worth five hundred and twenty-three dollars, something about the stock value or something, just some old scheme to get your money. I can't believe Madear paid all those years and we don't have enough insurance to bury her with. She wouldn't want us to have to take up a collection, but we just ain't got it."

"I understand. It's been tight for everybody. As long as them Republicans are in office, not too many of us are working. I'm so glad the Democrats won this last time. With Mr. Charlie out of office, things are going to start getting better."

"Who's Mr. Charlie?" Courtney asked.

"You don't know who Mr. Charlie is?" Aunt Cat's daughter laughed. "It's the 'white man.' " She laughed some more. "Times changing for you younger folks. I guess they don't teach you what you need to know in those fancy schools. I guess that's our job."

Growing up, it had been so easy to accept all she'd heard. It was black and white. Courtney hadn't given it much thought in the past. Being the third seat in a two-chair conversation gave her ample opportunity to listen. It was insightful, listening to the older women in her family. Life and race weren't quite as clear-cut as the women made them seem. Much of what she had heard, accepted, and based her decisions on about the ways of blacks and whites had become gray after getting to know Sebastian, beyond his color. It would be a lot of work, looking at people on a case-by-case basis. As far as the Young family was concerned, spending time pondering on how to improve race relations was a waste of time. The line between blacks and whites was clearly drawn and required no thought.

"And that's what we're going to do. We take care of our own." Aunt Sis held her cousin's hand. "Don't you worry about the money. We are family and will do what we have to do. You know Edwin, Courtney, Terry, and Deon have all been blessed. They have good jobs. We'll work this out."

Courtney pushed against the force in her neck that wanted to look up at Aunt Sis and say, *Don't include me in.* She felt like a fly on the wall. They talked as if she weren't in the room. Except for the constant ducking in and out of family seeking food, Courtney might as well have been alone.

"You all hungry? You see there's plenty of food," Aunt Cat's daughter told Courtney and Aunt Sis.

Courtney and Aunt Sis fixed a plate and ate at the table.

The loud talking coming from the front room and the chatters coming from out back required the women in the kitchen to speak up so they could hear one another.

"Anybody coming from your daddy's family?" Aunt Sis asked her cousin.

"I think Aunt Rochelle is."

"I haven't seen her and Ray in years. Their son should be about grown now."

"Her and Ray split up about seven years ago," Aunt Cat's daughter revealed.

"I didn't know they were divorced," Aunt Sis said with bewilderment.

"Oh no, I don't know about divorced. From what I know, they're just split up. Ain't neither one of them paying for no divorce. They still do that old mess down here."

"It's not much difference between here and up North. They do the same thing back at home. Who kept the son after they split? What's his name?"

"Troy," Courtney tossed in.

"That's right, little Troy," Aunt Sis agreed.

"You know Troy wasn't their natural child. They kept him from a baby and raised him like he was their own. He just went to the service about five months ago. A good boy."

"Can't do that anymore."

"What's that?" Aunt Cat's daughter questioned.

"Just get a child that needs a home and bring him in. They make you go through all kinds of questions and papers. You have to make so much money, have so many bedrooms. It's crazy. When a child needs a home, they need a home," Aunt Sis said in a firm voice, slightly elevated, but not as low as those in the front room.

"Many of the kids in the adoption system are black," Courtney added.

"That's because the 'white folks' have messed everything up," Aunt Cat's daughter said.

Courtney cringed inside and then relaxed. She wasn't at work and didn't have to protect anyone's ears from reality. Whenever Courtney heard the term "white folks" coming from the older heads of the family and "you people" coming from other races, it was a sure sign of danger. She wondered what similar term other races used to talk about blacks. Not like the slashing n-word used behind closed doors, but a more refined, less offensive version that could be spoken in public. What word did her coworkers use when she wasn't around, when they were huddled together in an office, without any peppered people sprinkled in the middle, talking about the black criminals featured on the local news? Whatever the word was, it couldn't be positive. Race was the most damaging four-letter word Courtney knew.

"We've been taking care of our children for generations. Whenever a mother needed help, there was a grandmother, aunt, mother, or cousin to help out," Aunt Sis preached.

"Or a neighbor."

"That's right. Any of them would raise the child and they didn't get paid for it either. They just did it. Now you have to do all of this paperwork while the kids sit in one of those orphanages waiting on somebody to get them. Don't make any sense. Courtney, break me off a piece of that cake box?" Aunt Sis asked, with her tongue trying to dislodge the culprit on one side of her back tooth and her pinky finger pushing from the other side. "I can't stand it when I get chicken caught in my teeth."

Courtney obliged her aunt.

"Did I tell you that Honey Babe is bringing them bad kids down from Virginia?" Aunt Cat's daughter asked Aunt Sis.

"Umph, you better have somebody stay and watch the house when we go to the funeral. Those kids have sticky fingers. If you're not careful, you won't have any of your mother's belongings left for yourself. I want you to take those quilts and put them in the back of our van. Get the keys from Edwin. That way I know nobody will be able to go through things until you've had time to sit down for a moment and decide what you want people to have." Aunt Sis got up and put her paper plate in the garbage bag that was running over. "Ooo, it makes me so mad when people come to a funeral looking for what they can take home like this is some kind of shopping trip."

"She didn't come to see Madear when she was up on her feet."

"Those the main ones you have to watch, coming here looking for a handout. You let me know anybody that gives you a hard time about your mother's stuff. I'll take care of them, because they know I don't play," Aunt Sis made clear to her cousin. "Right is right."

"That would sure be a help, Cuttin' Sis."

All Courtney could hear from the front room were "heys." She got up to see what all the commotion was about. The petite woman standing in the center of the room with the pearl-colored glasses on her nose was Big Mama.

"Who just come in, Courtney?" Aunt Sis asked Courtney.

"Nee-Nee and Big Mama."

"Cousin Emma done made it. Let me get on in there."

The house was filled. Aunt Sis pushed through to get up front.

"Cousin Emma," Aunt Sis screamed with her arms spread two states apart, positioned for a hug, "it's sure good to see you."

"Sho' good to see you, chile."

"You made it all right?"

"Long as God riding with me, ain't got anything to worry about."

"Amen" chimed in the group who, just sixty seconds ago, Courtney suspected hadn't included a single bit of God in any of their conversations, but then it wasn't Sunday. She leaned on the door frame and watched the people, older than she, but younger than Big Mama, fall in line. The few curses that had seeped out of the front room into the kitchen earlier were bottled up. When an old wise head like Big Mama entered a room, it was like Jesus on the mountaintop. Everybody got quiet and gave her respect. A few family members offered her a seat and she declined.

"It's been a long time, Cleora."

Since Big Mama was talking with Aunt Sis, the rest of the room went back to their own conversations.

"It has been, Cousin Emma. How long it's been since you been to Philadelphia?"

"Near about fifteen years."

"Has it been that long? I guess it has been. I remember when you came with that pretty little granddaughter of yours."

"She not little no mo'. Rachel is grown now."

Nee-Nee said, "Let's go in the kitchen. It's too crowded in here."

The line of Young women were in motion.

"Why don't you come up for a visit, Cousin Emma? I got plenty of room at the house. There's no one there but me since Ed passed."

"Ize sho' thank about it. Just might do that."

Every new family member to arrive would get the red-carpet welcome. Except for a few teary eyes and a missing Aunt Cat, no one would know that this reunion was for a funeral. The gut-wrenching cries and agonizing outbursts would be saved for the funeral on Sunday. Courtney was prepared.

Chapter 27

Standard time had kicked in, and it was already dark outside by the time Courtney got home around six-thirty. Next time she would use her preapproved day off instead of returning from North Carolina at five in the morning, going to work late, and getting off late. She was paying for the noble gesture now. She turned on lights in her apartment and hung her jacket in the closet. October might have rolled in with a vengeance but it was whimpering out like a lamb.

The sixty-degree weather outside left the room shivery. She dropped her keys on the table and hit the play button on the answering machine. She turned on the heat to knock the chill off and listened to the messages, waiting to hear Sebastian's voice. It was there.

"Courtney, it's Bas. Just checking on you. Give me a call when you get in."

She hit replay several times to hear his voice, which she'd grown accustomed to having nearby. She felt a little down and called Edwin for encouragement. Thank goodness he was home from work, which was unusual for him.

"I had to come home early. I'm tired. The drive wore me out," he told her. "You know, I'm glad you called. I wanted to find out how everything's going with you and Sebastian."

She sighed. "Well, we've talked, but I haven't seen him in a couple of weeks. I really haven't seen him much since that happened at Aunt

Sis's." Her voice wanted to choke up, but she resisted. "I didn't want to stop seeing him, but I have."

"You shouldn't let Mama stop you from seeing him if that's what you want to do."

"It wasn't just her. I'm not sure how I feel about being serious with a white guy. I just don't know. I've been praying, but I don't feel any wiser about it. I figured it would be easier to break it off, before anything gets serious, or more serious, I should say. There are plenty of other guys out there, black ones too."

"Is breaking it off with him the right thing to do?"

"I have no idea, but the drama is too much for me. I just want a nice quiet relationship, regular stuff."

"If you're serious about moving on, I can introduce you to Roger. I've been telling you he's a sharp brother. If you want, I can give him your work number. It can't hurt to go out with him."

"Look who's talking; when are you taking Sheila out?"

"We're not talking about me. We have to deal with one pitiful Young relationship at a time. This is your day."

Courtney and Edwin chuckled.

"I guess you can give him my number. I won't make any promises about going out with him. I'll just have to see how it goes if he calls me."

She finished up her call with Edwin and contemplated calling Sebastian, but it didn't make sense. If they spoke, he would want to go out and she'd have to find a way to say no without being direct. She couldn't hurt his feelings. She cared about him too much. Sitting in her apartment and being pitiful wasn't desirable either. Roger wasn't the solution for getting over Sebastian, but perhaps he could be a distraction in the interim. If he called, she would go out with him. Nothing serious, just a two-hour break from pining over Sebastian and dreaming of what couldn't be.

Sebastian knew Courtney was home by now and had gotten his message. He could show up on her doorstep unannounced, but it was risky. It was easy to see that she'd pulled back since the unfortunate event at her aunt's house. He'd seen her that Sunday evening, but not since. Two weeks without her was like being in solitary confinement, where the darkness dared the light to radiate. He was lonely and missed having her near.

He wanted to be forceful, but knew she couldn't be won over by might. The water was getting choppy, but he was determined to hang on to the revelation that he'd gotten from God; no matter what the situation looked like, he believed Courtney was to be his wife. How to get from her not wanting to see or talk to him was going to require faith and hope, which only came from one source. He would continue seeking God, but there was something else he decided to do. Tomorrow he would finally call Fifth Baptist and see if he could get on Reverend Tyler's calendar. It would be wise to talk with a man of God who also happened to be a friend of Courtney's family. He ached from not being able to see her tonight, but knew their day would come. He just had to endure the nights to come in the middle.

Chapter 28

Courtney stood in the waiting area of the downtown restaurant powdering her nose with the enlarged fluffy cotton puff that she kept neatly tucked inside her makeup case. She thumbed through her hair, one side at a time, with the hope of fluffing it into submission. She pulled the sides of her fitted suit down to ensure that it was lying properly across her straight-lined hips.

Roger seemed pleasant enough when he'd called on Tuesday. Making the suggestion to meet for lunch on a Thursday was smart. It wasn't prime time. An hour, good or bad, wasn't a sacrifice.

The butterflies in her stomach were manageable, much more so than if she'd chosen to go to dinner with Roger instead of lunch today. She had considered asking Edwin and Sheila to double-date with them, but didn't have the courage after that last fiasco. Edwin had messed up one too many times with Sheila. The group setting would have provided Courtney the cushion she desired. She was a rookie in the dating game. Paul and Sebastian were the only two men she'd spent significant time with. They were her same age. She knew them and felt comfortable with them. Going out with a man eight years older left her wondering what to expect.

Courtney took a deep breath and let it softly empty out of her lungs, taking her jitters along with it.

She constantly looked at her watch, even though Roger had clearly said his meeting ended at noon and he would catch a cab to the restaurant by twelve-fifteen. It was five after twelve and each minute seemed to have a weight attached.

She gave an extra look to every man approaching the door, wondering if it was Roger. He had described himself as six feet tall, one hundred and ninety pounds, brown-skinned with short hair faded on the side, wearing a gray suit. A man entered the restaurant wearing a pair of dark shades that accented his tall, coconut-colored skin. "Umph," Courtney grunted. She knew it had to be Roger, at least she hoped.

He pulled the door open with one hand and removed his shades with the other. She didn't know if she should walk up to him or pretend like she didn't see him so he would come to her.

Before she could work out a plan, Roger exposed a mouth of pearly whites.

"Courtney?"

He gave her a quick, loose hug.

The two shook hands.

"Roger."

"My meeting didn't end by noon. I hope you haven't been waiting long."

"No, it wasn't long at all," she said, although the fifteen minutes had seemed like an entire day.

"Let's get a table." He put his open-faced hand on the center of her back and slightly nudged her toward the hostess.

The hostess located their reservation and led them to their table. The waiter was already there with two glasses of water and menus. Roger pulled the chair out for Courtney. As she sat down, he pushed it in gently. He opened his suit jacket before taking his seat.

"So, Courtney Young. It is a pleasure to finally meet you."

She giggled and took a sip of water, feeling like a giddy schoolgirl being in the company of what she saw as an older refined gentleman.

The waiter interrupted long enough to take their orders and retrieve the menus. After he left, Roger leaned to one side, propped his elbow on the armed chair, tucked his thumb under his chin, and used the other fingers to cover his mouth. There was a short span of silence while he studied her face.

"Edwin has told me so much about you. You're like a sister to him."

She stopped stirring the straw in the glass of water long enough to look Roger in the eye and say, "What can I say? He's always been like an older brother to me."

Edwin didn't have a problem with Sebastian, but she hadn't expected him to. Edwin and Jamal were always letting her do whatever made her happy. If only Aunt Sis could do the same.

"Edwin is great and I love him. What about you, do you have any sisters or brothers?"

"One brother and one sister. I'm the oldest. What about you, where do you fall in the line?"

"You could say I'm the oldest, the youngest, and in the middle, all at the same time."

Roger had a perplexed look on his face.

"I'm an only child, so I get to be all of it," she said.

"That's probably not so bad since you have someone like Edwin looking out for you."

"He's good to me." She resumed stirring the straw slowly in the glass. "Did you meet Edwin at Yale?"

Sebastian had almost gone to Yale. She was glad he chose Penn instead.

"No, actually we met at Temple."

"I didn't realize you knew him from undergrad. I thought you met him more recently."

The waiter set the plates of food in front of Courtney and Roger without disrupting their conversation.

"Actually, we lost contact when he went to law school at Yale and I went to business school at Stanford. We didn't hook up again until I took this promotion at Chase last year and moved back to Philadelphia for a senior vice president position in the investment banking division."

Roger was a business school guy, just like Sebastian. He hadn't mentioned it, but she wondered if Sebastian was considering investment banking. He was exceptional when it came to finance and he seemed to do pretty well with watching the stocks in his own trust fund portfolio.

"Senior vice president! Wow, you're young to be in that position. That's quite an accomplishment."

Roger raised his eyebrow. "Perhaps, but I can't take any credit. I did the preparation and God opened the door. All I had to do was walk through it."

"So are you enjoying Philadelphia?"

"I am. It's kind of strange because I really don't remember a whole lot about it. Last year was the first time I'd been back since I left Temple eight years ago. I was a West Coast kid and had no reason to hang around. God didn't tell me to stay, so I was out of here."

"Looks like you're back."

"Looks like it and enjoying every minute. My job is good, life is great, and God is wonderful. So, tell me about the wonderful Ms. Young."

He took a bite of his sandwich while Courtney swished her mouth with a sip of water, before responding.

"Let's see, I was born and raised in Philadelphia. I already told you that I'm an only child. I got my marketing degree from Northwestern. I graduated in June and now I'm working as a marketing analyst in training."

"What does the in-training mean?"

She was determined to stay composed, regardless of how badly the lingering warmth of Sebastian's words tried to bubble up and spill over into a smile. The "in-training" had become an inside joke between them. He called her la marketer. A flash of sadness doused the warmth inside. Sebastian had invited her to check out Paris with him during spring break. He had painted the picture. They were going to take the boat from the base of the Eiffel Tower, ride along the Seine River, past the Notre Dame Cathedral, ending up at the Louvre to see the Mona Lisa. She had dared him to stand in the middle of the park, which stretched between the Louvre and the Millennium Ferris Wheel, and play his trumpet with the flare of a true Frenchman. He promised to take her to see the original black Statue of Liberty depicting a black female slave holding a broken chain in her left hand and broken chains of slavery at her feet. He said it was sculpted by Frédéric-Auguste Bartholdi. It didn't make any difference. She wasn't going with him. Sebastian couldn't be her focus.

"I'm on a fast track for management. I have a mentor that I work with on what they call hot projects. In two years, if all goes well, I will get promoted to an assistant manager's position, and then a full management position one year after that." Feeling like she'd answered the test correctly, she rewarded herself with a spoonful of minestrone soup.

"Impressive. So, you're intelligent, not that I expected anything less being related to Edwin, that genius."

Roger wiped his mouth and placed the napkin on top of his plate, empty except for a pickle left on it. He slid the plate up, creating enough space for him to rest his elbows on the table. Fingertips touching, he pressed his hands together.

"What do you like in the way of entertainment?"

Courtney hunched her shoulders, unprepared for the question. She hadn't given much thought to what would happen after today. Most of her energy had been spent on thinking about Sebastian and how he made her happy. That chapter of her life had to be closed. Here was her chance to start with a clean social preference slate, and her mind was blank.

"What about plays, do you like going to the theater?"

The movie theater in Society Hill was her favorite. That's where she and Sebastian got to hang out and get almond roca. Roger was talking about the real theater, the one with the thirty-foot red curtains that were pulled back slowly to show the stage. She and Paul had gone to one play in their six years together, and it was because she begged and pleaded. All of the other plays she'd seen had been with Edwin or with friends back at school.

"I saw *Dreamgirls* right before I left Chicago."

"Are you up for seeing a play this weekend?"

Courtney almost said she had plans for this weekend, but caught herself. Every weekend was going to be spent with Sebastian. It hadn't mattered what they did, as long as they got to hang out together. This would be the first weekend with someone else. She didn't respond immediately.

"Oh, forgive me for being so presumptuous. I'm sorry, I didn't ask if you were either interested or available this weekend."

"Yes, I am."

"Which, interested or available?"

"Both."

Roger bent his arm and slid his cuffed sleeve back so he could see the time on his Rolex watch.

"Sounds good. I'm looking forward to getting to know you. Lunch has been wonderful, but I need to get back for a two o'clock meeting. That's one thing about my job, I love what I do but it keeps me jumping. I'm sure you have the same situation. Right?"

"Pretty much."

He pulled his electronic organizer from his jacket pocket and removed the stylus from its resting place.

"Let's see here, I have your work number. Do you prefer that I call you there?"

"Work or home," she said, and then relayed the home number to him.

"I'll give you a call tonight to work out the details for this weekend. Ready?" Roger said, taking a long flattering look at Courtney, never losing sight of her eyes. He pulled out his American Express, grabbed the check, and said, "Let's go."

He stood up, shook his coat out, and helped Courtney to her feet by delicately pulling the chair back, giving her legroom to stand. He extended his arm behind her as if he were parting the waters for her to cross.

Lunch turned out to be more than she was looking for. Agreeing to meet Roger for lunch was partly a way to block out Sebastian while also an opportunity to rob loneliness of the time that it had sucked out of her in recent days.

His gestures didn't go unnoticed. Courtney savored every action. Sebastian was her measuring stick. He treated her like a queen with no shortage of courtesies. She was quick to recognize that as the kind of treatment and attention she wanted going forward.

Chapter 29

Courtney walked along Sixteenth Street allowing the mild autumn wind to tingle her face as it playfully rushed in and retreated like a child who came within an arm's reach and pulled away just in time to escape being tagged. Roger had offered to put her in a cab and pay for her five-block ride back to work. She had declined, looking forward to taking the leisurely walk and soaking up the moment, before jumping back into the corporate madhouse.

The afternoon was hectic and passed quickly. Courtney went home for the evening, got some sleep, and started over Friday morning. Roger had called last night as he promised and they'd agreed to go see *Phantom of the Opera*. It was a play Courtney had wanted to see for years and would surely have caught it in New York with Sebastian, given a few more weekends together.

She was drafting the minutes from her nine o'clock meeting when the security guard called her down to the lobby. She went down and her eyes danced when the guard told her the vase of long-stemmed yellow roses was for her.

For me? she thought. *Who, why? It's not my birthday.*

She carried the vase to her office and placed it on the corner of her desk. She searched for the card and found it tucked inside the thick patch of baby's breath. The card read:

> *Ms. Courtney Young,*
> *Funny, Beautiful, and Smart.*
> *What a combination!*
> *Had a great time. Thanks—Roger*

She spun around in her seat with her feet drawn in to avoid clipping the desk.

Sheila stopped by to see if Courtney wanted to go out for lunch.

"Ooooo, are those from Sebaaaastian?"

"No, they're not."

"Whoa, don't tell me." She got closer so no one else could hear. "Paul heard that you're seeing a white guy and he's trying to come back?"

"I haven't talked to Paul in . . . I don't know how long."

"Well, who are those from then?" Sheila said with her neck stiffened and head leaning to one side.

"They're from Roger, the guy that I went to lunch with yesterday." She pressed the card to her chest and covered it with both hands.

"Roger! What happened to Sebastian?"

"He was a friend, but this was a real date."

"What was Sebastian?"

"I told you, a friend."

"Oh, girlfriend, you're moving too fast for me. You have one in the drawer, one at lunch, and another waiting for dinner." Sheila reared back on her heels and framed her face with her hand. "Brice doesn't have anything on you."

"It's not like that."

"All I know is that you were all head-over-heels for this Sebastian guy and now you're getting flowers from this Roger. What happened?"

"I couldn't deal with the pressure. My family had a fit, or should I say my aunt had a natural-born fit about Sebastian coming into her house a few weeks ago."

"What was Edwin's reaction about you seeing Sebastian?"

"He's okay with it."

"From what I saw at the party, I guess he would be. Regardless, you can't let people tell you how to live. That's crazy."

"Edwin's mom is like a mother to me."

"Look, nothing against your aunt, but she seems to be in too many people's business. Every time Edwin canceled a date with me, it had something to do with Mama. She needs to leave you alone. That's why Edwin doesn't have anybody. Mandy is crazy too. When you told me she let your aunt and Edwin squeeze her into backseat, I didn't say a word because it was pathetic."

"I know. Can you believe that!"

"I would have told him and his mama that they could both keep my part of the baby seat. My behind needs a whole seat and then some. That's exactly why I have my own car, because I like peace. The day I have to reduce myself to get a man, just shoot me and put me out of my tired existence. Oooo, your aunt better be glad it didn't work out between Edwin and me, because I would have gotten her straight right from the beginning. Edwin can only cater to one woman at a time and if he's with me, you best believe it's going to be me. She wouldn't like me, because I don't believe in sharing a man. Not even with his mama. It sounds like she needs to get her own life and her own man. That's what fathers are for. Oooo." Sheila sighed and tensed her body with her fingers stretched apart and pulsating. "Enough with the madness. Tell me about this Roger."

The third member of the minigroup interrupted before Courtney could respond.

"Flowers, whoa. I underestimated the brother. I guess Paul is getting his act together after all," Brice said.

"These aren't from Paul."

"Hey, whey, whoa, they're not from Paul." Brice scratched his head, wearing a Cheshire Cat grin. "They better not be from Joe Bob around the corner."

Courtney sighed and said, "Why, what difference would it make?"

"Who sent those?"

"Why?"

"Okay, all I need to know is if they came from a brother."

"I still don't understand what difference it makes. You didn't send them."

"Are they from a brother or not?"

"Yes, not that I have to tell you, but since you won't leave me alone, yes, they are. Okay, you happy now?"

"That's all I need to know."

Brice got his answer and returned to the business he had been conducting before stumbling into Courtney's cubicle.

"Typical," Sheila said.

"What?"

"A brother can see whoever he wants to, any race, CEO, secretary, young, old, with or without children. Doesn't matter. Let a sister go out with another race and a brother can't stand it. They can't stand seeing 'the man' with a sister." Sheila leaned forward and rested her elbows on her thighs and spoke softly. "What's good for the goose is good for the gander. They better start getting used to it."

"Why do you say that?"

"We don't have enough brothers around here to supply the sisters as it is. Take us for instance. We have one Brice to split between the two of us and he's too much of a player for anybody, let alone the fact that he's not even our type. Whatever our type is, he's not it. So, who does that leave, Jason, Wally, and Adam? I don't think so, not for me, and not because they're white. I wouldn't want them because Jason is the only good-looking one out of the bunch. I can't reduce my standards either. I am too content by myself to do that."

Courtney had chosen to be with Paul for six years. With all of the guys pursuing her in college, she hadn't experienced the pains of a shortage. Truth be told, she had more suitors than she could ever have been interested in.

"You really think there's a shortage?"

"I do think there's a shortage, if you're looking. There are so many brothers that are erroneously locked up, on drugs, chasing women, gay, not interested in a sister, or held captive by their mamas."

"I honestly have to say I haven't experienced any kind of shortage," Courtney said.

"That's because you're still young, in shape, and not too far up the executive ladder. You're still moldable. I had all kinds of options when I was your age too, but that was eight years and three promotions ago. So, don't take this season of plenty for granted. Some of the men around here are clearly interested in you, like Jason," Sheila said in a playful tone.

"Don't start."

"He's cute, not to be a brother, that is. Don't you think he's cute?"

"I don't know."

"Well, you better start thinking about it."

"I'm not worried about finding a man."

"Could have fooled me. That might be what you're saying. The look on your face when I walked into this cubicle was called worry with a capital W."

"I was upset about what's happening, but I wouldn't say worried."

"Why, because you have Edwin on your side introducing you to wonderful men like Roger?"

"No, it's because I have the Lord on my side and whatever man he has for me will find me."

"Well, I can't say anything behind that. I might as well get my heathen behind on up from here and get some work done before I end up without a man and a job." Sheila stood up and yawned. "So what if he's white?"

"Who?"

"The man that God sends."

Courtney didn't know what to say.

"It's something to think about if you plan to move up around here. Look at me, I don't run into as many black men in management as you do. In the past six months I've probably been in a hundred meetings and only run into one or two brothers, not counting Hodges. That's it."

"That's interesting." Courtney remained quiet for a moment and then said, "Would you ever consider dating someone that's not black?"

"Like I told you before, that's not my thing, but don't let that stop you. Some people can handle hot spices, some people can't. An interracial relationship is too spicy for my blood, simple as that. But I know you love hot sauce, nice and *spiiiicy*," Sheila said, finishing off with a chuckle. "Now, that's something to think about, church lady." Sheila tapped on the metal frame of the cloth cubicle wall. "I'm out of here."

Sheila left and Courtney turned back to her computer, poking through her e-mail folder, pondering the question. She took a deep breath remembering that God wouldn't put more on her than she could bear. She believed that eliminated Sebastian and the battle stemming from being with him. Oh well, enough time wasted. She leaned over and drew in the aroma of the floral bouquet, allowing it to sweeten her thoughts. She had more tangible elements to dwell on, like her next date with a black Mr. Wonderful.

Chapter 30

Sebastian was thrilled to have a familiar face visiting him in Philadelphia. When his old buddy Bart had called a few days ago saying he would be in town for a tennis tournament, it was a given that he would stop by. He had buzzed Bart from the first-floor lobby and was waiting for him to arrive at his door. The rapping on the door could only be one out-of-control man. Sebastian opened it and there stood his fellow Andover alumnus.

"Hey, Bas, what's up, dude?"

"Bart, get in here, man. How are ya?"

Like magnets, the men drew close enough to bump chests and instantly repelled.

"Thanks for letting me crash here for a night." Bart snatched the duffel bag from his own shoulder and tossed it behind the door.

"Are you hungry or what?" Sebastian asked.

"Starved like you would not believe."

"Sandwich and chips okay?"

"Totally."

Sebastian went into his kitchen that opened into the living room on one side and the dining room on the other. Bart hung around the dining room area, which was more of an office, equipped with a laptop, printer, fax, file cabinet, and full-sized desk. Framed photos covered the corner section of the wall.

"So, is law school kicking you or what?" Bart asked, leaning over the file cabinet to get a closer look at the pictures.

Sebastian spoke up so Bart could hear him from the kitchen. "I don't start law school until the fall."

"So what are you doing now?"

Sebastian came out with turkey and cheese, lettuce, tomato, mustard, mayo, and a dash of oregano on a long Italian hoagie roll and handed it and a napkin to Bart. He set the bottle of ginger ale and chips on the coffee table. "I'm in the four-year joint-degree program. The first part is business school. It starts in January but I'm getting a jump on it by taking a couple of classes now."

"You totally rule, dude. You are like your dad's hero."

Sebastian sat in the recliner and Bart sat on the futon, pulling the coffee table closer.

"I wouldn't say that. He thinks I'm too laid-back and that I'm not taking life serious enough. Unless I'm billing seventy-plus hours per week, I'm a slacker."

"For sure. Our parents are like so out of it. My dad is having a conniption. I'm really busting my chops this year in order to get ranked high enough to make one of the Grand Slams. I just missed the U.S. Open this year."

"That's awesome, Bart."

"I know I can do this, dude. I am so geeked. I gotta stay focused. I'm holding off on taking a job with my dad's construction company. If I don't make one of the Opens in the next couple of years, it will be too late for me. This is my time now." He took a chomp from the sandwich and plopped it back down on the paper plate, zeroing in on a sheet of wallet-sized photos that had *Dave & Busters* boldly displayed across the bottom of each.

"Who's in the picture, Bas?"

"Oh, that's Courtney."

"Courtney," he said, shaking his head and chugging down another bite of the over-half-eaten sandwich and cramming chips into whatever empty space was left in his mouth. "Is she in one of your study groups?"

"No, she's my friend."

"Figures, you always were the most popular guy on campus. You always had tons of friends."

"She's not that kind of friend, she's a *fffriendd.*"

"What do you mean *fffriendd?* You don't mean a girlfriend!"

"Yes and no."

"No way, dude. She can't be your girlfriend."

"She isn't, not yet." He hadn't been able to see her in six weeks and ached for her presence. He had left messages, but she hadn't returned any of his calls. He didn't feel hopeless. He had grown up believing he could have whatever he wanted, could go anywhere and do anything. Once he accepted the Lord in college, he realized there were only certain places he wanted to be and a limited number of things he wanted to do. Knowing the Lord hadn't reduced his possibilities, just brought them into focus. In spite of what it looked like at the moment, he had faith that it would work out with Courtney. The peace that he felt was from God, something his father's money couldn't buy. "Well, she was like my girlfriend about a month ago, but she's not seeing me right now."

"Whoa, and my dad thinks I'm screwed up. You're really cruising for a bruising from your old man, Bas. Why can't I have a brother like you? You would make me look like the family star. First you totally flip out and get into this religious cult stuff and your parents lose it. Now, you're seeing a black chick. I bet your parents are *totally* losing it over you and her." He wiped his mouth with a napkin, balled it up, and tossed it onto the plate, which only had a few traces of lettuce and a few chip crumbs remaining.

"I haven't told them yet. I was waiting to tell them in person, when I go home for Thanksgiving. But what can they do? I like her and I'm going after her. I don't care what they say about it."

"I hear you, dude, but you have to tell me, how is she?"

"She's beautiful. She's smart, she's funny, and she's wonderful. No, she's *amazing!*"

"Come on, dude, you know what I mean, how is she?"

"What do you mean?"

"How is she in bed?"

"I have no idea."

"Oh, come on, you can tell me. We've swapped stories since freshman year in boarding school about everything, no sense buttoning up now. Come on, tell me."

"She's not like that. I'm not like that."

"I don't believe it, you're not going to tell me. Dude, it's me, Bart. Are they really as wild as they say?"

"I'm telling you, she's not like that," he said in a crisp voice, enunciating every word.

"Oh, come on. Every woman can be like that, especially the black chicks, I hear."

"Not every woman and definitely not Courtney, you moron, and I don't personally know every woman. Do you!"

"Whoa, listen to yourself, dude. You're like totally defensive. You've really fallen for this chick!"

"There's no one in the entire world like Courtney Young, no one."

"So how long are you going to try and sway her? There must be plenty of other babes at Penn if she won't give in."

"I'm not trying to sway her!"

"If it's not physical, what other reason could you possibly have for seeing her? You can't possibly be serious about her. That would be totally insane."

"Why would it be insane?"

"Because you are a Whittington. The only black people your family knows are the ones who work at your parents' house. You're from a rich family. Dude, there's no way your parents are going to let this happen."

"I've seen a lot more of the world than Boston. I have news for you, Bart. There are blacks everywhere. There's more people of color in the world than there are of us from European backgrounds."

"No way, dude. Even if it were true, doesn't mean crap. Our world is from Boston to Maine, old money and our parents. They call the shots."

"They can't stop me from seeing her if I want to see her."

"Sure they can. One swift stroke of the pen and, my boy, you're out of the will and the firm. Now let's be reasonable, no black chick is worth that much."

Sebastian knew that regardless of how he tried to articulate his feelings for Courtney, Bart wouldn't be able to understand the magnitude of his love and desire for her. Sometimes it was overwhelming to himself. If it hadn't been for God giving him the heart for her and confirmation in his spirit that she was the one for him, he probably would have found it hard to believe as well.

Chapter 31

It was getting late and she hadn't heard from Roger yet. It was only a matter of time. He would be calling. He had consistently done it since they started going out three weeks ago, even when he had to work late, like tonight. They didn't have much time together during the workweek, but lunches and weekends were commonplace. Being senior vice president came with a price, which could only be paid by sacrificing significant chunks of personal time, a price she wasn't ready to pay in her career yet.

She saw him as the complete package, fine, built, hardworking, intellectually brilliant, knew the Lord, and thank goodness, he was black. What more could she ask for in a man? He was a far cry from Paul. He didn't set off a spark with the mere touch of his hand like Sebastian did from the beginning. Then again, she couldn't compare them. One was an apple and the other an orange. Passion could come in time.

She pulled the blanket up across her shoulders and stretched out on the couch.

At nine-thirty the phone rang. Courtney answered it.

"Hello, you, right on time, as usual."

"Right on time for what?" Sebastian asked.

"Sebastian," she said, and let silence claim the moment, "it's good to hear from you."

She wanted to say hi, Sebastian. I am so glad you called. I've missed you like crazy. My project is going so well. I've already gotten the approval from Sheila to do my first marketing test plan. I am so excited. I can't wait to see you. I have so much to tell you. So much catching up to do, but she couldn't. Leave it like it was. "School going okay for you?"

Courtney's phone clicked, signaling that another call was coming in. She ignored it.

"It is. Not as much fun without you around. You're the life of the party."

She couldn't forget the first time they met at D&B, back in August. It didn't seem like three months ago, but it was. She closed her eyes and soared back to Penn Treaty Park. She held on to the memory. It was the first time she had glimpsed him as a man, not as a white man or black man, just a man.

"How about getting together over the next couple of days, before the holiday?"

"Nah, I won't be able to. I'm kind of seeing someone now."

"Oh, I see. Wow, I shouldn't be surprised. You are such an incredible woman. Who's the happy fellow?"

"Roger is an investment banker downtown."

"Roger, another business guy, can't get away from us types, can you?"

"I guess not." She could hear the disappointment in his voice. It hurt her to hurt him, but it was better to let him know now, before she got too far down the romantic road with Roger. "How are you, Sebastian, really?"

"Life is good, God is good."

"What are you doing for Thanksgiving?"

"I'm leaving for Boston Thanksgiving Day. Since you've never been to Boston, why don't you come with me?"

Her phone clicked again.

"What a sweet offer but I can't. One of my relatives might be coming from Detroit. We're having dinner at Aunt Sis's and I have to be there. You know how she is." Courtney wanted to snatch her words back but they were too far gone. Of all people, Sebastian knew too well how Aunt Sis could get. "I mean . . ." she began clarifying.

"It's okay, Courtney. I understand. Your aunt loves you and deep down she only wants the best for you. She just doesn't know what that is yet."

She wanted to elaborate and savor this time with Sebastian, but knew eventually the call, like the friendship, had to end. They talked for a little longer and said their good-byes.

She hadn't considered answering the incoming calls when Sebastian was on the line. If it was the same person calling, they had made several attempts to get through. She dialed the code to get the number of the last incoming call that she'd missed. It was Roger's number. She called him back.

"Did you call?"

"Sure did, lovely lady. I got in about an hour ago and tried to call you a couple of times."

"I'm sorry. I was on the phone with an old friend. I've known him since our freshman year at Northwestern."

"It's a him, hmm. Must be a good friend if you didn't want to interrupt the call."

"Don't worry, he's not my type."

"I'm hoping that I'm your type."

"Just might be."

"That's good news."

"Although I'd have to forgive you for not eating barbecued chicken pizza with pineapples and for being a Republican. Can you believe this? I didn't know any black Republicans until I went to college and met a bunch of black kids from families with money."

"I'm conservative but I wouldn't call myself a Republican. Actually, if I have to be labeled it would be Independent."

"Independent! Those are the little groups that wanna be political. They write their names in on Election Day and just hold up the voting line."

"Somebody should hold up the line."

"Yeah, right."

"Seriously. We need to make politicians accountable. My parents have always voted Democrat, regardless of who the candidate is or what they represent. Sometimes it has been a good choice and sometimes it hasn't."

"Mine do the same thing."

"Many blacks do, and sometimes the party takes it for granted. How many times have you seen the politicians flock to our churches around election time making all kinds of promises and then you don't see them again for another four years?"

"Reverend Tyler was just talking about that a few months ago."

"Is that why you go Independent or Republican?"

"I don't vote straight Republican either. They definitely don't meet all of my needs. They usually talk about cutting taxes, which I like."

"Especially for someone who makes as much as you do."

"Yes, the tax cuts are good, when they actually do them. But the problem is that right after they cut taxes, they give big corporations billions of dollars in breaks. Then they turn around and vote to cut out the two dollars' worth of social programs poor people need."

"Don't I know. The folks in my old neighborhood are always complaining about some meal plan or after-school program shutting down, but I don't see how any of those programs would affect somebody like you who is in such a high-income range."

"Every month I have to send my grandparents money because their prescriptions eat up their entire Social Security checks."

Courtney could relate because she remembered her parents used to talk about Aunt Cat having the same problem before she passed, except there was no one to send her money regularly.

"This is what you'd call the pains of African-American success."

"What do you mean?"

"We're getting educated, making more money. Our socioeconomic status is improving. Many of us are probably better off voting with the wealthy people, but the rest of our family is still in the trenches. That requires us to vote along liberal lines so they can get the government help they need."

"We're split down the middle."

"You got it. That's why I'm Independent. I vote on a case-by-case basis. I'm not automatically voting Democrat because I'm black and I'm definitely not voting Republican just because I have a six-figure net worth. Whoever gets my vote will have to meet my needs and my grandparents'."

"That's going to be hard to do."

"Well, one day I'll have to write my own name on the ballot."

"Go for it. You have my vote."

"Good, I'll keep that in mind. By the way, I can't make lunch tomorrow or Wednesday. The CFO is coming down from Wall Street right after the holiday and I need time to get my team ready. I know we don't usually go out on weeknights, but I would love to take you out tomorrow evening for a late dinner."

"Ah, I won't be able to go tomorrow. I've already committed to go to this Love Exchange at the Carver Center out in Norristown. My sorority sponsors a free day of shopping for the people in the community before the holiday. I have to help out. You're welcome to come with me."

"Go on without me. I'll see you afterward, or what about Wednesday night? We're having a special Thanksgiving service at my church. Why don't you come with me?"

"I can't. I promised to help Aunt Sis with the Thanksgiving dinner."

"The one that I'll be eating with with you?"

"That's the one."

"Well, I don't want to disrupt those plans, but one of these days you'll have to break away from Fifth Baptist and come to church with me."

"I will," she promised, and they talked a short while longer before concluding the call. She wondered how Faith Christian Center was getting along. She was becoming a regular there and missed going with Sebastian. No need to dwell. The dust was settling. Roger was the man of the hour. Her parents had met him when they were in town a few weeks ago and seemed to like him. Aunt Sis had heard nothing but wonderful things about him, and taking him to Fifth Baptist required no effort. It was all working out. She liked him too. What wasn't to like? Like could go a long way in a relationship. Perhaps passion was overrated.

Chapter 32

Sebastian hailed the cab knowing his mother would have a fit about him not calling the family driver to pick him up. He preferred to let George enjoy his holiday, but he would try to be somewhat considerate of his mother's feelings by not getting a yellow-colored cab. Any other color wouldn't look quite as bad pulling up to the house. Either way, she would get over it. She always did when he bucked tradition and went his own way. Repetition in the Whittingtons' world wasn't habit, more a way of life. Who he mingled with, where and what he ate, when, where, and how he traveled was already predetermined for him. He was a Whittington.

He took the twenty-minute ride from Boston's Logan Airport to the suburban Brookline area, a place where the average price of a home was well over a million dollars. The driver eased up the slight incline on the narrow circular drive. He stopped in front of the solid wood door serving as the gateway into the two-story brick home, which was visible from the street until the spring, when the patch of trees lining the perimeter redressed itself.

He paid the driver, giving him a five-dollar tip, and slung his duffel bag over his shoulder. The crisp fall New England air, which had traveled the short distance from the bay, had his nostrils throbbing. The air was fit for narrow-nosed aristocratic blue bloods, the natives who could trace their ancestry back to the *Mayflower.* An imposter, with nostrils wide enough to absorb the heat and dust from the African desert, would find it difficult to breathe comfortably. There were other parts of town more palatable for the less discerning nostril. He rubbed his nose and sniffed. Maybe he would take a walk over to George's area later, and say hello. The air wasn't quite as sharp in that part of town.

He walked up the side doorway and entered the house through the service door located next to the three-car garage. George wasn't in but more than likely, Shirley was. How else would they eat Thanksgiving dinner? The closest his mother had gotten to cooking a meal was making popcorn and brownies with him when he was a child. If there was to be food on the table today, Shirley was cooking it. He walked through the mudroom, leaving his coat and shoes, past the laundry room, the indoor gym, the butler's pantry, and into the kitchen. There she stood, a short stocky black woman whose sixty-five years had been kind to her. No wrinkles in her face or hunch in her back. A few strands of gray were the only clue that she was over forty-five. She had said over and over that her black skin protected her from the sun. That's the way she was made. She told him that's why black women didn't show their age so fast. Guess she was right.

"Shirleyyy."

"Sebastian, my baby."

Hugs and kisses commenced.

She was like a second mom, or would that be a third mom, since his first mom had died and his stepmom was his second mom. Whichever, Shirley had been around all of his life. She had known his real mom and used to tell him stories about her when he was younger. He often tried to draw her in his mind since there were no pictures of her in the house. Apparently his father took the grief hard and couldn't handle any lingering memories. Every childhood photo he had was with his dad and second mom. He never knew his real mom, but it would have been nice if his dad had kept just one picture to solidify her in his mind. Shirley was his memory bank. When he wanted to know something, he'd have to ask her. Problem was, as he got older, he stopped asking and she stopped telling.

"Where are the folks?"

"Getting dressed for dinner." She gave him a light spank on the behind. "You better do the same."

"Be right down."

He went up to greet his parents and to get dressed. A half hour later, they all came down for the three o'clock dinner. The formal dining room was the size of a classroom with a twelve-seat table in the middle. Every holiday Sebastian wondered why they had to eat at the huge table when there were only three of them. Shirley and George never ate with them because they preferred eating at home with their own families. There weren't any other close relatives, and if there were, he didn't know about them. Cousins didn't count. Unless your name was in the will, you weren't considered a close relative. They were too far removed from the inheritance pool.

Mrs. Whittington had prepared the Thanksgiving menu with poached pears and poppy-seed dressing over a bed of field greens and pumpkin bisque for starters, followed by rack of lamb, red roasted potatoes, asparagus with hollandaise sauce, and sealing the meal with homemade pumpkin pie. Sebastian could count on Shirley to sneak in a piece of sweet potato pie and corn-bread dressing for him every holiday. In the breadbasket was where he would collect his treat later in the evening.

Shirley served the food while the family talked, careful not to distract. Sebastian suspected that she was listening but not listening. It was probably a trait she had mastered over her twenty-seven years of service in the Whittington home. She had access to his father's personal office and papers. It wouldn't surprise him if she knew more than he did about the family, even the confidential stuff.

"I hardly hear from you anymore."

"Mom, you call me every other day and I can't always get back to you right away."

"I can't believe you're too busy for your mother."

Sebastian was sensitive when it came to dealing with his mother. She was a housewife who filled her time with the Rotary Club, numerous charities, a couple of hobby classes, and an intense workout program. Shirley ran the house taking care of the shopping, the cooking, the laundry, and the cleaning. Dad wasn't able to spend much time with his mother because he had to run the practice during the day and hobnob with other influential men in the business during the evening hours. Networking was part of the job. Mom tried to busy herself, but Sebastian realized her gaps of loneliness were reduced when he stayed in constant contact. He'd done the best he could for years, but that wasn't feasible now. He was a man and had to spend time building his own life.

"Tell us, darling, what has kept you so terribly occupied in Philadelphia?" Mrs. Whittington asked while cutting the piece of lamb on her plate.

"You can't be as challenged in business school as you would be in law school."

"I'm challenged just fine, Dad, and Mom, I'm keeping quite busy."

"You don't share information with me like you used to do before you went off to boarding school," Mrs. Whittington told Sebastian.

"Mom, I was a kid then."

"I'm still your mother. It's important for us to communicate."

"Mom, as much as I'd like to be in touch more, it's difficult to share every detail of my life with you over the phone, every other day."

"Precisely why you need to come home more often. I don't know why you couldn't have gone to Harvard, for goodness' sake." She took a sip of water from the crystal glass. "We miss having you here, don't we, dear?" she directed to her husband.

"Tell me, how was the game last month?"

"Excellent! The seats were wonderful, Dad."

"Don't keep us in suspense. Tell us about the young lady from Northwestern."

Sebastian set the fork next to his plate. "Courtney is an incredible person."

"Courtney, that's the first time we've heard her name. Courtney what?" Mrs. Whittington asked.

"Courtney Young."

"Young? I don't recognize her surname. Where in Europe is her family from?" Mr. Whittington inquired.

"I have no idea."

"No idea. Didn't you find that out first?" Mrs. Whittington wanted to know.

"Sure didn't, no reason to. I like her regardless of where her family came from. As a matter of fact, she's never been to Europe."

"That's hard to believe, but I've heard several members of the Rotary Club talk about family members who have yet to take their voyage to Europe to partake of their lineage. Perhaps Courtney will get a chance to do just that now with the two of you being together. Perhaps you will give her a guided tour since you have traveled extensively throughout Europe."

"I would love nothing better than to take her to Europe and the rest of the world too."

"This sounds serious, honey. We need to meet this Courtney and her parents."

"What type of business is her father in?" Mr. Whittington asked.

"They just retired from the gas and electric company."

"CEO, CFO, what?"

"Call taker supervisor."

"Call taker? I don't understand."

"They supervised a group of people who answered the phone when customers called in."

"I still don't understand. Was he a hands-on officer? Is that what you're having difficulty articulating?"

"Who is this 'they' you keep referring to?" Mrs. Whittington asked.

"They are Mr. and Mrs. Young."

"Surely, you don't mean the mother worked?"

"That's exactly what I mean, she did work."

"Settle down, Elizabeth. They probably owned some type of contracting service."

"No, it wasn't a contracting service, Dad. They were regular employees with the gas and electric company."

Mrs. Whittington choked on the asparagus and coughed several times, using the napkin to cover her mouth. "Shirley, could you please be a gem and bring me another napkin?"

"Yes, ma'am."

"It's becoming clear that we don't know anything about this girl."

"Son, not every family with a European heritage is appropriate for our family. There are people in this country that might look like us, but don't have the same, well, let's say, way of life," Mr. Whittington informed Sebastian.

"You mean not every white girl is appropriate for me, with our money and all."

"Excellent interpretation, counselor, hard to suppress those legal genes." Mr. Whittington laid his napkin on the table and leaned back in the armchair situated at the head of the table. "Working class and poor people can't appreciate the training and exposure you've had. I'm sure she's a blond beauty, but—"

"Dear!"

"It's okay, Elizabeth. It's okay, son, to spend your youthful years passing the time. You just can't marry someone like that."

"Well, I was going to suggest that both families take a trip to Europe together in the spring to get more acquainted. In light of this new information, that doesn't seem appropriate," Mrs. Whittington said.

"I still want to take Courtney to Paris or Rome in the spring if she'll go."

"Why wouldn't she? Women like her don't get many opportunities to travel, not like you have." She took a bite of the roasted potatoes. "If you must go on this, excursion, for goodness' sake take her somewhere more amenable, like an island or even Hawaii. Take her to a place where she wouldn't have to adjust to a foreign culture."

Shirley walked around the table refilling the water glasses.

"She wants to visit the African part of her heritage first."

"Africa! Is she Dutch from South Africa?" Mr. Whittington asked.

"No, just black from west Philadelphia."

His father looked up without saying a word.

"Sebastian, that's not funny! You've pulled so many preposterous feats. I thought you might be serious. Thank goodness you're joking," Mrs. Whittington said, fanning herself with the lined napkin.

"I'm serious."

"I mean it, Sebastian, let's not joke like this. I'm not finding this little session humorous."

"It's not supposed to be humorous, Mother. I am serious. Courtney is black."

"A black girl!"

"Elizabeth," Mr. Whittington said in a lowered tone, "let's talk about this after Shirley leaves. I don't want her to be offended."

The three ate their dinner with limited small talk. Shirley checked in periodically to see what needed refilling. When the plates were empty, she asked if they wanted more food brought to the table.

"No, Shirley, we're finished here. We'll take dessert in the parlor," Mrs. Whittington told her.

The group dragged to the parlor with no sign of enthusiasm. Shirley brought three slices of pumpkin pie and a squirt of whipped cream on the side into the parlor, handing one to each person. She set the silver platter holding the rest of the pie on the service cart.

"Excuse me," Shirley said, cutting into the silence, "do you mind if I leave after I finish the dishes? I would like to get home in time to have dinner with my family. We have about thirty people at my house waiting for me. I sure would appreciate leaving a little early."

"Don't worry about it, Shirley, I'll clean up," Sebastian offered.

"No, you won't," Shirley declined.

"Yes, I will, Shirley. I don't have anything else to do. Really, it's fine."

Mr. Whittington stepped in. "He's right. Go on home, Shirley, we'll be fine. Have a happy Thanksgiving and give Fred my regards."

"Thank you, Mr. Whittington. I will tell my husband you said hello, and, Sebastian, thank you for washing the dishes for me. I surely appreciate you doing them."

Sebastian got up to give Shirley a hug and to say bye personally. She gathered her belongings and made a final pass to the parlor. "Excuse me again, Mr. and Mrs. Whittington, I'll lock up the guest house and the garage when I leave, but my key is getting a little worn. Could you please pick me up a new one sometime next week, please?"

"Absolutely, Shirley," Mrs. Whittington assured her. "Now you go and enjoy the holiday with your family."

"Thank you and I'll see you tomorrow."

When the door closed, the family knew Shirley was gone and the conversation could be taken off pause.

"Honey, how can she be a black girl! Is this one of those rebellious phases? Why would you want to do something so outrageous? She can't be black. There must be some mistake." She slapped her linen napkin on her lap.

"Why not, Mom? What does it matter to you who I date?"

"It matters. We have so much at stake. The livelihood of our family is contingent upon you finishing law school, coming home, marrying well to carry on the family values, and taking over Whittington and Whittington some day. That's always been the plan for you. A black woman doesn't fit into the equation."

"Is my happiness part of the equation?"

"Don't you do that!" she cried out. "Don't try and make me be the bad person in this. You created this situation, Sebastian. You have to take ownership."

"Exactly what situation are you referring to, Mom?"

"Where did we go wrong? How could we fail you so horribly? I cannot believe that you hate us this much," she said, pushing past the sobbing.

She grabbed another napkin off the service cart.

"What are you talking about?"

"You're no longer worshipping in the faith we raised you in. You take off and travel around the world. You were in some godforsaken dump in Africa, putting all of us at risk when you were out there sleeping in the same places as those AIDS people, when you should have been in law school preparing to come home and join the family practice. You waste time blowing that toy you call a trumpet, for trinkets and baubles in those god-awful venues."

"They're called gigs, Mom, and I happen to enjoy playing my trumpet with a band every chance I get. It's a gift, a God-given talent."

"Don't you dare bring up God. We were the ones who spent money on lessons for you, letting you follow your childhood whim. Perhaps it is our fault. We let you have too much latitude in your development and this is how you repay us, with an African-black woman!"

"It's African-American or black, Mother."

"What's the difference? Half the time those people don't know themselves who they are. This is not what we want for you," she told him. Then: "Aren't you going to say something?" she asked her husband.

"No."

"I can't believe you're okay with this startling revelation that our son has brought home for the holiday."

"I'm not okay with it."

"So say something, for goodness' sake. Do something!"

"It's just a passing fancy. It's not serious. Dear, it's an exercise in testosterone."

"Excuse me but you're talking as if I'm not sitting here. Courtney is not an exercise in testosterone. She is an intelligent and beautiful woman who I happen to be madly in love with."

"That's not possible. You've never been around those people for any sizable period of time, except for Shirley and George, and they don't count. They're different, we're different," Mrs. Whittington said.

"You're like oil and vinegar, you might mix for a second but given enough time you'll separate. We have invested a fortune in your education. Surely you can't be serious. I won't tolerate this." Mr. Whittington scowled.

"What is this, a dictatorship? You cannot tell me who I can and can't see."

"This better be a passing fancy. Do you understand the damage such reckless abandonment would cause the family? You're my only child, my only heir. You have obligations."

"I didn't ask to be born into your family."

"I didn't ask for you either."

"Sebastian!" Mrs. Whittington cried out to her husband.

"But I deal with it. That's what we Whittingtons do. We make a wrong situation right. That's what you have to do with this business of yours. You could *never* work in our firm with a black women on your arm and in your bed."

"I'm okay with that! Law school is your plan for me. It's never been mine."

He scooted his chair back and stormed out the service door, snatching his coat off the hook in the mudroom, barely avoiding sending the intercom box crashing to the floor.

"Sebastian, wait," Mrs. Whittington yelled.

"Let him go. He'll be back."

"What makes you so sure?"

"He's a Whittington, where else can he go!"

The air was still jagged, but not as much as inside the house. The day would have to come when his parents accepted him for who he was and what he wanted. God had given him confirmation about Courtney. Given the choice, he was going to have to side with his loving father in heaven over the angry one in the house. Courtney's love wasn't going to come easy. There was a price to be paid.

What was she doing at this very minute? He wanted to bring her to Boston. Not to meet the family but to show her the sights. To see the Boston he knew. The one where they could find a quaint spot and let the bay and the wind play rhythmic tunes with the rocks on percussion. They could go downtown where the feel of intellectualism oozed out of every corner, since the city was overrun with top-tier schools. But an ice cream parlor, bookstore, and seafood restaurant on every corner helped to keep balance for the regular people. The aura of Europe with the narrow alleylike roads, cobblestone walkways, and generous helpings of imitation-glass lanterns created Christmas card material. That's what he loved about Boston. It was a book that couldn't be judged by its cover. It appeared to be one way on the surface. But when he took time to dig into the heart of the city and to get to know its soul, it was a treasure, just like his Courtney Young. The very thought of her seeing this Roger was confirmation to him that she didn't know how much he was willing to endure, just to be with her. She had to know and God had to be the one to tell her.

Chapter 33

The Youngs knew how to throw a get-together, and holidays were no exception. Courtney invited Roger to dinner with her family when he had decided, two weeks ago, not to take the six-hour bi-coastal flight home for Thanksgiving. He would go home for Christmas instead.

The couple turned onto Aunt Sis's block by two-thirty, in plenty of time for the three o'clock feasting hour. Courtney knew Aunt Sis's neighborhood as home, but didn't expect others to feel comfortable on the first visit. That had been an understatement for Sebastian. Wonder what he was doing in Boston. She stopped trying to put him out of her mind. All efforts to abandon her memories with him were fruitless. Whenever a thought of him came up, she let it run its course, each time leaving an affectionate feeling as payment.

Courtney and Roger inched along the street looking for a parking spot.

"This reminds me of my old neighborhood back home."

"I thought you grew up in the suburbs," she said.

"My parents moved to the suburbs when I was in high school. I lived in the ghetto before that."

"Ghetto! I didn't know that. How did you end up in Philadelphia for college?"

"My father was a big fan of college basketball and I played a little bit in high school. We were hoping I'd get a chance to try out for John Chaney's program."

Courtney saw a tight spot three doors from her aunt's house and pointed it out to Roger.

"Did you play?"

"No, I didn't. Me and forty other players had the same idea and they were a lot better than I was. I didn't make the team but it all worked out anyway. I got my degree in economics and went on to business school. The rest is history."

Economics was the same undergrad degree as Sebastian. What a coincidence. He was going to laugh when she told him. *Oh, that's right,* she remembered. They weren't talking, and on top of that, why would he want to know about some other guy? She was just so accustomed to sharing every tidbit in her day with him.

"So you're glad that you went to Temple?"

"Sure am. How else would I have met Edwin and eight years later meet you?"

Courtney exhaled.

He shut the engine off, put the parking brake on the Porsche Boxter, and unsnapped his driving gloves. He reached into the backseat to get the wrapped package. "Ready?"

Courtney was becoming familiar with his style. She waited in the car until he came around and opened her door. She clutched his hand as he extended it to help her out of the car. Arms locked in his, she strutted the short walk to Aunt Sis's and glided up the stairs like a princess being escorted by her prince.

She pushed the door open and announced they were coming in. Aunt Sis came into the front room for the introductions.

"Come on in here and get yourself a seat."

"Thank you for letting me share Thanksgiving dinner with your family. I am truly grateful. This is for you," Roger said, holding out the box.

"My goodness, what's this?" She brushed her hands along her apron several times before reaching for the gift. "You didn't have to bring anything."

"It's the least I could do."

Courtney took his coat and put it in the tiny closet near the door.

Aunt Sis ripped the paper off the gift and opened the lid. She dug into the mound of colorful tissue paper and drew in a deep breath.

"Oh my, this is something. Oh my. Thank you, Roger. You really didn't have to do this." She pulled the crystal from the box, and the ceiling light hit it, sending rainbows racing around the living room and dining room walls.

The door opened and it was Edwin. "Hey now, what's up, man?"

The two men embraced with a covered shake and hug combination. Edwin resorted to a hug for Courtney and a kiss on the cheek for his mother.

"Where's Jamal? He's always the last one," Edwin said.

"One of these times we're going to start without him."

"Yeah, sure, Mama. You always say it and every time you make us wait until your baby boy gets here. We're used to it."

"Well, he's still my baby. I'm going to look out for him when nobody else will. That's what a mama does. You know I'll do the same for you."

Regardless of how many times Jamal went to court, Aunt Sis was always in the front row with other mothers who got there the best way they could in order to be the one light of love in an otherwise dark legal system. Unconditional love didn't need to know the charge. It didn't need to know guilt or innocence. It didn't need to sit in judgment. It just needed to be what it was, pure, giving the ability to love without condoning the mistake. Funny thing about love, it didn't seem to play by society's rules. Aunt Sis was a master when it came to Jamal.

"Just don't let me starve. That's all I ask."

She leaned on the dining room chair and grinned. "Don't worry, he always shows up just in time."

Roger, Edwin, and Courtney stood around the dining room talking while Aunt Sis kept busy. The table was overflowing, but she managed to carve out space between the macaroni and cheese and the turkey stuffing to squeeze in the cinnamon-sprinkled yams.

"I was hoping your parents would change their mind and come on up anyway," she directed to Courtney.

"I talked to them yesterday. They're tired from all the running around they've been doing. They close on the new house tomorrow and Daddy didn't feel like getting up at two o'clock in the morning to drive back down there in time for their appointment."

"I forgot about the house."

"You know that I would have gone down there, but they're staying at Aunt Cat's house until they move into the new place this weekend. Between them and Nee-Nee's kids in there, I bet it's pretty tight," Courtney said. "I thought Big Mama was coming for Thanksgiving."

"If Cousin Emma's coming, it will be on Saturday, and that's a big if. She's taking the train from Detroit and it stops in Chicago. She's having Thanksgiving with her granddaughter and might stay there a while and come here afterward. She's not sure yet." She continued sliding the dishes around the table. "You ever been to North Carolina, Roger?"

"No, Mrs. Williams, I haven't. Mr. and Mrs. Young invited me to come visit once they get settled in their new house. I look forward to taking them up on their offer."

"You do that, because, honey, let me tell you, they sure like you. I don't know what you said to them, but they sure fell in love with you. They all but have Courtney married off to you."

"Aunt Sis!"

"What? I'm just saying what they said. That's nothing to be ashamed about. If you find a good man, keep him, isn't that right, Roger?"

"Yes, Mrs. Williams, I believe it is."

"Ohhh, please don't encourage her."

Aunt Sis stood in the dining room looking at her masterpiece. "Come on in the kitchen with me, Courtney. I could use a little help."

Life was back to normal in the Young family. The hurricane that blew in with Sebastian had passed, and Courtney knew Aunt Sis probably had a few lingering clouds of distaste, but overall, it was blue skies. After that horrific Sunday, she didn't bring his name up and Aunt Sis didn't either. It was better that way.

"Oooo-weee, he is a good-looking man," Aunt Sis said in a low voice as soon as she cleared the kitchen doorway. "Umph, umph, umph and he's got that big-time job. I can tell he knows how to treat a woman. Your mama says he goes to church too?"

"He knows the Lord."

Aunt Sis rocked her head, leaning against the counter. "She didn't know if he had any kids."

"He doesn't have any kids," Courtney told her aunt.

"He got another woman?"

"Not that I know of."

"That means no. A man like him wouldn't need to tip around with no woman. If he had somebody he'd have told you up front so you could know your place. No kids, no other women, and he's black," Aunt Sis said, and cut her eyes through Courtney and quickly returned to her cooking. "He got it all. You can't ask for any more in a man. Girl, you better not let this one get away. His kind doesn't show up every day, take it from your old aunt, who knows what she's talking about."

"I thought Paul was your favorite."

"He was, yesterday. Don't get me wrong, Paul's a nice boy, but Roger is a man. Paul will make a good husband for somebody down the road, just not you. You need more than he's got to offer. I see that now. You know Youngs don't marry low. We were always taught that we were going somewhere, and to marry somebody who didn't mind going with us."

"When did your opinion about Paul change?"

"After seeing your husband standing out there."

"Aunt Sis, don't say that."

"What! Claim him, girl, claim him before someone comes along and snatches him right out from under you."

Roger was one of the classics. Courtney liked him and enjoyed his company. He was more than Paul but he wasn't Sebastian, the one who ignited something deep inside and it wouldn't go out. Sebastian made her laugh when she felt like crying. He was a friend, a peer, and her equal. Roger was more like a mentor, kind of like a male Sheila. Ah, what a thought. Too bad she'd already wasted him.

"Women nowadays don't sit back and wait for a man to come to them. You should see the women chasing Edwin. It's a good thing he's not loose and giving in to all of these old wild women. Thank goodness my baby's got some sense."

Courtney thought about Sheila. She wasn't chasing Edwin and he didn't seem to be chasing her either. That's why they weren't getting anywhere.

"Paul's going to be hurt. He really likes you, Aunt Sis."

"I like him too. That hasn't changed. He's still welcome in my house and I can't say that for everybody," Aunt Sis said, opening the oven door and pulling out the hot rack of rolls and golden brown corn bread. "Paul just has to call first." She dumped the bread into a big bowl layered with a thin kitchen towel.

If only Sebastian were half as welcome. Such a reception would take a miracle, the kind requiring big, big faith along the lines of parting the Schuylkill River or raising up everybody in Burks Funeral Home. She knew about the miracles in the Bible, but those kinds just weren't happening every day around Philadelphia.

"Aunt Sis, that is so wrong," she said, chuckling.

Aunt Sis cut the corn bread into squares and ran the butter knife around the edge, to loosen any sections attached to the pan. One quick flip and the bread fell from the basket into the serving bowl.

"Hey, this train has to keep on rolling. Now let's go feed those hungry men out there before they get up and leave. Then we'll both be looking around like we've lost our minds."

The ladies each took a bowl into the dining room and wedged them on the crowded table. The door flew open and "Hey, hey, hey" flooded the living room.

Courtney looked at her watch. Three o'clock, right on time. Aunt Sis's face said it all. Courtney was glad to see her cousin too. He was one less man that she had to worry about, worry where he was and what he was doing for the holiday, leaving only one man that she cared about unaccounted for. Sebastian was someone far away, but close.

"Finally, now can we eat," Edwin said as the group took their seats around the table.

Chapter 34

Character was what Courtney liked about Roger's three-story brown-stone located in the upscale section of Center City, the heart of downtown Philadelphia. Her entire apartment could fit into his living room and dining room with space left over. The thick sofa and matching armchairs would have been swallowed up in his living room, large enough to comfortably hold five sets of furniture, had it not been for the Persian rugs sectioning off the sitting area, and large pieces of artwork and sculptures framing the space. Roger kept his home meticulous, which wasn't difficult to do with a housekeeper coming in weekly.

Courtney sat in what she had proclaimed as her chair, with one leg tucked under the other. She couldn't believe it had already been two months since she and Roger met for lunch the first time. From that moment on, their time together had been pleasant, like a gourmet meal with several courses, light lunches for the appetizer, theater after theater for the salad, well-seasoned conversation for the entrée, sprinkled with class and maturity, winding up with encouragement and support for the dessert. There wasn't a thing wrong with him.

Every time Courtney looked at Roger, he was attentive, absorbing every word she spoke. He was one of the nice ones and she studied him in amazement. He had already accomplished so much in his thirty years, a senior vice president. She hadn't been able to ignite that special feeling for him, but they did have God in common. Maybe that was the way to bridge some of the gap she was experiencing in their recent meetings. If God had put them together, the details would work out. She relaxed into her chair and let Roger continue along his normal course.

"Right after the new year I have to go to London for a business meeting. Why don't you come with me? We can hop over to Switzerland for the weekend. They have great skiing there."

Courtney rubbed her leg, which was peeking from under her pants, and thought back to Sebastian and the stories he had told her about skiing. She had told him it was too cold for her to be in the middle of some snowcapped anything, trying to ski. She did have to admit that the part about sitting in front of a fireplace drinking a mug of hot apple cider was tempting. She had told Sebastian black folks didn't ski. Maybe it was just the black people she knew, the ones who came from no money. Clearly she had been wrong. She'd have to correct herself with Sebastian some day. Roger had many traits similar to Sebastian. The only major differences were the color of their skin and the strength of their sparks.

"Ah, I can't go. I have a few tight deadlines next week, and I already have plans the first weekend in January. Remember I told you my sorority is having our Founders Day celebration that weekend?"

"That's right, you're still into college activities."

"This is a graduate chapter, not an undergrad one!"

Courtney just knew she and Roger would agree on most issues. Why not? They were born-again believers, submerged in corporate America, making good money, holding degrees from top-notch institutions, coming from solid families rooted in the community, and both black. Let Aunt Sis tell it, they were cut from the same cloth. The list of commonalities was long enough to make them identical twins, and in sync in the necessary areas. His comment about the sorority threw another bucket of sand on the flickering light, which had been trying to get started.

"I'm sorry. I didn't mean that it's just for young people. You know what I mean. I didn't mean anything by it," he said, taking her hand.

"I know. You're just an old man with this young woman," she said with a tinge of humor, while rolling his comment around in her mind. They did have at least one area of significant difference. He was older and might even be smarter, but she didn't like how his words often made her feel the distinction in their relationship. She was glaringly different from Sebastian, but he never made her feel the difference. People on the outside of their relationship had turned the racial knife in her gut, making her feel uncomfortable, but never Sebastian. He did just the opposite by building her up and making her feel exceptional, not inadequate or inferior. She was pretty sure Roger didn't mean to come across in a condescending way, but it was what it was.

He caressed her hand in his. "Beautiful and intelligent woman."

Courtney tried to let her shoulders relax back into place.

"If you want to come to London with me, you're invited," he said.

"Thanks for the invitation, but I think I'll pass. You'll get much more done if you don't have to cart me around. I'm sure you'll have a lot of work to do."

"You're right about the work but the offer stands if you want to change your mind. It will be difficult not having you around for the weekend." He took her hand again and wrapped his arms around her shoulders. "I'll be gone for the weekend, but don't get too comfortable without me. If I have to, I'll come and get you."

The words resonated and took her deep inside. Settling for a man just because he was wonderful wasn't much better than staying with Paul when he clearly wasn't equally yoked with her. Enough was enough. What was the purpose of serving God if she couldn't get the clarity she needed? She had been praying for guidance and direction for months, before and after Paul, before and since Sebastian, before and now with Roger. She was asking, but God wasn't answering clearly, or was he? Maybe the problem wasn't in the asking but in the hearing. It was too much confusion. Absence might not make the heart grow fonder, but it would sure give some much-needed peace about all of this dating business. It was time to step back and get some breathing room. Roger was one of the "good ones," for someone.

Chapter 35

January flew by and February was in hot pursuit. In the midst of the flurry, Courtney was trying to sort out her feelings. Sebastian visited her thoughts daily. He had stopped calling on a regular basis, but he sent a greeting card faithfully every week. She had read each card at least five times before tucking them neatly away in the nightstand next to her bed. He wouldn't go away and she wasn't trying to smother him anymore.

Roger hadn't missed a romantic beat in three months. During Courtney's stretch with Paul, Roger would have been more than she could have hoped for, but he wasn't enough to soothe her longing for Sebastian. It was clear as spring water, but how could she tell him? She had turned him down three out of the past five weekends, each time claiming to be too tired. It was true if being tired of dangling counted. There was something to passion after all.

Today was one of the toughest to be unattached. Flowers and goodies were bursting out of the office seams. The ladies bounced around to see who got what, some discreetly and others boldly sticking their heads in and out of cubicles. It was like a kid waking up at five o'clock in the morning and running to the Christmas tree to see what gifts he'd gotten. Everybody was happy, except for the one who didn't have a gift with her name on it. That's what it felt like this year. Even the three-stem carnation bouquet Paul had given for the past four years would have been a welcomed sight.

Sheila stuck her head in and took a quick survey of the cubicle. "Ah, you didn't get anything yet!"

Courtney shook her head no. "There's nobody to give me anything."

"Girlfriend, please. You have men falling out of your pocket when you walk. I know as perfect as Roger is, he's going to do something for you."

"I don't think so. I turned him down for lunch today because I had a short meeting with Cara. So, he probably won't do anything else."

"You turned him down? What's up with that?"

"Tired of pretending that he's the one I want to be with."

"Oh, so this is all about Sebaaaastian," she said, stirring in a pinch of humor.

"You are terrible."

"That's right but I keep it real. You know you like the man. I don't know why you don't just go for it. If I were in your shoes, I would."

"You would!"

"In a heartbeat. It's hard enough finding someone that you get along with. You have to consider the man if he's someone that you truly have feelings for and he returns the feelings."

"I miss him so much. You would not believe."

"That's why you need to handle your business and go for it."

"Deep down, my aunt is still tripping about him, but I don't care anymore."

"You know my thoughts about your aunt, but anyway, that's your aunt and I'll leave it alone. Now, about the rest of life, you're always going to have challenges in a relationship and they're probably tripled in an interracial one. Whenever a racially divided topic comes up, as they always do every three to four years, the two of you will have to work hard not to square off in your own racial corners. You'll have to deal with stuff the rest of us don't think about when we're around the 'folks.' Like, you know how we get upset when a black man is the first one to get killed in a movie."

"Or when the news reporter finds the most inarticulate, no-hair-combed, missing-toothed person on the scene and asks him to give an account of what happened," Courtney added.

"The news is the worst. You two won't be able to watch the news together, because it always has racial overtones, or at least you know we believe it does. I am so sick of seeing black criminals plastered on the screen. Do they only take mug shots in the middle of the night when the brother is looking his worst? They don't do that to other people. You can tell when the suspect is another race."

"How?"

"They just talk about the heinous crime, but most of the time they don't show a picture. When it's a brother, they dig up a mug shot or picture from somewhere, anywhere. I know with all of the Mafia, triad, and serial killings and barrio gangs, somebody else has to be committing crimes too."

"Those are regular blue-collar and no-collar criminals. What about the white-collar criminals ripping off people's life savings and getting a slap on the wrist for it?"

"Oh, we don't even want to get off into that. I'd be screaming up in here. A brother rips off a minimart and gets fifty dollars and five to ten. A CEO rips off his Fortune 500 company for five hundred million dollars and he gets a five-million-dollar fine and a thousand hours of community service. That's not race talking, that's purely money setting the standards."

"Poor people, no matter who they are, get the short end. It just so happens so many of the poor are black."

"But see, you won't be able to talk like this with Sebaaaastian. You'll have to think about what you do and what you say."

"I should be doing that anyway."

"Good point, church lady. You're held to a higher standard than me. I'm still a heathen. I can get mad at that crazy black entertainer who left his pregnant college sweetheart wife last month after twelve years of marriage and three kids, for an eighteen-year-old bleached-blond high school dropout who was working as a waitress when they met. Men like him make me sick to my stomach."

"Why, because of the race factor?"

"No, because he's stupid. I'm not sure about love, but ignorance is blind. Regardless of what color you are, that's a slap in the face to any married woman."

"Some of the things we blame on race are situations we all face. I really do think people are more alike than they are different. Women are women, men are men, broke is broke, and trifling is trifling. That guy was just crazy."

"It was bad enough cheating on his wife, who by the way was the one who helped to make him rich, but the woman was calling him at home and asking his wife if she could talk to him."

"Now you know that's bold."

"Can you believe that? In the interview I saw, the wife said the woman was driving past the house looking for him."

"And to add insult to injury, he moved the wife and the three kids out of their estate and moved the waitress into his wife's house."

"That is such a trip."

"But see, nothing good can come out of that much flagrant disrespect for another individual. As far as I'm concerned, the wife made out the best, by getting free from that mess. The jerk and the waitress deserve one another."

"That's too much drama."

"They were just ignorant for no reason. Don't worry, though. As long as you don't start off wrong, you won't have their kind of drama."

"If I'm going to do this, I'll just have to trust that God will work it out."

"In the meantime, I bet Jason sneaks you a gift over here." Sheila got up to leave. "Let me have whatever you don't want today. I need something to put on the desk in my fishbowl office."

"Maybe Hodges will send you something."

"Ooooo, now who's wrong?" she said, grinning and tapping the cubicle wall on her way out.

Courtney punched a few computer keys and straightened up in her chair. When security called her down to the lobby to pick up a delivery, she was caught off guard. Who could be sending something? Probably Mommy and Daddy, or maybe Roger? They weren't in a totally committed relationship, but receiving a gift would be a nice pick-me-up.

She stopped by Sheila's on the way downstairs. She knocked on the closed door and Sheila beckoned for her to come in.

"I have a package downstairs."

"I knew you would get something."

"Probably from my parents."

"Yeah, right, I know better."

"Why don't you walk down with me?"

Sheila set her pen down and got up. "Why not? I might as well live my Valentine's Day vicariously through you, since I'm sure I won't get anything."

The ladies hustled down to the lobby in anticipation.

Sebastian stood in the visitor center wearing a pair of worn jeans and a polo shirt, which was showing from underneath his down-filled ski jacket. He was cradling a dozen multicolored roses and a box of candy.

There was no shortage of flowers in the visitor center. Gentlemen accompanied some, while other bouquets waited patiently for their valentine to extract them from the traffic jam.

"Gee, those are huge roses. What a great day for the florist," Sebastian told one man standing near him who was wearing a tailored suit, accented with a matching belt and soft leather shoes. He was another one holding a dozen eighteen-inch long-stemmed red roses.

"That's the way it is."

"I thought mine were nice, but the buds on your roses are like bowls. I hope you're gone with those roses before my friend comes down to get these."

The man looked at the box Sebastian was holding. "You should be okay. You brought a gift plus some flowers, smart."

"Oh yeah. It's her favorite. Almond roca," Sebastian was quick to say.

"My girlfriend likes candy too. I should have gotten her a box, but I didn't think about it."

"Don't worry, you're a sure hit with a set of roses like that."

Courtney and Sheila opened the door to the visitor center. Courtney stopped cold in her tracks, causing Sheila to run into the back of her. Her eyes dilated and her body tensed.

"Roger, Sebastian!"

"Roger! You're Roger?" Sebastian said.

"Who are you?" Roger asked.

Courtney walked closer to the men standing in the middle of the room. Sheila stayed back, out of the line of fire.

"Roger, this is my friend Sebastian."

"Friend, what friend!"

"Uh, excuse me, Sebastian, can I talk with Roger in the lobby?"

Courtney didn't have the presence of mind to do the introductions for Sheila. That would have to come at a less heated time. Courtney felt her heart thumping in the lobby. The situation required no explanation. Two men in their respective corners, each holding blossoming bouquets, and her standing in the middle, did all of the talking.

"Who is he? Why is he here, Courtney?" Roger demanded.

"I'm sorry. I didn't know he was coming."

"I knew something was going on, because you kept canceling on me. I haven't pressured you about it. I figured you were pulling back because you needed time to think about our relationship."

"I did."

"Is this what you're doing with the time?"

"Roger, it isn't what you think."

"This doesn't require much thinking, Courtney. It's pretty obvious."

"I'm so sorry. I really am. I messed up. I wanted to talk to you but just couldn't figure out what to say."

"Now I know what's going on. What was the problem? I didn't make enough time for you during the week?"

"No, that's not it," she responded.

"What then?"

"It's nothing you did. You're a great guy. I just can't get past Sebastian." Her eyes watered. "My heart is with him."

"Courtney, I deserved more than this. You could have told me about this any time before now."

"You're right and not that it justifies this, but I didn't know he was coming today. We haven't talked in months."

"You knew I'd be here today."

"No, I didn't."

"Then you really don't know me." He handed her the roses and leaned down to kiss her on the cheek. "But I'm not mad at you, terribly disappointed, but not mad."

The rivers of her eyelids were threatening to spill their banks at any moment. "I haven't been true to you or even to myself. I've been in so much confusion and I'm finally getting to the place where I'm willing to step out on faith and go where I feel God is leading me. I'm so sorry it happened like this. I'm sorry I wasted so much of your time."

"You haven't wasted my time. I have enjoyed every minute of the time we've shared. I don't know why God allowed us to meet, but there must be a reason. Who knows what it is? But obviously a long-term relationship isn't it. I'm grateful for what it was, and that was good."

She hugged him and he embraced her tightly.

"Ms. Courtney Young, I have no intentions of getting in the middle of whatever God has going on. You do your thing. If you ever need me, you know how to find me. You take care, beautiful lady." He lifted her hand to his lips and gave her a kiss. As he pulled away, their hands stretched the distance.

Sheila opened the door and Sebastian walked into the lobby. "I apologize for showing up unannounced. I hope this doesn't create a problem for you."

Courtney had no place to put the other set of flowers and box he was holding.

Sheila came into the lobby. "Excuse me, Courtney," she said, giving a series of winks that Sebastian couldn't see, "why don't I take the flowers upstairs for you?"

Courtney knew Sheila was biting her tongue off and so desperately wanted to say something about this debacle. She would hear it later. Thank goodness Brice was nowhere to be found.

Sheila reached for Roger's bouquet and swooped in close to Courtney's ear long enough to grit her teeth and squeak out of one side, "Girl, they are both fine." She spoke up louder for Sebastian to hear. "Courtney, stop by when you get a chance later this afternoon."

Courtney and Sebastian were left alone. He handed his gifts to her.

"Thanks for the flowers. They're nice."

"Courtney, it's been four long months without you. Tell me that you don't have feelings for me and I'll leave."

She didn't say a word. The room was a canyon, deep, wide, and if she moved she was sure to slip off the edge, into an endless depth where there was no footing or comfort zone.

"Tell me you don't think about me. You're in my skin. You're in my thoughts. Courtney," he said, lifting her hand with the box of candy in it and placing it against his chest, "you're in my heart."

She squeezed tight inside to keep from bursting into tears, not knowing if it was from relief of the ordeal finally being over or if it was from being confused in the first place. "If you don't mind, I'm going back upstairs. I was in the middle of something before I came down."

"I understand," he said in a tone that sounded as if weights were on every word. "Happy Valentine's Day."

He took a long look at Courtney, winked, and walked toward the exit.

"Sebastian!" If she was ever going to take the step of faith and go over the edge, this was the time. She dashed to him and extended her gift-filled hands to embrace him. "I missed you so much. I am so glad to see you."

He hugged her tight while the guards looked on. She knew they were staring and acknowledged it, but didn't give it enough validity to sting. She cherished the tenderness and security of his hug. It was a soothing and peaceful feeling. She had finally figured out how to step out in faith and to move forward. She wasn't going to be the cat in the picture, stuck in limbo, not knowing how to go out or how to come in.

Chapter 36

Courtney was light as a feather. The pressure of choosing was behind her and all was well with Sebastian. They were taking it a step at a time but the path was clear. They wanted to be together, which included being in the same worship service. For the first time, they had gone to his church earlier in the morning as an official couple.

Courtney was settling into the relationship. Life with Sebastian was great but not perfect. Aunt Sis wanted the family over for dinner, but Courtney knew better than to set foot across her threshold with Sebastian, a definite no-no.

A shock to all, Jamal showed up a half hour early, instead of his normal practice of arriving right on time, not a minute too early or too late.

"Ce-Ce, what up, girl? How you rolling?"

"I'm doing okay for myself, cuz."

"All right now," he said, plopping down on the couch and flipping on the TV.

"What's going down at the firm, big bro?"

"Same ole, same ole. A brother trying to make a few things happen."

"All right now, player. Mama, when can we eat? I am hunggary."

Aunt Sis was at the dining room table wiping the plastic tablecloth and place mats.

"Boy, you are not going to worry me. You get here early one time and now you want to rush me. You won't starve and if you're in such a hurry, come on over here and set this table."

"Nah, I'm good."

"Um-hmm."

"And where were you this morning, Ms. Courtney? You weren't at church. Were you vacationing in town, young lady?"

"I visited another church this morning."

"What's all this business about going to some other church? What's wrong with Fifth Baptist?" Aunt Sis said, cutting her eyes toward Courtney. "It's been good enough for you all these years. Why, all of a sudden, you can't go to Fifth Baptist? Don't tell me Fifth Baptist isn't good enough for you, young lady. Now don't go and get uppity on your aunt."

"Aunt Sis, I love going to Fifth Baptist with the family. It's just, well, Sebastian goes to church too and he invited me to visit."

"Sebastian! Sebastian who? I know you can't be talking about that white boy that you brought over here. I can't possibly believe that you're talking about him. So, I'm wondering what other Sebastian it is!"

"That's him, Aunt Sis."

"I don't believe this. I don't believe you have the nerve to stand in my face, grown as you want to be, and tell me you're seeing someone behind our backs I told you not to see."

Aunt Sis took a step back and snapped her arms into a folded position across her chest.

"Mama, let's not get into this again," Edwin said, stepping in. "Let's just leave her alone"

"Oh no, you can't save her. I got her."

"No, you don't. Not while I'm up in here." Jamal put the TV on mute and bumped the remote against his thigh and rubbed the top of his bowed head. "You can't tell her what to do. Ce-Ce hasn't done anything to anybody from what I can see. Mama, you need to chill."

"Chill, who you talking to! You better come look in my face and see who you're talking to, because I'm not one of your running buddies. I don't care how old you all get, I'm still the oldest, and I will be heard."

"Mama, you have to think about what you're saying," Edwin eased in.

She cut him up and down with her eyes spitting fire. "I know they don't have you getting up in this too."

"We know you don't mean what you're saying."

Neck rocking and finger pointing, Aunt Sis wasn't keeping still. "Oh yes, I do, every word. I don't want that boy in my house. I don't want him on my block, in my family, or in my face. And I most surely do not want him in my niece's life. All he's going to do is bring a whole lot of trouble and pain to her and this family and we'll be the ones who have to help clean it up after he has moved on to the next tramp."

"Whoa, whoa, whoa, Mama, oh no," Jamal said, jumping up from the couch. "See, you've just gone too far! Ce-Ce is not a tramp and I'm not going to let *anybody* call her one, not even you!"

Edwin stood in the neutral zone, leaning more toward the wounded camp where Jamal and Courtney were pitted in the living room.

"Me either, Mama. I'm not going for it. I have let you say and do practically everything you want to because you're Mama, but this is too much. You need to think about what you're saying and you need to apologize to Courtney and I mean that."

Aunt Sis relaxed her arms and brushed them against her apron like she was trying to wipe away the strife. "I wasn't calling you a tramp, Courtney. You know better. See what I mean? He has us fighting." She tightened her fists back up and plugged them into her side, patting her foot enough times to count as a full-body aerobic workout. "He's not even here and he's already trying to tear up the family."

"I mean it, Mama, let it go!" Edwin said with enough sternness to shake the six-foot-long mirror in the dining room right off the wall, if there'd been one there.

Aunt Sis smeared the drying cloth across the tablecloth and mats to soak up the water residuals. "Let's just eat and leave all this other mess alone, at least for the day."

Courtney could see the fire was out on Aunt Sis's surface, but sensed it was smoldering inside, looking to burn out of control at any time, given the right amount of fuel.

Chapter 37

After Sebastian dropped Courtney off at home earlier in the afternoon, he'd taken a stroll along South Street in search of sheet music from one of the novelty shops. On the way back he stopped by Fresh Fields to get groceries. When he got home after four, there were nine messages on his answering service. At least one had to be from Courtney, although it seemed too early for her to be home if dinner at her aunt's house began at three. He set the grocery bags in the kitchen and hurried to hear the messages. All of them were from Mom asking him to call home as soon as he could. A lump of worry wanted to form in the pit of his stomach but he kept beating it down with positive thoughts. *They're both okay, Shirley's okay, everybody's okay.* He put the rest of the groceries away, dialed home, and his mother answered.

"Where have you been? I've been calling all day."

"I ran a few errands after I dropped Courtney off at home."

"You're seeing that, that girl again!"

"That 'girl' is named Courtney and you'd better get accustomed to saying her name, Mom, because she's not going anywhere."

"You told us you hadn't spoken with her in months."

"And that was true, but I saw her on Valentine's Day and we're working through her concerns."

"How dare you continue to see her when your father has forbidden you to do so! I refuse to acknowledge her."

"That's your decision, but I'm asking her to marry me when the time is right and I'd love for you to be a part of my happiness, but if you can't, well, so be it."

"Marriage, oh my goodness! Sebastian Alexander, this has gone far enough. This is preposterous. You've proven your point. You can stop this barbaric display of adolescence. If you want to finish business school and work on Wall Street or something like that for a while, fine. I'm sure we can collectively sit down and discuss this in a rational manner during a family meeting, like the adults we are, and come up with a reasonable plan."

"Mom, you don't get it, do you?"

"Yes, dear, I do. I finally do. You are more serious about this business school venture than we anticipated. Perhaps we have been a bit shortsighted when it comes to your academic and professional endeavors. We can fix this and I'm glad you have brought it to our attention. Your tactics have been a bit extreme, you must admit."

"You think my feelings for Courtney are part of some grand scheme to pursue a business career?"

"Absolutely. Why else would you go this far, threatening marriage for goodness' sake, Sebastian? I realize you've been trying to get our attention and it's okay. We haven't been listening."

"And you're still not. I love Courtney and we want to be together. One day I'm going to marry her. That's it. There's no other plan or motivation behind it."

"That's absurd! How could you ever put some fling above your family? I don't understand what's wrong with you. Ever since you got involved in that religious cult in Evanston, you haven't been the same. You're rebellious and have a flagrant disregard for us and for our way of life. Our biggest mistake was letting you go to Northwestern instead of sticking to our guns and making you go to Harvard or Yale where you would have been sheltered from these other elements that you have found yourself aligned with. Now we're paying a hefty price for our generosity. Your dad will be devastated and apparently that has no bearing on your decision."

"I'm doing what makes me happy and complete in the eyes of God. That comes first, Mom. Why can't you just be happy because I'm happy?"

"Happiness comes second to family. Do you have any idea of the far-reaching catastrophic impact such an act will have on all of us, especially to the firm? If you get married to this woman, you could end up with black children. Oh my goodness, I can't talk about this anymore. It's too devastating." Her fingers massaged the temple on one side of her head. "I feel a migraine coming on."

"Do you want me to talk to Dad or do you want to?"

"I refuse to share this with your father. It might give him a heart attack or worse. You will have to share this nightmare with him yourself."

"I'm sorry you see this as a bad thing. I'm so sorry about that."

"Well, we don't want your empty words of sympathy. If you really care about us, you'll do the right thing."

"That's exactly what I plan to do."

Chapter 38

The table was a sight of malnutrition compared to a meal at Aunt Sis's, but Courtney and Sebastian had worked hard preparing the roasted chicken in a light lemon sauce with spaghetti and a medley of steamed veggies. She pulled the piping-hot garlic bread from the oven and drew in a whiff, letting her eyes relax and her body follow, as she savored the tantalizing aroma. It wasn't homemade corn bread, but her palette would not be complaining.

Courtney was glad Sheila had accepted her dinner invitation, finally an opportunity to get her and Edwin together. A little help was all they needed.

Sheila leaned against the kitchen door frame. "What can I do to help you?"

"Nothing really. We've pretty much done everything in here. All that's left to do is to put the salad in the bowl and I can do that. You need to be out there with Edwin."

"See, don't you start," Sheila said, lowering her voice and emphasizing each word. "I came so I could meet Sebastian, not Edwin." She nabbed a carrot from the veggie tray that had been barely touched by the four of them. She swiped the carrot in the onion dip and glanced at Sebastian and Edwin sitting in the living room area talking, while the basketball game was playing in the background.

The conversation was winning out over the game with the men.

"I know my mother has given you a hard time about being with Courtney. I want you to know that I don't feel the same way about it. Courtney loves you and that's good enough for me," Edwin said.

"I'm glad to know that you support us. Support from your family is important to her."

"Who knows? Maybe my mother will come around at some point."

"That would be awesome, but it might take a while. My parents are resisting too. They've blown it way out of proportion. My mom has absolutely lost all ability to be rational about this whole situation. I love my mom, but I've made it clear that Courtney is the woman for me. She's the one God has sent to me and I'm not going to let my mother or even your mother prevent me from committing to Courtney. I love her like I've never loved anyone else."

"Sebastian, man, you have to do what you feel led to do. When it comes right down to it, it's all about what you and Courtney want to do. My mother means well, but sometimes she can get a little too involved with the affairs of her children, which includes Courtney."

"Boy, you don't have to tell me about that. My mother wants me to finish law school and come back home. She literally wants me to move back into my old room and pick up with life like it was when I was ten years old. There is no woman on the whole planet good enough for me, if you ask my mom."

Edwin thought about his own situation, different families but same mothers.

"The food is ready," Courtney announced.

There was a knock at the door.

Courtney looked at her watch. "You know it's Jamal. Can somebody get that, please?"

Sebastian went to the door and opened it after asking the visitor to identify himself.

"Hey, hey, hey. What's up, people?"

Sebastian reached out to shake Jamal's hand.

"Oh, that's right, you got that ole school shake," he said, laughing. "That ain't how we do it round here, man." He walked Sebastian through the slap, lock, flip, and knock routine. "That's what I'm talking about."

He made his rounds to Edwin and to Courtney, who came out of the kitchen when she heard him come in. She introduced him to Sheila last.

"Hey," Jamal said, covering his mouth and dipping his legs in a contorted fashion, making him look crippled, and coming back up with his hand stroking his chin. "Now who are you?"

"This is Sheila," Courtney squeezed in, knowing where Jamal was headed. "She's a friend of mine and Edwin's."

"Oh, oh, oh, oh, man," he said, turning to Edwin, "this you? I didn't know, man, my bad. You know I don't roll like that, pushing up on my brother's girl. Sorry about that, man."

No one, including Sheila or Edwin, said anything to refute or acknowledge Jamal's implications. It was dropped. The greetings ended and everybody got their hands washed and grabbed a seat at the table. Earlier Sebastian had pulled the table from the wall and temporarily relocated Courtney's portable office. He pulled the armchair in from the living room area for the fifth seat. Once he finished the prayer, they were off, gobbling the food like a tornado through a trailer park, leaving nothing but scraps and memories. Laughter and merriment pranced inside the apartment.

Courtney and Sebastian held hands under the table every chance they got. It was refreshing being accepted by the ones she loved, it felt normal.

Chapter 39

After dinner, Sebastian was helping Courtney clean the table and the dishes when Sheila told him she would help, releasing him to go hang out with the guys in the living room. The three men talked, interrupting only when superstar plays in the game had them oohing and ahhing.

"So, Jamal, Courtney tells me you got a new job at the Wal-Mart in Norristown? That's quite a haul without any wheels," Sebastian commented.

Jamal sighed. "You know it, man. I have to get up every morning at four in order to get to the bus stop by five. I catch one bus to Sixty-ninth Street and then another one to the transportation center in Norristown and then another bus to Wal-Mart. It takes me about three and a half hours each way, and that's when the buses are on time. Man, lately it's been *cccold* out there. You don't know," he said, shaking his head.

"You're probably the only one out there that early, I bet."

"You kidding me? Shoot, there's about thirty-five people on the stop with me every morning, all doing the same thing, trying to make that money in the burbs. That's where the jobs are."

Sebastian wondered if someone like Jamal would ever be validated in the eyes of his parents. They saw blacks as lazy, yet a long line of

Jamals were getting up in the early morning hours to catch public transportation to jobs far away from home for minimum wage. Candidates had turned down positions with his father's firm because the six-figure salary they were offering didn't have an expense account and a car service to the office.

"But it's all good because I got my license back."

"You did!" Edwin shouted out. "I didn't know. That's cool, man." He leaned toward the middle of the sofa and gave a slap and release acknowledgment.

"Yeah, I'm trying to get it together, man. Matter of fact, I got a ride downstairs I'm thinking about buying from this cat around the way. I mean, you know, it's not all that. I figure it will get me started, because I definitely need some transportation for this job, man. Why don't y'all come check it out with me? I got it downstairs."

"I'm going to have to bow out, man. I need to talk to Sheila," Edwin responded.

"Oh yeah, that's cool, man. What about you, partner? You want to roll with me?"

Sebastian thought about it and said, "Sure thing. I'd love to go for a test drive. Let me tell Courtney where we're going first."

Jamal grabbed his coat and gloves preparing to leave while Sebastian told Courtney.

"Do you have to go right now?" she asked.

"Don't worry about it, cuz. I'm not going to hurt your man. He's a big boy. He'll be all right."

"I thought we were going to play some cards."

"We're coming right back." Jamal draped his arm over Courtney's shoulder. "I'll take care of him. Don't worry. Come on, man, roll with me."

Sebastian gave Courtney a hug. "We're out of here."

"Don't you need a coat, dog?"

"No, I'm fine. My sweatshirt's enough."

Jamal and Sebastian got outside Courtney's apartment building, and the twenty-year-old Buick was parked out front wearing an ounce of paint more than rust. The rear door on the passenger's side was bashed in on the right side. The bumper was hanging six inches below where it should have been and was begging to be bolted down. Jamal pressed the alarm button on his key chain and the locks popped up.

Inside, the ceiling lining was drooping, barely leaving clearance for their heads. He started it up.

"She's got serious heat," he said, leaning close to the steering wheel, briskly rubbing his hands together and blowing on them.

Sebastian could agree since the blowers were blasting his knees.

"Man, I don't mean to be funny, but you 'white boys' are a trip. How can you wear shorts in this kind of weather with a sweatshirt? It's cold as a mug out here," Jamal said, sliding the heater gauge over to full red.

"The sun's out."

"Yeah, but so what? It's *cccold* out here. Y'all a trip, man, but you cool." He gave a few more blows to his hands for a quick dose of warmth.

An old lady, a few inches taller than a dwarf, walked toward the car with the little legs of her Chihuahua hustling along like he was running. Her gray hair was wrapped in a bun. Her flush red cheeks were dotted against skin the air had drained pale white.

Jamal saw her approaching in his rearview mirror. "Watch your elbows, man," he shouted out. *Thump, thump* sounded in the car as he locked the doors when the old lady got within earshot. "Man, you can never be too careful." The sound of the locks startled the woman, and the dog wet on himself and began barking at the car uncontrollably and scampering around aimlessly, dragging the little lady down the sidewalk, as she tried to regain control.

Jamal pulled off, fumbling with the radio. "I'm thinking about going ahead and getting this ride. I want some rims, but I'll wait until I get some other stuff done first."

"Cool."

"So you all in love with my lil' cuz, is that right, partner?"

"Guilty as charged."

"Yeah, well, it's all good. It's all good."

A car stopped next to them at the traffic light. *Boom, boom, boom* came from the car with patches of lyric and music filling the empty spots. Sebastian could barely hear Jamal over the bumping and thumping. The music from the other car had enough bass to send the vibration into their Buick. Careful not to stare, he glanced into the car and saw two teenage brunettes, one blonde, and one redhead bouncing to the sounds they were blasting into the streets.

"You don't have a problem with us being together, do you?"

"Nah, nah, homey. I mean you're not really my homey and all, but you all right for a 'white boy.' "

"I'm glad to hear that, Jamal. I love Courtney and I know how much she loves you and your family. I'm happy to know you're supporting her."

"It's like this, young blood, Courtney is like my little sister. I'm always going to look out for her. I like you 'cause she like you. But I will tell you this, partner, you better treat her right, and I do mean right. I don't care whether you're white, black, green, purple, or whatever, if you mess with my girl, you mess with me and I mean that, dog. I ain't playing. I ain't somebody to play with. I will get down when I have to. You know what I'm saying, right? Right?"

"I understand your position and I respect your loyalty to her."

"Position, loyalty, whatever, homey," Jamal said, chuckling, "long as you know what's up, Johnny Law. We gotta change your name, though, man. You can't hang out in the hood with a name like Sebastian. Brothers don't roll with a name like that. What's your nickname?"

"I don't have one, unless you count Bas."

"Nah, man. What kind of a nickname is Bas? Don't worry about it, man, I'll give you a name. From now on I'm calling you Nilla."

"Nilla?"

"Yeah, you know, like short for vanilla. Yeah, Nilla, I like that."

Sebastian was humored and enjoyed Jamal's free spirit, but had no intention of endorsing the new name he had been given, beyond the confines of this Buick.

"And I heard about what happened with my mom and, man, I'm sorry about all of it. You know, she be tripping about stuff all of the time, but she's my mama, man. I just deal with her until she goes too far, like she did with Ce-Ce. I don't play that."

"It was a very unpleasant scene at your mother's but I'm trusting that God's going to somehow work out the details."

"Oh, so you into that religion stuff too. Ah, man, and here I thought you were all cool and everythang and you have to drop this on me."

"I'm not religious, Jamal. I'm a believer who has a personal relationship with the Lord."

"Yeah, yeah, right, man. You are one of those Holy Rollers, sitting up in the church every Sunday, talking about cats like me who everybody thinks is making trouble for everybody else. That's why I stopped going to church, because of all those hypocrites up in there who lie, steal, and cheat all week long and try to act all righteous on Sunday. They be tripping and I ain't wasting my time with nonsense. If God is going to dog me the same as 'the man,' then why should I go to church?"

"I don't know what church you're going to, but God isn't about belittling you or using your mistakes to hold over your head. He does just the opposite."

"Not if you listen to the church folks at Fifth Baptist."

"I don't mean to slight anyone at Fifth Baptist or any other church, but going to church is not the same as accepting Christ as your personal savior and developing a relationship with him."

"So what are you saying, I can have a relationship and not have to go to church? Because that sounds like me."

"Kind of, but not really."

Jamal had a confused look on his face.

"What I mean, Jamal, is that when you accept the Lord, you don't have to go to church, but you will want to go in order to learn more about him and to be around other believers. It's like you being a Sixers fan. It's great watching the game alone, but when you're at a game with thousands of other people, all excited about the same team at the same time, it's totally awesome. It gets you really pumped up."

"Yeah, okay, I can see that."

"On the other hand, not everybody in church has a relationship with God. Some of them go because they think being in church automatically makes them connected to God. Since we can't look at somebody's heart and spirit like God can, the only indication of where someone is, spiritually, is too look at their actions and conversation. Just like at the game, anybody can sit on the Sixers side and profess to be a fan, but you don't really know if they are a committed fan until it's time to start cheering and supporting the team, even when they're struggling."

"Fair-weather fans."

"Exactly, that's how some of the religious people are. They're okay with God and the Bible so long as everything is in place. When challenges or uncomfortable positions arise, they pull back."

"Makes sense, Nilla. You're the first to really put it to me like this. You all right."

"It's easy to talk about God. He is so incredible. That's why I can endure everything that's happening with me and Courtney."

"Yeah, well, just don't come to Fifth Baptist."

"Believe it or not, my church isn't too different when it comes to racial matters. We might do a better job of hiding it, but even those who have accepted salvation and live by the leading of the Lord struggle with major areas in their life. In this country it happens to be race. So, Courtney and I won't have it easy anywhere."

"And you still want to do this, dog?"

"Without a moment of hesitation. When God blesses you with someone like Courtney, you have to take it and run with it."

"You're deep, man." Jamal was quiet for a moment.

"Are there blessings left for anybody else?" he asked.

"Absolutely. Tons and tons of them. He is no respecter of person, meaning that whatever good things he has for me, he has it for others and probably more."

"Yeah, I could deal with some good right about now."

"The gift of salvation is free."

"Ain't nothing free, man."

"This is." Sebastian wasn't sure if Jamal was asking about salvation. If he was, Sebastian didn't want to lose the opportunity to tell him about the loving Savior he knew, the one who had given him a heart for Courtney and had faithfully brought them together, against all odds. A God who could part the Red Sea, if necessary, in order to bring him and Courtney together, had to be shared with Jamal.

"There's something about you, Nilla. I don't know what it is, but you're all right."

"Getting saved by receiving God's gift is easy. All you would have to do is ask God to forgive your sins. Confess that Jesus is the Son of God. That he died on the cross for your sins. That Jesus Christ, our Lord and Savior, was raised from the dead and lives with our Father in heaven. That's it, that's all you have to do to receive the gift of eternal life. Easy."

"Yeah, man, but nah, I'm not in a position to do that at this moment. I got some stuff to work out first."

"That's the whole beauty of accepting Christ, he helps you work out the areas in your life that need it. He knows we're not perfect and accepts us anyway, just as we are."

"Yeah, but God is nobody to play with. Even I know that. Nah, I'm going to wait until I get a few things straightened out in my life before I go there. I ain't ready for the hookup, but you still all right with me, Reverend Nilla, and I appreciate you trying to get a brother saved. On the serious tip, I mean that."

No pressure. God knew where Jamal was and how to reach him. Sebastian believed in his heart one day Jamal would accept Christ. He made a mental note to pray for Jamal's salvation in the meantime. "No problem, you'll do it when it's right."

"No doubt." Jamal did a double-fist bump with Sebastian to seal the deal. He turned onto City Line Avenue. The police car turned behind them. He eyed the car but said nothing. Jamal sat straight up and went slow, making sure he did nothing to distract Five-O. The flashing red, white, and blue lights streaked across the front grill, looking like a Christmas tree. Before pulling over, he checked out the surroundings. At least it was broad daylight. He remembered his upbringing. One of the rules of life he'd gotten from his family, when he first got his driver's license, was never to stop for a police officer in a remote location. Stories about what had happened to blacks in such situations made it necessary for parents to pass the word of caution down to their children like a rite of passage. He knew to drive, with the flashers on if necessary, to a well-lit area, where at least someone else could see what was going on. Although he had to admit that times had changed and cops were bolder, and audiences didn't deter their wrath.

Sebastian glimpsed the lights flashing behind them and felt no reason to tense up around the police. There were good and bad cops in every town, but by and large he knew them to be friendly officers of the law, empowered by the commonwealth to keep citizens safe.

One officer approached the driver's side and another stood near the rear of the car, on the passenger side, with his arm bent back, allowing his hand to rest on the butt of his holstered gun.

"Registration and license, please."

Jamal reached into the glove compartment and fished for the registration, which was buried under a coffee cup and a stack of loose papers that had no order. He reached into his pocket and pulled out his license.

The officer studied the documents Jamal gave him. He unsnapped his holster and took a step back from the car.

"Please step out of the car, sir."

"Why?" Sebastian asked.

The officer paid no attention to Sebastian. He mumbled into the two-way radio braced on his shoulder.

Jamal hesitated, but knew he had to follow orders. He unbuckled his seat belt.

"Officer, I asked you what for," Sebastian demanded again.

"Let me see your identification," the officer asked.

Sebastian fumbled in his pockets, and then it hit him. He'd left his wallet at Courtney's in the pocket of his coat.

"Officer, I left my wallet at my girlfriend's apartment."

"Step out of the car, gentlemen."

Neither Jamal nor Sebastian was eager to respond.

The officer snatched the door open and ripped Jamal from his seat, while the backup officer stepped behind the car, aiming the gun through the back window.

Three tons of cement dropping from a two-story building was what it felt like when the officer smashed him into the hood of the car. Jamal begged his lungs to breathe, while his heart tried to keep the body functioning on what little air it had managed to siphon, before the shortage was put into affect.

Cars crept by gaping at the mayhem. Some yelled obscenities at the police as they drove by, but no one stopped.

The officer clamped on the cuffs. Without warning, the other officer drew his stick and with the force of a home run, hit Jamal across the back of his knees causing him to buckle to the ground.

Like a magnet, his hands gravitated toward the cuffs, a familiar path.

Sebastian didn't move. When his speech, arms, and legs were able to work in unison, he pushed the door open and jumped out. The officer drew his gun and aimed it at Sebastian from the rear of the car.

"Don't move. You're under arrest."

"There must be some mistake here, Officer."

"I said, don't move. You're under arrest," the officer said while easing around to the side of the car, his partner coming around the front. "Get your hands up."

"Officer, please, there is some mistake. We have not violated the law. I'm a student."

"You're an armed robber, that's what you are. So, shut up. You speak when I say speak."

Sebastian was new to the workings of an arrest. He'd heard his father and grandfather both speak so fondly of the great American legal system, and he was mildly looking forward to studying the intricacies of it in law school. His thoughts scampered around, not knowing what should be pieced together. Of all the classes and world traveling he'd been exposed to, he couldn't think of one element that had prepared him for how it felt to be kicked to the other side of the law. Innocent until proven guilty was acceptable in theory, but not on the street where the law was real, where someone was getting arrested for being in the wrong place at the wrong time. Best now to go along with the officers until he could talk with the police chief and get this straightened out. He slowly raised his arms and clasped his fingers behind his head with legs spread apart.

One officer pounced in and put the cuffs on while the other officer kept his firearm in position. Sebastian was subdued and the officer gave him a knee to the groin, causing him to buckle over.

Police sirens got louder and the street crowded with cars coming from everywhere. The other officers jumped in to help toss Jamal and Sebastian into the patrol car, banging their heads on the doorway in the process. The excitement was over and the officers stood around laughing and talking, as if it were the winding-down of a football match.

"This is absurd. Who do they think they are?"

Jamal relaxed in his seat. Sebastian squirmed around.

"Don't let them get to you. This is just a little game they play. It's all about power, that's all it is. As long as they have a gun and a badge they think they're above the law."

"I've never been arrested before. This doesn't feel comfortable."

"Don't even trip about this. You'll be out before it gets dark. Just take it easy."

"I'm not taking it easy. This is wrong and I'm not going to stand for it."

The sirens were silenced and the lights turned off. The other seven squad cars pulled away from the scene of the crime. The officers escorting Jamal and Sebastian to jail got into the squad car and drove toward downtown.

Sebastian couldn't wait to get downtown and see someone in charge. This sort of behavior wasn't to be tolerated by an officer sworn to uphold the law. Officers speeding and turning on their sirens to get through a red light was one thing, but this was at a totally different level. He spewed at the officers, "What are we being charged with?"

"Armed robbery."

"Armed robbery! I have no idea what you're talking about," Sebastian yelled.

"Oh, so you just happened to be in a car that was involved in a robbery, but you had nothing to do with it?"

"That's right. You've made a mistake arresting us."

"I told you to shut up. All we need is more guys like you trying to act like you're one of them." He took the stick and within seconds, Sebastian was doubled over and groaning.

"What's that for, man! You already have him locked down. What's up!" Jamal said.

"If you need help getting quiet, I will be more than happy to oblige you too," the officer offered.

"Happy to oblige me," Jamal mocked, "if you didn't have that stick."

"What, what would you do, tough guy? Pull over," he told the officer that was driving. "Let's teach these boys how to respect the law."

"Let's just take them downtown, Jim. Why bother with these guys?" the officer who was driving said, trying to dissuade his angered partner.

"What are you afraid of? Even if they tell, nobody's going to believe them. Come on, pull over, and this time you're getting in on the action. I don't want you to be some innocent witness sitting on the witness stand ratting me out," he said, laughing from the pit of his stomach.

The squad car turned off Belmont Avenue into Fairmount Park, winding around the roadway in search of a location to do the deed.

Sebastian's hands and forehead popped with sweat. His fear wanted to run but couldn't shake loose from the cuffs. *Lord, you are my shepherd and I shall not want,* he repeated in his head. One of his favorite scriptures dropped in his spirit so boldly that it seemed to be painted across the windshield. Psalms 91. He devoured as much of it as he could pull from memory. *He who dwells in the shelter of the Most High . . . He is my refuge and fortress, my God, in whom I trust . . . He will cover you with his feathers, and under his wings you will find refuge . . . If you make the Most High your dwelling . . . then no harm will befall you, no disaster will come near . . .*

Sebastian Alexander Whittington, Junior, couldn't help him at this critical moment, but his other father could.

Chapter 40

Sebastian took the cloth and rubbed his fingers fiercely to remove the fingerprint ink before it seeped into his soul.

"This is a total misunderstanding."

"Don't tell me, you're innocent, right?" the processing officer asked.

"That's right. We weren't party to any armed robbery. The car didn't belong to us. This is all just some huge mistake. If I could speak with the chief or whoever is in charge, we can get this whole matter taken care of very quickly."

"Yeah, and I want a raise and a trip to the Bahamas but I'm not getting that either."

The aching in his stomach area that made it difficult to turn around or lean over felt like it was coming from his ribs. He closed his eyes between the shooting pains, telling himself, *Please don't be broken.*

"We were assaulted by one of the officers that arrested us. I'm going to need medical attention."

"It happens when you resist arrest."

"Resist arrest! We were already arrested and cuffed when we were assaulted by the officer."

"Where are the marks?"

Sebastian massaged his lower rib cage, froze, winced, took a deep breath, and snapped his hand back, as if he'd touched a hot pan on the stove. The officer had been careful to do most of the work on the body. It was easier to conceal. A cut above the lip and a bruise across the eyebrow were the only visible signs of distress.

"You look fine to me."

"If you don't believe me, ask the other officer. He didn't attack us, but he was there, watching his partner."

"Sure, I'll ask him. If your story is true, I'm sure the officer will side with you over a fellow officer," she said, smirking.

How could he expect any other reaction? Everybody protects their own. Cops weren't any different. It was crystal clear that this wasn't where he wanted to be, a place where innocence didn't carry any clout. No one was willing to hear his story. He was in custody and that meant guilty until proven otherwise. Mutual respect was desired but didn't seem to be coming. He couldn't take it anymore. He had to get out without hesitation, and staying overnight wasn't an option. He had already been inconvenienced enough.

"When do I get my phone call?"

"We're just about finished booking you in. You'll get that call in a few minutes."

Photos, fingerprints, a few basic questions answered, and the process was complete. Now he could make the call, but to whom? Courtney would be worried to no end. Better to get out first and then fill her in, once he was out and she could see that he was okay.

He was innocent. If he could just get before the right person, this could be resolved in moments. The charges could be dropped without having to go before the judge, but it would take legal firepower to speed the process along. He dialed home and Mrs. Whittington answered.

"Mom, is Dad around?"

"He's in the gym. Why haven't I heard from you in the past four days? It's that black girl, isn't it? Now that you're frolicking with her again, you don't have time for us. I knew this would happen," Mrs. Whittington said.

"You have about three minutes," the guard announced.

"Mom, Mom, I don't have time to talk with you right now. It's urgent that I talk with Dad. Can you please buzz him on the intercom?"

She gasped and exhaled into the phone, causing him to move the receiver away from his ear. The officer stood guard, close enough to hear every word. The exchange rate was one lifetime for every ten seconds. That's what the waiting seemed like. Finally, a voice on the other end.

"Yes, Sebastian, your mom said this is urgent. What can I do for you?" he said, breathing heavily.

"Dad, we're in jail."

"Jail! On what charge?"

"They're charging us with armed robbery."

"Armed robbery!"

"But it's all a mix-up. The car that was involved doesn't belong to us."

"By us, do you mean the black girl?"

"No, not Courtney, Dad, her name is Courtney. Me and her cousin are the ones in custody."

"Less than two minutes left," the officer yelled.

"I knew it. This is what happens when you consort outside your element. Now you can appreciate my position on this entire sordid business."

"Dad, I only have a couple of minutes left. Are you going to help us or not?"

"You have shown blatant disregard for the family and have exercised poor judgment in the process and now it has landed you in this precarious set of circumstances," he said, and took a pause before continuing. "But you are still my son and I will take care of this for you. Give me the information."

Sebastian rattled off the jail location and other details his father would need. "Dad, we were also brutally attacked by one of the arresting officers. I'm going to need medical attention." He tried to rub the spot again, with not much more success.

"What! This is outrageous. Don't worry, you'll be out in less than an hour."

"Thanks, Dad, for helping us."

"Us! No, son, you're my only concern."

"Your time is up. You have to end the call. I need to get you to the holding cell," the officer said, taking the receiver from Sebastian and disconnecting the call.

"Cell! But my dad will be taking care of this within the hour."

"Fine, but you still have to go to the cell."

"If he's doing it within the hour, why do I need to go to the cell?"

"Because that's how this works. You get arrested, you get booked, and then you go to the cell until you go before the judge and get arraigned. Enough questions, let's go." The officer grabbed his arm and gave a slight pull toward the door.

"Wait a minute, I can post my own bail."

"Bail hasn't been set yet. I told you, this is how this works. You get arrested. You get booked and next is the holding cell. That's it. If you have more questions, save them for the judge. Let's go."

Sebastian acquiesced and took his walk into the place he'd never expected to see from this side of the law. He was a man who knew the Lord, but he was human too. He'd heard the horror stories of men being victimized in prison. He couldn't fully imagine the reception a guy with his background would get from a host of other victims that saw him as Mr. Oppressor. The rush of fear tried to reestablish a grip on his spirit, draining the stride in his step and the peace in his thoughts. Where was Jamal? Was he okay? Did Courtney know? Was she worried? He had to get out and get to her. He desperately had to get out for himself.

The metal bars slid open and the guard prodded him into a closet-sized area surrounded by bars in front of him, bars behind, and high walls on the side with no grates, windows, or any other identifiable features. The bars closed behind him in the caged area, enabling the ones in front of him to open. The sliding bars clanged shut. *This is temporary. This is temporary.* The Apostle Paul had endured his bouts with prison. He'd written most of the epistles in the Bible while being wrongfully held in prison. Faith had turned his adversities into productive times. Perhaps Sebastian could do the same, but how? He wasn't Paul and wasn't claiming to have his faith, but then he couldn't deny that they had the same God. If God had told Jeremiah that he knew him before he was formed in the womb, then surely God knew Sebastian was locked up on a bogus charge at the Roundhouse in Center City, Philadelphia. Sebastian began praying silently. Peace rushed from his mind, careening through his veins, heading for his feet, driving out every hint of fear, even that hiding in the crevices of his soul. His father would get him out. He just needed to trust and wait. All he had to do was keep tapping into the generator of faith God had established just for him, and the surges of peace would continue flowing during his time of tremendous need.

Chapter 41

Phones were jumping off the hook in Boston, D.C., Philadelphia, and Harrisburg. The situation was heating up and had to be cooled down, before it boiled over.

"Thank you for bringing this to my attention, Mr. Mayor."

"Good day, sir."

The police chief immediately called a captain into his office.

"I just got off the phone with the mayor. Apparently there has been some misconduct from two officers in our department."

"How did the mayor get involved?"

"Seems like he got a call from the governor, who got a call from the attorney general, who happens to be friends or college buddies with a Mr. Whittington. I'm not quite sure about all of the connections, but it's something like that. Bottom line is, we have a problem. One or two of our officers allegedly attacked two suspects when they were arresting them. One of the suspects is a graduate student at Penn, for goodness' sake."

"What's the charge?"

"Armed robbery."

"Doesn't sound like he fits the profile. Are we sure we didn't arrest the wrong people?"

"It's possible, but there's heat on this one."

"You mean a lawsuit?"

"That's the least of it. I'm talking publicity, which leads to resignations, and there's no way I'm putting my head on the chopping block for this. Check the report and make sure every detail is in order. We need to make sure our behinds are covered. This has to be by the book. I don't like this kind of attention. Geez, the attorney general is involved."

"What about the second suspect?"

"I don't know. They only mentioned one. Check the other one out just to be safe."

"I'll take care of it."

"And swiftly. Remember, this is an election year for the mayor. I don't want the media getting wind of this before we have an opportunity to put our own positive spin on it. That's all we need is for the mayor or the governor's office to come down on the entire department. We still haven't recovered from how we handled those people with the MOVE group. The last thing I want on my watch is another public outcry of excessive use of force."

"I'm on it, sir."

"Good, let me know when it's fixed so I can inform the mayor. Then he can get the governor and the attorney general off our backs. Once you've addressed it, I want to call a press conference to play up the fact that we are swift and absolute when it comes to enforcing the law, even when it comes down to reprimanding one of our own. That should buy us some favor with the mayor and the citizens. Not only can we salvage this mess up, I think we might even be able to capitalize on it." The chief leaned back in his chair with his fingers locked behind his head. "I just love the wheels of justice."

The captain hustled to his office, with the administrative assistant in tow, to put the plan into affect.

"I need the arrest file on two suspects immediately. One is a Mr. Sebastian Alexander Whittington the Third, and I need to know who the other one is. I also need you to get hold of someone in whatever holding area he's in. They have to get release papers processed for Mr. Sebastian Alexander Whittington the Third right away. Then get the two arresting officers in my office pronto, along with internal affairs and a set of disciplinary papers," the captain told the administrative assistant.

"Which papers?"

"Active probation with the intent to fire pending an investigation of misconduct."

Chapter 42

The local Young family was back together under one roof. It wasn't a funeral or a formal reunion, but it was party time. Jamal's new job and his reinstated driver's license were being celebrated as other accomplishments in the family had. The house was full of well-wishers. Enjoyment was the order of the day. The recent arrest could have put a damper on the festivities, but it didn't stop Aunt Sis from pressing forward with the get-together.

Uncle Raymond sat in a chair that was pushed into the corner in the dining room. The headline of his newspaper read:

CRIMINAL CHARGES AGAINST LOCAL OFFICERS
CIVIL SUIT FILED AGAINST POLICE DEPARTMENT

"Hey, hey, player in the house," Jamal said, hoisting his bike over his head and taking it to the basement, with the family showering him with kudos along the way and none mentioning his last run-in with the law. He was glad to be out. It wasn't over, but at least he didn't have to wait it out downtown. Edwin had managed to get him out of jail on house arrest with a curfew and an ankle monitor. No time to be wasted jumping into the party.

"Boy, what's that on your leg, looking like some kind of dog collar? What kind of a getup is that?"

"It's an ankle monitor, Uncle Raymond."

"Ankle monitor. What you got that on for?"

"My big bro worked out some kind of deal with Johnny Law so I could get out. I gotta wear this until all my business gets straightened out."

"Are you supposed to be out like that, with that thing on your leg?"

"I got clearance to go to work and to come over here for a few hours. It's all good, Unc."

"If you say so." Uncle Raymond scratched his gray-haired head with slow massaging scrapes. "I saw in the paper this morning where them police gone lose their jobs behind this mess and y'all gone sue them on top of it. You don't see that too much. Cops get away with all kind of foolishness and they always jacking up somebody. They can shoot somebody a hundred times and all the poor fellow got in his hand is a toothbrush. When you do catch them rascals on tape, they always talking about we didn't see the first part of the tape. Any time ten police beat somebody with those nightsticks, after they already got them down and cuffed, I don't need to see the rest of the tape. It doesn't take a rocket scientist to know they just beating 'cause they can."

"And they always get away with it," Jamal said.

"Now I ain't saying they all like that, but it only takes one bad apple to spoil the bunch. Some of them cops don't do the beating, but they watch the other police do it. You ask me, they just as guilty. Well, the old folks down home would say you might get by, but you don't get away. I'm sho' hoping they don't get away this time with y'all's case. Who y'all got, Johnnie?"

"Nah, Unc, that ain't me. I don't have a civil case going. Sebastian and his pops got some lawyer out of Boston. I ain't in it. I'm still trying to get them to drop the charges, since I ain't done none of what they trying to say that I did. The car in the robbery ain't even mine."

"Whose was it?"

"Malik Abdul, Mrs. Jones's son."

"Lou Ada's boy?"

"That's him."

"Oh Lawdy. He done gone and changed his name to some mess that he can't spell. He ain't nobody but little Leroy Jones to me. That's what his folks named him and that's what he always gone be to me. I sho' didn't know he the one who got you into this world of trouble, trying to sell you a hot car. He ought to know better. I know they raised him better. I don't know what happened to that boy. He got off into some crazy mess, that's what he did. Nothing a good hard day's work won't cure." Uncle Raymond turned a few pages in the newspaper. "You didn't have none of that dope in the car, did you?"

"Dope! Unc, I keep telling you I don't have anything to do with drugs. I've been telling you that for years."

"Yeah, I know, but where there's enough smoke, there's bound to be some fire. I can't believe those cops just keep arresting you for nothing. Now, you have to be doing something."

Jamal knew there was no convincing people that he was innocent, most of the time. He had accepted, a long time ago, that in the eyes of the public, the church members, and some family members, he must be guilty if the police said so. All he could do was keep pushing forward and working on getting himself straightened out the best way he knew how.

"Does Sable have one of those getups around his leg too?" Uncle Raymond asked Jamal.

"Who you talking about now, Unc?"

"You know, the boy your cousin with."

"You talking about Sebastian?"

"That's what I said, didn't I? Did Sable get one of them there leg doohickeys too?"

"Nah, I doubt it. You know his pops ain't having none of that. He's one of those high rollers up in Boston or somewhere around that way."

"Well, one of these days, them cops are going to get tired of bothering you and go do some real work around here."

Jamal hugged Uncle Raymond around his neck.

"Watch out there now, boy." Uncle Raymond's gold tooth made an appearance during his short grin and then retreated into the sparsely populated mouth of teeth. "I don't want that thing to explode on me and have the police jumping out of trees and bushes round here. You know how they did those MOVE people, burning up the whole block, including the women and kids."

"And then they shot up everybody in the alley that they didn't burn."

"I tell you, that was a shame. I don't care what the police say. You just can't kill that many people and have it be an accident. These cops just ain't going to quit beating up black folks 'cause they know they can get away with it. They sho' ought to be glad Johnnie wasn't around here when the police got all of them MOVE people. The two or three people they didn't kill would have owned the Liberty Bell and the Ben Franklin Bridge by now, 'cause you know that Johnnie don't play when it comes to getting paid. That's who your Uncle Cletus should have called when he got burnt by them fries."

Every mouth in the house was either flapping in conversation or being stuffed with food. The party was in high gear when Courtney walked through the front door, alone. Jamal was on one side of the room and Edwin was talking with Terry on the other when they saw Courtney come in. They both made beelines to Aunt Sis, who was in the kitchen.

"Mama, Ce-Ce is here."

"Please, don't start in on her."

"I invited her and Nilla. I didn't see him come in yet, but he might 'cause I invited him. If you don't want them here, I'll leave with them. I ain't playing, Mama."

Aunt Sis was stirring sauce on the stove. She removed the pot of spaghetti from the heat and poured it into the strainer sitting in the sink. Her head turned to avoid the wave of rising steam, which was sure to scald her if she wasn't careful.

"Why didn't he get a leg monitor? You two got arrested at the same time, for the same reason. You still getting treated like a criminal and he's out, footloose and fancy-free."

"Mama, leave it alone. You gotta quit all of this," Edwin pleaded.

"That ain't his fault, Mama. His daddy got the hookup and got him out. So what? If you got it like that, it's cool," Jamal explained to his mother.

Edwin wanted to have the hookup. He'd worked hard in the legal realm to get where and what he needed, to be effective. He was a pro at saving corporations billions of dollars in frivolous lawsuits, but he didn't have enough clout to get his brother out of the local jail, completely free on a bunch of bogus charges. When it came right down to it, he had the credentials and the track record, but he wasn't "the man." He was a brother from west Philly still trying to get into a game of double Dutch jump rope, and the good ole boys were turning the ropes at lightning speed, offering him no breaks. He was an attorney, a licensed officer of the court, and couldn't save his own brother from being harassed by the local police. Get an education, save yourself. That's what he grew up believing. The old homeys in the neighborhood had another way of protecting their own. Maybe he needed to think about that the next time he wanted to rattle off those empty words of motivation to a set of young brothers who were idolizing his two-seater convertible sports car.

Edwin stayed in the kitchen a little longer and Jamal came out to see his cousin.

"Ce-Ce, what's up, girl?"

The greetings were extended, Young style.

"Where's Nilla?"

"Nilla?"

"Ah, you know that's my new name for Sebastian. You know he couldn't walk around here with a name like that. Nilla is all right, though. Where is he? I invited him too."

"He wanted to come but you know how Aunt Sis gets. With you guys getting locked up last weekend, he didn't think it would be smart to come over here just yet. He did send you this gift, though," she said, handing the wrapped box to Jamal.

"That's too bad because I wanted to holla at him. It's all good, though. But, uh, you don't have to worry about Mama. If she trips with you or him from now on, she knows I'm out of here and she ain't trying to have me leave."

Courtney leaned on Jamal and thanked him for supporting her, while tears rolled down her cheek to his shoulder.

"Look, if I'm not tripping about Nilla, Mama definitely shouldn't be. If you're happy with him, cuz, that's all that I need to hear. I got your back."

When the front door opened, it wasn't Sebastian, but it was a face that lit up Courtney's spirit. "Big Mama's here," she said loud enough for people in the kitchen to hear while wiping her eyes and lifting her head from Jamal's shoulder.

Aunt Sis heard the ruckus and came into the living room wiping her hands on a towel that she stuffed into her apron pocket.

"Cousin Emma, you finally made it."

"Ize sho' did. Ize know ya didn't think I was gone make it, but God says this a good time, so Ize here."

"Get up from that chair, Deon, and let Cousin Emma have a seat."

Aunt Sis turned her head toward Big Mama's ear and said under her breath, "He acts like he's lost his home training since he married that woman."

"We all lose something when we get married, according to the Word, but it don't compare to what we gain." Big Mama put her hand out toward Deon. "You don't have to get up for me, baby. Ize been sitting on the train for hours. My legs feel good standing up. You sit down and enjoy yourself."

"Well, Deon, get her bag at least."

"No," Big Mama said, extending her hand again. "This bag gone be fine. Ize gone put it in the corner and that's gone be that. This supposed to be a party. Don't mind me none. Get back to what ya was doing."

"You should have called us. Edwin would have picked you up."

"Ize didn't want that young man having to run around after an ole woman like me. If'n he gone have a woman riding in his car, it ought to be someone young, more his speed, not ole women like us, Cleora. I likes getting around myself anyhow, without having to put myself off on somebody. They got a heap of cabs down there and Ize got one of them just fine."

"Edwin wouldn't have minded at all and you know it."

"Oh no, chile. The Lord done give me my health and my strength. I ain't having him driving me around, lessen it's an emergency, and this wasn't no emergency."

Big Mama would make her rounds, but Courtney was first.

Courtney's tears had dried, leaving no external evidence of her inward concern for the rift between the man she loved and the aunt she respected and adored. She was taller than Big Mama, but Courtney managed to squeeze in tight during the embrace.

"What's wrong, chile?" Big Mama pulled back and looked into Courtney's eyes. "Everybody else round here look to be happy. Ya might be smiling on the outside, but something ain't cooking right on the inside."

It hurt so badly to think it might not work with Sebastian. Around some, they were just hot and cold, day and night. How long could she endure this much tension? There was so much bothering her, and Courtney didn't know where to begin. "There's a lot going on."

"Don't worry, chile. Ya can talk to Big Mama."

"I don't know if talking is going to help this problem. It's pretty big."

"Well, it ain't nothing a little faith can't work out." Big Mama held Courtney's hands. " 'Tween me and you calling on God, it's gone be all right."

Chapter 43

Jamal squeezed his bike into the narrow sliver separating the wall from his bed. He had attended numerous Young celebrations in the past, but none had been in his honor since his eighth grade graduation. He felt satisfied. Life was looking up. Wal-Mart was a steady gig with benefits. It was nice having medical and dental insurance, even if he didn't use it. A retirement plan was something for Deon, Edwin, and Terry. Who would have thought that he, Jamal Williams, would have a 401K? It was all coming together. He wanted to work on the Jesus relationship Nilla had talked about, but he needed time to make a move that big. Next week he would go to the car lots at the auto mall by the airport and roll away with a set of wheels. He might even get a loan and build up some of that credit stuff. Never know, if some of those blessings came his way, a new place might be in the cards too. Right now, there was only one plan on the table. It was Saturday night and the Sixers were in the playoffs. The next three hours was dedicated time.

Four minutes into the second quarter, there was a bang on the door.

Jamal ignored it and turned the sound up on the TV set. Nothing or no crazy person was going to interrupt this heated bout. After all of the injuries and slow starts his team had endured in the beginning of the season, there was no way he planned to miss a single moment of the game. It was a miracle they had made it this far and were doing so well. When he did get serious about God, one of the first prayers he'd kick off would be for something he loved, his prized Sixers, couldn't hurt. The banging continued.

Jamal popped up from the bed and jerked the door open. "What!"

"Good to see you too, Mr. Williams."

"Man, come on. Don't you have anything else to do but bug me? Look, I ain't got time for this. Unless you got a warrant, step," Jamal told Detectives Crawford and Holmes, pointing toward the door.

Crawford came in and kicked the door shut. "Getting pretty uppity, aren't you? I guess since you had that little altercation with Officers Hotchkins and Cole, you're feeling pretty good about yourself."

"Who's Hotchkins and Cole?"

"Oh, come on, you know them. They're the ones the rich boy got fired, and on top of that, he brought heat down on the department. Now how can a little punk like you manage to be in a stolen car with someone holding that kind of power? What are you, his dealer?" Crawford rubbed his hands together briskly before resting his chin on the butt of his palms and then pointing his fingers toward Jamal. "It's your lucky day. You won't get many of these. We're not going to arrest you this time. Consider it like a get-out-of-jail-free card, but don't worry, when the heat cools down, we'll be back for our regular chats." Crawford patted Jamal on the shoulder. "You and me, we go way back, don't we? And they say whites and blacks can't get along. Look at us."

Jamal looked angry.

"Oh, I'm sorry. Hey, Sam, I think I've upset Mr. Williams. I'm sorry, Mr. Williams, did I use the wrong word? Can't do that. I don't want him getting some high-priced lawyer to sue my politically incorrect behind. Sam, what is it this week, African-American, black, Afro-American, Negro, Negroid, or what? It's so hard to keep up."

Sam Holmes frowned but kept quiet.

"Man, you a stone trip," Jamal told Holmes. "How you gone let him talk about me like that? He's talking about you too. You're a brother. What's up with that? Man, get out of here, you ain't nothing but his flunky."

Crawford pushed the racial comments to the edge, and Holmes took it because he didn't want to be labeled as the black man on the force crying about mistreatment. There wasn't a lot he could do about Crawford, but Mr. Williams was a different story. Holmes was a man too, and Crawford and Williams had better recognize that. He couldn't let his partner and this punk humiliate him at the same time.

It was as if a magnet drew the butt of his gun to a spot on the side of Jamal's head. He knew the crack was coming and prepared like all of the other times. The headache would last a day or two but that was it. He felt the blow and his brain waves short-circuited, causing him to slump on his feet.

His body went limp and fluttered to the floor, striking his head on the corner of the TV. Unexpectedly, the rickety leg of the table supporting the TV plummeted to the floor. The TV, which had endured so many attacks, finally gave way to the pressure and went crashing to the floor too. The screen and antenna were broken once it reached its final resting place.

"Usually you leave all of the fun for me, Sam. I guess you couldn't resist any longer." Crawford snapped the cuffs on in case Jamal recovered with a notion of retaliation. "There's nothing like a good hunt."

Holmes lodged the gun under Jamal's neck and forced it up, bringing his head with him.

"Get up, Mr. Williams. Get up."

There was no movement. Crawford kicked Jamal's feet. Still no movement.

"Check his pulse, Sam," Crawford said with a crack in his voice.

Detective Holmes moved his fingers around Jamal's neck and then felt around his wrist. He looked up with his eyes wide. "I don't feel a pulse."

"What!" Crawford rubbed his hands together briskly and blew on them, pacing. "I know, take his cuffs off, quick."

Sam fumbled with his keys.

Crawford ravaged his coat pocket for his cell phone. Finally, he had it. He punched in dispatch, asking for an ambulance and declining backup. There was much to do in a short time. Although the ambulance wasn't known for fast arrivals in this area, it might be just the time when one showed up as quickly as it did in the suburbs. The place had to be tidied. No loose ends. This wasn't the scenario he'd hoped for, not now, not while the eyes were glaring down on the department. He'd be ruined. Twenty years on the force would be down the drain, without thinking about jail time, and who knows what else? This situation had to be cleaned.

"What do we do with the TV?" Holmes asked.

"I don't know, push it in the closet. Just get it out of sight. This has to look like a routine arrest," Crawford said.

"But it wasn't an arrest, remember? We came over to let him know that he better not have had anything to do with Hotchkins and Cole losing their jobs. We don't have any legitimate reason to be over here. Ah, man, what are we going to do now?"

"I guess you better start trying to give him mouth-to-mouth. He can't die on us. You don't want some fancy lawyer charging you with aggravated assault or worse," Crawford said, looking down at the life-less body.

"Me! Why you say me?" Holmes questioned with his voice elevating.

"Sam, you're the one that cracked him over the head with the gun. That was a bad move."

"You've hit him with the stick many times."

"Sure, but I never had him down like this. I came to get information on the pending case with his buddy, Pee Wee Muhammad. I'm sorry, Sam, but someone might have to take the fall for this one. We'll stick together for as long as we can, but I have a family to feed. I can't lose twenty years on the force behind some punk like this."

Sam stood in the middle of the room with his eyes fixed on Jamal.

The sirens blasted in the rooming house, signaling the detectives to begin the CPR process and to finish any last-minute arrangements.

The paramedics rushed into room number 10, with a gob of other residents next to the gurney, peering into the cramped doorway for a look. Chattering and clambering ensued.

One paramedic cocked his head toward his shoulder to talk with the dispatcher through his radio. "I have a black male, looks to be in his mid-twenties, unconscious."

"What happened?" the other paramedic asked while checking Jamal's pulse and breathing.

Holmes began to respond when Crawford jumped in with a con-flicting account.

"So he fell onto the TV, hit his head, and it knocked him out. Is that it?"

"That's about it."

The paramedic's face scrunched as he looked at the two men. He pressed in for a pulse twice and held still. "I have a faint pulse. We have to get him on oxygen and get him out of here."

The other paramedic stared at the men and rolled his eyes before getting on the radio. "We're coming in with a trauma to the head, possible concussion, brain damage, or maybe some internal bleeding. We just don't know. The patient is still unconscious. We're on our way in."

Jamal was strapped in. The gurney was in motion, rolling down the narrow hallway that was holding light hostage and refused to let a glimmer of hope seep through the cracks.

Holmes and Crawford braced themselves against the doorway, watching Jamal roll farther and farther away. They were good at turning criminals into victims.

"A little too much spice too often spoils the soup," Crawford rattled.

They had gotten by so many times with their premeditated acts of violence, but would their streak hold up, allowing them to get away once again?

"I pray he's okay," Holmes said in a weak tone.

"Forget about him, we better make sure our story is straight if we're going to beat this one. I hope he doesn't remember any of this, or your behind is on the line, partner. Let's take a ride to the hospital. We have work to do."

Chapter 44

The breaking news story was everywhere. A twenty-six-year-old black man with a long history of crime was hospitalized yesterday evening after an altercation with the police. He was listed in critical condition. The incident was being investigated, but no charges of misconduct were expected to be filed against the two decorated police detectives.

Courtney tried to watch the news, but it kept making her cry. She knew what had really happened, no matter what kind of story the police were telling. How could they do this to Jamal? Just yesterday he was at the party, enjoying himself. He was so proud of his job at Wal-Mart. Everything was looking up for him, finally. Why did this have to happen? She wanted to hate the cops, but deep down she knew it would be a blatant display of prejudice and would violate the godly principle she was trying to live by, love thy neighbor, even the ones who grew up on the other side of town. It was hard not to give in to her desire and judge an entire group of people based on her opinion and experiences of a few. Which police would she include anyway, short ones, tall ones, Irish ones, black ones, abusive ones, uneducated ones? There were so many, all with something in common, but different. Only prayer and faith, the parting-of-rivers kind, could get her beyond this moment of agony.

Thank God for Sebastian. From the second she had come back from the hospital around midnight, Sebastian had been there for her, finally going home a few hours ago. She wanted to stay with him and hide herself in his protective love. Instead, he would go to their church without her, and she'd catch up with him at the hospital later.

She got herself together and went to Fifth Baptist. It would have been nice to escape the upcoming emotions and hurt swirling around church this morning, but this was definitely a family day. The Young family would have a united front and show themselves strong in the face of adversity. Walking down the aisle felt like being in a fog. It was all a blur. Jamal was okay. The family was fine. She and Sebastian were on track. When Courtney approached the Young section and saw Aunt Sis boo-hooing, the firm hand of reality slapped her in the face, reminding her that the anguish curdling in the pit of her stomach was no dream.

Aunt Sis didn't look good. She would have been at the hospital all day and night, but Reverend Tyler had asked the family to show up today for a special service of support. The morning moved in slow motion, but when ten-thirty came, the show began.

It was young adult Sunday, which meant the music was going to be lively. The choir knew how to get people on their feet. They could lead the congregation into the spirit and right on out the back door if they weren't careful. She recalled a few times when they were rocking so hard Reverend Tyler gave a look to the choir director that seemed to ask if they were still in worship. A little too much bass and dancing in the aisles caused him to raise the question. Overall Reverend Tyler ran a tight ship around Fifth Baptist. His favorite saying was that the church needed to be right before God.

The service got under way. The music was no less entertaining than Courtney had expected, and midway through the program Tyler took his platform and skimmed the Word of God as part of his warmup to the main attraction, getting the people motivated to fight for the cause.

She didn't have a notebook, but then Reverend Tyler's messages didn't really call for one if you were a regular member. Over time she'd heard most of his sermons. It wasn't the words so much that intrigued her, more so his delivery, kind of like an entertainer. She enjoyed his ability to move around the sanctuary with the energy of a lion and the grace of a gazelle. The congregation gobbled his show up.

"By now, we all have heard about Sister Cleora's son Jamal being hospitalized by a bunch of rogue cops. To Sister Williams and to the rest of the family, we want you to know Fifth Baptist is behind you. We are praying for your strength in the Lord. Amen." Reverend Tyler unwrapped the microphone cord and moved toward the center of the stage. "I don't know about you, Brother Henry, but I'm ashamed to say that we're all to blame for young Brother Jamal's beating. We each have watched the police brutalize him over the years and we haven't done a thing to stop it."

"That's right, Reverends" and "um-hmms" leaped from every pew.

"It's time we took a stand." He banged on the podium, refolded his handkerchief, and pressed into the microphone. "Do you hear what I say? It's time to stand up for our brothers and sisters. We don't have to let 'the man' hold a shotgun over our head no more. We got power, Oh, Lord. Yeah-ahhh. Power, you don't hear me. Power."

"Go on, Reverend," Sister Johnson bellowed out, leaping to her feet and waving her hand so enthusiastically that Sister Jones was forced to hold her hat in place.

"They might not be burning crosses in our yards, thanks be to God, but not too much has changed."

"Yeah-ah, preach on, Reverend," someone yelled.

"They tell me Peter and Paul had a problem with the law back in the Bible, well, and uh, he didn't know what to do. Well, the Lord sent an angel, yes, he did. Oh, oh, welllll."

Reverend Tyler put it in fifth gear and ran the aisles, leaving not a silent patron in the place except for Big Mama, Courtney, and old Mr. Hicks, who took a nap at sermon time every Sunday and woke up when the cheering rose to its peak around twelve forty-five. Reverend Tyler dropped back to second gear after a few laps and a couple of Bible parables, and after about four church folks collapsed from being overcome with some kind of spirit. Tyler was back in the pulpit with sweat popping from his temples that he wiped with his faithful hanky.

"We need to come out tomorrow night and have a prayer rally, first at the hospital and then down to the police station. We're going to let them know this isn't business as usual. Amen. Church, I want you to know that I got a call this morning from Sebastian Whittington. Some of you know him. He's in law school here in Philadelphia and he went to school with our own Courtney. He's also the one who's been in the news for filing the law suit against the police department."

Courtney wasn't prepared for an announcement concerning Sebastian. She was shocked that Sebastian had called Reverend Tyler without mentioning it to her. She sat straight up in her seat, bracing herself for whatever was coming.

"Well, he has offered to get us connected with a big attorney out of Boston. Amen. Isn't God good?"

"Amens" commenced. Reverend Tyler had spoken.

"You never know where your blessings are going to come from. I don't know how many of you have met Sebastian, but I tell you, he's a strong man of God. Church, we need more young men in the body of Christ like him. I invited him to the rally tomorrow. When you see him there, I want you to extend a word of encouragement to him, Fifth Baptist. Don't forget, church, I want to see everyone that can come out tomorrow night at six o'clock sharp. We can make a difference in numbers."

Courtney knew the call to arms was as good as done. Reverend Tyler might not draw a crowd of faithful followers like Malcolm X, who could fill a stadium on short notice, but there would be more than enough to make a statement.

Reverend Tyler preached another twenty minutes and the service came to a close around one-thirty. A flood of members surrounded Aunt Sis with words of support and prayers. Other members dashed to the vestibule where Reverend Tyler religiously stood at the back door and greeted people as they left.

"Mighty fine message, Reverend, and you are sure right. We need to stand up. I'm tired of hearing about all of what these police are doing. This is as bad as it was in the sixties. I thought those days were past but I guess they aren't," said one member.

"We'll see you at the march tomorrow."

"Sure will, Reverend. My family will be there."

Courtney stood in the back of church, to the side of the open doors leading into the vestibule, to catch a few moments of solitude. She could hear several people talking.

"That's what happen when 'black folks' get uppity and start trying to act like 'white folks.' It's a crying shame is what it is. See how she got all this mess stirred up, instead of staying with a nice man like Paul, one of her own kind?"

"Oh no, honey. I guess when you go to those big-name schools they wash all of the black and sense right out of you."

The ladies cackled and gathered their belongings as they approached Tyler's receiving line.

"I keep saying that 'white folks' and 'black folks' don't need to be mixing. If they stay out there in the whoops and we stay in the city, everything will be all right. Start messing with that picture and a whole lot of ugly stuff happens."

Six months ago Courtney would have kept out of sight and ducked out the back way, avoiding eye-to-eye contact with those who weren't trying to wish her well. Reverend Tyler was right. It was time to take a stand. God had dealt her and Sebastian the race card and they intended to play it, happily, all the way to the altar. Anyone who had a problem with it was going to have to seek God for their own peace. She wasn't carrying the weight anymore. Even Aunt Sis's blistering eyes, sure to be burning hate red as coals, didn't break her spirit or rock her faith. Head raised and stride in her step, she graced the vestibule. The women who were deep in conversation saw her coming.

"Courtney, we're so sorry to hear about your cousin. We'll be praying for your family," one of the cackling ladies said.

Courtney grinned, keeping her comments bolted down inside. Prayers were appreciated, but some who offered had too much of their own baggage. It didn't seem like they would be able to get one for her past the ceiling. Better to stick with her own prayers. Besides, she was on a first-name basis with God.

She was pleasantly surprised when a host of members approached her to give words of encouragement for her and Sebastian. She was touched and couldn't wait to tell him. Maybe now he could come to Fifth Baptist and be all right.

The vestibule line was still thick. Aunt Sis was introducing Big Mama to some of her church friends. They made their way to the back of the church and were waiting in the reception line too.

"Reverend Tyler can sure go, can't he?" Aunt Sis asked Big Mama.

"Sho' can go. He gets a lot of exercise. That ought to be good for his heart."

"Cousin Emma, you didn't like his preaching!"

"The preaching was just fine, but what Ize sees is that ya'll pastor got a special anointing on him for getting folks together." Big Mama took Aunt Sis's hand and patted it. "He sho' right, ya don't know how God gone send ya a blessing. Don't let ya anger block ya blessing, Cleora. After we speak to ya pastor, let's go to the hospital and see ya baby. I believe God got a miracle on the way and ain't no need waiting round here when it's over yonder."

Chapter 45

Courtney's anguish would have been enough to make Sebastian ache, but he knew Jamal for himself and called him a friend. Sebastian prayed to God this incident wouldn't derail his relationship with Courtney. They had finally gotten to a place of peace, a place of hope.

This nightmare couldn't be happening. Jamal was making strides to get his life turned around, but had he accepted Christ yet? Sebastian was in agony, wondering if maybe he should have pushed harder to get Jamal saved when he had the chance. But then, he remembered that he didn't have the power to save Jamal. That was God's job. He couldn't die.

He fiddled with the mouthpiece of his trumpet. No sense playing it. No sound could dip down far enough into his soul to calm the restless waters. He hadn't known what to do, only that doing nothing wasn't an option. He had given it some thought earlier and had come up with an idea to help the protest Reverend Tyler was staging. He had called Reverend Tyler and offered legal assistance. Now he had to follow up with a call to his father. Sebastian was happy that he'd taken the time out to meet with Tyler back in October. It hadn't been a long discussion and Tyler didn't have any concrete ideas on how to mend fences with Aunt Sis, other than prayer. Talking to the reverend was positive and Sebastian had felt comfortable calling him.

Appeal wasn't the term for what he had to do with his father. It would be more like begging for help. Jamal deserved justice and Mr. Whittington knew how to get it. He picked up the phone and held it before dialing home. His parents were still angry about him getting arrested. He couldn't quite figure out if they were mad at him, Jamal, the system, Courtney, or just mad to be mad. He humbled himself and called his dad in hopes of lending a helping hand to his friend and brother in the Lord.

"Whittington residence."

"Shirley, it's been a long time."

"It sure has, Sebastian. I hope Philadelphia is treating you okay."

"I'm hanging in here." He picked up the framed picture lying on the coffee table, showing him and Courtney at D&B. Eight months seemed like ages ago. They'd been through so much since then and had, apparently, experienced only the tip of the iceberg.

"How's the young lady you've been seeing?"

A flood of light poured into his eyes, illuminating his apartment. He was overjoyed to have someone from home care enough about his happiness to ask. No one else in his family had. "Courtney is awesome. You have to meet her one day."

"I'm sure I will."

"As always, it's good talking to you, Shirley. Take care of yourself and tell George I sent a big hello his way. Is my dad around, by any chance?"

"He sure is, but before I get him, I want you to know how proud I am of you, Sebastian. You haven't had it as easy as many would think but you've done all right for yourself. You're a smart man. It's not always what's on the outside. When God sends you a blessing, I'm sure you know how to grab it. If you get to know her, you might be shocked just how much you have in common, more than you know. I love you, Sebastian, whatever what you do or whoever you see. You remember that."

"I will, Shirley, and thank you for the support. I really needed to hear those words right now and I love you too."

"Hold on, I'll get your dad."

She paged Mr. Whittington on the intercom. He took the call in his office and participated in the cordial greetings.

"Dad, the guy who got arrested with me was victimized by the police last night. They were probably retaliating for the lawsuit and the other disciplinary actions taken against their fellow officers. Anyway, my friend Jamal is in the hospital, barely hanging on, and the police are getting away with it. Not one charge has been raised against them."

"And this doesn't sound like an issue I have to be privy to."

"Come on, Dad, you did a huge thing for me with the police. Can't you wage some kind of legal battle, on his behalf, to make the department accountable for the actions of these two rogue cops who have violated Jamal's civil rights?"

"Why would I? The people you're fraternizing with don't need me in their affairs, and I certainly don't need them wallowing in mine. Is this woman worth being degraded to a life plagued with headlines and perpetual run-ins with the law?" he spewed without excuse.

"I don't understand why you have so much animosity against someone you've never met."

"I've known her kind, intimately."

"What does that mean? What's her kind, funny, smart, what?"

"Black!" he bellowed through gritted teeth.

"Dad, why can't you understand she's more than just black? She's also a woman, a Northwestern graduate, and an all-around great person." He left a key attribute out, the fact that she loved the Lord, suspecting any reference to spirituality would be a conversation-buster. He reared his head back in the chair, giving his body a stretch. Both elbows bent and the phone in the air, he took a sigh. "It takes a long list of characteristics to describe who Courtney is, not just her skin color."

"Fine, but at the end of the day, she's black and that is unacceptable to me. I can never accept someone like her into my family."

"How do you know if you never give yourself a chance to get to know her?"

"Don't need to. I've seen firsthand the kind of damage 'their kind' can cause in our lives and I won't stand for them doing to you what was done to me." His words were sharp and deliberate.

"Dad, I'm not following." Sebastian scooted to the edge of his chair.

"Your mother."

"Mom, what about Mom? I know she's upset about Courtney too and she's being unreasonable right now, but it will pass."

"I'm not talking about your stepmom. I'm referring to your birth mother."

"What about her? I know she died when I was a baby. What does she have to do with this?"

"Your mother didn't die." The man kept quiet, letting seconds circle the room, uninterrupted. "She left."

"*What!* What are you talking about, she left?" He was on his feet, standing in the living room with his mouth hanging, open before he realized what was going on. "And what do you mean she didn't die?"

Mr. Whittington's words had hopped the train out of town and were slow about returning to the conversation. "I forced her to leave in order to save our family."

"I don't understand anything you're telling me. What are you talking about?" The vessels in Sebastian's temples vibrated. He gripped the phone with adequate pressure to squeeze the truth out.

"I know this will be difficult to understand, but your mother was black."

"Black! What do you mean black! You mean tanned or dark-toned, what?"

"When I met her, she was white with a liberal arts degree from Swarthmore and a graduate degree from Yale. We moved in the same elite circles. I fell in love with her, never realizing she was really a black woman."

"How could you not know?" He paced the apartment, taking sweeping rubs across his forehead.

"She concealed it. We didn't spend much time with her family, but the ones I did meet looked normal."

"This makes no sense, Dad. I can't believe you're telling me this now, after all of these years." Sebastian held his tongue, wanting to corral any unfiltered thought from escaping before it could be purified by the haphazard praying he was doing in the midst of this thunderstorm. He leaned on the kitchen counter. "When did you find out?"

"Right before you were born, she told me her grandmother was Dutch and African. Her grandmother married white and then the son she had married white, which led to your mother's birth. She tried to explain how her grandmother was conceived on a plantation in South Carolina, being the product of an owner and a field hand, but I didn't want to hear any of the sordid details. She was black and that was enough for me. The only reason she told me was out of fear that some of your traits might come out black. She recognized that her bloodline could have been dominating enough to pull characteristics from generations back. When I found out, she had to leave immediately after you were born. She didn't want to leave you, but her entire life would have been ruined if the truth came out. Whittington and Whittington wouldn't have been able to stand the potential scandal such a story presented either. So you see why I had to demand that she leave."

"You kicked my mother out to save face!"

"I protected your inheritance from a deceptive woman," Mr. Whittington defended in a stern voice.

"But I'm part of her. That makes me black too."

"That's a reality I have absolutely no control over." His words didn't go through the same filtering process as his son's. Nothing was spared. "Thank goodness your features are pure enough not to raise any red flags."

"Are you saying I'm okay because I look white enough to meet the seal of approval from you and your country club friends? No, don't even answer." The anger wanted to rise up, but he wouldn't let it, he couldn't. If it ever got to the surface, there might not be a way to control it, and that wasn't who God was developing him to be. The spirit of the Lord was deep inside and that's where he had to go to hold his peace. "Does Mom know?"

"She only knows what is necessary. This was not a matter she needed to be concerned with."

"Oh, so my mother lied and you kicked her out, no matter how it affected me, and now you've lied to Mom. What a vicious cycle."

"Look, Sebastian, I didn't ask for this set of circumstances," he yelled. "Yet, I have dealt with them, maintaining integrity and discretion. You should be grateful I didn't send you packing with that mother of yours."

"Perhaps you should have," he responded, letting each word linger in its own spotlight.

It was all making sense now. That's why he had to go to boarding school when he didn't want to go. It was an ultimatum of which he had had no input. Did Shirley know about this all along? She knew pretty much everything else that happened in the Whittington household and had for years, back when Mother was around. Maybe that's why she always told stories about Mother and went out of her way to show him love at times when it seemed like no one else would.

"My, my, aren't we a bit condescending. Wasn't it just last week when you called, needing my help?"

"And I'm grateful to God for you."

"God! Where was your God when I got you out of jail?"

"He showed up."

"No, I showed up."

"He sent you on his behalf."

Sebastian pumped and pumped into the well of his words, but came up dry. Not a single drop of understanding came out, so he hung up. He slumped in the chair. What was his father saying? How could this be? He stroked the back of his hand, up to his elbow. He looked the same as he had twenty minutes ago, back when he was white. What would change? It might help with Aunt Sis. Then again, she was basing her opinion of him on how he looked, not what he was made from. He might have black genes flowing in his body, but he looked white. There was a price to be paid on either side and there was nothing he could do about it.

Who was his mother? Where was she? How would he tell Courtney? This was too much to absorb in one shot. Thank God he knew Jesus, the one who saw his heart and appreciated the inner him, the true man living below the skin.

Chapter 46

It would have been easy to stay at home and sulk in his own sea of woes, but Sebastian wanted to take what energy he'd siphoned from the tête-à-tête with his father earlier and spend it on encouraging Jamal. Instead of going to church late, he would go to the hospital. Aunt Sis should be at Fifth Baptist, so this would be the ideal time to visit.

The corridors seemed cool and serene as he made his way to room 321, bed number 2. By some fluke, Aunt Sis might have come to the hospital before church. When he arrived, the room was empty, allowing his palpitating heart to slow down. Thank God she wasn't there.

Sebastian had prepared himself for a host of wires and tubes cascading from Jamal's body. Much to his surprise, there was an IV and a small tube coming from the back of his head, giving the only indication that Jamal's closed eyes were doing more than taking a simple rest.

He was thankful to Jamal for treating him like a man from the beginning, making no issue of his race. He had detected Jamal's intelligence right away. It was probably hard for outsiders to believe, those who didn't take time to get to know him. They saw him as a shiftless criminal, in and out of trouble, not living up to his potential. Chalk it up to fate. Jamal was born into an environment where breaks didn't come easily. Sebastian had to wonder if their resources had been switched growing up, where would they both be now. He believed that if he had been a seasoned criminal, with a tie and briefcase, he would have fit right in with the Center City executives. It wasn't that easy for someone like Jamal, who didn't have the luxuries of adapting his physical appearance like a chameleon, and rolling into society and being seen as a productive citizen. Jamal wasn't staying down. He was proud of Jamal for having the determination to make lemonade out of a truckload of lemons that had been dumped into his life.

The nurse came in the room and checked Jamal's pulse and vital signs.

"Any improvement?"

"Are you family?" the nurse asked with a puzzled look, lifting the chart from the holder on the door.

"Yes, I am, future in-law."

"Oh! Well, like I told Mrs. Williams last night, Jamal is resting comfortably. The CAT scan did reveal a skull fracture, hemorrhaging, and some blood clots."

"How serious is it?"

"The blood clot alone can be fatal, but we're doing everything we can to prevent that."

The nurse did something to the IV that increased the dripping pace.

"What do you do for something like that?"

"We put in what's called a burr hole to drain the fluid off his spine. That will help relieve the pressure. We'll keep trying meds through the IV to continue relieving the pressure, and to get the swelling down around the brain, while his body tries to repair the damage." She made notes on the clipboard chart. "It's all wait-and-see for now."

"Could he have brain damage?"

"This type of injury is much like having a stroke." She took a pause and drew in a breath. "It would be unusual for a patient to recover completely." The nurse put the chart back in the holder on the door and said, "Let's hope for the best," on the way out.

Lord, I believe, through faith, that Jamal is going to be well, in the name of Jesus. He wasn't sure if Jamal could hear, but God could. He continued praying and reading scriptures while his friend slept. A few hours passed. When Sebastian woke up from his short nap, it was nearly two o'clock. He jumped up and grabbed his Bible off the rolling table next to the bed. He said a quick prayer and a few words to Jamal, who was still sleeping. Sebastian rushed down the hall. He couldn't believe nearly three hours had gone so quickly. He got to the lobby and much to his dismay, Aunt Sis was coming in the entryway.

The Young family entourage, coming in with her, cleared the doorway and moved to one side of the lobby. Courtney reached for Sebastian's hand and they connected.

"I don't know what else I have to do to get you out of my face," Aunt Sis told Sebastian. "Every time I turn around, there you are. Don't you have anywhere else to go, somebody else to bother? I have enough to worry about without having to settle my stomach on the likes of you."

"Aunt Sis, he cares about Jamal too, why can't he come here and pray for him like the rest of us?" Courtney asked.

"Because unlike you, I don't need a white man to do anything for me, especially pray."

"But Jamal does."

Aunt Sis grunted and locked her arms across her chest. "I don't know why you don't get this. Your cousin is lying in the bed upstairs with his head bashed in by one of his kind."

"Mama, there were two cops and one of them was black," Edwin clarified.

"Doesn't make any difference. He was probably just an Uncle Tom, walking around beating up on black folks just because he got a little power. He just an overseer the master hired to keep us cookies in lines. That's how they do us. Hmmph. That's what happens when you forget where you come from," Aunt Sis hissed at Courtney.

"We need to try and work together, Aunt Sis."

"If God had wanted all of us together, he wouldn't have separated us, confused our language, and put us so far apart in the world," Aunt Sis threw out.

"It wasn't 'cause he didn't want us together. It was 'cause them people in the Bible had a whole lot of foolishness in their hearts, trying to build a tower that would reach to heaven. God knew that if'n the people worked together, nothing would be impossible to them. If'n we gets it together we could get rid of a heap of our troubles," Big Mama responded.

"Integration hasn't done a thing for us. All we've done is picked up the bad ways of 'white folks.' We're not the ones that run around killing ourselves, and everybody in the house, including the dog and the fish. We didn't used to jump out windows and slice our wrists because we lost our jobs. We used to just get by, making ends meet by having a few hustles on the side. We have always been the last ones to get hired and the first ones to get a pink slip. But now 'black folks' act like they can hardly survive without a million-dollar job and the rest act like they can't find one. We've never been lazy people. We've always wanted to work, had to work. Slavery made sure of that."

"You can't generalize about all people," Edwin told his mother.

"I can about enough of them. It's best if they stay in their place and I'll stay in mine. Separate but equal is what I want. We got the separate, but there's nothing equal about our neighborhoods and theirs."

Courtney reflected on her days in Chicago. Aunt Sis would have been at home. She could have gone to the South Side, the black suburbs, and been among plenty of people with grand houses, manicured lawns, and a steadfast determination to stay put, even if they did have to commute an hour to an hour and a half to work. The alternative didn't beat out their utopia.

"They got everything. We've had our hair cornrowed since King Tut sat on his mama's knee, but now they call it French braids. There is nothing French about a plait. They steal everything. Haven't left us a thing to call our own. We don't have a decent school or a decent grocery store. All we have is those foreigners coming in with them little nasty stores. We can't have anything. They've been taking our men and now they're after our women again. You'd think they had enough with all of these mixed folks running around here, don't half know if they're black or white. Just all confused and messed up." Her arms were folded tightly with fingers drilling into biceps that were protected by her jacket. "Sister Jones told me the soul food restaurant in Atlanta is owned by Asians. Now you know it's a sad day when we can't call ham hocks, collard greens, and sweet potato pie our own. I'll go without before I spend one red dime at one of those places. Hmmph. Give us some of the government programs they get and we can open our own stores in our neighborhood. Before I die, just once I want to buy bread and some hair grease from somebody on the other side of the counter who looks like me. Is that too much to ask?"

"Cuttin' Cleora, is ya finished?"

"I've said all I need to for the moment, but nothing has changed. I want him gone and anybody else in here that wants to protect him can hit the door too. That's okay with me today," she directed to Edwin and Courtney.

"If'n he done something against ya and the family, sho' let me know and Ize be the first one to gets down on my knees and cry out to the Lord above that he send a batch of angels here to carry this young man right on out of here. Now, if'n he ain't done nothing, then ya needs to put ya mind on prayers, 'cause that's the only way ya gone gets ya boy to raise up and walk out of here. Ya got to let this foolishness go. You're a woman of God. Wherever two or three are gathered together in his name, God says he's gone be in the midst. If'n God in here and Ize knows he is, is this how ya wants to act in front of him? If'n it is, Ize sho' don't want ya standing next to me, 'cause ya gone drain the spirit right out of me." Big Mama peered over the top of her glasses.

Aunt Sis drew in her insults and slithered to the other side of Big Mama, away from Sebastian.

Sensing the coast was clear, Sebastian pressed in closer to Courtney.

"Did the Lord confirm in ya spirits that ya for each other?" asked Big Mama.

Both nodded and grabbed hands again.

"Then that settles it."

"There is no way God put them together, not with all of these nice black men around here for her," said Aunt Sis.

"What ya cares for? Ya ain't got to live with him." She turned, facing Courtney and Sebastian. "Chile, let me tell ya, if'n ya got to go through meat and lean, likes we all got to do from time to time, then ya better be with somebody ya likes and ya know ya called to be with. Choosing ya man just 'cause they's one color or another don't mean it's going to be right."

"It's right in my book."

"Well, see, that's why Ize ain't living by ya book, Cuttin' Cleora. Ize living by the Word of God. Whoever ya is or wherever ya come from, once ya accept the Lord, that's it, you're all the same in the eyes of God. In the book that Ize going by, Galatians, chapter three, verses twenty-eight and twenty-nine, say, 'There is neither Jew nor Greek, slave nor free, male nor female, for you're all one in Christ Jesus.' If'n ya belong to Christ, then you're Abraham's seed, and heirs according to the promise."

"Well, I'm not Greek or Jewish, so that does not apply to me."

"Be mighty careful, Cleora. Ya ain't spouting off at me." Big Mama shook the Bible in the air. "Back when this was written down, Greeks and Jewish people were fighting just like blacks and whites are today. There's nothing new under the sun, the Bible says."

"If they don't bother me, I won't be bothering them."

"Hear what the Word say. Ya know what ya want to and don't want to believe. Ize can lead ya to the water, but ya got to drink on your own."

Sebastian was prepared for his mother and father, actually all of Boston, to disapprove of his relationship with Courtney, to the point of being boldly racist or at least mildly prejudiced. Aunt Sis had thrown him for a complete loop. Who knew blacks could be prejudiced too?

"My horoscope told me somebody or something was going to upset me today. It was right."

"Is that the book ya talking about ya living by? Cuttin' Cleora, is ya putting the word of a soothsayer up against the Word of God? If'n ya is, that the answer to most of your problems. Ain't no fortune-teller, soothsayer, man in the moon, cowbell ringer, or root doctor never gone tell ya more than the Word and the Holy Spirit. There's no shortcut for hearing from God. Ya got to take time to go before him, press in, and wait to hear from him. There's only one God giving out directions about that there life of yours. Ya better check 'cause Ize don't know who's given out your horoscope answers."

"Well, I don't need any horoscope to tell me they don't belong together. Why would God put them together? Nah, that's all her own doing."

"Well, one thing for sho'. God ain't gone tell ya something for them and won't tell them too. He says he will confirm his word for ya among two or three witnesses." Big Mama turned to Sebastian and Courtney and put their coupled hands between hers. "Don't let nobody bring ya no news about what God done said for ya until ya ask him for ya self and get in agreement on it for ya self. Ize ain't saying ya won't get a word from time to time, but go to ya Father and check on it for ya self." She did a firm shake and smiled light into their bond.

It was the first positive confirmation Courtney had gotten from someone anointed of God. Big Mama's words soaked in slowly, covering her fragile spiritual areas. She knew the Lord, true enough, but only six months ago she was like an embryo-Aunt Sis, with her own biases and prejudices. She had participated in enough racially oriented conversations and taken the "black" position on plenty of topics behind closed doors, among those living in the same cultural place. She realized that being called to an interracial relationship was like going to the mission fields in a foreign land, estranged from family and loved ones, speaking a different language, and living a different culture. Love might be blind, but racism and prejudices had twenty-twenty vision. Thriving in the relationship with Sebastian would take more than love. It required big faith, the parting-of-the-waters kind. She squeezed his hand a little tighter, refusing to let go, come joy or pain, knowing fully well Aunt Sis was capable of inflicting the latter.

"Doing God's will is right, but now that don't mean that it's gone be easy. Ya may not get support likes ya want. Some people just ain't gone be able to help ya. They ain't got the heart for your calling. Do you understand what I'm telling ya?"

The couple nodded.

"Jesus asked the disciples to wait up with him one hour before the persecutors came to get him. They went to sleep, leaving Jesus to wait on his own. Even for Jesus, the disciples couldn't understand the weight of his calling 'cause it wasn't they calling to hang on the cross. Love those that are going to persecute ya so that ya don't grow the same kind of hatred in your heart that they got to work with. Only Jesus could have done what he was created to do. Only the two of ya can do together what God done created ya to do together. Ize don't know what it is he has for ya to do, but ya be obedient to his Word and to ya calling. Ya got to step out in faith and trust God, even when it seems like ya headed down the road blind together. God knows where ya is and where ya going. Okay?"

Courtney and Sebastian embraced Big Mama in a circle hug.

"Ize wants ya to remember how Moses' family acted when they didn't take too kindly to his mixed kind of marriage. Oh, they showed out but God had the final say. Ya remember that. Put God first, each other next, and everything gone be all right."

"How is she going to put someone ahead of her family? He just came into her life," Aunt Sis wanted to know. "Family comes first. That's all there is to it."

"Ize says God come first."

"Well, we've known her all of her life. Don't that count for anything?"

"Cuttin' Cleora, they ain't gone stay children forever. They got to grow up and gets on they own. Anybody stay up under they mama's wings ain't grown, they's children. Ain't no three people in a marriage. Mama and Daddy got to find they own happiness and let these kids enjoy they lives without having to worry about ole gray-heads like us. Ize don't know about ya, but Ize don't want to be a burden and have to depend on my grandbaby. That would be selling my God too short and Ize ain't aiming to do that. Let these babies go, Cleora!"

"I can't help it if I need help from my kids at times. They don't mind doing for me."

"Shame on ya for needing their help. Ya ought to be in a place where they can bless ya without ya having to need it. They ought not have to tell ya when they tired of helping. They ain't ya source or your savior. Ya got to look up for that. Ya need to get ya house in order, Cleora."

Edwin kept quiet, but he fidgeted the entire time Big Mama spoke.

"Still, we don't mean nothing to her now that she's gotten her college degree. I guess we're Bo-Bo the clown, because she's treating us like we're fools."

"Mama, Courtney hasn't done anything. She's not the one embarrassing me and making me feel like a fool."

"Oh, so what are you saying? Is that your way of telling me I'm making you look like a fool? I know you're not talking to me like that. I know better. You're not that grown."

"The man look mighty grown to me."

"See? This is what I'm talking about. See what you're doing, causing us to fight? See? Our kids don't talk back and curse at their parents like your kind does. Our kids didn't do this until they start mixing around you all, picking up your old nasty ways."

"Cuttin' Cleora, Edwin gone get older, but he ain't gone get no growner. Cleora, ooo-weee, ya sho' got a mess of something pinned up in ya. Maybe you're the one we needs to be praying for first, 'cause ya spirit is blocking a heap of light in here."

"I'm trying to look out for my family. God helps those who help themselves."

"Is that right?"

"Um-hmm"

"Well, Ize done been back and forth through the Bible more times than Ize can remember and Ize ain't never seen where God says he helps those who help themselves. Jesus came to help those who couldn't help themselves."

Aunt Sis stuck her hand on her hip and patted her foot, but no rebuttal came forth. There was silence in her space.

"Ize don't know about ya, but Ize came to praise the Lord and to send some prayers up that's bound to shake heaven's doors. Ize wants my God to know that Ize in the Pennsylvania Hospital right here in Philadelphia and Ize don't aims to go anywhere until God either comes down himself or sends somebody that's got some healing power in their touch. Oh, glory. Hallelujah." She shook her fist in the air. "Anybody who wants to catch this train that's heading for glory, come on with me."

Big Mama moved forward to the bank of elevators with Edwin, Courtney, and Sebastian following. Aunt Sis stood in the same spot, with her lips poked out for an instant. She blew out a sigh with force sufficient to ruffle papers in the information kiosk. No one hovered or pushed backward to meet her. She rolled her eyes and took slow stomps toward the group.

Chapter 47

Being in the presence of Big Mama was enough to shake off the heaviness and feel some good old-fashioned joy. Courtney was refreshed, confident, and excited about her relationship with Sebastian, and hopefully about Jamal's recovery, thanks to Big Mama. Even Aunt Sis's bitterness couldn't pierce the peace that had saturated the hospital room earlier in the day.

"I know that Jamal is going to get better. He has to," Courtney said with her legs doubled up on the couch in Sebastian's apartment.

Sebastian's entire being was ready, willing, and able to hold Courtney up through this time of struggle. He also needed to tell her about his recent revelation, hoping and praying it wouldn't affect her feelings for him. He wanted to share every aspect of his life with her, regardless of how embarrassing or complicated it was. No secrets between them. All he could do was trust in her love, believing she saw and loved the true him, the one thriving below his black and white skin.

"Courtney, I have something important to tell you. It's something I found out this morning, talking to my dad. It was a really heated discussion, like you would not believe."

"About what or do I even want to ask?"

"I called him this morning, to see if he'd be willing to help Jamal on the legal front."

"Oh yeah, I'm sorry to interrupt, but Reverend Tyler announced at church today that you were offering legal support. I remember you telling me you spoke with him months ago, but I was so shocked when he said your name."

"I didn't think about calling him until after you and I had spoken this morning."

"Well, he spoke very highly of you. A few people came up to me afterward and told me they appreciate the help you're giving the church and my family. It was a nice feeling coming from some of the members. You know, if Reverend Tyler likes you, you're in, and he seems to like you."

"So much for that ray of light. I couldn't get my dad to help me at all. He was totally against it. Actually, he totally went off the deep end with a crock of racial epithets and I really didn't want to hear it. I asked him to put aside his racial biases, for once, and help his son do something that's right. We had a total wipeout and then he dropped this huge bomb in my lap, out of left field, that I wouldn't have guessed in a million years."

"Your dad and Aunt Sis have a lot in common. I bet they'd just love to hear that," she said with a grin.

Sitting in his chair, with his eyes closed, he slowly brushed his hands down his head. "You have no idea. Get this, my mom isn't dead or at least she wasn't twenty-three years ago, like I've been told all my life. Is that far-out or what?"

"Oh my gosh," Courtney gasped, throwing her open hands across her mouth. "Are you serrrious?"

"And the real kicker is, she was part black."

Courtney took a deep breath and her eyes enlarged like a balloon filling with air. *"What!* That can't be true!"

"That's why he kicked her out." It hurt to know that his father had lied about who he was for his entire life and that he himself was the very element in society his father despised. How long had he looked up to his father, wanting to please him, like every other son? It was crushing to know he would never be able to please his father, because his beginning, in which he had no input, put him two drops of black blood too far from the unconditional reach of his father's love. "This is out of control." He pressed his palms up from his eyebrows to his hairline, feeling no relief. He wanted to wail it out, to go deep and stab it out, the pain and self-pity that tempted to fester below. He was determined not to let it hold him. He couldn't let it. He closed his eyes and let his head droop. It all made sense now. That's why God had consistently put in his spirit that he was his father, that he was his father, over and over since he accepted Christ nearly four years ago. God knew this day would come. "I should hate my dad for all of his self-righteous pious deception, but I don't. I love him . . ."

Courtney got up and sat on the edge of the chair, stroking his hair and letting him lean on her. She had felt grief before and knew its calling card. Best to let him guide the conversation. She would sit there and just be supportive. This was his journey.

". . . even if he can't truly love me." He began to sob, at first quietly and controlled, but the pain picked up momentum and he cried openly, grabbing the sides of Courtney's sweatshirt and pressing into her stomach.

His crying made her cry. "It won't change anything between us, Sebastian."

He couldn't get a coherent phrase past his muffled words.

"I love you so much. If we can endure Aunt Sis, we can get past anything."

He sniffed a couple of times, brushed the tears from his cheeks in a strong, manly way. He didn't want Courtney to think he was a crybaby. He shook the sullen moment off, but hung on to Courtney a bit longer. It was comforting and where he needed to be, where he was destined to be.

"I knew we would be together the first time I laid eyes on you," he said. "It's no coincidence that we met at Northwestern when we did. I truly believe God arranged our entire meeting."

"If God wanted us together, then why did we have to go through all of this craziness?" Sensing that Sebastian was okay for the moment, she went back to the couch.

"The craziness wasn't God. That was our free will kicking in with a surge. He can direct us, but we're the ones who have to trust his guidance and step out in faith."

"I went through so much confusion and still have moments, but you have hung in there the entire time, never wavering."

"That's all God. I can't take credit for it. I had to pray over and over for him to keep me totally focused. I didn't want to waver. I so desperately want to be with you. When God created me, I know he had you in mind. We could have gone to any school in the world, but he put us at Northwestern in Evanston, Illinois, at the exact same time.

Of all of the billions, probably trillions of people that have ever walked this earth, he had the precision to place us there at the exact same time."

"That is pretty amazing when you think about it like that. But, what if I hadn't been on the cheerleading squad or you in the band? I might not have run into you and we would have missed out."

"I don't think so."

"No!" she questioned.

"Uh-Uh. I don't believe I would have missed you and here's why. Think about it like this. Let's say you and I are destined to meet somewhere and you're coming by train and I'm on foot. If your train gets there five minutes late, God would stop the clocks of time just so you could catch up, and run into at the exact, preordained moment."

"Yeah, right."

"I mean it, maybe not literally but definitely spiritually. I truly believe God wants to bless us with his perfect will that much. That's why I can endure potshots from your aunt, my dad, the people from Fifth Baptist, and anybody else who thinks God runs a segregated heaven. Hey, if Moses can survive a bicultural marriage, then I figure we're in good company."

"Moses could speak directly to God, and God could talk to the people that were tripping with him. Unless God comes down to dinner and tells Aunt Sis face-to-face to back off, it's not happening. That much we can trust."

"Maybe now that I'm part black, she'll be more accepting," he said, blowing out a deep breath, clearing the path for laughter.

Courtney joined in. "Yeah, right." She knew Sebastian was about as black to Aunt Sis as Abraham Lincoln. If he did have black in him, it wasn't showing, and what he looked like was all that counted. All that talk about digging down and judging a person by character and not color was foreign to Aunt Sis. Martin Luther King had a dream about equality and the coming together of races, but anyone hanging around Aunt Sis's house would be led to believe that his dream pretty much died with him.

"Ah, wishful thinking, huh?"

"I think so."

"Then we just have to understand her and pray for a change in her heart, because we both understand that I haven't known her long enough to be the source of so much of her anger. I will respect her but I'm not going to receive her lashing out as a reflection of my character, and I hope you're okay with that."

"Hey, I'm fine with it. Right is right and wrong is wrong. This time my Aunt Sis is big-time wrong."

"Good, because when we get the okay from God to get married, she's going to be really stuck with me."

Courtney hoped they would get married one day and felt equipped for the journey, but was curious about certain aspects of the race thing. She knew it would be an adjustment in their lives, regarding friends, church, and daily practices. It would be hard for others to accept them. Why not? She still found herself noticing interracial couples in public. She was more conscious not to stare and had actually gone too far in the opposite direction by looking past them altogether, making no eye-to-eye contact or offering a hello, as she had done all of her life with blacks that she ran into at work and on the street. Accepting or not, color was always going to be noticeable. "When you look at me, don't you see black?"

"Yeah, I do. When someone, anyone looks at you, they're sure to notice that you're black, a woman, and incredibly beautiful."

On occasion, Courtney had meetings with coworkers at other sites. In order to find one another, they would describe themselves to her and she, in turn, would do the same. She was often amazed that race or skin color wasn't included in the description, although it is a distinctive characteristic. It was always part of her description. Why not? she figured. She was as much black as she was from the Young family and a woman and a born-again believer and a bunch of other things. All attributes contributed to the making of her unique self.

"I also see your heart beating in perfect harmony with mine and you have to get past color to see that kind of love."

Sebastian stood up with his arms open and Courtney stood too, falling into his embrace.

He sensed where she was coming from and added, "The only way to narrow the gap between whites and blacks is to love one person at a time, and I choose you," he said, "and I am so happy about that."

Even with the wait-and-see that was going on with Jamal, being with Sebastian gave her a time of relief from the stress. She spent another couple of hours with him before going home for the evening.

Chapter 48

The night was rough. Courtney tossed and turned most of the time, falling asleep, waking up, checking the clock to find out that one hour, at the most, had elapsed. She didn't know if the phone would ring or not, and if it did, would it be good news about Jamal? He had been no better off but no worse off either when she checked with Edwin and the hospital this morning before going into the office. She would continue to think positive thoughts and pray on and off during the day. Sebastian had asked her to consider fasting, leading into the rally.

"What's up, what's up?"

Courtney didn't need to see him to know who it was. "Good morning, Brice."

"Get out of the way, crazy man, so I can sit down. Hey, girlfriend." Sheila came in with her cup of coffee and took the same seat she always did. Brice stretched and took a chair.

"How was your weekend?" Sheila asked Courtney.

"It was tough, had a lot going on." Courtney would have been comfortable telling Sheila about Jamal's predicament, but was not quite sure about Brice. Sharing racial information was one thing, but telling coworkers about her cousin being in and out of jail and beaten by the police on multiple occasions was something else. Many of the professionals in the office wouldn't understand it, black or white.

Many of them never saw the courtroom or jail-visiting-room side of the law packed with poor people, mostly ones from the other side of the socioeconomic divide. That was the imaginary line that separated the haves from the have-nots, and was as divisive, at times, in society as race. If he was arrested, then he must be guilty. If the TV news or the paper did the story, as they always seemed to do for the accused black, then it must be true and he was automatically deemed guilty. But it wasn't always true, especially not in Jamal's case. It wouldn't be fair to tell part of Jamal's story and not all of it. They would judge him, and she feared they would judge her.

"Umph, don't we all," Sheila attested.

"Check this out, did you see the news last night? There's a big rally happening at Pennsylvania Hospital and the police station tonight. I might check it out, my chance to get down like the sixties," Brice said.

"I only watch world news. The local stuff is too depressing. What's the rally for?" Sheila asked.

"Five-O beat down a brother in town and the church folks aren't having it. They claim they were investigating a case and the man committed an unprovoked assault on the officers, and they acted in self-defense. I don't know how you can attack two officers and end up in the hospital almost dead."

The word "dead" chilled Courtney. She could have broken down and cried at the thought but stayed strong, as she so often had to do at work, like the other times her personal life had fought for exposure.

She leaned on the chair arm and dangled the necklace around her neck.

"Why are you so quiet?" Sheila asked her.

"Because that was my cousin."

"Oh, for real! That's you? Oh man, Courtney," Brice said, scratching his head.

Sheila choked on the coffee she was swallowing and pushed the cup away from her without a drop spilling on her suit. "What cousin!"

"Jamal."

"Oh, Courtney," Sheila said, setting the cup down and going over to hug her. "I had no idea, none. Oh boy. How's he doing?"

"Hanging in there. We believe he's going to be all right. We have to wait for him to wake up and I hope it's soon."

"I'll say a prayer for you," Sheila offered.

"I will too," Brice said.

"Man, please," Sheila said, "you don't know anything about praying."

"What, just because I'm not one of those Holy Rollers that goes to church every Sunday, I know a little something about God. Don't all blacks?"

Courtney looked at Brice and chuckled. He was so Brice, living somewhere between black and white. She would accept him for who he was and let God shelter her from the rest.

They continued talking among themselves for a few minutes until Jason came around the corner.

"Courtney, I see you're busy. I'll come back later."

Sheila picked up her cup of coffee and took a sip, leaving her laughing eyes for Courtney to see.

"Hi, Sheila and Bri."

Brice's chuckling turned into an all-out roaring laughter. "Bri! Who is Bri!"

He continued chuckling while Jason's face continued to be crayoned in red, darker and darker, brighter and brighter. Sheila kept the cup to her mouth while Courtney's eyes watered and lips quivered.

Brice got up to go. "I'll see you ladies later." He patted Jason on the shoulder. "Look here, Jason, let's talk."

"That boy is crazy," Sheila said when the two men had left.

Courtney nodded in agreement.

"Are you okay?"

"I'm getting better."

"If you need the time off, take it and don't worry about it. This place will be here when you get back."

"No, really, I'm fine. As a matter of fact, some parts of my life are great," she said, rocking softly from side to side in her seat.

"What?"

"Sebastian is wonderful."

"You go, girl. I'm happy for you."

"Now, we have to pray for your Mr. Right to come along."

"You never know, he just might. In the meantime, I have work to do since nobody else is going to be paying my bills." She got up to leave. "If you need me, let me know."

They hugged and Sheila left.

On the way back to her office, she thought about Edwin. She'd had a nice talk with him at Courtney's. If he could draw some boundaries in his life with his mother, then maybe he was someone she would be interested in getting to know. Before it was a big if, but speaking with him a week ago, it seemed like a possibility. Anyway, she would call him to offer her support for Jamal. She got to her fishbowl, closed the door, and called Edwin. His secretary put her through.

"Sheila, what a very nice surprise."

"Yes, well, Courtney told me about what happened to Jamal and I wanted to let you know you and your family are in my thoughts."

"I appreciate it."

"If there's anything I can do or say or whatever, let me know. I'm here."

Big Mama had said a mouthful yesterday, not just for Sebastian and Courtney, but for him too. He needed to start leading his own life and walking his own path, without his mother doing all of the steering. He had bent over backward for her in the past because he didn't want to feel guilty for saying no at times. So he did everything she'd asked him to do. It had seemed like the right approach at the time, but not anymore. She had grown totally dependent on him and that wasn't good for her.

"Actually, there is something. I'd like for you to come to the rally with me tonight."

"I've never been to a rally." She hesitated before answering and spun her pen around the desktop. "I guess so, yes, why not?" She accepted, hunching her shoulders and scrunching her face. "Where and what time?"

"I'll pick you up around five-thirty from your place."

"Sure, fine with me, five-thirty it is. Do you still know how to get to my place?"

"Sure do."

"Great. I'll see you soon."

Edwin reared back in his chair and let his hand glide over his head, front to back, several times. He leaned forward and wrenched his hands, bobbing his head. Changes were coming.

The secretary told Edwin his mother was on line one.

He grabbed it, wondering if something had changed in Jamal's condition. "Mama, what's going on?"

"The hospital called and said Jamal isn't awake yet, but they said his brain patterns are good, his heart rate is strong, and they have gotten the swelling and pressure down. The tests show the bleeding has stopped and they don't see any clots. They say my baby is doing good, praise God," she yelled. "When he wakes up, they say he'll be in a lot of pain, but I'm not worried about that. I just want him to wake up."

"This is great news, Mama. Really good news."

"So, what time are you picking me up for the rally?"

"Uhm, I thought you said you weren't going to the rally. You wanted to stay at the hospital with Jamal."

"I know I said that before, but since he's made this big turn for the better, I want to be out there at that rally."

"Well, Mama, I won't be able to pick you up. I'm picking up Sheila."

"Sheila! What do you mean you can't pick me up?"

Edwin felt that if he kept giving her fish, she'd never learn to fish on her own. She'd never have to go to God for help as long as he was enabling her. In a way, it kind of felt like he was hindering her growth in God, because she didn't have to go to God for her needs, she came to him. If she had to go to God more often, she just might get to know him and then maybe God could speak to her heart about the way she was treating Sebastian and Courtney. One day he would be married with a wife and kids and wouldn't be able to help her like he'd been doing. Might as well start weaning her now.

"It's a two-seater and there's not enough room, unless you want to sit in the back, but it's awfully tight."

"Huh, I won't ever sit in that backseat. That's for those other women, not your mama."

Edwin wouldn't forget the humiliation that came with squeezing Mandy in the backseat. She had been very understanding, probably too understanding. To treat such a dear friend that way was wrong. He valued her as a friend, knowing that was all they would ever be. Like Big Mama had said, taking the easy road didn't make it right. Mandy wasn't what he wanted. It wasn't about her color. He just wasn't romantically attracted to every woman in the world. She happened to be one that he wasn't. He couldn't explain it, but Sheila was another story. Her fiery personality drew him.

"Why don't you check with Courtney and Sebastian? They might be going. Maybe you can get a ride with them."

"Hmmph. I can't believe you. They have finally gotten to you, turning against me this way."

"Mama, I am not turning against you. I'm just not going to change my plans because you changed yours. I love you, but I'm sorry."

"Fine, I have to go see my baby. I'll talk with you later."

"See you later, Mama. I love—" he was able to get out before she hung up. "Oh well. She's going to be okay and so am I." He dialed the phone to give Courtney the good news about Jamal.

Courtney wanted to jump for joy after hearing Jamal had taken a turn for the better. She knew God was going to do something great. She had felt it and Big Mama had prophesied it. Life couldn't get any more complicated and rewarding all at the same time. It was like sweet and sour mixing on the same plate.

Cara came in to see if she wanted to go to lunch later.

"I'm going to pass today but let's do it tomorrow."

"Sounds good. Where do you want to go, your choice?"

"The Caribbean restaurant?"

"Fine, we're on. Let's say twelvish."

Courtney was a bit startled that Cara had agreed to go to the restaurant so willingly. Perhaps she had misjudged her in the past. Maybe she had assumed Cara needed to be shielded from her world, mixed with whites and blacks, churchgoers and not, wealthy and broke. The more she thought about it, she hadn't given herself an opportunity to get to know Cara, outside of work. Perhaps it was time. The next time Cara had an art party or invited her to dinner or something, she was going to take her up on it. Sebastian was right, the only way to work on race relations was by getting to know one person at a time, and Cara was a good place to start.

Courtney swung around in her seat after Cara left.

Life was forever changed. She took the photo from her briefcase and put it inside the desk hutch. It was a big step to expose her relationship to coworkers, but she was ready. Between the love of God and the love of Sebastian, anything was possible. Nothing in the world was going to keep her from receiving the blessing that God had given to her in Sebastian. It would be like walking blindly down the road of life together, not knowing who or what was going to try and judge or derail them, but through their love for one another and faith in God's promises, she was trusting that they were headed for green pastures and warm winds blowing like trumpets across the heavenly spring skies, and that was good enough for her.

EPILOGUE

SPRING OF THE FOLLOWING YEAR

Mrs. Whittington stood in the doorway of their home office, holding her son's wedding invitation. "I've made myself absolutely nauseous over this," she told her husband, trying to keep her streaming flow of tears under control with a handful of tissue. " I have agonized over what to do and I've decided to go to the wedding."

"You can't be serious!" Mr. Whittington responded.

"I am. We have to go. There is no other way to salvage any kind of productive relationship with our son."

"I refuse to endorse this farce by showing up," he shouted.

"I'm talking about supporting our son! My goodness, are you this bent on completely alienating him?"

"I resent your accusation."

"Face it, Sebastian, this is the path he's chosen, despite our disapproval. We lost, now we have to accept his decision and live with it."

"How regal coming from you dear? Your hands aren't clean in creating this strife with him."

"I admit that I'm not fully denouncing my feelings on the matter, but my son's happiness is important to me." She pinched her nostrils shut with the tissue, and pressed her eyelids together to squeeze out any remaining tears. "I'm going with or without you. I refuse to shut the door when my son's life is just beginning."

"Then you will be going alone."

"Sebastian, I can't believe you're allowing this bias to completely cloud your ability to support your son, our only son. If you don't go to our son's wedding, he might not forgive you. I won't forgive you."

"Elizabeth, why are you making such a big deal out of this? He's not even your son."

"How dare you!" She sucked in a gush of air to gain composure. "He is my son, in every way that counts. Sebastian, you do what you can live with," she threw at him and ran away.

Mrs. Whittington prepared to make the trip alone, since George and Shirley had left with their families, before daybreak, to get the five-hour drive behind them. Mrs. Whittington got dressed quickly and the limousine service, which she had called earlier, was waiting at the front door. She stopped in to see Mr. Whittington before leaving. "I know we've said some harsh words to one another. I want us to be able to survive this. It's not too late to go."

"Have a safe trip," Mr. Whittington told her, without lifting his eyes from the document he was drafting at his desk.

Sebastian stood tall in the lobby of Fifth Baptist Church, with his black tuxedo and red rose contrasting against his tanned skin. The day had finally come and he couldn't wait to exchange vows with Courtney. Bart, Jamal, Edwin, and a few old friends rounded off his groomsmen quite nicely. He thought it would be easy to do this without his parents, but the gnaw on his heart led him to believe that he'd miscalculated.

"Ya parents done made it here yet?" Big Mama asked.

Sebastian looked down at the floor and let his head bounce back up. "I don't get to talk to my parents much anymore. I'm sure they aren't coming, but I do have someone on my family's side of the church. George and Shirley are here and a bunch of my old friends. That will have to do for my family."

Big Mama took his hands and sheltered them in hers. "Don't ya worry none. Give it time. They gone come around. Ize can tell you that a heap love, a mess of time, and a whole lots of Holy Ghost will work a situation out. You just gotta keep the faith. It's gonna be all right and don't you worry about my family. Anybody gives ya back talk, tell them to come see me. Ize straighten them out," Big Mama teased, closing with a roll of laughter that ignited from deep in the pit of her stomach. She wrapped her arms around him. "Welcome to the family, and we is family."

Sebastian was grateful for Big Mama's acceptance and encourage-ment. He couldn't help but to think about his parents. Would they ever be able to love him beyond their point of disapproval about the choices he'd made for his life? If they did, it would have to come by the grace of God and that's where he would have to leave it. His par-ents needed to seek their own peace because today was his day. At long last, he was marrying his sweetheart, the woman he had been drawn to for five years.

Courtney stood in Reverend Tyler's private hallway and peered into the crowd, through the small round window. The church was filled with a mixture of well-wishers, with everybody from some of her loud family members to Sebastian's ritzy entourage from boarding school, co-workers, church members, professed heathens, and every-thing in between. There was a smorgasbord of people: some poor, some rich, some smart, some not, some crooks, some professionals, some that approved of her and Sebastian, and some that didn't. But for her, they were all family and she was taught not to disown any of them. It still blew her mind every time she thought about how she'd ended up with Sebastian, in light of all the controversy surrounding their relationship.

Among the hundreds of guests, she saw her sorority sisters, a small group from Northwestern, including Larry, Big Mama's granddaughter, Rachel, with her companion, Neal. Next to Rachel was Uncle Raymond, who'd probably had a nip of liquor before coming, to steady his nerves. He was sharp wearing his polyester double-breasted suit. After meeting Ashley at the rehearsal dinner last night, he was captivated by her and had vowed to get a dance at the reception. Aunt Sis had told him to leave that young girl alone since he was barking up a tree way over his head. Looked like Uncle Raymond didn't listen because Mommy said he had doused an extra squirt of Old Spice, which would probably cause people to leave open seats directly to the left and right of him during the service. Seated behind Rachel were the school board director and his wife. Running up and down the aisle was Honey Babe's kids. Aunt Sis, and a few of the other older women, caught wind of it and shut the activity down after the second lap. That

hadn't been the only drama of the day. According to Deon, Aunt Sis
had caused a stir earlier in the morning, when the eight-car caravan
had arrived from North Carolina. Apparently Aunt Sis asked Little
Mama to leave all of her bags and any uninvited creatures in the car
during the wedding and reception. Little Mama hadn't taken too
kindly to the implication, but settled down after Daddy threatened to
kick both of them out of the ceremony if there was a problem they
couldn't get resolved in a hurry.

Courtney saw Brice standing near the back of the church and his
eyes were roving down the seam of Cara's bridesmaid dress. She could
only imagine what he was saying.

"Very nice . . . ," he said to Cara, without making eye contact and
taking time to complete his visual tour, "dress."

Cara blushed and said, "Why, thank you, Brice."

Brice had his suspicions about Cara passing. He had to stay true to
his people, so the only way he could pursue Cara would be for her to
be black. There was only one way to find out, according to Sheila's
theory, since his roots test hadn't been definitive. "So, do you come
from a big family like Courtney?"

"Oh my gosh, no. Courtney has a huge family."

"What about your grandmother, do you have a picture of her?"

Cara looked bewildered and excused herself to go and see if Courtney
needed help.

"I'm going to find out," Brice said as she left. "She likes me." Un-
affected, he blended into the crowd to see who else might be worthy
of his attention.

Two of Aunt Sis's friends from Fifth Baptist huddled in the back
corner of the church, chatting in a low tone. "Look over there. Aren't
they those relatives from Courtney's mother's side of the family? You
know, the ones with the big house over there off the mainline."

"Oh yeah, I see Mr. and Mrs. Thang. You know they won't speak to
us common folks."

"This is barking right up their tree, marrying white. I heard their
daughter will be coming right behind Courtney."

"You know that's how they are. Soon as they get some money,
blacks aren't good enough for them."

"Huh, well, we better get our seats. It's about to get started."

Courtney giggled softly thinking about her family and friends.
Some things in life just didn't change, Brice and Aunt Sis were two of

them. Times hadn't been easy for Aunt Sis, once Edwin and Sheila began dating nearly a year ago. Ever since Edwin got Aunt Sis straight, several months back, about his relationship with Sheila, she hadn't been too happy. Sheila had made it clear to Edwin that she wasn't putting up with Aunt Sis's treatment, the way Mandy had. Sheila promised Edwin she'd be respectful to his mother but no doormat. In return, he promised to protect her feelings when it came to his mother. Who knows what the future would hold for them, but they were both happy at the moment.

Aunt Sis did have something to be happy about, Jamal. His full recovery had been a miracle; no brain damage was more than the family could have expected. The bigger miracle was the shock of him finally being able to live without the police bothering him all the time. After the so-called accident with the two detectives, last spring, the police hadn't arrested him since, or paid him a visit in nearly a year. Courtney dabbed the tears from her eyes, careful not to smear her eyeliner or smudge the wedding gown. Life had changed so dramatically in the past two years, but it was all for the better.

No amount of drama, stares, gawking, or flat out mean-spiritedness could shake her confidence in the upcoming marriage to Sebastian Alexander Whittington III, which was only minutes away. She was sure the burning fire of opposition had molded their lives into a love that could endure the many tests to come. If God had been able to bring them together, surely he was able to keep them together. Courtney heard Brendon laying on the organ, giving the signal that the show was about to begin. She took one last look as Sebastian and Bart followed Reverend Tyler down the aisle. Sheila, Cara, Ashley, and the other two bridesmaids came down the hall to get her. It was time, and Courtney was ready. Although Sebastian's family wasn't able to come, she said a silent prayer that one day they would come around.

A limousine pulled in front of the Fifth Baptist and Mrs. Whittington took her time about getting out, partly ashamed that her husband wasn't by her side. She opened the door and took a big step, all the while, hoping her husband would be able to do the same some day.

Mr. Whittington sat in his office, with the curtains still drawn. He flipped to the letter D in his legal directory and then dialed the phone.

"Alan, Sebastian Whittington here. It's been a long time. How's life at Harvard?"

"Good to hear. Listen, I know of a case in Philadelphia that might be of interest to you, or some of your colleagues. It deals with a constitutional rights violation by the police department. I think you just might be able to provide some assistance to a young man by the name of Jamal Williams."

MAKES YOU GO HMMM!

Thought-Provoking Questions for Discussion

Now that you have read *Blind Faith*, let's talk about some of the issues addressed. Grab your reading buddies and have fun.

1. One cliché states that if a man is good to his mom, he'll be a good husband. Yet, when a man gives his mother too much attention, he's called a "momma's boy." What's the right balance? When does a mother-son relationship cross the line? How'd you characterize Edwin and Aunt Sis's relationship?

2. Courtney didn't like the piercing stares she received from passers-by. Why do you think so many people stared? What does it take to survive an interracial relationship? What do you think will be the major challenges for Courtney and Sebastian?

3. How do you feel when you see a man of your race married to someone of another race? What about when you see a man of another race with a woman of another race? What about a man with money? Specifically, a white man with a black woman? A black man with a white woman? How did you feel about Courtney and Sebastian vs. Edwin and Mandy—felt same or different? What's more divisive in this country, race or money?

4. Sheila said that some issues had nothing to do with race. What were your thoughts about Mr. Hodges sexually harassing Sheila? Were you surprised to find out that he was black?

5. Are there any interracial couples in your church? How do you feel they're treated? What did you like/dislike about Fifth Baptist? Faith Christian Center? Reverend Tyler? Which church will be more accepting of Courtney and Sebastian?

6. Do you believe there is truth to the stereotype that women, in some cultures, are more accommodating to men than others? What about Courtney? Sheila? Mandy?

7. Aunt Sis and Mrs. Whittington have strong opinions about the women in their son's lives. Although from distinctively different lifestyles and backgrounds, the two women are very similar.

Describe their commonalities. Was Aunt Sis's anger justified? What will Courtney and Sebastian have to do in order to deal with the ongoing resistance of key family members in their lives?

8. What did Edwin have in common with Sheila? With Mandy? Is it more important to date someone in your same race or socio-economic status? Based on social, financial, educational, religious, and romantic factors, was Courtney more compatible with Paul, Sebastian, or Roger? Why?

9. How important was a relationship to Sheila? What do you think was the main reason she wasn't in a serious relationship? What area in her personality do you think needs development?

10. What's Big Mama's message? What makes her so likeable and respected by Sebastian, Courtney, and Aunt Sis? Who's the Big Mama in your life—the person you call on when times get tough and you need compassionate advice?

11. What constitutes police brutality? Based on your own feelings/experiences, is an officer like Crawford rare or common? Did you expect Detective Holmes to be black? What emotions arise for you when a police car pulls up behind you? Would it be a sense of peace like Sebastian or fear/concern like Jamal?

12. What aspects of Brice's personality reminded you of Jamal? What does the future hold for a guy like Jamal? How does he overcome the weight of having a record? Do you think his poverty level or his race will be his biggest limitation? Which factor contributed most to Crawford's harassment?

13. Courtney seemed to be too black to interact completely with coworkers and too white to embrace relationships at home, causing her not to really fit in either group. She found Brice, Sheila, and her friends at Northwestern to be her peers. Was she bourgeoisie? If so, is that a good or bad thing? How do first- and second-generation educated blacks find their places in society? How could Courtney fit in, without compromising herself by going to happy hour and the pool hall? Was Paul right about her being uppity? Have you ever had an experience like the one she had at work, happy hour, or at Fifth Baptist?

14. Does the concept of "passing," whereby an individual of known

black heritage assimilates into society as a white person, exist today? Do you think Cara was passing? What would Sebastian's natural mother have to have done in order to pass indefinitely? Do you think Shirley, the housekeeper, knew about Sebastian's mom?

15. The TV in Jamal's room is a metaphor. What does it represent?

Dear Readers:

Thank you for obtaining a copy of *Blind Faith*. I hope you found the story entertaining. Perhaps it also motivated you to assess your own views on prejudices and stereotypes, based on race, religion, and socioeconomic differences. You might not share the extreme positions of an Aunt Sis or a Mrs. Whittington, but any stones we toss into rivers of discord cause a ripple.

> Dear friends, let us love one another, for love comes
> from God. Everyone who loves has been born of God
> and knows God. Whoever does not love does not
> know God, because God is love.
> —1 John 4:7

Take a moment and post a review or note on the website and let me know your thoughts about the story. Also, don't forget to pick up a copy of my other titles, *No Regrets, Nobody's Perfect,* and a faith-based anthology called *Blessed Assurance.*

Thank you for the support. Keep reading, and I look forward to hearing from you.

WWW.PATRICIAHALEY.COM